Ragdale

is a non-profit artists' community located 30 miles north of Chicago. Emerging and established artists, writers, and composers are supported through the residency program. Deadlines for the competitive application process are January 15th and June 1st. The application fee is $20 and the residency fee is $15/day. Fifty-five acres of prairie adjoin the historical buildings where 8 writer's rooms, 3 visual art studios and one composer's studio are located. For information email: mosher@ragdale. org, call 847.234.1063, ext. 206, send an SASE to: Ragdale Admissions, 1260 N. Green Bay Road, Lake Forest, IL 60045 or go to www.ragdale.org.

Editor-in-Chief & Publisher:	M. M. M. Hayes
Associate Editors:	Dan Gutstein, Kathryn Hughes
Contributing Editors:	Allison Amend, J. T. Barbarese, Will Boast, Chloe Bolan, MacDonald Caputo, Mary Dalton, Xoaquima Diaz, Paul Eberly, Donald G. Evans, Joan Gillespie, Joyce Gordon, Amy Greenberg, Kit Coyne Irwin, Brenda Kilianski, Richard Lange, Miriam Lykke, Annie McGravie, James O'Laughlin, Katherine Seigenthaler, Lynn Sloan, Judy Smith, Deb Olin Unferth, Virginia Watts, Julie Will
International Editor:	Thomas Kennedy
Life Subscribers' Editor:	Suzanne Ross
Business Manager:	John O'Shaughnessy
Production Manager:	Chris Fojtek
Interns:	Chris Fojtek, Karen Russell, Mary South (Northwestern University, Evanston, IL) Matt Hamity (UPenn, Philadelphia, PA)
Advisory Board:	Charles Baxter, Robert Olen Butler, John Callaway, Stephen Dixon, Andre Dubus III, James Klise, James McManus, G. E. Murray, Pamela Painter, Melissa Pritchard, Fred Shafer
Founding Editors:	Tom Bracken, F. R. Katz, Pamela Painter, Thalia Selz

STORYQUARTERLY, founded in 1975, is an independent magazine of the short story published by an Illinois non-profit corporation. Editors welcome short story submissions from October 1 thru March 31. Send on-line submissions only, via *Submissions* link at our website: http://www.storyquarterly.com. Member of COSMEP, CLMP, indexed in American Humanities Index. Opinions expressed herein are not necessarily those of the editors. For subscriptions and advertising rates, contact *StoryQuarterly* at: storyquarterly@yahoo.com. Single copy: $10; 2 years: $18; 5 years: $40; Student/Group rate: 5/$30; Life Subscriptions: $250; Sample copy: $8. See further information at http://www.storyquarterly.com

Distrubuted by:
Ingram Periodicals
117 Heil Quaker Blvd.
P. O. Box 7000
LaVergne, TN 37086
615-793-5000

B. DeBoer
113 Centre St.
Nutley, NJ 07110
201-665-9300

© 2003 by StoryQuarterly, Inc. All rights reserved.
ISBN: 0-9722-444-1-7   ISSN: 0361-0144

Cover design by Marylee MacDonald

STORYQUARTERLY 39

Congratulations to Our Authors!

Patricia Lear's "Nirvana" (SQ38) received a 2003 Illinois Arts Council Award, and will be included in *New Stories From the South: Best of 2003*, edited by Shannon Ravenel.

Amanda Rae Holzer's "Love and Other Catastrophes: A Mix Tape" (SQ38) will be included in *Best American Nonrequired Reading 2003*, edited by Dave Eggers. This was Amanda's first published story.

Robert Olen Butler's "Mother in the Trenches" (SQ38) was reprinted by *Harper's Magazine* in their February 2003 issue.

First Robie Macauley Award winner Edward Schwarzschild (SQ37) signed a two-book contract with Algonquin Press, for a story collection and novel built around his SQ37 story. Another Wolinsky story won the 2003 Moment/Karma Foundation Short Fiction Prize.

Many Thanks Too go to the following schools which used StoryQuarterly in literature and writing classes:

    Antioch University, Marina del Rey, CA
    DePaul University, Chicago: Anne Calcagno
    Columbia College, Chicago: Kathryn Hughes
    Harper College, Palatine, IL: Greg Herriges
    Loyola University, Chicago: Chloe Bolan, Annie McGravie
    Northeastern University, Chicago: Tom Bracken
    Northwestern University, Evanston, IL: Jim O'Laughlin
    Eastern Oregon University: Jodie Varon
    San Diego State University, CA: Duff Brenna
    Wichita State U, KS: Margaret Dawe
    School of Young Chicago Writers

The English Department at Northwestern University in Evanston provided us with spectacular interns who enlivened our work while they organized it. Matt Hamity, from UPenn, was also a huge help.

Third Annual
Robie Macauley Award for Fiction
$500

TO:

"A Correspondence"

by

Sylvia Sellers-Garcia

Judged by
Richard Ford

"'A Correspondence' is excellent and is my selection. This story is sustained and serious, and the complex fictive world it reveals is entirely persuasive and pleasingly under the writer's authority. Importantly too, it is a very interesting story to read."

—*Richard Ford*

Manuscripts submitted to Richard Ford were sent blind; i.e. all had author names removed.

Sweetest of all this year was the success of our authors. Our first Robie Macauley Prize Winner, Ed Schwarzschild, acquired one of many agents who called about his winning story. She auctioned his work and he signed a two-book contract with Algonquin Press for a collection and a novel about the characters in his SQ37 story. His novel is due out in 2004.

Our second Macauley Award Winner, Emily Rapp-Seitz, won her prize mid-MFA and mid-novel. She put up a Wait-a-Minute sign to many agents calling about her award-winning IRA story. When she's ready, we expect similar recognition for Emily's stunning ability to enter the life of the Other—in SQ38, an unexpected underbelly of terrorist life in Belfast.

Our current, and third winner, Sylvia Sellers-Garcia, emerges as a fascinating mix of erudition and passion. Her Borges-style story unspools in Guatemala and, to the amazement of all here at SQ, is her first published fiction. A mesmerizing performance it is too, and we expect it to attract similar attention, something we hope becomes a tradition for our Macauley Award Winners.

Other SQ authors hit milestone marks too, and we are as pleased as any parent. Our regular Past Contributors' Notes Section keeps us—and you—up to date on what they've done lately (p. 538).

Another birth this issue, our first translation, realizes a passionate goal of our Editor-in-Chief, M. M. M. Hayes, who has long maintained that the United States is already bi-lingual, speaking English and Spanish. This issue introduces to a North American audience the contemporary Mexican feminist, Angeles Mastretta, whose highly independent "aunts" reveal an author's understanding and love of her characters, however flawed. A sensation in the 1990s when *Mujeres de Ojos Grandes*, or *Women With Big Eyes* became a best-seller in Mexico (where translator Amy Schildhouse Greenberg discovered her), Angeles Mastretta appears here, appropriately, in both Spanish and English.

Our online submissions worked near-perfectly this year, thanks to the database and design of our web designer *par excellence*, Kit Irwin, so next year we will take submissions online only and eliminate much of the very time-consuming clerical work of keeping track of all the manuscripts. The online database does all of that for us. We'll make a few exceptions for people who have no email, or for novel excerpts too long to send online.

Next year? Well, an essay by J.T. Barbarese, a Harry Potter scholar (Yes! There is one), a farce about dinosaurs, and lots of serendipity, we're sure.

Submitters often ask what we look for in a story, and it's good that they do, for we still know that it's the questions that engage our intellect, not the answers. And we couldn't agree on an easy answer anyway, having as a matter of principle chosen fiction editors who represent widely different schools of What's Good. We read read read—roughly eight thousand submissions a year since we began taking stories online—and we do it for that magic moment of resonance when we slip unsuspecting into intensity, mystery—into subjects that either live on the larger stage the world has become, or that question conventional wisdom and explore its limits. Such stories, when we stumble onto them, do demand surrender: we can see them dance, we can hear them sing.

Join us there.

SQ

Amanda Rae Holzer

AMANDA RAE HOLZER'S "Love and Other Catastrophes: A Mix Tape" will be included in *The Best American Nonrequired Reading 2003*, edited by Dave Eggers, as well as an updated edition of *What If?* edited by Pamela Painter and Anne Bernays. Holzer completed her B.A. in literature from Emerson College in 2002. "This story for me involved quite a bit of maniacal humming and singing, with the occasional call to an unimpressed friend asking, 'Oh, who sang that one, you know, with the word *love* in it?' In that sense I considered it a research project of sorts that built its own momentum until it felt like I was just plugging in song titles that already belonged in a predestined order. Although I experimented here with a far more light-hearted style, I consider most of my writing to be serious and dramatic. I do admit, I had fun."

Patricia Lear

PATRICIA LEAR's story in *SQ38*, "Nirvana," won a 2003 Illinois Arts Council Award and was chosen for *New Stories From the South: Best of 2003*. Her first story collection, *Stardust, 7-Eleven, Route 57, A&W and So Forth*, was included on the *New York Times Book Review Summer Reading List*, *Editor's Choice* and *Notable Books of the Year*. Her fiction has been anthologized in *O.Henry Prize*, *New Stories From the South*, *Ten Years of Best of the South*, *The Antioch Review Anniversary Issue* and *Chicago Works*. "I cobbled 'Nirvana' together from a scrap here and a scrap there, and then started making it add up to something. Stories need to work on so many different levels and each level has to be attended to, always looking back to what came before and then asking: what does this story demand now? Quiet, loud, raucous, tranquility? What? I whittled, carved and sanded, and blew off the sawdust. The ending came to me, one of those rare writing gifts delivered whole and right, slippery and perfect. And the title? Hey, I like rock music." Lear is expanding "Nirvana" into a novel.

StoryQuarterly 39

THIRD ROBIE MACAULEY FICTION AWARD

to

Sylvia Sellers-Garcia for "A Correspondence"

judged by

RICHARD FORD

RICHARD FORD	Remembrance	11
SYLVIA SELLERS-GARCIA	A Correspondence	14
CHRIS ABANI	Weeping Madonna	56
BRIGID PASULKA	The Lemon Tree	63
MORGAN MCDERMOTT	Traction	84
KATHERINE SHONK	Kitchen Friends	103
PENNY NEWBURY	How I Discovered America	132
DREW JOHNSON	Delta Interval	151
CHRIS ABANI	Blooding	164
DAN O'BRIEN	Apocrypha	170
RICHARD NEWMAN	Movie Moguls Resurrect Gristlehead	185
CHARLES JOHNSON	Dr. King's Refrigerator	186
KEITH LEE MORRIS	San Diego Dreams	193
STEVE ALMOND	Hillary Falls	206
	Rumors of Myself	207
	Mr. Albert's Remedy	209
JEFFERY RENARD ALLEN	Mississippi Story	211
N. S. KÖENINGS	Pearls to Swine	231
CHRISTY KARPINSKI	Viewpoints: A Photo Essay	263
JOHN CASEY	What's Funny? An Essay	270

KATE HILL CANTRILL	Guess Who Was At The Party?	289
MICHAEL KNIGHT	Smash and Grab	294
KAUI HART HEMMINGS	Minor Wars	308
JOAN CORWIN	Sinners	326
J. T. BARBARESE	Jesus and Magdalene As Children	342
AMY SCHILDHOUSE GREENBERG	Angeles Mastretta	347
ANGELES MASTRETTA	Tía Eloísa	348
	Tía Mónica	350
	Tía Amalia	354
	Tía Pilar y Tía Marta	356
translated by:	AMY SCHILDHOUSE GREENBERG	
RAMU NAGAPPAN	Blue Boy	360
MICHAEL POORE	Chief Next Lightning's Phantom Hand	381
HELEN CHANDRA	Under Ganesh's Gaze	392
TERRY THUEMLING	Alfalfa	410
MIKA TANNER	Christmas Cake	411
CAROLYN ALESSIO	Blue Roses	438
STEPHEN DIXON	Go	448
SHARON BALENTINE	The Stones Also Are the River	460
ENID BARON	Margery's Will	464
ANDREW PORTER	Storms	478
LARA JK WILSON	Touch	497
KIM PONDERS	How Bluegrass Saved My Life	514
CONTRIBUTORS' NOTES		534
PAST CONTRIBUTORS' NEWS		542

Robie Macauley
May 13, 1919 – November 20, 1995

Editor for the *Kenyon Review*, fiction editor for *Playboy*, and executive editor for Houghton Mifflin, Robie was the Recipient of a Furioso Prize, *Benjamin Franklin Magazine* Awards Citation, *Kenyon Review* and Rockefeller Foundation Fellowships, a Guggenheim Fellowship, a Fulbright Research Fellowship at the University of London, an O. Henry Prize. Several times anthologized in *Best American Short Stories*, he also won *The Paris Review*'s John Train Award.

Remembrance

Richard Ford

When I was twenty-seven, we lived in Chicago—my wife and me. I was trying to start my writing life in a nicer-than-we-could-afford loft apartment on East Scott Street, behind the Gold Coast. The year before, when I was still in school, I'd had a novice story accepted for an anthology edited by Robie Macauley, who was known to me as the fiction editor of *Playboy*, and whose name was memorable to me because it was very agreeable to the ear, almost melodic. Back then, it seemed to me that the world of writing, the world I wanted into, was full of men with noble-sounding, euphonious names–Galway Kinnell, Rust Hills, Oakley Hall, Baxter Hathaway, Donald Justice, E.L. Doctorow. Robie Macauley.

On a day during the spring—it was 1971—the actual anthology that included my story arrived in the mail, and I could for the first time see what a story I'd written looked like in print, with my name up front. Very good, I thought. I was pleased. It was only ten in the morning when the mail arrived, but I had a drink anyway to celebrate. I called my wife at work. And then I remembered that the Playboy Building was just a few blocks down Michigan, and that possibly the same Robie Macauley was right there, and if I was worth anything, I'd just go down there, ask to see him, walk in and personally express to him my gratitude for choosing my story. I thought he'd be surprised but appreciate it.

And that is exactly what I did. Ten-thirty. I walked down there (I'd had a couple more celebratory drinks), looked Robie Macauley up on the lobby directory, got on the elevator, went up to his floor and told the receptionist I was a writer, and wanted to see Mr. Macauley because he'd published a story of mine. The receptionist smiled, said just a minute, and disappeared down a long hallway of office doors. (You can tell how long ago this occurred by how easy it was to gain precious access to people who obviously needed protection from people like me.)

I waited. And in less than two minutes the receptionist came back and asked me to come along down the hall with her, and brought me into a rather small, book-lined office that looked down onto Michigan Avenue. Mr. Macauley was sitting behind a desk. Hello, I said—or something to that effect—I'm Richard Ford, and you published my story in *Intro III*, and I'm just here to say how much I appreciate it. Mr. Macauley seemed not puzzled, only slightly not to be expecting me. He'd, moments before, been thinking about something else, I guess. But he collected himself right away, asked me to sit down and said that he remembered my story and that it was one he had particularly liked, and that he was very glad to meet me and appreciated my coming to see him. I was, myself, rather touched by my own gesture, and I sat there in front of Robie Macauley (a man I didn't know and would never see again) and simply let the nice moment sink in on me while the effects of having had some drinks quite early in the day began to wear off. He asked me what I was doing in Chicago, he asked me about my former teacher—an extremely good writer he knew; he asked me what I was working on. I seem to remember he said I should submit something to *Playboy* and that he'd love to read it, though I may have made that up. And then he looked at me and smiled in a way that was both friendly and also serious about something that didn't involve me. Following which I had the good timing and good sense to stand up, shake his hand again, thank him again and say good-bye.

I think of that morning now with a mixture of pleasure, and satisfaction underlaid by something hollow. I'm happy I did it, to be sure, though nothing ever came of our unusual meeting. I never submitted a story to Robie Macauley. And I didn't really believe him when he, generously, said mine was a memorable story (I knew it wasn't). It was more than noble of him to see me right off the street and tipsy, and to ask me about myself. It let me know that nobility of some everyday kind could in fact characterize the world I was trying to enter.

But when I got back to my empty apartment at about eleven, a bit hung over, there was this same hollow feeling already waiting for me. It was the flat-footed, now-where-was-I sensation of having to face again the proper task I'd been happy to jump up and leave an hour before, and face it with the certainty that nothing was going to help—not having an early drink, not having a mediocre story published in an anthology probably no one would read, not visiting a famous editor. Nothing was going to help—and I attribute this lesson to Robie Macauley—except that I stay where I was, do my work, persuade myself I was lucky to get to do it, and then afterwards let whatever would happen, happen.

Sylvia Sellers-Garcia

SYLVIA SELLERS-GARCIA writes: "This story takes place in Guatemala, where my mother's family is from. Over the years I've met many people who were directly or indirectly involved in the armed conflict, and the number of different perspectives on this patch of history is eye-opening. Some people—incredibly—persist in believing that the armed conflict in Guatemala never happened. When the idea for this story first occurred, I was thinking about people on the fringes of the conflict. Most Guatemalans fall into this category: they were indirectly affected, not protagonists. Nonetheless, the course of the fighting made deep impressions. Thinking of similar conflicts elsewhere in Latin America and in other parts of the world, I wanted to study what people do—individually and collectively—with such memories. Speaking with people in Guatemala—and elsewhere, I am sure—makes evident how memories are shaped so that they might be compatible with a social agenda, or adaptable to one's self-image, or simply bearable." Sellers-Garcia is a fact-checker for *The New Yorker* and begins a Ph.D. in History at Berkeley this fall.

Third Annual Robie Macauley Fiction Award Winner

A Correspondence

Sylvia Sellers-Garcia

The first letter arrived on a Monday. When I returned from the office, I opened the gate and picked up the mail from the walkway. There wasn't much: a letter from the bank, a catalogue, a brochure for a vacation spot in Mexico, and an envelope with my address but no name printed above it, no return address, and postmarked in the city at the central station. I did not open the letter right away, because it was already past eight, and I was used to eating at seven. After hanging my jacket and hat and leaving my briefcase in the study, I put the mail alongside the newspaper on the kitchen table and prepared my dinner. As it happened, I became engrossed in an article about the future of the glass industry in Quetzaltenango and I ate my dinner without making it through the paper. So it wasn't until much later, when I was drinking tea in the study and clearing my desk, that I turned to the envelope.

It was already late, and I was beginning to feel sleepy. The only light in the room came from the desk lamp, a frosted globe with fine etchings that threw an amber glow across the room. I often

A Correspondence

spent two or three hours at the end of the day sitting behind the desk or in the leather armchair on the other side of the room. By eleven, the sound of the traffic on the highway would die away, and I would sit quietly, waiting for a dog to bark or looking into the corners of the study where the darkness prevented me from recognizing the books on the bookshelves. I sat in the leather armchair and opened the letter. As I cracked open the paper, I observed to myself that my eyelids were drooping and that it was time to go to bed. The moment I saw the typewritten pages my pulse quickened and my drowsiness faded.

> *Don't bother turning to the end of the letter; you won't find a signature. I know it will frustrate you. You'll make a list of people in your mind and make hypotheses. You'll skip ahead, skimming for evidence, and read the most insignificant details as clues. I suggest you not bother and imagine me instead: the color of my beard, the car I drive, the state of my handkerchiefs, the way I hold my fork, the pattern of my curtains—stripes, trellises, it doesn't matter. In a page or two you will begin to ask yourself why I can't speak to you in person. I'm not the only one who can't. There are others—many, I would guess—who are in the same situation. In the beginning, when everyone clamored for an answer, we were unavailable—occupied with love, or debt, or fear. And then years later, when everyone knew what had happened, we wrestled with confusion, or estrangement, or shame. And now, when everyone wants to forget, we realize that it is too late. We must go quietly, invisibly, in a way that will afflict no one, but with the kind of memories that instead of fading, grow louder and louder like the ringing of a bell between one's ears. It would not be enough to write these letters and then throw them away, or write them and send them to an address I picked at random out of the phonebook. If I had not known a judge, I would have*

found one for the purpose of writing to him. But I happen to know you. I write to ask whether you will reconsider a judgment that was passed a long time ago.

More than twenty-five years ago, I was a student of politics at the university. My parents always hoped that I would become a doctor, but I became interested in government, and in particular, politics. As you know, it was difficult at that time for an ordinary person, let alone a student of politics, to be unaware of the tension that boiled at the edges and threatened to blow the lid off of ordered society altogether. I studied politics, but increasingly became most interested in political history, and I am embarrassed to say that I had no clear opinions of my own about what was going on around me. On this point, my parents could offer no guidance; in fact, they seemed to be even more ignorant than I was.

I discovered that I would have to form my own opinions one evening during my first year at the university. I was having dinner at my parents' house, and my mother was in the uncomfortable position of having to cook and serve dinner by herself before joining my father and me at the table. When she finally sat down, she was frazzled and full of complaints about the maid, who had vanished unexpectedly the day before. My father was silent on the subject. "She must have run off with the guerrillas," I offered. "Ha!" my mother laughed. "The what?" I felt a dull surprise, a disorientation, as though I had tried to run through a screen door. "Well, I don't know any myself, but they say that the guerrillas are all over—not just up in the mountains, but here in the city, too. At the university they talk of nothing else. There are all kinds of student organizations and people are getting together, planning things, getting organized." My parents stopped eating and stared at me in silence. My father said, "Don't be ridiculous. No such thing exists." He calmly recommended cutting his meat. I tried to say more, but my mother cut me off, saying, "I suppose that's why she took the emeralds your father gave me for our anniversary. Camouflage." She laughed to herself while my father chewed and raised his eyebrows at his plate.

But rumor of an organized movement seeped into every corner of campus: a thick fog that concealed its own doubtful outlines as well as it did the original nature and purpose of the university. Gradually, I grew to sympathize with it, or what I could make of it. I criticized the government for censoring the press, I mocked it for being a puppet in the hands of North American powers, and I resented it for having reverted to a set of policies that were irrelevant to my own life but that seemed to me, at the time, extremely significant.

The first two years did not feel uneventful at the time, but in retrospect I realize that they were. I was getting to know my field, befriending a few of the younger professors, and staking out my own intellectual ground. I began by studying the history of recent politics, and each semester took me further and further away from the present, so that by my third year I found myself focusing on the political history of the colonial period: material that could be examined with several centuries' hindsight. It was no coincidence that this kind of study of politics was as far removed from the actual, living politics of the country as conceivably possible. I wanted to remain sympathetic but uninvolved. Nonetheless, I knew that this distinction was apparent only to me. I was caught in the midst of something: a fish is more like a man than he is like the lake he lives in, but he is indistinguishable from it to someone standing on the shore. And if the lake were to be drained, the fish would go with it.

After my second year of university, things changed. One afternoon in October, I attended an economics class, and during the discussion the professor chose me, I believe at random, to comment on another student's argument. I explained why the argument was unsound, and concluded–convincingly–that the country would never become prosperous if its scholars and counselors sacrificed fundamental economic logic for the sake of idealism. The discussion moved on and I forgot all about my comment until after class, when I found the student I had responded to waiting for me outside of the classroom. Many months later, Claudia would confess to me that she hated my manner of arguing. "You don't get angry!" she cried. "Get angry, you must get angry. There is nothing more offensive to me than how you sit there, talking calmly, as if you don't care at all what I say." I told her that her anger always upset me. "Then why don't you shout?" she hollered. Claudia accused me of trying to make her more argumentative by failing to put a proper amount of passion into our arguments. "If you don't shout then I'm going to shout enough for both of us." And yet, that first time, I was sure that she liked me for how I responded. As soon as I walked out of the door, she pushed her face into mine and hissed, "Aren't you embarrassed?" I mumbled something of an apology and walked away. "You know what for," she said, more loudly, as she walked beside me. "For playing up to the professor at my expense–at the expense of the only student who tries to stand up to him. Sure, it's easy to insult my ideas when everyone else in the room agrees with you. Did you think for a second about how difficult it was for me to express a difference of opinion? You probably did, but you didn't care. You just wanted to tell him what he wanted to hear. You're ashamed; I know you are. Do you have anything to say for yourself?" I stopped walking and looked at her in silence for a moment. "I don't know," I said. For a moment I thought her anger would overwhelm me. I had a vision of her fists pounding into my stomach over and over again until I fell to the ground, her face purpling with rage and her wild hair suffocating me. But then Claudia began to laugh. She laughed hard and leaned on the wall to keep from falling. "You've never been yelled at like that before, have you?" she asked, in a different voice. I laughed lightly in response. "Well, you know what to do if you want more." She laughed again and handed me her books. I was forced to buy Claudia dinner to apologize, and by the time I dropped her off at home, after midnight, my impression of her had changed.

She may sound hard to you, but Claudia was in reality quite gentle. The day after I met her, I was walking to one of my classes and saw her again. She ran towards me with her jacket open and her neck and cheeks red with exertion. When she stopped in front of me, her hair collapsed all around her face. She grabbed my arms, squeezed her eyes together, and told me breathlessly that she needed my car. As she dragged me towards the parking lot she explained about the woman she'd met by the bus stop. "She missed the bus," Claudia cried. "And she's on her way to her brother's funeral with her children. And there won't be any more buses to Rabinal until the evening and then the funeral will be over." The woman stood by the bus station with a boy under each arm. She wore traditional dress, her head sash filthy, and both she and her children went barefoot. When she climbed into the car, her stolid face neither looked at me nor spoke. I drove them all the way to Rabinal from the capital with Claudia in the front seat. For several hours, the road wound through clusters of cement houses with aluminum roofs and then plunged into hills of overgrown jungle. Occasionally Claudia turned and said something to the woman, who stared out the window and blinked placidly in response. Her two children, both less than five years old, sat next to each other silently and gazed at me in the rearview mirror, resembling not so much two boys as their impassive ghosts.

By the time we dropped them off in the center of Rabinal and started to make our way back to the city, dark had fallen and I had missed all my classes. Claudia looked exhausted but elated. I decided to mention what had been bothering me from the time we picked the woman up at the bus station. "Claudia, she wasn't going to a funeral, was she?" She was quiet for half a minute, and then asked why I doubted it. "Well, she wasn't wearing the kind of clothes you wear to a funeral. And she wasn't crying. She just wanted a ride, didn't she?"

Claudia spoke quietly. "They don't wear black like we do for funerals. And they don't grieve like we do either. You could see the pain all over her face."

The next day, something similar happened, and the day after that, another something. Claudia asked things of me—every day and always more. And I always wanted to give her what she demanded. I was not used to being asked for so much. If you were to press me now, I would not be able to tell you which qualities of Claudia's I found so compelling. She had a plain, somewhat round face, and wavy unkempt hair. Short in the legs, a bit wide in the hips, with a ferocious strength in her arms, she appeared as unremarkable clothed as naked. She could be very childish and petty when things did not go her way, and had an irritating way of asserting herself when others were trying to accommodate, while letting herself get run over by people whom she trusted unwisely. Perhaps she was not a very good judge of character, but I began to notice that when I was not with her, I felt left out of something. Surrounded by people on the street or in class, I nonetheless felt stranded, alone, far away from a place where people were expecting me and wondering what had happened to me. I would grow impatient, then anxious. With her, I awoke to find myself safely back where I was supposed to be.

A Correspondence

*

I fell asleep in my chair after reading the letter for the third time, so that Tuesday morning I felt stiff and my neck ached. I dressed slowly and with some difficulty. When I had finally straightened my tie, I realized that I had forgotten to shave and so I was forced to remove both my shirt and tie and spend fifteen minutes with my neck craned painfully over the sink. This process at last concluded, I fried two eggs and made toast. I ate with more appetite than I usually did. Despite the discomfort caused by an awkward night's sleep, I was feeling surprisingly alert. I washed the breakfast dishes, left them to dry in the wooden rack beside the sink, and prepared my briefcase for work. On impulse, I walked into the study to glance again at the letter, which was sitting where I had left it on the armchair. I looked around the room and wondered when I had last opened the curtains in the study. Though I had lived in the house for decades, I could not remember ever once seeing them open. It suddenly seemed ridiculous to keep the room so dark. No doubt the tobacco and the odor of pages mildewed by humidity had been absorbed so thoroughly by every object in the house that I no longer noticed. I spent so much time in the study that I too probably smelled of smoke and mold. This thought prompted me to open the heavy green curtains that covered the sliding doors, and a pale, bitter light fell against me. As I looked down to avoid the glare, I noticed with surprise that the rug was filthy. I examined the pale, cloud-shaped stains with a sense of dismay. There was no doubt the room had been kept closed for too long.

After my eyes adjusted to the light, I opened the sliding door and stepped out onto the narrow concrete step. I couldn't remember having looked into the backyard before. It was completely unfamiliar to me. I saw about two meters of coarse crabgrass and then a whitewashed concrete wall blocked my view. At the top of the wall was a coil of barbed wire. I could barely see the upper story of a house on the other side of the wall. The second floor of the house had a wide balcony where a few desiccated palms sat partially obstructed by two long lines of laundry. When I looked to the right I noticed a laundry line in my yard as well; two of my shirts and a set of pajamas were hanging from it. For a single panicked moment, I couldn't understand how my clothes had come to be hanging there. With alarm, I imagined myself doing things in my own home—perhaps even outside of my home—that I later had no memory of, as though walking and acting in my sleep.

A moment later, of course, I realized that my clothing had been put there by the maid, who cleaned, washed, and prepared dinner for me during the day. I had turned on the step to leave the yard when I heard a door pulled open and saw the top half of a woman emerge onto the balcony of the neighboring house. She was wearing a towel and a pair of large sunglasses that hid half her face. Her long black hair was wet, and the drying fringes had begun to curl. The woman bent out of view for a moment and when she stood up again she no longer wore the towel. She switched the radio on and for a few moments stood, head cocked, as if getting her bearings. Then she turned away and, swinging back and forth gently to the music, took down the laundry. When her back was to me I stepped into the study. This had the confusing effect of bringing more of the woman into view, so that I could clearly see her buttocks swaying with the slow, rocking movement of her step. I closed the sliding door as quietly as possible, but felt unable to tear my glance from the gentle, irregular dance of the woman as she folded her laundry. After I had been standing in this way for at least a minute, an object flew towards me and crashed against the glass of the sliding door. My heart jumped, and I immediately thought someone on the balcony had caught me watching and thrown a rock at the window. But then I saw that the window was undamaged and that a bird no larger than my fist lay motionless on the concrete step. I crouched down and stared at it through the glass of the sliding door. The bird shuddered slightly and its eye gleamed. I watched, with my hand tensed on the handle of the sliding door. Once I began to pull it open, but then changed my mind and closed it again. When I stood up, the woman who had been on the balcony was gone.

On the way to the office, I began to feel well again. I sat in the back of the car, protected from the sunlight by the tinted windows and watching the city stir gradually into action. The man at the fruit stall by the end of the boulevard was taking a nap under his newspaper. Along the highway, rows of buses stopped to spew exhaust and discharge ordered streams of people in clothing that had been starched, pressed, then crumpled during the long journey into the city. The sign for a breakfast restaurant with a yoghurt theme advertised juices and pancakes in neon lettering. In its empty parking lot, plastic bags were swept up by the wind and constellated against the chain-link fence. By the time I arrived at my office, the weak sunlight and the mist had given way to a hot morning. Adela had prepared coffee that sat on my desk in a porcelain saucer. She had organized my desk and set a stack of files before the chair. I was not at all late—Adela was just coming in with the cream and sugar. She smiled at me, took my jacket, and left me to make my way through the morning paperwork.

*

There was another envelope marked only with my address when I returned to my house that evening. The letter was once again several typewritten pages. It began abruptly where it had left off the day before.

> *A few months later, Claudia moved in with me. My parents had bought me a house close to the university so that I would not have to make the long drive from their house to arrive in time for my*

classes. It was an unusual arrangement at the time; most young people lived with their parents until they were married. In my case, my parents could afford the house and they felt that I would benefit from the independence. But young people rarely lived together before getting married–it was bohemian, even indecent–and so I decided not to mention it. Claudia and I knew we would be married eventually, and in the meantime we began to feel that it was not enough to see each other during classes and after we had finished our work. Once Claudia moved in, the anxiety that I felt when she was not around subsided. Whenever she was absent, I knew for certain that I would see her again soon. We settled into a comfortable rhythm, leaving for school together, working at the library, and heading home together at night. My parents didn't ask any questions, and my contact with them dwindled to just the meeting each Sunday when they pulled together our closest family members for a long afternoon meal.

During this time, I began to shift from being obsessed with politics at the university to being involved in them. This shift happened almost without my noticing. At one point, Claudia asked me, "Why don't you come to the meetings with me?" I told her that the student meetings always seemed attended by people who actually knew what they were doing. She laughed. "If you went to them, you would know what you were doing, too." I expected that going to the meetings would make all the talk about the guerrillas and the government less remote, but I was mistaken. After going to more than a dozen meetings, those subjects seemed just as abstract as they always had. But perhaps this was my own fault for being too involved in my work. Whatever I was studying always became so absorbing that I thought of it constantly and related everything around me to it, almost to the point where the material ceased to be an interesting complement to my observations and instead became confusedly intertwined with them.

A Correspondence

I was, when Claudia asked me to go to the meetings, reading "Rabinal-Achí," the ancient ballet-drama of the Maya Quiché. The truth is that I was having difficulty understanding or even envisioning the play, and I took some comfort from a part of the prologue in which Luis Cardoza y Aragón admits that he was profoundly bored the first time he saw the play reenacted in 1966. He points out that if he had been able to see it in Rabinal, performed by its inhabitants, the impression would have been different. "But of course," he wrote, "we cannot really connect, in any way, no matter how hard we try, with the mentality, the psychology, the sensibilities, the idiosyncrasies, of the people of Rabinal, of the Quiché prior to Spanish colonization." For months, I grappled with "Rabinal-Achí," and as this period coincided with the time when Claudia convinced me to attend the student meetings, I inevitably had the play in mind as I sat among the other students, listening to the arguments that arose each time, such that the meetings and the play became entangled and I formed the unavoidable impression that I, like Cardoza y Aragón, was watching a dull and terribly inexpressive modern rendition of the old drama.

The vacation passed and classes recommenced the next year. The meetings became more frequent; twice, sometimes three times a week, I found myself going with Claudia to the cramped classroom where the giant spider plants hung side by side against the frosted window. Claudia began to take on a more important role. There was some talk of sending her to teach classes in a rural village, and I, of course, said I would go with her. We were in our last year, and Claudia began to plan for our departure from the city when we graduated in the spring. I participated in the planning, but Claudia was in charge, and I deferred to her judgment—in large part because I was less informed than she. For example, once I had to ask Claudia if she knew what our future address would be. She looked at me suspiciously and asked me why I needed to know. I told her that I wanted to give my parents the address so that they could send a few boxes of books. For several seconds, Claudia stared at me, frowning. "You can't give your parents the address," she said slowly. I asked her why. She said that we weren't allowed to give anyone our address–it was too dangerous. "We're not retiring to our country estate, we're moving to a dirty patch of woods with no running water, no electricity, and absolutely no mail service. Even if there were mail service, there would be nothing to send in or out, because no one there can read anyway. Perhaps you forgot. That's why we're going." I thought about this. Claudia shook her head. "Have you been listening at the meetings at all?" We were standing in the kitchen. Claudia was in the middle of the room with her arms crossed and I had paused in the middle of chopping a green onion. The sound of the blood rushing in my ears surprised me. I put the knife down and went to open one of the cabinets over the stove and then closed it. Then I opened a drawer, closed it, and went to look in the pantry. "Would you stop that?" Claudia said. "What are you looking for?" "I think I cut myself," I said. "Let me see." "I'm looking for the bandages." Claudia stepped in my way. "Let me see your hand. Show me where you cut it." For several seconds, Claudia stood in front of me, waiting. I held my hand out towards her, palm upward, and turned it slowly. We both looked at it. There was no mark on it anywhere. Claudia turned away. "I have been listening," I said. "I'm going with you."

  Then, at the beginning of our last semester, the nature of the meetings changed. There was no meeting called for two weeks. Sixteen days after the last meeting, I was sitting in the yard under the lemon tree, flipping through a few books, when I heard Claudia slam the front door. I lay quietly on the blanket, listening as she ran through the house, slamming doors and calling out my name. Finally she ran out into the yard, her hands trembling, her face discolored from crying, and she immediately tried to pull me to my feet. "Get up. Get inside," she cried. When she found me too slow to respond, she began flailing at me and pulling my clothes. "What, Claudia? What?" I said. "Get out of here–get inside–get inside now!" She succeeded in dragging me into the house. After she had locked the back door, pulled me into the bedroom, closed the curtains, and sat me on the bed, she told me what she had learned from a friend at the university. Ten days earlier, two students had been pursued at night by a car as they were leaving the university. After being chased through the network of roads around the campus, they had been cornered separately and shot. Their bodies had been found a couple of days later. The authorities made a statement accusing the armed guerrillas, but another student, who had seen them followed as they left, swore that the car had been a military vehicle. To me, the conclusion was clear. But Claudia did not see it the same way. "They're afraid of us," she said. "Finally." As she repeated this, her face, frozen in a grimace of combined horror and wrath, was bathed in a thick band of afternoon sun that came in from between the curtains. For a moment she seemed like a creature caught in the middle of a transformation. The right side of her, untouched by the light, remained alive–soft, rumpled, dark–but her left side had already turned to bronze. In a few moments the metal sheen on her hair and face would spread slowly across her nose and down her neck to her body, leaving her a lovely, rigid statue. I reached out and wiped her cheeks with my fingers. "Claudia," I said to her, speaking very softly, "who really cares if they're afraid of us?" She looked at me blankly. "It could have been you or me," I said. Claudia frowned, and a sharpness settled in her eyes. She pushed my hand away from her face. Looking down at the bedspread that we were sitting on, she began troubling a loose thread with her fingers. Then she spoke very quietly, almost absent-mindedly, as though commenting on the broken seam of the coverlet. "Coward." She turned away from the window and I lost the illusion of the bronze woman; with her face down and her forehead creased, she seemed very real—preoccupied but calm.

*

Adela had something to say to me on Wednesday. She came in to clear the coffee things and paused, smiling at me in her restrained way. I had hired her two years earlier because she was organized and disciplined and my experience with young women had taught me that this was rare. She spoke on the telephone with her mother once a day to make plans for dinner, and otherwise worked methodically and quietly from morning to afternoon. Her systematic and tidy way of approaching every task extended into her manner of movement and dress. I never saw her in anything other than a pair of low heels and a mid-length skirt. She wore cheap but pretty little earrings that matched her blouse. There was something comforting and simple about her appearance. When she moved through the office rooms, neatly stepping in and out with a quiet and economic step, I felt sure everything was running as efficiently and smoothly as possible.

"I don't know what you are doing with yourself this week," she said to me, still smiling, "but keep it up. Even if you tried to convince me that you had started exercising, I wouldn't believe it. Or maybe you've met someone? I wouldn't put it past you." With that she raised her eyebrows at me and walked out of the room. I shook my head. Adela was always teasing me in this way, and it was understood that I was supposed to ignore her comments and act tolerantly fed up. But she usually teased me by saying that I looked as though I hadn't slept enough. Adela was sometimes silly but she was perceptive.

A Correspondence

Cheered by her comment, I walked over to the office window. My offices were located on the first floor of an old municipal building overlooking the central plaza. When it was warm, as it was on that Wednesday, Adela opened the wooden shutters and the windows. They knocked against the cabinets if there was a light breeze. The meter-thick stone wall made of the window a little balcony, and I leaned out against it towards the plaza. Renovation of the plaza had long been in the planning stage. A dry fountain splattered with pigeon excrement stood in the center. The stones were slowly being pushed out of place by coarse weeds, and the tiles surrounding the fountain were chipped and faded. The fountain was unfortunately shaped: too tall and narrow for the base, the center spout stood like an awkward white limb sticking out of a bunched-up pant leg. It was terribly hot, and the plaza was almost deserted. A lone man sat in the shadow of the skinny fountain, feeding a mass of pigeons that crowded, pecked, and circled anxiously.

"Adela," I said, turning from the window. After a moment she walked in from the other room. "Don't bother to prepare lunch. I am going out today."

Adela's eyes widened. "You're going out? Where will you eat?"

I responded with some annoyance. "There are plenty of places to have lunch."

"Yes, but you've never been to any of them."

I waved my hand at her.

"Fine. But just in case," she said gently, "if you don't find anything, lunch will still be here." After a look from me she retreated.

*

I walked close to the inside edge of the sidewalk, in the shade of the trees that stretched over the walls and into the street. Under the jacarandas, the hot still air was stirred by a sweet and chilling dampness. The streets were quiet; I walked away from the plaza and through several side streets towards the Italian restaurant. From the outside, the restaurant was uninviting. I suppose at some point it must have been an office building. Then the offices closed, and the windows were shuttered and swallowed up by bougainvillea. The double glass doors looked in on what seemed to be an abandoned entryway. But as soon as you entered the building, the restaurant took on a different aspect. Walking in through the low foyer, you suddenly had the impression that you had ducked into a covered alleyway between two stone houses. The square awaited on the other side. To the right, a fruit vendor sat behind his cart swatting at flies. A bread vendor piled hot bread on his cart to the left. Further on you could see rows and rows of olive oil bottles through the glass windows of a storefront. A hat shop was visible across the square; a woman was trying on a pale yellow hat and looking at herself in a mirror. Buildings clustered around the square had their windows open. Through them you could see a woman carrying a baby, a baker kneading, a shoe repairman at his bench, a man grinding meat for sausages. The windows on the top floors were lined with flowerpots and the occasional line of laundry was stretched out from one window to another. In the center of the square, a little fountain spouted water that glittered in the bright sunlight. People bustled through the square, eating at the round metal tables, purchasing bread and vegetables, or tossing coins at the old accordion player, who sat in the far corner playing his instrument.

Of course, after only a moment, the true nature of the square became apparent. The bread and fruit stands were mere decorations; the lazy waiters leaned on them and poked carelessly at the unused food. The windows had been set into the wall and their scenes painted onto the surface. The shutters, never opened or closed, were covered with a thin film of dust and cobwebs. There was no sunlight, but a blue dome cleverly illuminated at its perimeter with bright lights. In fact, the fountain, the accordion player, and the food on the metal tables were the only genuine articles in the square. Everything else was only a half-hearted effort to create a brief illusion for the restaurant's patrons. When the illusion vanished, all that remained was the unpleasant contrast between the façade and the expectation excited in the visitor's mind by the momentary vision. Nonetheless, there was something appealing about the false Italian square. If you were able to revive the brief image of the square as it had first appeared, you realized that it was perfect; it was unchanging, utterly dependable: at any moment you could return to the restaurant and be assured that the Italian square remained just as you remembered it.

 I walked in between the sagging carts and waited by the side of the room until a waiter led me to one of the tables at the far end. After ordering my food, I sat back to listen to the fountain and the accordion. Most of the other people sitting at the tables were couples. They were older than I had expected them to be. The accordion player was rendering a piece by Piazzola that sounded like a sharp, tremulous complaint. It seemed to me for a moment that the woman painted into the window of the hat shop had smiled at herself in the mirror. She turned and impulsively purchased the hat from the storekeeper, whom I could not see from where I was sitting. And in fact the hat suited her perfectly. As she flounced out of the shop, holding the pale yellow hat against her black hair and taking tiny, exaggerated steps, in time to the music, my foot began to tap lightly. She held her hand out to me and I followed, stepping around the fountain and holding her waist against mine. When the tango turned more clamorous she pulled herself free and laughingly dipped her hat into the water. Before I could stop her she was tossing the water onto my face, onto my suit, and all the while she was laughing.

 "You like this tango?" The accordion player was standing near my table, smiling.

"Yes, thank you, it's very pleasant."

"I think it must bring back memories for you." He laughed. "For old men like us, what doesn't bring back memories?"

I nodded at him vaguely. "No, no memories. Just a lovely tango. Thank you."

He kept smiling, looking at me amicably. Then his eyes grew thoughtful and he looked more closely. "You look very familiar. I think we must know each other. Did you used to come here often?"

"No, I don't think so."

He squinted at me and reached out his hand tentatively. "Are you sure? I feel certain I know you."

"You must be mistaken. I'm sorry." I motioned for the waiter. When he reached me, I spoke to him apologetically. "I lost track of the time—I'm sorry. Would you be so kind as to wrap my lunch so that I can take it with me?" He nodded and moved away.

Though I was looking away from him, the accordion player showed no sign of leaving. In fact, his curiosity seemed to grow by the second. "It's just in back there, I've almost got it," he murmured, his hand outstretched cautiously, as if pushing aside the tissue paper surrounding something very fragile.

"Excuse me," I said to him, with some impatience. I had to step around him to get out of the corner and across the room to where the waiter stood by the cash register. He handed me my lunch in a brown paper bag. I had one last look at the faded Italian square before I stepped back out into the midday sun.

It was around that time that I began to see more of Pepe. I had not been in contact with him for many years. Pepe's father and my father were friends, and our parents were part of the same social circle. There were five families in all, and half a dozen boys of about the same age. So Pepe and I saw each other every other weekend, and on these occasions I was very friendly with the

A Correspondence

other boys. We also attended school together. I was always polite to the other boys in class, but we did not continue our friendship there. In fact, our interaction outside of the weekend gatherings was limited to the occasional polite greeting; sometimes, I must admit, I actually turned a different way or pretended not to notice them in order to avoid any awkwardness. When I went to college, Pepe went to work with his father, who was an investor. The family gatherings petered out and I lost touch with Pepe completely.

During the fall that Claudia and I were attending meetings, I ran into Pepe again. I was in a bookstore downtown, looking for a novel. I had been having trouble sleeping and Claudia suggested I read something to distract myself before going to bed. When I turned the corner of a shelf, half-engrossed in a book, I bumped into someone. The book fell to the floor. I looked up, and it was Pepe. For a moment, I had the urge to pick up the book and walk away without saying anything, but then the moment passed. A broad smile spread across his face and I saw that times had changed. Pepe embraced me warmly. I forgot about the book, and Pepe and I went to get a drink. He told me about doing investment work with his father, and I told him about Claudia and the university.

I found that Pepe and I had more in common than I thought. Or perhaps it was not that we had things in common, but we felt comfortable with the same things. I remember that spending time with Pepe caused me to contemplate for the first time how unlike my family Claudia's was. Pepe's family, on the other hand, was very similar to mine. There was something about the way we conducted ourselves in the world that was in common and different from Claudia's way. Perhaps, I thought, it came down to the simple fact that Pepe and I had the same manners. Whenever Claudia and I ate at a restaurant, she had a habit of thanking the waiter for anything, no matter how small: if he placed silverware, took an empty glass, or made room for a plate, she made a point of interrupting our conversation to thank him, leaving me with the awkward choice of remaining rudely silent or thanking him as well. But I didn't think it was necessary to thank the waiter for everything–in fact, it probably annoyed him. Pepe seemed to understand this, or he naturally acted the same way I did. As we sat and talked that first time, the waiter brought our coffee, arranged milk and sugar, and brought spoons; the whole while Pepe and I conversed, uninterrupted.

  The second time I got together with Pepe, I was a little late returning home. Claudia was waiting for me at the window. She ran to open the door and clasped my cheeks in her hands. "Where have you been?" she cried. I told her. "Don't do that to me," she said. "I get so worried about you. You can't come home late. I've been absolutely crazy." She clung to my hand and pulled me near her. As she rested her head on my shoulder, she released a sigh that felt like a tiny balloon deflating in my hand. I was surprised by this extreme show of affection, and I realized that she was feeling more anxiety than she expressed. For days, I was consumed with comforting Claudia, and she gradually returned to normal. When Pepe called again, I had forgotten all about him. "You need to get out of your house for a while," he remonstrated. I tried to make an excuse, but he continued to press me. "Claudia gets upset when I go out," I confessed. She was standing a few feet away, stirring hot chocolate over the stove. Without looking up, she waved her hand dismissively. "Don't exaggerate," she said, "I don't care if you go out. Go out, please. Maybe I'll get some work done."

  I told Claudia that I would return by five in the afternoon and went to meet Pepe at the Bar Banana. At five, Pepe suggested that we go down the street to La Condesa, and I agreed. La

A Correspondence

Condesa was packed, and it took us almost thirty-five minutes to get drinks. So it was past seven when I parked the car in front of the house. Claudia was sitting on the doorstep resting her chin on her knees and wearing one of my sweaters. When I got out of the car she ran up to me and threw her arms around me. "I'm sorry," I said to her. She kissed me all over and scolded me and kissed me again. For days she would not let me out of her sight.

Whenever Pepe and I got together, we talked about general topics, and he often asked me about Claudia. I spoke to him openly and without embarrassment because I soon realized he didn't really understand my relationship with Claudia at all. Usually he would ask me a question and then let me talk, nodding me on, and the few comments he made seemed so inapt that I wondered whether he actually listened to me. Once, I remember, Pepe asked me whether I thought Claudia was right for me. "I can't imagine life without her," I said. Pepe nodded. "It's just that she seems to make you nervous." "You mean the meetings and all that—oh yes, certainly." "No," Pepe said, "I mean her." I laughed. "I never know what to expect with her. She surprised me from the beginning. But that's what I like about her." We were sitting at an outdoor restaurant at the time, and Pepe was serving us wine. He filled my glass and then his own and took a sip. "I think we should get some pastries," Pepe said thoughtfully. I did not respond, but remained quiet for some time. "No, she doesn't make me nervous at all," I said. Pepe smiled and raised his glass. "Who?" he asked. There are some friendships that arise because both people are in circumstances where they want not so much to be understood as to have an opportunity to speak. Under these circumstances, a listener's lack of insight is not disappointing. On the contrary, there is even something pleasurable in knowing that one is safe from the unsettling penetration of an astute friend. I developed this kind of friendship with Pepe. And so I felt completely easy talking to him.

I can't remember what Pepe talked to me about. It is the nature of these friendships that one absorbs very little of the other person's thoughts and conversation.

*

Thursday afternoon was unusually hot. Adela had opened the windows in our rooms. I was finding it difficult to concentrate on my work. The plaza was completely deserted, and only a very few cars made their way cautiously around the perimeter as if their tires were in danger of melting. Adela had turned off the lights in the rooms to keep the air from getting too warm. As I sat in my leather desk chair with a sheaf of papers in front of me on the olive desk mat, a powerful drowsiness came over me. I felt an irrational desire to remove my shoes and socks so that my feet, which were feeling sweaty and swollen, could rest on the cool tile floor under the desk. Moving the papers to one side, I rested my forehead on the desk mat, crushing my nose slightly and letting my arms hang between my legs. It seemed that I blinked for only a moment. When I opened my eyes, I was disgusted to find a pool of spit on the desk mat. I stood up, eyeing the easy chair in the corner that I sometimes sat in to read, and found that I had, in fact, removed my shoes already. For a moment I paused, frowning, certain that I had thought about removing my shoes and socks but decided it would be inappropriate. Now that they were off, however, it was certainly too delicious to feel the cold tiles. I walked over to the easy chair and rested my head against the side. The list of things I had to do that afternoon flashed briefly through my mind, but I quickly let each item evaporate—there was nothing that could not be done on Friday. When my eyes were closed and I felt settled in the chair, a wave of relief washed over me. I was in a corner away from the sun; I felt only a light, cloudy sleepiness and none of the abrupt exhaustion that had left me pressed so uncomfortably face down on the desk. I had been resting this way for only a few moments when I suddenly began to feel uncontrollably irritated by my belt. My collar, too, was cutting unpleasantly into my neck. The door was closed. Adela would not disturb me and I would stay safely in my room. There was no reason not to remove my belt. I stood somewhat groggily and removed my belt, un-tucked my shirt, and opened my collar. The moment I opened my collar I felt that I would go crazy if I did not remove the shirt altogether. The sleeves felt unbelievably constricting—all the cloth had bunched up under my arms when I slid into the chair. I removed the shirt, put it and the belt on the side table, and happily dropped back into the armchair wearing only my pants and my undershirt. It seemed to me at that moment that there could be no greater pleasure than to sit this way, in relative comfort, and take a short nap while the sun was at its strongest. I rested my head against the side of the armchair once again and closed my eyes.

I had been snoozing this way for a few minutes when I suddenly had a thought: in the sitting room, there was a round leather footstool sitting between the two armchairs near the far wall that separated the sitting room from Adela's office. As soon as I had thought of the footstool, my legs and feet began to feel itchy with discomfort. I sighed, and tried to rearrange myself so that I would forget about the footstool, but it was no use.

Rising heavily, I walked barefooted across the room. I opened the door very quietly so that Adela would not hear me. The door to her office was closed. I would simply walk across the sitting room quietly, take the footstool, and return to my office. I began to tip-toe across the room, but stopped halfway. Why was it that I could hear nothing from Adela's room? The walls were thick, and I ordinarily never heard Adela, but the quiet seemed unnatural. I stood still on the carpet in the center of the room and strained to hear. Suddenly I heard the voice of a man coming from Adela's office. It began quite abruptly. I could not distinguish any words, but there was no mistaking the low, muted rumble. Tiptoeing carefully, I crossed the room and pressed my ear against the wall. The voice continued. Even with my ear against the wall, I was unable to make out what he was saying, but the voice began to have an unpleasant effect on me. He was speaking monotonously—there was no urgency in his tone—but something about it set me on edge. I began to feel a gnawing in my stomach, and as I struggled unsuccessfully to identify either the speaker or the cause of my dislike for him, I felt the anxiety building in my tightening chest. The more I thought about it, the more it seemed to me that I knew the voice. But I could not place it at all. And as the minutes went by and my anxiety rose, I could not even seem to pinpoint what disturbed me about the sound of his voice. I crouched as close as possible to the door and pressed my ear against the wall. In the minutes that followed—I do not know how many they were—I pushed my memory to its limit.

It often happens that I am struck by an emotion for which I cannot immediately recall a cause. For example, I will be pausing on a corner and crossing a street, and I will sense in the back of my mind a certain unidentifiable unpleasantness, a bitter atmosphere, but I will be unable to remember what has caused it. I will poke around in my memory and dispel the unpleasant fog until I remember: ah yes, when I was walking in the morning I ran into an acquaintance, who waved from across the street and called me by name. And after a few minutes of conversation, I asked him how his wife was doing, only to remember as the question was rolling off my tongue that his wife had left him six months earlier with their accountant. And after his face closed in and he answered that he didn't know, I was left with the sourness between us that is certain to remain with me until, after resurfacing again and again in my mind, it can finally begin to lose its rancidness and fade to become yet another flavorless image from this morning, or yesterday, or last

A Correspondence

month. But often the shadow cast by the incident—either bitter or sweet—will be long, and one will feel the anonymous emotion trickling to the front of one's mind again and again, unbidden.

The man in Adela's room had such an effect. The disturbing emotion conjured by his voice was deeply familiar, and this made my inability to identify him all the more distressing. For several moments, I was adrift: without a name or reference or memory to anchor the man's voice, I could only float helplessly in the various emotions provoked by it. Had I been able to say, *Ah yes–it's the director of the Society For Historic Preservation, who always comes to pester me for donations*, then I would have been able to address the unpleasant feeling and put it to rest at once. As it was, I could only flounder through the emotions that swept through me for some clue that would lead me to their origin. First and foremost, I felt a near terror of confrontation. The last thing I wanted was to speak to the man face to face. But I also felt a curious kind of embarrassment, as though something deeply shameful to both of us had occurred and we were both eager to put it to rest. At the same time, I felt suspicious. I knew, clearer than I knew anything, that he had no reason to be in Adela's office. It was, in fact, impossible that he should be in Adela's office. As this was the one thing I knew for certain, I pursued it in my mind, but succeeded only in causing myself greater anxiety: knowing that he should not be in Adela's office but that he indubitably was in her office began to fill me with irrational fear. Would there be a consequence to his being in Adela's office? I could not remember. And then, a strange unrelated sentiment that seemed to streak through the others like a flash of silver on a gray horizon: a kind of excitement, almost elation, at hearing him. Yet upon closer examination, this feeling was not caused by the man, but by knowing that the man and I were separated sturdily by the thick wall between the two rooms. I struggled to make sense of the kaleidoscopic emotions; I could only conclude that the man was familiar but damaging to me and that my sole consolation came from knowing some separation, however slim, remained between us. At this moment, when my desperate clawing through my memory had reached its most frenzied point, the man stopped speaking, quite suddenly. I held my breath. For several minutes, silence. I thought I would hear Adela speak, or, if I were very lucky, the sound of the door opening and closing as he left the room. (Would he leave at last?) But I heard nothing. Then, unexpectedly, Adela's chair creaked, and I heard her sharp heels on the floor. She was walking in the direction of the sitting room! I stood up quickly, my heart pounding, and flattened myself against the wall. There was no time to get behind the door. Adela was approaching the door, she was reaching the door, she had opened it.

She stepped briskly into the room, then stopped for a moment and turned around slowly. She looked at me with amazement and then a guarded concern. I remembered at that moment that I was barefoot and in my undershirt. But I could not be bothered to care. I gestured to Adela wildly so that she would close the door. After several moments of shocked silence, she walked back and shut it quietly. "Is he gone?" I whispered. She stared at me, seemingly without comprehending. "What are you talking about?" she whispered, looking openly worried. "The man who was talking to you. . . is he gone?" For what seemed like several minutes, Adela looked at me in astonishment. Finally, she shifted her feet, as if bracing herself for a sudden tremor, and said, "There was no one here. I was taking down the notes you dictated. There are more than a dozen letters to be transcribed and sent by this afternoon." As soon as Adela spoke, the memory of my anxiety seemed to vanish. All I could think of was my ridiculous state of disarray: what would Adela think, finding me barefoot and shirtless in the sitting room? It was not even appropriate for a young woman to see a man of my age in such a state of undress. "I'm sorry Adela, it is terribly hot. I had to

A Correspondence

take off my shirt for fear of suffocation." After a moment, she nodded slightly. "Would you please bring me some water? I will be back in my room. Dressed, of course. Please excuse me." I padded lightly back into my room and after several seconds I heard Adela's clicking heels as she left the sitting room and headed down the hall for some fresh water.

In early December, three of the organizers from Claudia's group went missing. They were last seen on campus, separately, though it is possible that they had come together unseen at some point later in the day. At first, their families and friends expected them to reappear. But after one week and then two weeks went by, it became increasingly clear that the students were either captive somewhere or dead. The group responded as it had before: the meetings became more clandestine and more determined than ever.

When I next saw Pepe, in mid-December, I complained to him about the meetings. "Does Claudia know?" he asked. "She knows," I said. "Why do you go then, if you don't want to be there?" I protested that Claudia could not go by herself. "Well, why does she have to go?" I thought about how to answer him. "Claudia is the type who will always love a cause more than a person. She feels for me as much as she's capable of feeling for anyone." "Is that it?" Pepe murmured. "I must meet her," he said confidently, as if meeting her would make it possible to change her. I thought it was a good idea. "I can go to your house the next time we get together," Pepe said. I reflected that Claudia would respond badly to Pepe if it were just the three of us. "She's better in groups," I said to him. "Why don't you come to the next meeting? It's the only occasion that she goes out for nowadays." The moment I finished speaking, I blushed with embarrassment. "Forgive me for being so thoughtless," I said. "I'm so used to disregarding my own safety that I seem to have forgotten that I can't do the same for everyone else. We'll find some other way for you to meet each other." But Pepe responded with a sympathy that I had not known him capable of. "Please," he said quietly, as if ashamed. "You and I are friends. We've been friends since childhood and now we're even closer. If you can go to look after Claudia, why can't I go to look after you?" He spoke with such sincerity that I could not bring myself to argue. We agreed that he would attend the next meeting, and I gave him the instructions that he would need to join us.

I'm not sure why I decided not to tell Claudia that Pepe was going to be at the meeting. Mostly likely when I arrived home all thoughts of Pepe vanished, as usual, and when I next thought of him, both he and his attendance at the meeting seemed so insignificant that I felt they weren't worth mentioning. But then again, I wasn't entirely sure how Claudia would react to Pepe. There was still the chance that Pepe would decide not to show up, and so it seemed silly to upset her in advance only to discover that Pepe had not appeared.

We arrived late that day. On the way to the designated meeting place, we stopped at a light near a large intersection. There were two children on the street, putting on a little performance and begging for change. The younger child sat on the shoulders of his brother, wearing an oversized mask of an American president that covered his whole head. They were wearing, between them, a baggy, dirt-smudged suit that flapped awkwardly as the older child staggered around under the weight of his brother. The little boy wearing the mask was juggling what looked to be painted eggs. Together, the pair presented a pathetic and hilarious image: a bedraggled politician, drunkenly juggling his last possessions on the streets of a tiny country whose name he had probably been unable to pronounce correctly before his fall from grace. As they stumbled towards us, Claudia and I were both watching with our mouths

A Correspondence

half-open, half-smiling. Suddenly, one of the eggs tumbled out of the child's hand and onto our windshield. The glass cracked instantly and a maze of opaque lines streaked across the pane.

When I had assured that the glass was only cracked and not broken, I stepped out of the car. I had expected the children to be long gone, but they stood by the side of the road: two separate and tiny people in oversized clothes, giving the impression that the politician had been the victim of a powerful spell. They looked at me blankly. One of them gestured towards the car and asked for the egg. Speechlessly, I leaned over the car and found it still embedded in the windshield. When I had picked it out carefully, I discovered that it was made of polished stone—marble perhaps—and quite heavy. I handed the egg back to the top half of the politician, who was holding his head upside-down at his side, and then both he and his other half ran away and into the traffic. By this time, we had caused a major traffic jam with the car, and Claudia was in tears. I climbed back into the car and by sticking my head out of the side window was able to drive slowly out of the intersection.

When we finally arrived at the meeting, which was taking place in the storeroom of a roadside restaurant, the opening announcements were well under way. Everyone turned to look at us when we walked in. I saw Pepe sitting by himself on the other side of the room and nodded to him. He nodded slightly and smiled. Claudia and I took our places at the back of the room between two shelves. I usually found it difficult to keep my mind on the meeting, especially when an argument ensued and everyone spent hours elaborating and clarifying their opinions. That day was no exception. I was particularly distracted by the series of events that had caused our minor accident at the intersection. It reminded me of something, some memory, but I was unable to recall it. The announcements were concluded; the room began to grow very warm. We were not allowed to open the windows in the storeroom. In fact, they were covered carefully with both shutters and thick curtains. A single phosphorescent bulb in the center of the ceiling cast a raw, surgical glow over us. As I watched the young man who was speaking, I tried to stay awake by concentrating on the memory that was eluding me. I had an odd sensation about the memory: before knowing what it was, I sensed the feelings associated with it. A sense of confused indignation and uneasiness seemed to spring from the memory, which I could not yet identify from the grab-bag of images that presented themselves to me. I sifted through them unhurriedly, trying to match the strange emotions with their source. The young man's speech seemed to reach a concluding point. A young woman next to him spoke. They were taking a vote. I looked at Claudia and raised my hand when she did. I glanced across the room and noticed that Pepe had moved. He was standing by the door. I observed too that he did not vote.

Then the memory appeared before me, as if summoned. It was something that had occurred more than a decade earlier and that even then had probably remained in my mind for no more than a few hours. Nonetheless, the memory now came to me vividly, and as I recalled its details, the emotions they were charged with released their full power, as if they had been grains of pepper packed long ago, air-tight, that were now being crushed before my face.

I could have been no more than eleven when the first few family gatherings with my parents and the parents of the other boys took place. On the third or fourth meeting, we met at my house. After dinner, the adults sat in the living room, and all of the children went to my room. There was one older girl–she might have been sixteen or seventeen–who always ended up looking after two toddlers. Most of the time, she kept them apart from us boys or else

A Correspondence

stayed with the adults if the toddlers had been left at home. But that night she came along with us. Everyone politely inspected the things in my room. We played some music. After a while we simply sat around, talking and joking about things. At one point, when we were getting sleepy, Pepe said he had a very funny game to show everyone. He asked me if I would volunteer to help.

Pepe followed me to my parents' room, where Pepe chose one of my father's striped shirts in the wardrobe. We stood in front of the mirror, and Pepe had me hold the shirt against my chest, backwards, as if I were going to button it in the back. Then he went to stand behind me, slipped his arms under mine, and pulled the sleeves onto his arms. With the shirt pulled tight against me, it looked as though Pepe's arms were mine. He poked my cheek. We both doubled over, giggling, at what looked like me poking myself.

Back in my room, Pepe pulled my hair, rubbed my belly, and made all sorts of ridiculous movements, which made everyone in the room wild with laughter. "Talk about something," he whispered to me. Flushed and excited, I began to talk about whatever occurred to me. For some reason, perhaps because we were wearing my father's shirt, I took on the persona of some stiff, older man. Pepe accordingly crossed his arms, waved his finger reprovingly, and fiddled compulsively with the shirt collar. At some point, I later supposed, the joke probably began to wear thin. The laughter grew reluctant, as if everyone had suddenly become very tired. But I didn't notice. I kept talking, and my monologue became more outrageous and more exaggerated. The room went completely silent, but still I could not contain my excitement. I was sure that if I spoke animatedly enough, their great, spontaneous, uncontrollable laughter would resurge.

Miraculously, it did. People looked up, and suddenly giggled. One boy snickered, then laughed into his hand. The children looked me in the eye with curiosity. Then the older girl, standing near the back of the room, spoke softly. "Stop that, Pepe." For some reason, the other children in the room seemed to think this an invitation to laugh louder. "Pepe, stop it," she repeated, more firmly. I faltered, and my monologue derailed. I could not think what had upset her. The baby she was holding started to whimper and cry. I stopped speaking altogether, and the room settled into a low murmur of snickering laughter. The girl walked up to us and tore off my shirt. "Help me take them back to their mother," she said, handing me the crying baby. "I get lost in this huge house of yours." I took the baby and followed her out. Pepe shrugged at me, and I left him and the rest of the boys alone in my room.

The memory had set me on edge. Inadvertently, I glanced at Pepe, to dispel the unpleasant recollection with the image of how I now knew him. He was gazing across the room with a look of bored and contented vacancy. I turned to Claudia. Her eyes were on the speaker and she was wearing a look of grim concentration. I knew she wouldn't like it, but I leaned over anyway and gave her a little kiss on the cheek to make myself feel better. Surprised, she blinked at me and gave me a flicker of a smile. It was at that moment, when I was still leaning in and watching the unexpected smile, that the meeting ended. The door burst open. There were shouts and screams, which seemed to come from very far away, and the sound of automatic gunfire. A streak of sunlight filled the room, and I turned to see people yanking the curtains and shutters off of the windows. Tables and chairs were overturned. Claudia and I were frozen—we had both instinctively crouched near the ground. I threw myself over her and pressed us both against the floor. For several minutes, I saw nothing and only heard the shots being fired and the commotion of those who were trying to get away.

When the gunfire stopped, we stayed on the ground. I could feel Claudia trembling underneath me. Someone near the windows was howling, "Ay, ay, ay . . . ." There were two short bursts of fire and the wailing stopped. When someone grabbed me by my shirt collar and pulled me up, I did not resist. I released Claudia, who was similarly dragged upright, and stood as I was instructed to. Claudia began to cry silently, and I glanced around the room. About half of the people who had been at the meeting were standing as we were. Most of them were staring down at the ground. Of the other half, perhaps only four or five had gotten away through the window. The rest lay in various positions around the room: entangled in their chairs, slumped in what had been crouching positions beneath the tables, or sprawled against the wall by the windows. The soldiers stood stiffly around the room, pointing their weapons at those of us who were standing. For some reason, they struck me as very small. Only their weapons seemed disproportionately huge. Their faces were calm, and I had the momentary impression that they had nothing to do with the shooting, but had only rushed in afterwards to guard us. There were two men walking around the room, surveying the damage, inspecting the members of the meeting who were standing, and occasionally speaking to each other in low voices. One of them, a man in uniform, was clearly the one in charge of the soldiers. The other one was Pepe.

We were in the storeroom for only a few minutes more. I had the sense for years afterwards that I had not actually been at the meeting, but simply watched the brief series of events during and after the meeting through a crack in one of the windows. In trying to recall what I felt, I drew a complete blank. The only real sensation I could identify was the sense of stifling heat and anxiety that simmered in me during the meeting as I recalled what had happened in my room that night, years ago, with the other children. That feeling of stuffiness, the dry smell of flour and cardboard that was released as the storeroom grew warmer, was the *only memory that truly assured me that I had been present at the meeting.*

But of course I was not at the window but there, in the room, watching as people were led away one by one. The man in uniform and Pepe walked up to each of the standing members of the meeting, and Pepe said something briefly in the man's ear. As they approached us, I realized that he was telling the man each person's name. The man nodded, as if adding the name to some internal register, and then moved on to the next person. As he was left behind, the person who had just been named was taken away by a soldier. They reached Claudia before they reached me. Pepe leaned in towards the older man and said her name, very firmly and distinctly. He nodded, and they moved on to me. A soldier who had been standing in front of Claudia walked up to her and pulled her towards the door. She turned to look at me over her shoulder, and I met her gaze. I felt it move into me, forcefully, as if something had plunged into my stomach. I struggled to decipher the expression in her eyes, but understood nothing. Then she turned her head and stumbled out the door of the storeroom.

Pepe looked at me with his familiar, detached expression. He leaned in towards the older man, but did not say my name. Instead, he said, "This one is different. He's here against his will." The older man looked at him questioningly, as if to ask how such a thing could be possible. "Out of devotion to the woman, purely. He has no mind for politics. On his own, he's quite useless." There was a pause, during which both men seemed to assess me. The older man appeared less to be doubting Pepe than wondering how it was possible for me to exist. He seemed disgusted. Pepe leaned towards me slightly. "Am I wrong?" he asked me quietly. They both waited, Pepe with interest, the officer with barely-concealed repugnance. I said nothing. After a long pause, the officer motioned to a soldier nearby and said, "Make sure he gets in his car." Then they moved on to the next man.

Escorted by the soldier, I walked out to the car. I could see no military vehicles or other evidence outside the restaurant of what was going on within. The soldier's face was motionless as I unlocked the car and got into the driver's seat. I sat there for a little while behind the shattered windshield. I was looking up at the soldier questioningly, waiting for his instructions. After a few moments, he blinked and gave me a grim smile, as if apologizing that he could not go with me. Then he waved his gun in the direction of the road. I started the car and rolled up the hill, out of the restaurant's driveway and onto the main road.

The meeting place was on the outskirts of the city, so it took me nearly forty minutes to reach the center. It seemed too much of an effort, or perhaps it simply did not occur to me, to lean my head out of the window as I drove home. Everything before me was distorted by the opaque fissures in the glass. The lights doubled; the road split absurdly in opposite, impossible directions; the buildings hung in the air, their lower halves missing, like torn photographs. On a highway near the center of the city, a police officer stopped me. I pulled over by the side of the road and waited for him to approach. He looked critically at the car and then down at me through the car door window. "What are you driving around with a broken windshield for?" he asked. I told him that I was just trying to get home. "It just happened," I said. "Just a minute ago, the whole thing shattered." "You can't drive around like that," he said. "There's an auto shop around the corner. Drop it off there before you cause another accident." Just to make sure, he followed me around the corner and watched me give my keys to the attendant. After leaving my name and address on a tag for the keys, I walked to the corner and looked at the bus schedules to find one that would take me home.

I decided to stay in the same house. After a couple of years I put Claudia's things away in one of the rooms. I could not bring myself to get rid of them, nor could I see my way to selling the house. I finished my degree at the university. In fact, I went on to get two other degrees. By the time I was in my late twenties I had a secure job with a good salary. I had a few acquaintances at work, but I did not cultivate any friendships. I went out with women once in a while, but I didn't have any serious relationships and I never got married. The weekend meetings with my parents continued. Occasionally I went on short trips with them for a long weekend or a week at a time. I don't believe I ever saw Pepe again, but I can't be sure; there are often times, to this day, when I feel certain that I have caught a glimpse of him in a crowd. I'm sure this kind of life sounds dull, but it hasn't been. I think perhaps the few years with Claudia contained, in a concentrated form, enough excitement and anxiety to fill a lifetime. This must be the case, as I find that I spend much of my time thinking about those years and reliving small segments of them over and over in my mind, as if extracting a tiny drop of their concentrated substance to last over several days.

*

It was past midnight when I finished reading. I carefully folded the letter and put it back in its envelope. Then I lifted myself out of the old leather armchair and walked over to the desk. The four letters were there, in their envelopes, stacked neatly. I sat in the desk chair and opened the middle drawer, which held pens, clips, stamps, envelopes, and boxes of writing paper. I selected a gray paper and took my good pen out of its case. After testing the pen and reordering the paper several times, I sat for a few minutes, gazing at the impression left in the cracked leather armchair. Then I began to write.

A Correspondence

I have taken your advice, and imagined you, little by little, as some person, known but unknown, who moves through his life in an ordinary way. I have imagined an address, and a house, and a conventional set of clothes, and a neatly-trimmed beard and a pair of wire-rimmed glasses.

In the first letter you sent me, you asked me to reconsider a judgment. After reading all four of your letters, I am not certain which judgment you mean. That of your parents? Of the children you knew when you were young? That of Claudia? If so, which? Was it her first impression of you or her last that really counted? Or is it the judgment of Pepe, of the officer who was in the storeroom, that really matters to you? Do you mean to ask whether their judgment was fair? Or do you mean to ask whether they could have been avoided?

But what else could you have done? You had to form your own opinions; you had to be a student; you had to fall in love with Claudia. Once you had fallen in love with her, you had to follow her. Once you had followed her, you had to defend yourself from her. When Pepe said to you, "Am I wrong?" it didn't occur to you to contradict him because he wasn't wrong. You would never have been there if it hadn't been for Claudia, and you were there against your will. In fact, you could not know where they were taking Claudia. Perhaps it was not immediately apparent what you would gain by following her, once more. Perhaps, somewhere in the back of your mind, you had the idea that you might do her more good if you were released.

Of course, Pepe was not really asking whether you were there against your will. If you remember, the way he looked you straight in the eye and paused, he was really asking, "Do you want to go with Claudia?" And in this sense, too, you answered truthfully. The difficulty lies in all the other times, prior to that day, that you did not. How many times did the question come to mind?

Each time you replied "yes" when you meant "no." Of all the hundreds of times the question arose, you answered honestly only once.

Of course, the question looked quite different that day in the storeroom. When Pepe said to you, "Am I wrong?" you were not thinking of Claudia's face as she was pushed through the door. You were thinking about the face of the student who had fallen by the windows and rolled onto a sack of flour. The sack, cut through by bullets, had released a thick cloud that rose and settled on his skin and clothes. You were thinking of his face: a white mask punctured by the red opening of his mouth.

And then again, you were not thinking of Claudia's face as she was pushed out the door because that was not the last time that you saw her. Or heard her, in any case. Are you forgetting that as Pepe spoke to the officer, you heard her voice from behind the door through which she had just vanished? It was Claudia's voice–she did not say anything–it was simply a cry. So that when Pepe asked, "Am I wrong?" the sound of Claudia's cry was still ringing in your ears. In fact, hearing her as you stared at the student on the ground, you could not help confusing the two in your mind.

*

I had just paused to wipe the perspiration from my forehead when I heard the phone in the corridor ring. It rang twice, three times: a shrill, distant sound muffled by the heavy door of the study. I decided to leave the call unanswered. It rang on, fifteen, sixteen, seventeen times. Finally, at the twenty-fifth ring, I lost my patience and threw my pen down. I stood heavily, pushing the desk chair back, and walked across the study. When I reached the door, the phone was still ringing. I walked out under the stairs and around the corner to the little table where the phone sat next to a vase of plastic flowers. It was ringing for the thirty-eighth time when I lifted the receiver. "Yes," I said, the impatience coming out in my voice. There was an uncertain pause, and then a man's voice: "May I speak with Claudia?" I was silent. The man on the other end of the line waited. Then he spoke again. "Excuse me, can you hear me? Is Claudia..." I interrupted him. "Claudia isn't here." I hung up.

I took my handkerchief from my pocket and wiped my face carefully. Then I folded it and replaced it in my pocket. I stood in the corridor and looked at the phone. It was a white phone with buttons and a small light illuminating the time, which was digitally displayed in the center. After several minutes, I walked back to the study, turned off the light, and went to bed.

*

The next day Adela had not made the coffee. I sat in my chair and waited pointedly for her to arrive with it. When she finally walked in, she was so startled that she almost dropped the tray. "You're here so early," she exclaimed. I pointed at the coffee tray. She jumped back into motion, carrying the tray to the desk and serving me coffee before she turned to leave the room. When she had reached the door, she paused and turned. "It's no good coming in early if you're not going to get anything done. You should go back home and go to sleep." I waved my hand at her and she walked away across the sitting room. It promised to be another unbearably hot day. Taking my coffee with me, I walked to the windows and opened the shutters slowly. A line of children in uniform was making its way across the square. They must have been in about the fourth grade-all of them girls, all of them wearing pleated blue skirts and white blouses. Their teacher was already out of sight as they wound around the fountain and over the uneven stones. For the most part, they walked with impressive coordination, in pairs, holding hands.

As I watched them, one little girl shook her hand free of her classmate's and stepped out of line. She glanced ahead for a moment, to make certain that the teacher had not seen her, and then ran over to the fountain. She squatted down close to the ground so that her skirt dragged and her cap tilted forward precariously. The line of children left the square, and she remained, inspecting closely whatever it was she had found. She poked it delicately with a stick.

I heard Adela's heels on the tiles as she walked back into the room. "Leave the coffee things," I said to her, without turning. The little girl lifted what she had found very carefully with the tip of the stick. She held it up and slowly straightened herself, holding her cap with the other hand the whole while. Then she turned towards the fountain as if preparing to drop her find in its base. As she could not reach over the lip of the fountain's base, she released her hat and unsteadily tried to push herself up onto the ledge. Still holding the stick, she rested her stomach on the edge of the fountain and for several moments teetered like a spoon balanced on the edge of a bowl. "The fountain is empty," I said quietly. "Yes, they'll never fill it," I heard Adela say. "Will you sign this, please?" I turned away from the window and walked to the table. Adela held out the letter and I signed it without reading it. She nodded crisply and clattered out of the room, carrying the mail and a set of tapes for dictation. When she had left the room, I returned to the window. The square was deserted; the girl was gone. The fountain looked the same as it had before. I closed the shutters to keep out the oppressive sunlight and walked back to the desk. After pouring myself another cup of coffee, I sat down to begin the day's paperwork.

Weeping Madonna

Chris Abani

> *This is the journey the kola must make. The eldest man, in presenting the kola nut to the gathered guests, must say, 'This is the King's kola'. The youngest boy in the gathering then takes the bowl and passes it to the eldest guest and says, 'Will you break the King's kola?'*

The alabaster Madonna wept bullet holes. They traced a jagged pattern down her face and robes to collect in a pool of spent shell casings at her feet. She trampled a serpent underfoot which seemed to be drowning in the brass waves. Her arms, folded over her immaculate heart, kept it from flying out of her chest. Her face, cast lovingly towards heaven, wore a sad smile. Sitting among the shell casings at her feet, a thirteen-year-old Innocent sucked on a battered harmonica. The sound whispered out of the honeycombed back, floating up, past the Madonna to an askew Christ on the cross. It went in through the wound in his side, worming around and out the nails in his feet, condensing on the walls of the pock-marked church in a dew of hope.

In the burnt out skeleton of the church, in the reluctant shadows cast by the walls, a group of soldiers, rifles in arms, bristled. They were young, the oldest no more than fifteen. The sweet smell of marijuana floated past them mixing with the smell of stale sex, warm blood, burnt wood and flesh, rising in an incense offering to God. Cicadas hummed and the very air, hot and humid, crackled with the electric sigh of restless spirits. The smoker, seventeen, the oldest person in the platoon, was known simply as Captain. He stubbed out the spliff he was smoking, grinding it into the dry crumbly earth. It was 1969 and they were part of the Biafran Army's Boys Brigade.

The harmonica sang breathily as Innocent teased a hymn from it. The notes fluttered hopefully, hesitantly, a fragile thing. But as the sun warmed them, they rose steadily. Some of the soldiers in the shade who were familiar with the catholic hymn hummed along. The hymn brought back memories of a different time, a different place.

"Hey, music boy! Play me another song," Captain shouted.

Innocent stopped sucking on his harmonica.

"Like what?" he asked.

"You know de Beach Boys? Play dat." Captain laughed loudly.

Innocent turned away and went back to playing the hymn. There was no love lost between him and Captain. Mostly because out of everyone in the platoon, Innocent was the one he chose to bully the most. Across from him, tied to a tree, were the corpses of the Catholic priests who used to run this parish. Their white soutans were caped in crimson. On the floor near them, one dead, one whimpering in shock, were two nuns that had been raped by Captain. The dead one had tried to struggle. Innocent had watched, afraid to intercede. Afraid of what Captain would do to him. He had stared into the nun's eyes that were as grey as a fading blackboard, watched her implore him as her life ebbed away, steeling himself. Like Captain said, "War is war."

The rest of the carnage, the shooting of the priests, the burning of the church and the slaughter of the congregation who had been worshipping inside it, had been done before they got there. Most of the dead had been refugees fleeing from the advancing federal troops. Innocent could no longer tell the difference between rebel and federal controlled territory. The lines kept shifting.

It was harmattan and everything was coated in fine red dust. A sloughed-off fragment of another hymn popped into Innocent's head, the words flooding: *Are you washed, in the blood, in the soul cleansing blood of the lamb?* He shrugged it away and went back to his playing. The other boys in the platoon rippled towards Captain. They were hungry and wanted permission to go scavenging. Innocent took the harmonica out of his mouth and gazed past them.

Off to the right was the priests' house. A one-story structure with big sweeping verandahs and a balcony that wore a lovely ornate wrought-iron balustrade. Bougainvillea crept up the walls in green and purple lushness. The building's brilliant whitewash surprised the red earth of the courtyard. To the left stood two low bungalows that had been the school. In the middle, behind him was the smoking remains of a church, its once white walls mascaraed in black tear tracks. In the quadrangle between the buildings rose the statue of the Virgin shadowed by the statute of Christ on the cross perched in front of the church. Towering above the Madonna and Christ was a bamboo flagpole. White twine beat forlornly on it in the wind, wishing for a flag.

Some bodies littered the road into the church compound and on the dry grass that was tenaciously holding on to the hard earth. There were some men, mostly women and even a few children. Some of them had been shot. Others had been hacked to death with machetes. A few had been clubbed. Blood stained their clothes. The whitewashed stones lining the road were flecked with the dried blood, like teeth stained with pink dental dye. There were still pools of blood clotting flies into a knobby black crust. The earth was baked so hard it couldn't absorb any more blood. It refused to soak it up.

Even though the enemy had been responsible for this massacre, Innocent knew the rebels weren't much better. He had long since lost any belief in the inherent goodness of the rebel cause and the evil of the enemy. Once he had been driven by deep idealism. Now he just wanted to survive. He had seen Captain commit enough atrocities to realize that they were all infected by the insanity of blood fever.

He looked at the dead bodies. They had probably converged on the church compound believing they would be safe here. Protected by God's benevolence and man's reputed fear of Him. How wrong they had been. He could have told them that. There is only one God in war. The gun. One religion. Genocide. He looked up to see Captain studying him intently.

"Oi, music boy!" Captain called. "Music boy!"

Innocent ignored him.

"Oh, music boy is angry dat we defiled God's servants. He believes God is going to punish us. Dat's why he is playing his mouth-organ, to ease de souls of the dead mercenary priests to heaven or hell," Captain said, bursting into deep laughter.

Innocent stopped playing. He was suddenly nervous; something dangerous in the way Captain laughed. Still laughing, Captain got up and walked over to Innocent. Innocent sprung up and walked away. Captain stopped and turned to one of the boys in the group.

"James."

"Sar."

"James, aim at dis bagger and fire on command."

James hefted his Mark IV rifle up, rammed a bullet into the breach and pointed it at Innocent's chest.

"At yar command, Sar!" he said.

"Do you see? Do you see obedient, eh? Next time I call you, you jump up, run over and say Yes Sar! Do you understand me?"

"Yes Sar!" Innocent said snapping to attention. He knew Captain was a little crazy and capable of killing him.

"Good. Music boy!"

"Yes Sar!"

Captain laughed. Turning to James he said: "Ajiwaya," a Biafran Army term that meant, "As you were." James lowered the rifle. It was still cocked. He held it gingerly. Having no safety catch, it was extremely dangerous to carry once cocked. James spoke up, deflecting Captain's attention from Innocent.

"Sar. Permission to speak, Sar!" he said.

Captain gave him a perfunctory nod.

"We are hungry, Sar. Can we sarch de priests' house to see if we can find food, Sar."

"Go on," Captain said.

The group broke rank and with whoops of glee tripped their way to the priests' house. It had not been burnt and that made Innocent suspicious. The whole place was probably booby-trapped. He shouted a warning but nobody listened. They were too hungry. None of them had had anything more substantial than wild fruit foraged in the forest. No meat since most of the animals had fled deep into the jungle to hide. Innocent remembered the last time they had meat.

One of the boys had shot a monkey. They had done it before. Shot monkeys. Cooked them into a pepper-soup that smelt delicious. But Innocent could never eat any. The monkey had looked so human, the small hands so like a child's, scraping the side of the container used as a pot. One monkey, obviously not dead, had jumped up after being shot. One of the boys had crushed its skull under the butt of his rifle, cutting off its baby squeal. Everyone teased Innocent about not eating the monkey. Called him a coward. A woman. Not a warrior. He pointed out how much like cannibalism it all seemed. Captain swore at him, saying he would make him eat the next dead enemy soldier they came across. The boys hooted with laughter. The last time however, only a few weeks ago, he had given in to the taunting and taken a piece of the meat. Later he was sick, but he couldn't get the taste of it out of his mouth. The frightening thing was, he had enjoyed it.

A few minutes later, the boys emerged with tins of pork, stale bread, bottles of hot beer and altar wine. They had been left behind by the federal troops who were Muslims. They brought the loot to Captain and only when he had selected what he wanted did they pounce on the rest. Tins were bayoneted open. Hot beer boiled over roughly opened bottles. Nobody paid any attention to Innocent, or offered him any food. There was only one motto here: "We shall survive."

Innocent got up and walked up the three steps into the burnt out shell of the church. The fire hadn't consumed everything. Three walls, the roof—three quarters of the church—had been burnt. In the still smoking pews he saw the roasted corpses of the congregation. They had been shot, clubbed or macheteed to death, and then tied to the pews to roast with the church. The air was heavy with the stench of roasted meat, not nauseous, but actually mouth watering. Innocent wondered if they had all been dead or whether some had survived the shots, clubs and machetes, to be consumed screaming by the fire. Did dying in a church guarantee you a place in heaven, he wondered, walking up the aisle crunching soot, ash and charcoal underfoot.

The altar had miraculously survived. It was still set for mass. White altarcloth, chalice, communion wafers still stuffed into the chasuble, water, wine, candles, flowers and an open missal. Innocent walked round the altar and read the open page. He used to be an altar boy and the Latin was not difficult for him to read. *Kyrie Eleison, Christe Eleison, Kyrie Eleison.*

Behind the altar, not wearing a single bullet hole, and only slightly cracked from the heat, was a stained glass window. It filtered the harsh sunlight in soft blues, yellows, pinks, oranges and greens. Innocent noticed that the floor, the altar, the missal and his body had become a patchwork of colour. He licked the tip of a blue finger and peeled away a red page, an orange one and a green one. He paused and read. *Agnus Dei qui tollis peccata mundi, miserere nobis, Agnus Dei qui tollis peccata mundi, dona nobis pacem.* He smiled at the last line. *Grant us peace.*

His stomach rumbled and he wished he had fought with the others for some morsel. He looked out. The rest of the platoon was now gorging on paw-paws plucked from a nearby tree. His eyes took in the now barren tree, so much for that idea. He turned back to the altar. Nobody was going to miss the communion wafers and he was sure God didn't want him starving to death. Carefully hoisting his rifle onto his back and dropping his harmonica into his pocket, he picked up the chasuble and began stuffing his mouth full of the sweet white circles of bread. Finishing it off, he emptied water into the wine in the chalice. Saying a silent prayer for forgiveness, he reached for the chalice. Even as he picked it up, he heard the click of the bomb arming itself. The bastards had booby-trapped the altar.

Copyright © 2003 by Chris Abani

The Lemon Tree

Brigid Pasulka

There was a limousine waiting outside the prison gate the day Vova got out. A proper limousine—long and black, with a boomerang antenna and a young, gap-toothed driver leaning against one of the doors. Behind the limo were only bare green hills, losing their footing and slipping into the Volga River about twenty kilometers distant. The other prisoners hooted through the wire mesh up above.

"Driver! Driver! I'll be right down!"

"Yeah, yeah. Just need to get my dinner jacket."

"Yeah, my dinner jacket and my whore."

"Yeah, be right down."

The gap-toothed driver advanced toward Vova, reaching out with both hands to take the small sapling cradled in the crook of his arm. "Vladimir Borisovich?" he asked.

"Did Poprok send you?" Vova clasped both hands around the root ball, weaving the handle of a dangling plastic bag between his fingertips. He wore the same jeans, the same blue hooded sweatshirt that he had worn the morning he had been arrested, the morning he found out that Poprok had turned him in.

"Mr. Poprok thought you'd be more comfortable in a limousine than taking the train."

Vova laughed and shook his head. He bumped the sapling up on his hip like a child too big to be carried.

The Lemon Tree

"You work for Poprok?"

"Yes, sir."

Vova squinted at the boy, at his gelled hair and his clear eyes. "Watch your back."

The boy shifted his weight and cleared his throat. "Sir?"

"Tell Poprok I'd rather walk." He started down the road, stiff-legged so as not to splash mud on the back of his trousers.

The young driver followed closely behind, nearly tripping over Vova's heels. "Wait. You don't understand. I've come all the way from Moscow. Mr. Poprok will be upset if I come back without you ... I could lose my job.... Come on, man."

Prisoners shouted from above. "What the hell're you doing, Vova?"

"I told you he wasn't right in the head."

"Hey, free limo everybody! Free limo!"

The driver looked up at the windows of the prison, wide as the spine of a book and covered by chicken wire. Still, he hurried back to the limousine, scrambled into the front seat and turned the ignition.

"Wait, driver!" the prisoners continued to shout. "Wait right there! I'll be right down ... in another three and a half years. Wait!"

"Vova, you fucking *durak!*"

The black limousine crept after Vova for about a kilometer, the driver shouting out the window at Vova. "Vladimir Borisovich, be reasonable! Vladimir Borisovich!"

Vova smiled. He stretched his head back to look up at the sky and felt the sun on his throat, the lemon sapling under his arm, the plastic bag hitting his leg. He was no longer a prisoner or even an ex-con. For all anyone could tell, he was simply a man returning from a weekend at the *dacha*.

"Forget you then." The limousine driver peeled off, spitting mud.

*

Vova was not ungrateful for Poprok's help while he was in prison. He simply considered it what he was owed—no more, no less.

Thanks to Poprok and his connections on the outside, Vova had quickly developed a reputation in the prison as the one who could arrange anything: cigarettes, pens, pinups, vodka, blades, pantyhose, presents delivered to children on the outside, and Vaseline against the winter wind whistling through the chicken wire.

Shortly after he arrived, the leader of the thief faction had wished out loud for a spoonful of Astrakhan caviar. A week later, a soccer ball came sailing over the chain-link fence and into the yard, wobbling like an obese dove. When the nearest prisoner bent down to retrieve it, he saw the black ink curling into the name of the thief leader and threw it to the ground. Inside were two kilograms of Astrakhan caviar, stored safely within several layers of plastic bags.

When the thief leader found out who the supplier was, he approached Vova in the yard, two deputies deployed in formation behind him. "I'm not paying you," he said, clapping a hand on Vova's shoulder.

He was short, and Vova stared straight over his head at the small crowd gathered a safe distance back. "It was a gift."

"A gift?" The thief leader raised an eyebrow. "Are you blue?"

"No," Vova answered. "I only do women."

"Good," the thief leader said, massaging Vova's shoulder. "I only do straight guys." One of the deputies chuckled, and the thief leader held up a hand to silence him.

"I only do business face to face," Vova countered unflinchingly.

The thief leader laughed. Vova laughed. And for the rest of Vova's sentence, the thief leader's hand on his shoulder had the effect of a knighting or a canonization. Vova was untouchable, simply going about his business, paying for the thief leader's gifts with the business from the other prisoners, with a little left over in the middle for himself.

The Lemon Tree

In all the time Vova spent arranging things for others, though, he only arranged two things for himself: a TB vaccine; and a lemon every month.

"What is it with you and the fucking lemons?" one of the newcomers would inevitably ask, trying to make conversation.

Vova carefully turned the lemon around in his hand, dragging a homemade knife around the equator, then along one of the meridians. He held the lemon under his nose as he pulled the four equal slices of rind from the white underneath. His tongue darted along the corners of his newly-grown beard, collecting the droplets of juice like mercury, and it was as if he could taste a different life. Not his old life—he'd never seen a lemon tree before he'd grown his own—but a different one.

Vova shrugged. "Don't want to get fucking scurvy."

"So...." the newcomer asked. "Who can I talk to about getting some fucking lemons in this place?"

Other prisoners eventually tried to grow the lemon seeds into trees too, but Vova was the only one whose patience could outlast the winter. He'd fashioned a double-layer of burlap for a pot, tied at the top and filled with a careful compost of yard dirt and manure, and he'd acquired an extra wool blanket and sewn it to his own along the edge. At night, he'd stow the seedling under a stool he kept next to his cot, draping one end of the long blanket over the stool and the other end over his own bed, using the heat of his body to warm the seedling. It would remain under the makeshift greenhouse all day long, except for a couple of afternoons a week that Vova had arranged for it to sit in the tiny, glassed window of the guard room. All this came for a price, of course, but with his side business, Vova could afford to pay.

*

As Vova walked down the road away from the prison, it was as if the walls and the ceiling of the world had been flung away, and he felt an incredible urge to make tight turns off the road and carve out a smaller, more manageable plot for himself. The expanse of sky was nearly unbearable, and Vova looked at it with the same anticipation as when his mother used to snap the duvet over him and his brother Kolya, waiting for the blissful moment when it would drift down and cover them, settling in the spaces between their limbs. But the sky overhead refused to comply.

The roots of the lemon sapling scratched at his side through the burlap. They had long outgrown the sack, and instead of procuring another one, Vova had poured out a teaspoonful of dirt each day in the yard. Eventually, the roots had snaked around and around, forming a prickly, dense sphere.

"Don't worry," he whispered to the sapling. "I'll get you into some ground as soon as I can."

After half an hour, a hard, brown kernel of a town appeared on the horizon. Vova's legs ached from the long strides and the spring mud sucking at his heels after four long years of shuffling around the prison yard. It was Saturday morning, and as he neared the town, he passed people walking along the side of the main road, milk and *kefir*, cheese and bread straining their string bags like pale, netted fish. Women and children, even the men, whispering a quiet innocence that now seemed to Vova a different language. Vova walked among them gingerly so as not to disrupt their idyll. At the ticket window in the station, he softened his usual voice, melting the words at the edges. The woman behind the counter glanced at his hands as he slid the money to her, and looked at him strangely before pushing his ticket back under the glass.

*

On the train, Vova rented a set of sheets from the *babushka*. The train was direct, an overnight that would have him back in Moscow by the next afternoon. He found his seat in second class—an open car with fold-down bunks jutting out from every wall at every

The Lemon Tree

height. Like submarine quarters, except for the teenagers flirting desperately at the other end of the car. Vova's ticket matched with the number on one of the bottom bunks in an alcove of four. A young couple sat on the cot opposite, both of the boy's hands gently cupping one of the girl's as if it were a moth. The girl had a round face, with a blood and milk complexion, and sturdy arms and legs. The boy was slighter than she was, with rounded shoulders and toddler's hair—tiny, even curls at the nape as if painstakingly wound around pencils each night. Other passengers passed by, leaning into the alcove, squinting at the numbers, and every so often Vova's ears picked up an argument going on somewhere else in the car.

Vova stood up and unbuckled his belt, whipping it swiftly out of the loops. The girl blushed and stared determinedly out the window; the boy looked alarmed but did nothing more than tighten his grip on the girl's hand, his eyes following Vova's movements. Vova nodded at the boy, but the boy wouldn't acknowledge him. He threaded his belt through the metal rail next to his cot and wound the ends around the trunk of the sapling—now hard and thick as a large garden snake—before buckling it securely. The boy seemed to relax and spoke softly into the girl's ear; she only nodded, her strawberry-blond hair brushing gently against his cheek.

The train pulled out of the station just as the light was beginning to leach from the sky and streak the land. Vova kicked off his shoes and tucked them into the plastic bag with the rest of his belongings, wedging them beneath his head. As the train picked up speed, the boy's voice in the girl's ear and even the arguments at the other end of the car were lost in the rush of iron wheels and rails and countryside.

After a couple of hours, the boy stood up, taking a large mug with him. He cast a look like a net over Vova as he left, just in case. The girl folded her hands in her lap and stared at them, every so often raising her eyes to look in Vova's direction. He guessed she was no more than seventeen—about the age of Isadora, his favorite of his six sisters. He wanted to tell the girl about Isadora, how she looked every time she saw him. About the surprise in her eye, the tension of her lithe body let loose like a spring as she hurled herself at him and twisted her skinny arms around him like vines. He looked over at the girl, at her arms, thick as rolled blankets, at the plateau of sweater stretched between her breasts, at the crucifix dangling against it, bouncing against the sweater in time with the rhythm of the wheels against the rails.

A startled look crossed her face. She folded her arms in front of her, and he could feel her fear bricking up the small space between their knees. He caught her staring at his ring finger, and he slid his hand sideways between his knees to cover it. She blushed and quickly looked away.

He'd gotten it tattooed while he was in prison—a cross curled all the way around his finger, the sign of the thief gang. For protection on the inside. Right before he'd left, the thief leader, who he'd supplied with soccer balls and caviar and regular visits from prostitutes—it turned out he was devoutly straight—had insisted on giving him another tattoo. A three-domed church with three crosses perched on top—the sign of a prison leader. For protection on the outside, he'd said. It had taken the thief gang's regular tattoo artist six weeks of ten-minute spurts in the courtyard, using a sewing needle wrapped with a thread reservoir, the tip sterilized match by match. Vova touched his chest, convinced he could almost feel the lines through his sweatshirt. He wished for the pale, clean skin underneath.

The boyfriend returned with a steaming mug of water from the *samovar* and a pile of white sheets. He glanced at Vova before pulling down the top bunk and flopping the sheets onto it. The girl unpacked a small string bag and arranged and rearranged the contents precariously on the narrow shelf beneath the window. With a small pocketknife, she sawed half a loaf of bread into slices, arranged them on a sheet of folded tinfoil, and spread them with butter and *pashtet*. She opened two small, plastic margarine tubs and fluffed up the mayonnaise salads inside with a fork. She poured half the steaming mug into a small glass jar and took turns dunking a teabag first into one and then the other, making sure the color was even in both. Meanwhile, the boy climbed the bunk, struggling to feel out footholds and handholds, to pull and tuck the sheets around the top mattress as best he could. The two worked peacefully and efficiently; they could have run an entire farm, just the two of them, unripe as they were.

When the boyfriend was satisfied, he sat down on the bottom bunk, hunching, his elbows on his knees so as not to hit his head. The girl smoothed a cloth napkin on the sheets next to him and doled out the rations of food. They ate in silence, with nowhere to look except directly across at Vova. Vova obliged, spreading his sheets out and lying down, facing the wall. He had forgotten to buy anything to eat in the station, and hunger scratched at his stomach like a hen in the dirt. The lemon sapling was secured next to his head, and he reached out to stroke the leaves.

"Go to bed," the tightly wound voice of a teenage boy ordered from the other end of the car. Three boys—two supporting the third—stumbled up the aisle, stopping at the head of Vova's bunk. Vova's body automatically clenched, and his eyes snapped open. Their faces were obscured by the top bunk.

"Nye... nyet.... Jus' lemme...jus' lemme...."

"Come on, Alex, you're legless. She's not going to let you get into her bunk."

"Is too... is too... she... just... just...."

Vova heard the couple cleaning up: rustle of tinfoil, clomp of plastic tub against plastic tub, clink of silverware.

"Alex, come on, don't be a dog. Go to bed. Come on...get his left side...his left side. Left."

Vova watched as the two teenage boys hoisted the third onto the top bunk.

He fell to the floor. "Ow! Balls!"

"Well, if you could get up on your own...." They hurled him upwards again, and the top bunk heaved when he landed. Vova stretched his hand up to support it.

"Thank fuck," one boy said. The boy on the top bunk mumbled.

"See you in the morning, *durak*." They laughed, and their voices trailed off to the end of the car.

Vova shifted to his back, his eyes cracked open enough to watch the silhouettes of the couple weaving between his eyelashes as they smacked a chaste kiss and climbed into their separate bunks, the boyfriend on top, the girl on the bottom. The car shushed except for the clumsy swearing and laughing of the teenagers at the end of the car, and the rhythm of the wheels and the rasping of the boy up above managed to lull Vova to sleep.

*

He awoke disoriented. The lemon smell was more pungent than usual, and the moon sliced through the window at a different angle than in his prison cell. It took a few moments for Vova to recognize the wheels ringing against the rails, and to place the gruff voices that had woken him as coming from the bunk opposite. They were muffled by the thick silence, which Vova carefully peeled back in order to discern the individual words.

"*Dyevushka...dyevushka.*" Girl..girl. Hidden, Vova rolled over slowly. Two men, one larger than the other, were sitting at the foot of the girl's bunk. "*Dyevushka...dyevushka.*" The larger one leaned over and put his hand on the bundle of sheets and blankets.

The girl jerked awake with a gasp, and sat up, hitting her head against the top bunk. She pulled her knees up to her chest and remained there, her chin on her knees, her wide eyes locked on the man's hand as he placed it on her leg.

"You don't mind if we sit here, do you?" The girl didn't respond. "I didn't think so." He nudged the other man and they both chuckled.

"Sasch! Sasch!" the girl tried calling to her boyfriend, but she was unable to apply her voice to it, and all that came out was a rustle of air. The boy was fast asleep on the top bunk, the sheets and blanket lumped on his torso, his limbs poking out like a turtle.

The man ran his hand up to the girl's knee, and put two fingers on her plump cheek. "I *like* them well fed." She jerked her head to the side.

"Go away," she said, but the words emerged almost as a question. "Go away before I call the conductor."

The man laughed. He moved his hand to her foot and turned to his friend. "You hear that? She's gonna call the conductor. She's gonna call the conductor on me."

He twisted his body back to the girl, this time ducking his head under the top bunk. "Go ahead, li'l girl," he slurred. "Go ahead and call the conductor. He's a friend of ours, and I'm sure he'd want his turn, too."

Vova quietly unzipped his sweatshirt and unbuttoned his shirt underneath. He traced his fingers over the tattoo, and his heart flung itself impatiently against his chest.

"Come on, girl." The man's voice was more insistent now. "Come on, don't be such a prude." Vova coughed and let his hand dangle off the side of the bunk, the tattoo weighing on his ring finger. He coughed again, almost had to fake an entire fit of coughing before he heard one of the men utter the word he was waiting for. "*Vor.*" Thief.

"*Vor*...hey, *vor*," the smaller man said again. Vova swung his legs to the ground and sat up, ducking his head, balancing his elbows on his knees.

"Brother," the thinner one said, holding out his hands, palm side down, the cross twisted around his finger more noticeable this way. The larger one turned his attention away from the girl for a moment and grasped her foot. He held his other hand out in the same way as the other man, the same cross snaking around his finger. The girl's eyes widened, and she began to shake. It was Vova's turn. Vova flattened his hand as they had, then stood up and let his shirt fall open. The men's eyes traced the lines of the three domes, and they pulled back their hands and waited.

"This isn't your seat," Vova said calmly.

"Come on, brother, we were just trying to have some fun. We didn't know she was yours."

"This isn't your seat," Vova repeated, settling his eyes on the larger one, who slowly removed his hand from the girl's foot and stood up.

"Come on," he said to the smaller one. "I didn't like the view here anyway."

Vova watched their backs as they walked down the aisle and disappeared into the next car. The girl looked up at him, still cowering, her expression a mixture of gratefulness and fear. Vova went over to the window and leaned his forehead against it, propping his arms up on the ledge. He stared out at the moon in the velvet sky, nestled there as if by a magician's slight of hand. He felt the girl's eyes on him, and he was ashamed of what he knew she saw.

"He's a sound sleeper, yes?" Vova indicated the boyfriend, still sprawled out on the top bunk. She nodded. Vova turned back toward the window to give her privacy. He heard the rustling of the starched sheets as she stretched out beneath them and eventually fell asleep.

"Hey...hey...." The drunk boy on the bunk above Vova was now wide awake, his back propped against the wall, the soles of his shoes reaching into the aisle, near Vova's head. Vova tapped his shoes and the boy quickly moved them.

The Lemon Tree

"You were in the trap?" the boy asked. "Cool."

"No. It wasn't."

"Come on, man. Show me your tattoos. I didn't get a good look at them." The boy was about fifteen, and his voice still strained against itself. Vova turned back toward the window.

"I hear you guys got a whole system of tattoos," the boy tried again. "And if you make a mistake and show the wrong person the wrong tattoo...." In the reflection of the window, the boy put two fingers to his neck and drew them across his throat.

"Look, don't you want to sleep off some of that vodka?"

The boy fell silent for a moment. "Can't you teach me some prison words?"

Vova shook his head at his reflection in the window.

"Come on, just one word. Like what do you call an ass-kicking in prison slang?"

Vova spun around and seized the boy's foot. "Look. Mind your own business and go the fuck back to sleep."

The boy stiffened, his face bleached with fear. Vova let go of his foot and took a step backwards.

"Sorry," Vova said. "Sorry."

The boyfriend across the aisle was suddenly awake now too. "Hey! You leave that boy alone. Pick on one of your own kind."

Vova ignored him, but the words echoed in his head. He buttoned up his shirt, ducked into his bunk and lay down, the scent of the sapling seeping into his dreams.

*

Vova awoke to a windowful of dawn. The murmurings on the other side of the partition were not the same jagged voices he had awoken to in prison every morning for four years. The others in his alcove were all peacefully asleep, and Vova quietly unclipped his belt from the railing and lifted the sapling from the corner of his bunk. He joined the line for the bathroom—rumpled grandmothers, sleep-subdued teenagers all rubbing at their eyes, pulling at their skin to awaken whatever was beneath. When it was his turn, he slipped inside, set the sapling on the floor and bolted the door. He took off his sweatshirt and tied it around his waist. He pumped the foot pedal until water came out, and with a sliver of soap and the homemade blade he had once used to cut the lemons, set about the task of shaving.

"Hurry up! What's taking you so long?" The shrill voice of the *babushka* pierced the dull bass line of her fists pounding against the door. "You think you are better than the rest of us—us workers—you elitist snob! What would Grandfather Lenin say? Hmmm?"

Vova hurried to finish. He pumped the foot pedal a few more times to wash the hairs from the sink, and held the root ball under the faucet for a couple of seconds until the burlap was saturated.

"Sorry, *babushka*. Sorry, grandmother," he said to the old woman waiting outside the door. The *babushka* shrank, backing into the next person in line. Vova felt a trickling sensation on his cheek and reached up to wipe it with his sleeve. His sleeve returned soaked with blood, and Vova again pressed it to his cheek, at the same time trying to slip his fingers inside the cuff so the tattoo would not be visible. The old woman, her face still taut with fear, grabbed the door and slipped inside the bathroom. She pulled the door behind her until only a thin slice of her nose and lips remained visible through the crack.

"Criminal! Monster!" she hissed, and slammed and bolted the door.

Vova went into the vestibule. There were a couple of boys sitting against the opposite wall, chain-smoking. Their eyes were stamped with dark circles as if they hadn't slept all night, and their jeans were soft from dirt. Vova nodded at them as he sat down, and one of them handed him a cigarette and lit it for him. Vova set the lemon sapling next to him, being careful to blow the smoke away from it. He thought about going back to his bunk—he'd left the sheets and would lose the deposit. He thought of the girl and her boyfriend getting up to prepare breakfast and unmake the beds, the drunken boy with his hangover struggling to climb down from the top bunk and rejoin his friends. He remembered their eyes, accusing him of things he hadn't even done.

In the end, he decided that he'd rather stay where he was, breathing in the clouds of smoke, feeling the cold, ribbed steel melding with the seat of his pants, pulling up his knees and making apologies every time there was a stop. All he could hope was that when the train pulled into Moscow, Shrubek and the rest of his friends, his sister Isadora and his mother, would greet a different man and welcome him home.

*

It was early evening when the train arrived in Moscow. Shrubek was parked in a crappy tan Lada at the back entrance of Kievskaya Station, where the market stalls squatted shoulder-to-shoulder.

"How does it feel to be a free man?" Shrubek asked as Vova secured the sapling in the back seat.

"Fuck me if there aren't scarier people on the train than there were in the trap."

Shrubek put the car into gear and pulled away from the curb. "I thought Poprok was going to send a limo to come pick you up."

"He did."

Shrubek stared at Vova. "And?"

"And I told him to go to hell. I'm cutting all contact with Poprok," Vova snapped.

"Vova, you've got to let it go. He's apologized."

"I don't have to let anything go," he said. "Besides, I'm not a part of that anymore."

Shrubek exhaled and shook his head.

"You're getting laid again regularly, aren't you?" Vova asked.

"What?"

"It's the end of the winter in Moscow and your cheeks are glowing like a baboon's ass in heat. Who is it?"

Shrubek smiled. "Would you believe? Nastya and I got back together."

"Ah, for fuck's sake," Vova said, leaning his head on the back of the seat. "Here we go again."

"I know," Shrubek said. "I know. I'm going to be careful this time, though."

"Careful?" Vova practically shouted. "Careful's a condom. You need the whole fucking Iron Curtain to protect yourself from her. Did you forget what she did to you?"

Shrubek braked hard. "Lay off," he said. The car behind honked. Silence wedged itself in like a third person in the front seat.

"So what are you going to do now that you're out?" Shrubek asked.

Vova shrugged. "I don't know. Get an honest job. Maybe something outdoors."

"You? Get an honest job?" Shrubek laughed.

"What do you mean by that?"

"I'm just saying...I mean, you've never had an honest job in your life."

Vova shrugged. "People change."

Shrubek reached between his feet and pulled out a can of beer. "Here, I thought maybe you'd want this."

Vova crossed his arms across his chest. "I don't drink anymore."

"You what?"

"I don't drink anymore. I gave it up."

Shrubek laughed. "What does that mean, you don't drink anymore? You've been drinking since the fifth grade."

"I gave it up."

"Gave it up? Jesus-Mary, what the hell happened to you in there?"

"Why does something have to happen? Why does there have to be some crisis every time a guy wants to make the smallest fucking change in his life?" Vova turned away.

"I'll save this for you," Shrubek said, tucking the beer back under the seat.

Vova stared out the window. The city was brighter than before, almost blinding, the gray façades stooping under the weight of all the signs and advertisements.

"When did they put that movie theater in?"

"That one?" Shrubek said. "A while ago. It's been there a while."

He pulled up onto the sidewalk and parked in front of the Fish Bar. The gray stucco façade, the crumbling steps leading down to the cellar, the flickering candles balanced on the stones protruding from the walls—enough to light the entire room. It was all still the same as before, and Vova relaxed.

"You're back!" The owner, Ilya, greeted him. "Good to see you. How are things?"

"The place looks good," Vova said. "Exactly the same."

"Yeah, yeah. I put off renovating until I could get the money together, and by then all the tourists and New Russians started telling me how quaint and retro it was, so I decided just to leave it. Good marketing, yes?"

Vova nodded. "Good marketing."

Vova recognized the voices coming from the corner table, and instinctively walked toward it, scanning the faces: Malvina, Katya, Nastya, and his brother Kolya.

"Kolya! What the hell are you doing here?" Vova shouted. His brother stood up, his arms outstretched. Vova set the sapling down on the table and hugged him. "Kolya, what are you doing here?" he repeated.

"Katya told me. Had to find out somehow, since you don't seem to know what a stamp is. Break our mother's heart."

"How do you know Katya?"

"We've met," Kolya said, putting his arm around her. "Around."

Nastya intercepted Vova and threw her arms around him, kissing the air next to his cheeks. "Oh, Vova," she gushed. "It's been so long! It just hasn't been the same without you. We've missed you terribly."

"Hey, Nastya." Vova turned to Malvina and Katya, kissing each one warmly on the cheek.

"Careful girls," Kolya warned. "It's been a while since he's seen a woman."

Shrubek stood up. "All right. Who wants something to drink? Vova, you want a, I don't know, juice or something?"

"Juice?" Malvina slapped the table. Her short, black hair glinted in the candlelight, and her eyes widened behind her glasses. "Juice?"

Vova shrugged. "Sure, I guess so."

Malvina reached across the table and grabbed Vova by the shirt collar. "What have you done to Vova? Where have you taken him? Let us talk to your leaders!" She trembled with laughter, releasing his shirt, leaving the imprints of her tiny fingers in his collar like rain in sand. A smile plucked at the corner of Vova's mouth.

"What's with the tree?" Kolya asked.

"It's a lemon sapling," Vova said.

"Where'd you get it?"

"I grew it."

"You grew it? You?"

"Yeah," Vova said. "But it's getting too big for the burlap. I thought I'd go out to the *dacha* tomorrow and plant it."

"Mom sold the *dacha*," Kolya said.

"She sold it?"

"Yeah, none of us wanted to go out there anymore," Kolya said. "You'd know if you'd ever written."

Vova stared at the sapling, absentmindedly plucking a few of the dried leaves. He picked up the paperback book that was lying on the table, riffling the pages between his fingers. "What's this?"

"It's Katya's and my latest book," Malvina said.
"You two have a book?" Vova asked. "Together?"
"Didn't Shrubek tell you?"
Vova looked at the cover. "*War and Peace?* I think that guy, Tolstoy, beat you to it."
"No, no. Read some of it."
Vova cleared his throat.

> The militiawomen, an elite cadre composed only of fair, young, blond virgins, carried Prince Andrei to the forest, where the wagons were sheltered and where the field hospital had been established. As they carried Prince Andrei, the birch branches caught at their translucent silk uniforms, tearing at them until the virgins were nearly naked. "I can't... I can't breathe," Prince Andrei gasped. The virgins laid him down on the soft floor of the forest and commenced fighting over who was to revive Prince Andrei by kissing him over the entire length of his body. The other soldiers lay on their stretchers and gazed steadily, as if trying to live vicariously through the wonderful spectacle. "I can't . . . I can't breathe,"nearly all of them shouted in unison. In a matter of minutes from all the tents could be heard, loud, fierce, pitiful groans..."

"Malvina, what the hell is this?"
"Russian Classics Done Right. That's our slogan."
"This is our second," Katya added. "We already put out a soft porn version of *Eugene Onegin.*"
"In verse," Malvina said.
"What about teaching?" Vova asked.
"This pays much better," Malvina said.
"What about your students?"
Malvina shrugged. "What about them?"
"So, did Shruby pick you up in the BMW?" Nastya asked.

"BMW?" Vova asked. "Shrubek has a BMW?"

"Mmm-hmm," Nastya said, smiling. "My Shruby's sure come a long way since the old days, hasn't he?"

"Your Shruby."

Nastya smiled and sipped at her drink with her straw.

"What'd he do, steal it?" Vova asked. "Where the hell did Shrubek get a BMW?"

The table went quiet.

"What? What is it?" Vova demanded.

"Shruby's in business with Poprok," Nastya said proudly.

The room blurred. Shrubek appeared, setting the drinks down on the table. "Vova, I was going to tell you," he said. "I was going to tell you."

Vova picked up the sapling from the table. "I can't believe you'd do this."

"Things change," Shrubek said. "Like you said, Vova, things change."

Vova was on his feet, the sapling tucked under his arm.

"Vova," Malvina pleaded, "listen to Shrubek. Let him explain."

He shook her hand from his arm. "No, you listen to me. You have all sold out. Sold out!" He headed for the door, lifting the sapling above his head, twisting his body between the backs of chairs.

"Let him go." It was his brother's voice. "Just let him go."

*

The night was cold for April, and Vova stuffed his free hand into his pocket as he walked down Tverskaya Street. He thought he'd go home and surprise his mother and his sister Isadora. He wanted to taste his mother's cooking and feel his sister's arms around him. He tucked further inside himself and tried to ignore the blaring signs and the crowds. A McDonald's loomed ahead. The broad windows had a turquoise cast to them, and the polished chrome trim and railings slithered across the façade. The light from the McDonald's was so brilliant it must have been imported, shipped over in huge crates from somewhere south of the Black Sea, and it choked out the filmy, low-wattage street light that was so familiar to Vova, that meant home.

Vova edged over on the sidewalk as if passing a hulking stranger on a dark street, and concentrated on the red neon sign marking the metro in the distance, across the Ring Road. He pressed the root ball firmly against his side, the dry roots scraping through his sweatshirt like the fingernails of a frightened child. The sky overhead was so flat and hard, he could have hammered a nail into it, and the buildings on both sides of the street slowly began to close in around him.

"Hey! Hey!"

Vova hunched his shoulders.

"Hey! Guy with the tree! You!"

Vova turned. It was the drunken boy from the train and a line of his friends, balanced on the chrome railing running the length of the patio at the McDonald's. The kid launched himself down to the pavement below. Vova quickened his pace.

"Hey, brother! Wait up!" He tugged at Vova's sleeve, and Vova spun around, snatching his arm back and tucking it close to his chest. The boy smelled of beer.

"Don't call me brother."

"Okay, okay. Calm, calm. I just figured that's what you were used to in the trap."

"I don't remember seeing you there." Vova continued walking.

"Jesus-Mary, would you slow down! You won't even talk to me for a second." Vova stopped in the middle of the sidewalk. In the halo of the McDonald's, Vova noticed the boy's friends now off the railing, hands rammed into their pockets, craning their necks, keeping their distance.

"What do you want?" Vova demanded.

"Just come and meet my friends. They don't believe that I was hanging out with a thief-prisoner. Just one minute. Come on."

"*Ex* thief. *Ex* prisoner. And we weren't *hanging out*," Vova said.

"You don't have to play clean with me," the boy replied. "I ain't gonna rat you out."

In a flash, Vova dropped the sapling and had the boy by the collar. His eyes swarmed. "Rat me out? I haven't done anything. I'm not a criminal. Do you hear me? Do you hear me?"

The boy screwed his eyes shut, bracing his face to absorb a blow, and his friends inched forward. Vova set the boy down and tried to fix his collar, but the boy covered his face, backing away toward the McDonald's.

"Look," Vova began. "You've got the wrong idea. I'm not...you just have the wrong idea."

The boy's friends were already clustered around him, asking if he was okay.

"I would have punched the shit out of him if he'd kept ahold of you for one more second."

"No you wouldn't have. You almost shit your pants you were so scared."

"Did not."

Vova checked the lemon sapling for damage. The burlap sack had split, and the remaining dirt from the prison yard had spilled onto the sidewalk. He crouched like an animal, brushing the dirt into a pile, scooping it back into the gaping sack, lashing the edges of the hole together with the lace from his shoe. As Vova worked, he wondered where and when he would finally find the ground to plant it. As he worked, the leaves brushed his face, and the lemon scent filled his nostrils, reminding him of the nights underneath the two wool blankets, making him long for the days in the prison yard. At least there he knew who to look out for and where the fence stood.

Traction

Morgan McDermott

Ridge watches *Antiques Roadshow* because he needs proof that love endures. Veronique watches because she likes to know how much old stuff is worth. *Value is what you talk someone into believing*, Veronique will say, usually with a shrug when an old table turns out to be worth a mint. *Value is the financial equivalent of faith.*

Ridge enjoys the celebration of craftsmanship that is each appraisal on the show. He admires how love and patience applied to gold or celedon or mahogany creates something special. Veronique enjoys calling out each dollar amount before it appears on the screen. She and Ridge have been both sleeping together and watching the show together for almost a year, but since his accident she has been calling the numbers nonchalantly, as though bored. Ridge wonders if this should bother him. He wonders if it should bother him more than the fact that she is his brother's wife.

Days ago, when she put an art deco statuette at six figures and had the price almost to the penny, Ridge had been kneading her shoulders. There was no tension present, no trace of anticipation. They were in a rut. He could feel it there beneath his fingers.

It's not an issue of value, Veronique said, looking away from the television. I can't say how much he values you. I just don't think he has the money to buy a new truck.

He's lucky I'm alive, Ridge said. With those bald tires, that girl could sue him. She could sue the company and win.

Veronique shrugged his hands off her neck. He realized he had made a mistake.

It's a good thing I'm still alive, Ridge said. Isn't it?

I think you're lucky, she said. Maybe I'm lucky, too. I don't know any more.

Maybe? he said. He withdrew his arm. She shifted to the other end of the couch.

I just can't say if Archer thinks *he's* lucky, she said.

You really know how to hurt a guy's feelings.

I used to like your feelings, she said.

Ridge's forehead was still tender. A knot lay at his hairline where it met the windshield. Late in January he crashed the company pickup into an elm. He had been at a club, had struck up a conversation with a girl. He offered her a ride home, assured her he was safe. But freezing rain had slicked the roads, a rain that looked like nothing on descent but after a few hours brought down power lines. Ridge had forgotten how something so gentle could devastate so thoroughly. He had not lived in Chicago for twenty years, had spent the last decade in Lebanon, Kuwait, east Africa. He had forgotten how to tread on thin ice. After twenty years in war zones, improper traction on a suburban street had nearly killed him.

Why don't you call your girl from the nightclub? Veronique said. Ask her how you might get the money.

His head ached constantly since the accident. He closed his eyes. Veronique poked Ridge in his ribs with her naked toe, demanding attention. It was her way. Sometimes she inflicted a little pain to get what she wanted.

Why don't you? she said.

When he did not respond, she ignored him in return, reached for the oversized photograph book on the floor.

For your information, I am not a hurtful person, she said, flipping pages. I give to the United Way.

On the television, an expert evaluated letters written by Teddy Roosevelt to his young wife. The expert explained how romantic correspondence fetched such high prices because it so rarely survived either second thoughts or the second-hand. Ridge watched the collector of the letters nod as the expert praised their quality, the amount of time dedicated to archiving them in acid-free folders. So much communication was ruined by acidity, the expert said. The episode had been filmed in the West. The collector wore a white cowboy shirt open at the neck, its collar spread like gull wings. He wore a turquoise necklace and a turquoise bracelet on each wrist, his sleeves rolled up to the elbows to reveal dragon tattoos. Navy, Ridge thought. East Asia.

Roseland, Veronique whispered. Who wouldn't live in The Roseland?

Ridge pretended not to hear.

She leafed through her book detailing Chicago neighborhoods at their pinnacle, studying intently the pictures of stately houses and grand apartment buildings. The book was not a connection to the past, but a guide to her future. He had bought the book for her at Christmas. He told her she had to know more if she was going to call herself The Realtor With the Answer.

The Roseland she said, teeth bared, biting on the words like they were gold coins. On the television, bells announced the valuation of the Roosevelt letters. Veronique looked up. The number was very long.

Those are so sold, she said.

She was in a rare moment of stasis. Veronique did not rest so much as cease fidgeting. Usually when she came to his apartment they made love urgently, the moments stolen from her schedule. Ridge understood. To become a player in North Shore real estate she had to live and breathe the game; she spent much of her day in various states of foreplay. When she came to Ridge she needed relief. He did not take it personally. When they finished, Veronique would nap. He would watch. Though she slept briefly, he could have watched for hours. Ridge had been trained to sit immobile for days with a rifle in hand and scope to his eye, trained to blend into the background, to disappear in the trees or grass or sand. He hardly breathed as he watched, and when Veronique woke it was always with fearful eyes and furrowed brow. She would sit up startled, unaware of where she was. She would look at him hard, her eyes wide, then narrow. He loved those moments of recognition, the rosy relief that colored her face.

Avalon Park, she said, and flipped the page. *The Avalon?*

When she saw he would not answer, she slapped the book closed. She sat up, replaced the book on the floor. Her skin was very pale and Ridge could see blue veins running north and south like interstates drawn on a road map.

She dressed. Watching her, Ridge recalled the carnival attraction in which a person stands in a glass box filled with whirling, wind-blown dollar bills. Veronique moved as if confined in that clear box, yearning for the dollars swirling around her.

Sometimes I wonder who you are, Ridge said.

Take a number, she said, her eyes on the television, where bells were ringing.

*

"Absolutely not," Archer says. "No way. We're bleeding money."

Ridge tosses the brochure for the pickup truck to the floor. It is a beautiful truck. It has anti-lock brakes and an electronic traction system designed to keep a man in control.

"You drive crazy," Archer says.

"Forget it," Ridge says. "Watch your game."

Archer comes to Ridge's apartment to watch basketball. It is their attempt at re-connecting after so long apart. Sales have flatlined. Archer spends too much time pacing his apartment, a four-bedroom unit on a top floor of The Denmark. It is a short walk down to Ridge's level.

"New truck," Archer says, the words a foul phrase in a foreign tongue.

"Drop it."

"I have to say No, so I'm the bad guy," Archer says. "Congratulations."

The brothers communicated little in twenty years. They reunited only once, at their mother's funeral. Ridge had a twenty-four hour pass. His unit was in war games in the Caribbean. When their father died, Archer cremated the body without ceremony and spent the following weeks burning clothes, documents, photographs—any evidence that the elder Devlin ever existed.

Archer is still unnerved by Ridge's presence. When Ridge returned from the Middle East with only discharge papers, three day's beard and a duffel, he had forced the younger man to take on a role, to be their father. Archer put Ridge up in a small unit in The Denmark, gave him a job. He set simple parameters: Archer had the maturity and responsibilities, Ridge had the machismo. Archer had the family business and the stability, Ridge had the war stories.

Archer had the wife.

On the television, players in turquoise chase players in teal. Everyone sweats profusely, as if part of the competition is to look the most like a winner.

"It's a miracle you didn't kill that girl," Archer says.

Twenty years a Marine, Ridge has wrecked many automobiles. A few of them belonged to married women; married women couldn't stay away from his easy smile, his lead-footed abandon. His uniform increased his value, made him either more special, or more interchangeable. It made him more dangerous, or less, depending on the woman. There was a type—organized, responsible, yet longing for adventure—who could not get enough of him once he revealed his trade. Such women were riveted when he described what it was like to feel the traction of a carved rifle stock against the cheek as one took aim on an enemy of democracy.

He is still figuring out whether or not Veronique is one of these women.

"You drive like there's no tomorrow," Archer says.

When Ridge returned to Evanston it was in dress blues, and Veronique jumped at the chance to drive him around town in her Mercedes. Ridge was field-trained to move with stealth; the slightest noise, the faintest emanation of sweat, was a potential threat to his life. Women responded to his self-control. Once, outside Kassala, on a ridge overlooking the Blue Nile, he had lain for forty hours beneath a heavy layer of sand and soil, waiting for his shot on a Sudanese war criminal. Emulating dirt had deleterious effects on a man; Ridge cut loose when in civilization, drove fast when presented with open road. In San Diego, Ridge tooled around with his commanding officer's wife until the man rotated to Japan. The woman drove a new Seville: small and cream, with a smart V-8 engine. He missed that car greatly. When Ridge started sleeping with Veronique he tried to convince himself that she and her Mercedes were like any of his maneuvers. He tried to stay calm, to view it as a quick spin around the block, just running a little gas through the lines. At the three-month mark, the time he usually lost the new-car feel, he realized he was in love.

"I always get there in one piece," Ridge says.

*

Paint over it, Veronique said, watching Ridge steam the wallpaper. A dozen layers covered each wall in Ridge's apartment, a hundred years of history. Ridge knew he had to steam down to plaster to make proper repairs. He had come home to make repairs. He wanted to make at least some properly.

The Denmark was thirty apartments when Archer and his wife took possession. It would be twenty loft condominiums after Archer's men gutted it of everything that made it a landmark. Under Veronique's guidance, Archer had shifted the focus of *Devlin and Son* from building new homes to conversions along the lake.

Her projects had more sex appeal and riskier profit margins, but she believed her approach would make the business millions. Her approach was simple: buyers want *vintage*, but not *old*. The charm of ornate plasterwork, French windows, and roofline gargoyles was magnified when accompanied by central air, Jacuzzis, and programmable dishwashers.

Time is money, Veronique said. She wore a dark suit. Her arms were crossed.

My time is money, she said.

They made love on the couch. She first hung her suit over the fireplace with care. The garment hovered in the air, retaining her curves like armor.

Archer wants to sell this unit, Veronique said when they were finished. She lay on her back, her head on his lap.

He figures your living here without rent has been fair compensation.

Ridge had his hand spread open on Veronique's naked belly like a lie detector. She had prominent muscles, and Ridge liked to read them with his fingers as they talked, feeling her moods. Her muscles were tense at the moment. It either did or did not mean she wanted him to stay.

What happened to family loyalty? Ridge said.

She did not speak. Ridge was crazy about Veronique when she was in the nude. He had trouble with her only when she was clothed. Veronique had a master's degree in management. She had been taught by expert managers to select a wardrobe that would project an image. She favored black suits, severe heels, jewelry of Mexican gold. When she was in uniform she was impenetrable.

You'll need to install a dishwasher then, Ridge said. And one of those fancy tubs. He removed his hand.

*

The basketball game is over. Archer rises, looks at his watch, then places his hands on the small of his back. Archer is thirty-two, and is already starting to stoop. Ridge watches Archer grimace. He has seen the man's back brace, the soft attachment Archer wears beneath his shirt.

"I have to change clothes," Archer says.

"I have to find somewhere to live," Ridge says.

Archer bares his teeth, grimacing. His face reddens. It is the same way their father responded when confronted. Ridge spent most of his time in the Marines exorcising the old man's spiteful words and gestures from his own muscle and bone until almost everything he said and did came from him, and not from the past. It was a slow process, like working off an indentured servitude.

"That was just an idea," Archer says. "A contingency. We might all have to give up on this place. I'm going to meet the Bank tonight."

"What bank is open at night?"

Archer's teeth grind from the pain as he twists himself upright. "We're broke come the twenty-eighth. Your accident didn't help with the insurance. I might have to lay off the Romanians."

"A tragedy," Ridge says. Ridge despises communists in general, and this group of former Marxists in particular for their sloppy work and lack of pride. Archer's Romanians trample the tradition of European craftsmanship each day they show up to butcher the building. But they work cheap.

"I'm not kidding," Archer says. He looks around Ridge's apartment, at the flawless walls. "We could go broke. Then you wouldn't have a place to creep around at night like a tomcat."

Ridge watches his brother survey the room with contempt for both what he does not value, and what he cannot buy.

"You go broke, you go broke," Ridge says. "At least you don't have mouths to feed."

The words slap his brother in the face. Ridge feels ashamed. It is something their old man would have said.

Traction

*

Archer and his wife had set about fashioning a child like business professionals. They chose power names, procured daycare, opened a Roth IRA. They painted the guest room, bought a crib, put their dog to sleep.

And then nothing happened. The deal was never closed. That was three years ago. Two years ago, Archer and Veronique formed a limited partnership to purchase The Denmark. They were project-oriented people; when one project stalled, they found another.

Stop saying you love me, Veronique said.

She straddled Ridge, still wearing her shell and suit jacket. Her skirt lay over a chair. The Denmark had an open house shortly; she presented the model condominium each Sunday afternoon, arranging cookies on a tray and a smile on her lips. As the months passed with dwindling interest, both the cookies and the smile were growing stale.

I love your body, Ridge said.

Veronique slid off him. She reached for the skirt.

You're coming upstairs, she said, zipping up.

It was a game they played. Ridge hovered until potential buyers entered, then Veronique engaged him in conversation as though they were strangers. Veronique enticed Ridge as Archer looked on. She would flirt, touch Ridge's arm, his muscles. A year ago none of them would have played such roles, but times were tight. They were growing desperate.

Dress your age, Veronique said. Her eyes flicked to the top of his head. Ridge knew she assumed he dyed his hair. He took it as a compliment. Archer was already salt-and-pepper.

I need you to look your best, she said, smoothing her wrinkles. Otherwise none of this makes a bit of sense, she said.

*

After Archer leaves, Ridge does five hundred pushups, then showers. He combs his wet hair, dresses, slips into his black field jacket.

He places a flashlight in his pocket, as most of the building's electricity is shut off at the main. The flashlight is long and heavy, purchased at the PX at Camp Butler. He liked to take late walks in Okinawa; night in southern Japan was inky-dark and still, every sound and smell intensified. He used the light sparingly, found his way down narrow streets in the pitch, tracking the movements of other pedestrians by sound or scent alone. It was as though he had no body, no form. It made him feel like a spirit, or an angel. Yet the night presented problems. Bars expelled rowdy drunks, young jarheads who thought basic training had made them into the heavyweight champions of the world. His flashlight doubled nicely as a sap.

Ridge steps out his back door into the rear courtyard of The Denmark. It is early February, but it is surprisingly warm. He wears his jacket anyway, knowing Valentine's month in Chicago is not to be trusted.

Ridge likes The Denmark best at twilight. The three-story brick building is a stately U-shape. The Romanians have allowed its courtyard to grow lush with dandelions. At twilight, birds and rabbits forage in the high grass and there are no Romanian curses shouted down stairwells. There is no tinkle of breaking glass, no chatter of power saws. The Denmark is noble in silence, a handsome man eating alone in a fine restaurant. Ridge enjoys exploring the building when it is quiet enough to read the tales built into each of its stories.

The Romanians are demolishing his favorite section, mid-sized apartments with windows providing views into the surrounding buildings. It is from these apartments that Ridge watches the neighborhood. He likes to sit still and survey his surroundings. Trained not to smoke, not to give his position away, he likes invisibility. He climbs three flights of stairs, opens the door to the top floor apartment.

"You're a real secretive bastard."

Caught in the moment between the assumption that he is alone and the realization that he is not, Ridge douses his flashlight, freezes.

"She's really something," Archer says.

Ridge has been trained to minimize his profile when discovered. He bends, turns his body, alters his shape. Ridge wonders first how Archer discovered the affair, then how the younger man will attack in retribution. Ridge's heartbeat slows. His pulse settles. His feet spread; his boots gain traction in the dust.

"Really," Archer says.

Ridge spots Archer in the living room, looking into the windows of the apartment building opposite The Denmark. Archer sits on a five-gallon paint bucket, eye-level with the window.

"You could always keep a secret," Archer says.

"How did you know I would come here?" Ridge says, relaxing. His brother is still in the dark. Ridge has maintained his position undetected.

"I see you come and go," Archer says. "I thought they taught hit men to be sly."

Twenty yards across the street, a woman about Veronique's age watches television in her living room. The couch upon which she lies faces the set and, beyond, her windows. The building opposite The Denmark is twenty years younger and is in very good condition. It rents expensive to young professional couples, themselves very desirable. The woman's hair is wild-curly and falls around her shoulders. She wears a tight, stylish shirt and baggy shorts. Her bare legs are extended. She rests her head against the arm of the couch. She is beautiful at this distance, just far enough to hide any flaw.

"It's like you could open your mouth and talk to her," Archer says.

Ridge steps closer. Cellophane crunches beneath his boot. The Romanians take breaks in the apartment. Five-gallon buckets form a circle. In its center lie crushed cigarette butts, soda cans, wrappers to snack cakes. It is an encampment. The wrappers are the kind of spoor Ridge is trained to read when hunting the enemy. He is in enemy territory. Archer is not his friend. All Ridge knows about Archer is that he either does or does not enjoy basketball, and that he either does or does not enjoy construction, and that he either does or does not love his wife.

"She ever get naked?" Archer says.

"Yes," Ridge says. He has seen her exposed, sitting sideways on her couch, her vulnerable points in shadow as she conversed with a naked young man. Trained to read battlefield gestures, Ridge has followed many of their conversations across the expanse. He has watched the young woman's breasts rise and fall in time to her hands as she established a perimeter with the young man, motioned for a halt, called for a retreat.

Ridge pulls a bucket from the circle, sits next to his brother.

"Look." Archer slaps Ridge on the arm. Ridge looks. The girl rises from the couch, moves to her television set. She bends for just a moment, turns, returns to her recline.

"Did she just get up to change the channel?" Archer says.

"Appears so."

"I didn't know people did that anymore."

Archer tries to read his wristwatch in the dark, holding it to the windows for illumination. It is the gold Rolex, with a metallic face difficult to read in good light. Ridge knows. Ridge wears it when he plays the buyer, when Veronique wants him to make an impression.

*

Try something on, Veronique said from her bed. I can't get him to wear nice clothes any more. I bring them home, they hang in the closet. I bought him a Zenga suit.

A what? Ridge said. He stood naked in front of his brother's open closet.

Ermenegildo Zenga, she said. It's a kind of suit. Don't you read magazines?

Ridge fingered the row of silk shirts. Their texture surprised him. Expecting a smooth surface, Ridge found rough threads, nubs. *India silk*, the labels read.

He hasn't worn a tie since our wedding, she said. Help yourself.

Ridge wandered to Archer's dresser. Its glass-top surface was spartan: a wedding photograph in a silver frame, a comb, a golden dollar coin. The Rolex lay in a souvenir ashtray bearing the rippled, three-dimensional faces of Mount Rushmore. He set the coin in the tray, obscuring Thomas Jefferson, and picked up the watch.

Nice, he said.

I bought that, she said. He never wears it.

Ridge slipped the Rolex around his wrist, snapped its bracelet closed. It was loose. Though he had forty pounds on Archer, the parts designed to be lean on a man were lean on Ridge. He appraised himself in the dresser mirror, hand held to chin.

You try things, she said.

He never told you about the time he took my watch.

When?

He was ten. I had a digital watch, one of the first. Liquid crystal. Archer took it to school and busted it good.

Ridge watched her in the mirror, behind him on the bed.

That doesn't sound like Archer, she said.

Not now, Ridge said. The old man threw him down the stairs when he heard.

He watched her stillness, a cat. She was waiting. So he told her how the old man had been when they were boys, constructing a boxing ring in the back yard of their house in Evanston. The old man marked off the space, winding rope around trees.

Time to learn to stay on your feet, their father said. You have to learn not to be afraid to square off with a man face-to-face.

He took it easy on Ridge, bloodying the boy's nose, bruising his ribs. Ridge learned to hit the ground and stay down and, eventually, to not be at home at all. He learned to finish high school through the mail, learned the Marine Corps welcomed a well-spoken suburban boy. Archer, who was much younger, was not so lucky.

The old man put Archer in traction, Ridge said.

He never said a word, she said.

And worse, Ridge said. I have the teeth somewhere to prove it.

Teeth, she said, nodding.

Ridge took his time unfastening the clasp, watching her the whole time. She made no move to call him. She made no move to cover up. He had spent many years reading people from a distance, but she was tough.

Archer never learned to take a dive, Ridge said.

What about you? she said.

He hefted the watch in his palm. It was heavy for its size. It was clearly valuable.

I turned eighteen in boot camp, he said. I learned how to hurt people from a distance.

Smart boy, she said.

I thought so at the time, he said.

At the time.

Archer learned to read chin music, he said. I think if the old man loved anything other than building, it was that Archer could take a punch and keep coming.

Ridge set the watch down on the glass, and then, without thinking, pressed his hand down on the flat, cool surface. He left heavy, sweaty handprints: first one, then another, then another, until he formed a path, animal tracks across a beach.

That's the man you married, he said. Just so you know.

Thank you.

You're not going to tell him I told you.

I'm not?

Just like you're not going to tell him that I love you.

He watched Veronique reach for the sheet, pull it over her body.

You're going to mess everything up, she said. You're that kind of man who messes up everything he touches.

*

"It's early," Ridge says as his brother struggles with the watch. "Your meeting didn't go well?"

"I should have eaten something during the game," Archer says. "I get hungry, I lose all my confidence."

Across the street, the young woman stretches, yawns. Her arms move above her head. Her shirt rides up, and they see her belly. The absence of right in what they are doing electrifies the innocent flash of skin.

"Invest in a new truck," Ridge says. "You should trust me."

"Trust you," Archer says. "He would have left you the whole business. You could have been a rich man."

"No," Ridge says. "I could either be rich, or be a man."

The young woman sits up abruptly. A person enters the frame of the windowpanes: a young man in a suit, still slim enough to be more suit than man. His hair is clipped short. He looks like he smells nice. He bends for a kiss.

"Can't do it," Archer says. "In fact, we need to sell Veronique's Mercedes. The bank says from now on, no frills."

"The bank," Ridge says.

"Truth is, Veronique wants us to cut you loose. She says you abuse privileges and she doesn't know if she can trust you."

Across the street, the young man strips. Ridge has seen the process before. The young woman nods, speaking as he removes his coat, then tie, then shirt. Archer turns to watch, his body stiff on the plastic bucket. Ridge cringes at the arthritic crunch of Archer's vertebrae. As soon as Ridge fled for boot camp, his father dropped a letter. The name of the family business changed from *Devlin and Sons* to *Devlin and Son*. The old man mailed him one of the new business cards at Parris Island. No note, just the card sliding around loose in a long envelope. It was a message. Nobody could take anything from a Devlin without paying.

"When did she say this?" Ridge asks.

"A while ago," Archer says. "When you had the accident."

"When I had the accident *when*, exactly?"

"I don't know," Archer says. "You were still in the hospital."

Across the street, the young woman stands. The young man removes his trousers. She takes them, smoothing them along the crease. She picks lint off them with care.

"Look," Archer says. "Look at the pecs on that guy."

"Rehab," Ridge says.

"Did I tell you Veronique wants me with muscles? She bought me a SoloFlex. She doesn't even think about my back."

Ridge watches the young man and woman as he listens, silent.

"I knew it was a mistake to have you around," Archer says. "You give her ideas."

Commuter trains arrive and leave. The train station is a block from The Denmark. The rumble bounces between buildings. Since returning to the North Shore, Ridge has had to acquaint himself with the schedules real people keep. Outside, it is now the hour to rush, the hour in which a real man hurries home to the family he loves.

"Keep a secret," Archer says, standing. "I think she's seeing someone."

Archer wobbles, unsteadied by his own news. Ridge does not say a word. Cars roar to life on the street. Horns beep as men and women begin to struggle for position.

"She's careful, but you know what you know," Archer says.

Ridge places his hands over his head, fingers locked, as if he has just finished a long run, or is being arrested. Across the street, the young man stands naked in the middle of his living room. The young woman holds a tub of salve in one hand. It is a large tub: white, medicinal. Even across the divide, Ridge recognizes the gnarls of pink and white flesh across the young man's chest. Ridge knows the scars of deeply-penetrating wounds, from mortar rounds, and from auto accidents, and from bullets. He cannot tell the origin of the story on the young man's skin, but it is skin with a story.

"I'm going to build houses again," Archer says. "The bank thinks he can unload this place to some Russians if we can't make it go. We sell the Mercedes, some stocks."

Ridge realizes Archer is dressed in a suit and what, in the scant light, appears to be a shirt of India silk. Archer is wearing a tie.

"I'm going to start over," Archer says. "I can't stand the sales end."

"She's good at it, though," Ridge says. "Your wife."

"Good," Archer says. "She's Da Vinci. But it hurts my mouth to smile that much."

Ridge hears the *thwok* in the dark; the sloppy, wet suction as his brother removes the bridge. Archer sighs in relief. It is a large device. Archer is missing every visible upper tooth.

"I want a clean slate," Archer says, voice altered without the false teeth. It is now the voice of an old man, the consonants, crushed. "I'm due. I'm going to buy V a little car, something sporty."

The young man tenses as the woman runs her hands over him. She rubs roughly, intently, the strain showing between her eyebrows. The young man faces Ridge and Archer, his body rocking as she works his hide. The young man stares straight ahead, as if looking Ridge in the eye.

"Clean slate," Ridge says, and thinks of Veronique. He thinks of her with a chalkboard eraser in hand, wonders how thorough his erasure will be. "What kind?"

Reinserting his bridge, Archer bends to pick up Ridge's flashlight. "What kind of what?"

"Car," Ridge says. "What kind of car is sportier than a new truck?"

Archer's keys clip-clop as he taps the flashlight against his leg. It is a winter sound, of holidays and buggies drawn by teams of horses. Ridge pictures white holiday lights strung in trees up and down the shore and thinks of the last letter Archer ever wrote him. It found Ridge in the Canal Zone. At the time, Ridge was courting the wife of a Naval aviator. He hardly thought of his brother then. Ridge was twenty-three at the time, and his past was something he could take or leave as he pleased. Archer's letter was a single enormous sheet of blueprint paper, thin parchment folded again, and again, and again. Archer endured much pain to print in an exact hand, placing slashes through each "o," as though it were a zero, as though each letter had a value larger than the word it cooperated with others to form.

"A girlie car," Archer says. "You know, something cute and cheap."

"You're the boss," Ridge says. "You'll work it out."

Archer started his Christmas letter where any seventeen-year-old would: their father was dead. The old man's body lay frozen in the ring. Archer wrote that the old man had pushed the high school boy to a breaking point. Archer described how the snow that fell relentlessly that season only extended the fights; the old man considered snow extra padding, reasoned even a lazy boy could not help but return to his feet. Their father had pledged to make Archer a man or die trying. In the bulky letter Archer enclosed his two incisors, as though the message had been posted to the Tooth Fairy. Archer concluded where anyone would whose hands and fingers were swollen and bloody. Succinctly.

Help me, the letter read. There was no signature.

"I'll tell you one thing, Veronique would never be seen in a truck," Archer says.

Across the way, the young woman focuses her attention on a particular point of the man's back, a trouble spot in the skin. Ridge notes the star-shaped scar on the man's chest at the same level. Something substantial that entered the man's breast had left in a hurry. At this moment, Ridge can understand the feeling.

Archer flips his wrist out, pulls his shirtsleeve back to expose his watch. Before Ridge can act, Archer switches on the flashlight.

The effect is immediate. The sudden illumination, the vision of the well-dressed stranger in the window so close, startles the young man to action. The young man moves out of instinct, his reflexes sharp. He reaches the wall switch in a flash, cloaks the apartment in darkness.

Exit wounds, Ridge thinks.

The dark windows of the apartment reflect the streetlights. Flickers become illusions of flesh, of movement, as Ridge peers ahead.

"She's gone," Archer says. "First thing in the morning, she's measuring for blinds to shut you out. No reason to ever come back here."

Ridge stands very still, focuses on the windows. He senses that the young man and woman have not fled. He senses the stirring, the ragged breathing, as they wait in the shadows. The two of them are not gone. Like Ridge, they are simply trying to figure out what to do next.

Kitchen Friends

Katherine Shonk

On a high-ozone morning in Moscow, midsummer 1996, Leslie stood among a clutch of Russians at the corner of Prospect Mira and Novoalekseevskaya Street, squinting dreamily at the sky-blue number 48 trolleybus that was slowly rumbling toward them through the haze. Past the bus, the broad avenue sloped gently upward, dissolving into the oversized kitsch and clutter of the All-Russia Exhibition of Economic Achievements. Leslie could make out the upper loop of the gigantic Ferris wheel, the menacing hook of the sickle brandished by the enormous steel collective-farm girl, and the rocket at the top of the Sputnik Obelisk, blasting perpetually into space on a titanium trail.

The next moment, Leslie was lying flat on the sidewalk amid an explosion so loud it seemed to come from everywhere. Suddenly conscious of the shape of the earth and of her body riding it like the pointer of a compass, she clawed the pavement, certain that if she released her grip, she would tumble into the stratosphere. The blast bore down upon her, and all she could think was that gravity had been sucked up by a black hole that had spun, tornado-like, too close to earth.

Other people were scattered about the street, while some wobbled on their feet, perilously vertical. As the boom began to subside, Leslie was aware of matched tangs of pressure just inside her ears.

Kitchen Friends

The air was pungent with the scent of fireworks. She could make out screams and shouts, horns and car alarms, squealing brakes, but the noises were far away, tweeting and delicate.

Words hurtled through Leslie's mind and gathered into thoughts. Her theory about the disappearance of gravity was replaced with the suspicion that a bomb had exploded nearby. This suspicion was given credence when a man shouted: "*Bomba!*"

Leslie lifted her head slightly. The man pointed north. She followed an imaginary string from his fingertip into a cloud of black smoke billowing from the trolleybus that a few moments before had been clattering toward the corner where she now lay.

All around Leslie, people began to lurch up from the earth, arms spread wide, like children imitating flowers in a school play. Wait for me, Leslie thought. Surveying her arms and legs, she found her limbs intact. Slowly she rose, a tender shoot blossoming to full height. Pulling loose from the street, she faced the bus and took her first steps on this new, wondrous earth.

*

Smoke-charred passengers clambered from the rear of the bus, arms flapping wildly. As they staggered away, cleaner passersby and would-be riders descended upon them. A young man in a red blazer chased a woman with charcoal handprints on her face, her skirt ripped to her waist. Only a few people lay bleeding on the ground, tended by police. Several women sat weeping on the curb, rubbing their eyes with dirty knuckles, while others muttered to themselves and wandered close to the traffic. Men took off their soiled shirts and strutted around the crumpled carcass of the trolleybus, gesturing and pointing.

Leslie draped her arm around one of the wandering women and told her not to worry. "I can't hear! I've gone deaf!" the woman shouted. An officer hailing passing cars guided Leslie and the woman into the back seat of a red Zhiguli driven by a small man with narrow eyes. The driver swerved madly, his rear end bobbing above the seat like a jockey's, his blaring horn a fly diving in and out of Leslie's ear. The woman gripped Leslie's hand. She looked familiar beneath the ash that veiled her flesh: middle-aged, plump, with brown-rooted orange hair—the liquor saleswoman at Produkti, the local state grocery store. Leslie, who only drank socially, had never spoken to her before.

Just a day earlier, Leslie remembered, several people had been injured in another bombing of a Moscow trolleybus. A passenger had brought an unattended bag of potatoes to the driver seconds before the device hidden inside exploded. No one had claimed responsibility, but government officials blamed Chechen rebels. Russia's war against Chechen independence, put on hold during the Yeltsin reelection blitz, was raging again.

Leslie thought of her Russian grandfather, Grandpa Serge, dead now for almost a year. What would he think if he could see her, speeding away from a terrorist attack in a gypsy cab, rubbing the arm of a shell-shocked saleswoman? A Simonov, surrounded by commoners, on the run again in their native land! He would be appalled. Leslie relaxed against the seat, her alarm settling into a pleasant buzz of alertness.

She had lived in Moscow for four years, but Leslie's Russian odyssey began in childhood. Every summer her parents, each thrice divorced by her sixteenth birthday, would chuck their only child off to her émigré grandfather's estate in Malibu. Day after day, as Grandpa Serge worked on his tan, Leslie had lain on a deck chair beside him, listening groggily to his lectures about the Simonovs' proud heritage and noble blood, which he authenticated by citing the flaws of other Russian aristocrats. "The Sheremetevs? Nothing but lackeys," Grandpa Serge snorted, as if eleven-year-old Leslie—sprawled in a two-piece swimsuit, sucking compote cocktail through a twisty straw—had argued otherwise.

Kitchen Friends

"The Nabokovs were poseurs, every last one!" Her parents' stormy loving and leaving made Leslie feel disposable. From Grandpa Serge, she learned of a better class of Simonov, those who banded together against the whims and indignities of the outside world. Her grandfather's virulent strain of Russian seeped into her brain and clung there stubbornly, fending off the timorous advances of Wisconsin middle-school French. In her twenties, Leslie established an identity as a true Russophile, known for her love of Tolstoy, her painstaking dissections of glasnost and perestroika, and the dramatically patterned shawls she wore through Milwaukee winters.

In 1992 Grandpa Serge urged Leslie to travel to Moscow to research a book that would educate the newly uncloistered citizenry about their most important displaced family. Leslie seized on the plan. She imagined herself a minor celebrity, admired for her charming blend of Russian pedigree and American free spirit. But when she arrived in Moscow and began poring over historical documents in the state archives, her exhilaration fizzled. Her ancestors had been not benevolent patrons, but barons of the most nefarious kind—thieves, murderers, and tax cheats. In the mid-nineteenth century they had even rounded up a rogue army of their own peasants and launched a mini-revolt against the abolition of serfdom.

Visiting the family estate, Leslie found that the main house had long ago been converted into a sock factory. She was invited back for a privatization ceremony in which Moscow Light Industrial Manufacturing Plant #53 was renamed the Black Cat Joint-Stock Company. Addressing the Black Cat employees from the porch of the main house, Leslie spoke of "the importance of a truly *benevolent* leadership." As a token acknowledgement of the plant's history, the director presented her with one hundred dollars' worth of stock and ten pairs of glittering caramel-colored panty hose. The ceremony was the only bright spot in Leslie's research.

"Traitors!" Grandpa Serge raged from his deck chair that summer, shaking a pair of Black Cat panty hose in the air. The lenses of his sunglasses reflected Leslie's face back to herself—stricken twins. "A mockery! A mockery of our family honor!"

Leslie remembered how the workers, swapping whispers and cigarettes on the factory lawn, had transmogrified before her eyes into their forebears, lugging sacks of grain and leaning on wooden rakes. Dizzy with shame, she had doubled over the pool and vomited.

Back in Moscow that fall, Leslie confided to her diary her horror over her family's crimes and her disillusionment with her grandfather, whose sense of *noblesse oblige* had proven as infectious as his native tongue. When she finished her outpouring, she realized that she had composed the type of slice-of-life-in-Russia columns that expatriates published week after week for other expatriates to read. She abandoned her book project and found an unpaid position as a columnist with the *Moscow Sparrow*, the third-largest English-language newspaper in the city. Supported by the allowance Grandpa Serge's accountant sent each month, Leslie told her story alongside the *Sparrow's* wire stories and advertorials: an American discovering her homeland, befriending the descendants of those her ancestors had enslaved. She wrote of the famous hospitality of Russians and their willingness to speak *po dusham*—from the soul—with near strangers.

By the time her grandfather died, of malignant melanoma, Leslie viewed her use of her trust fund as a subversive act. When the trolleybus bomb exploded, she had been heading to the newspaper office to deliver a column urging her readers to get to know their Russian neighbors and co-workers, her favorite theme.

At the hospital, Leslie was released within an hour by a doctor who assured her that the ringing in her ears was a sign of healing. She found her traveling companion propped up in a bed in the emergency ward, still in her tattered street clothes, but her face had been washed, and her expression of horror had calcified into grim resignation. Two doe-eyed young women in tank tops and miniskirts perched on each side of the woman, stroking her arm and gazing at the tiny television at the foot of the bed.

"That's the foreigner who rescued me!" the woman shouted, pointing at Leslie.

The young women gasped and ushered Leslie onto the bed. Larisa Mikhailovna introduced herself and her daughters, Ksenia and Irina. Hearing loss, Irina told Leslie, was their mother's only symptom as well.

While the daughters cooed over her, Leslie explained that, although it was true she was technically a foreigner, she was more than just an American abroad, more than just half Russian. "I'm an ordinary citizen, like you."

"Of course, of course, you're Russian, too...in a manner of speaking." Larisa Mikhailovna's face clouded, then cleared. "At least, you're not one of them."

"What do you mean, Larisa Mikhailovna?" Leslie said.

"Call me Lara." The woman elaborated. "I mean to say, you're not a terrorist." Lara squinted at Leslie. "Right?"

"Of course not!" Leslie cried. "Do you...Do you think the Chechens are responsible?"

"Who else?" scoffed Ksenia, the elder daughter.

Though Leslie hated to jump to conclusions, she had to admit that Chechen separatists were the most likely culprits.

"A survivor knows," Lara said. "Just think of how we were tossed out of our seats like popcorn. How we fought to breathe."

"I wasn't actually on the bus," Leslie confessed.

"But you *almost* were," Lara said. Leslie was riveted by the intensity of her new friend's gaze. Lara's eyes were wide set, and one of them was a lighter brown than the other, giving Leslie the sensation that the eyes belonged to two different women whose faces had swum together, as in a film dissolve. "And then you saved me!" Lara shouted.

"Well..." Leslie said.

"It's true! You stepped in when my own daughters couldn't. You're almost like family."

"Family?" Leslie echoed.

Lara, Ksenia, and Irina nodded, and slowly Leslie also began to nod. She relaxed against the rough sheet. Together the four of them stared at the lanky, colorfully dressed host of Name That Tune, bouncing from one edge of the television screen to the other like a metronome. Lara sang along with the orchestra's snippets of Russian folk songs in a high, quavering voice. Leslie sighed as the daughters stroked her arms with fingers smooth as satin. It had been so long since she touched someone, since someone touched her; even in the stores, money was passed back and forth on a dish.

Leslie had expected to accumulate a host of Russian friends in the course of her daily life, as she expected the love of a sensitive and passionate Russian man and two well-behaved Russian children. These riches eluded her. When she reported in her columns the wry truisms of her *kukhonnie druz'ya*—her kitchen friends—she might be quoting the overheard small talk of a neighbor or the girl who sold her bread. Over the years, a number of Russian men had written to express their admiration for Leslie's beauty (a fuzzy, unflattering headshot ran beside her column). They tended to propose marriage on the first date, and when Leslie demurred, they fell into sulky silence and let her pick up the check. The men had formed a composite in her memory: balding, with a brown moustache and sad, droopy eyes. Leslie was thirty-five now; was it time to cut her losses and go home? Very few people would even note her departure from Russia—perhaps as few as would mark her return to America. She couldn't help but wonder if today she had been given a reprieve.

A nurse burst through the curtain brandishing a rubber-headed hammer and shooed the visitors from the bed. Before Leslie left, Lara asked her what she did for a living.

Kitchen Friends

"I'm a writer," Leslie said.

"Then you must write about this," the woman bellowed.

*

"This week I will not be writing about a visit to a new supermarket, or to Pasternak's grave, or to the animal marketplace," Leslie scrawled in her notebook as she rode the subway home. (Though she could afford to take cabs, she wanted to face the same risks as the rest of the population.) "Today I witnessed something that altered my life in a way I do not yet understand. Today I witnessed the explosion of a bomb on a Moscow trolleybus."

Leslie hesitated. Numerous monumental events had taken place during her years in Russia: the failed Communist *putsch* of 1993, the first "democratic election" earlier in the month, and the Chechen conflict, that endless bout of Whack-a-Mole. Other Western columnists called on the Russian government to reduce the indiscriminate killing of Chechen civilians and to allow the republic some degree of self-determination, but Leslie had avoided writing about the war, reluctant to tell Russians what to do. She had allowed turmoil and controversy to skirt her quiet life, but the bomb had changed that, as surely as if it had been meant for her. "The contrast between the cowardly terrorists," she wrote, "united by their bloodlust, and their victims, isolated and suffering in hospitals across the capital, is striking."

The sky above Prospect Mira was a dingy white that might be peeled away in layers, like ancient insulation batting, to expose a bruised and angry sun. The ruined trolleybus attracted Leslie like a magnet. The mayor of Moscow, a round little man with rolled-up shirtsleeves, was surveying the damage. "We're witnessing a pattern of terrorist acts," he informed the reporters who encircled him. Workers in orange vests swept up broken glass and scraps of twisted metal. A Fuji advertisement still clung to the rear panel of the bus, but its right front side lolled on the sidewalk like an abandoned larval skin. Beyond the shattered windows, lamps twirled from the ceiling, flying saucer models. "We're going to have to do something about the Chechen diaspora," the mayor said as Leslie scuttled away, spooked by the wreckage, its contrast to her own unbroken flesh.

That night on the TV news, Leslie spied herself and Larisa Mikhailovna ducking into the Zhiguli like hounded celebrities. Witnessing the birth of their friendship, tears sprang to Leslie's eyes. No one had died in the explosion, the anchor reported, but two passengers were hospitalized in serious condition; many of the remaining twenty-six had suffered sprains and hearing loss. The authorities were investigating bomb threats and called on citizens to report unattended packages in public places. The mayor ordered police to check the documents of anyone suspicious-looking—the same Arab-featured men they always stopped, Leslie supposed—and President Yeltsin declared Moscow "infested with terrorists." Meanwhile, Russian artillery and helicopter gunships bombarded villages in southern Chechnya.

In bed that night, jerking from the edge of sleep, Leslie relived the terror of dislocation, of being ripped from time and space. She pictured the felled trolleybus's live wire snaking down Prospect Mira, the electricity jolting the bomb's victims upright one by one. Together but apart, they were each battling this first, sleepless night. A new conviction surged through Leslie: by reaching out to these troubled souls, she could begin to make amends for the wrongs her ancestors had inflicted on their peasant predecessors. And in the process of absolving her guilt, she thought as she slid into a leaden, dreamless sleep, she might discover the close-knit circle of family and friends she had never had. She might even discover a reason to stay.

*

The next day at the *Sparrow* office, Jason, Leslie's editor, a twenty-two-year-old from Florida, frowned as he leafed through the twelve pages she had written on the explosion. But when Leslie showed him that the column was organized into sections of similar length, he agreed to publish it as a three-day series.

That afternoon, Leslie visited Larisa Mikhailovna's high-rise, near the exhibition center. Ksenia and Irina pulled her into the apartment, which trapped the heat of the steamy day. They had incredible news. The city had promised their mother $1,000 as compensation for her pain and suffering. And thanks to a hearing apparatus on loan from the hospital, she could hear much better and no longer needed to shout.

In the kitchen, Lara was pointing at the television screen, mouth agape. A slender beige cord draped from her bulbous hearing aid, which was squealing like a teakettle. On TV, a bearded man wearing black sunglasses, a beret, and military garb was speaking calmly to the camera, his fingers laced on a cloth-covered table, a pitcher of ice water at his side.

"It's S.R.!" Lara said, identifying a Chechen military commander. "He came back to life!"

He was one of the most extreme rebel leaders, Irina explained. A few months ago the government reported that S.R. had been killed, but as it turned out, he only lost an eye. He had sneaked off to Germany and disguised himself with plastic surgery.

"His friends staged the trolleybus explosions in honor of his return to Chechnya," said Lara, her voice oozing disgust. She dislodged the hearing aid and rapped it on the kitchen table. The squealing tapered off, and she shoved it back in her ear. "Didn't we tell you it was them?"

They had. How naïve Leslie must seem!

On the screen, rusted cars and trucks stacked high with furniture crept across a muddy field. Two old men trudged along on foot. A little girl stared through a car window jagged with broken glass.

"Just look at those beards, that dirty skin," said Lara.

What did Lara mean by dirty skin? Leslie wondered uneasily.

"Most foreigners don't understand." Lara patted Leslie's hand. "But you're not like them, are you?"

"No!" Leslie said. "No, I'm not!"

"Those French, those Swedes and all, the only thing they talk about is human rights." Lara's voice slid into a growl. "What about my right to ride a bus to work without being blown up?"

As the news turned to interviews with frightened Muscovites who were boycotting trolleybuses, Lara chose a bottle of wine from the carton in the kitchen—evidently a perk of her job. She began to tell Leslie about her life, speaking in a mournful voice, *po dusham*, each of her eyes staring with distinct yet equal force. She told Leslie the story of her husband's affairs, her own affair, and their subsequent divorce ten years ago. She complained about her mundane and ill-paying job as a salesclerk. Then she spoke at great length about the death of her lifelong dream of becoming an airport ground controller. Though she had graduated near the top of her class at the aviation institute, she failed the certification test because of a "mental condition" that prevented her from knowing right from left. This failure had haunted her ever since. Her daughters, silent shadows, nodded. Lara spoke late into the night, filling and refilling Leslie's glass with syrupy Moldovian wine. In great detail she described the thrill of guiding planes homeward with lighted batons. The ringing of Lara's hearing aid accompanied her somber voice like wind whistling through cracks in a wooden house, and Leslie grew woozy and limp-limbed, gazing from one to the other of the woman's mesmerizing eyes, feeling transported to the very heart of Russia.

*

The next morning, a photograph of S.R. covered the front page of all the newspapers. As Leslie approached the entrance to the subway, she stared at the rebel leader. He was smiling, his left hand raised in a half wave, half salute, the contours of his face hidden by his thick beard, his eyes shielded by impenetrable aviator sunglasses. Leslie bought a paper. When she returned home, she clipped the photograph, without knowing why, and tucked it in a drawer.

With another deadline approaching, Leslie wrote about the resurfacing of S.R. "It is difficult to accept that we live in a world where the followers of a Chechen commander celebrate his homecoming by bombing busloads of civilians. Russians and expatriates alike must unite against such cold-blooded evil."

In a burst of inspiration, Leslie also typed up a flyer:

> Dear Prospect Mira Trolleybus Bombing Survivor:
> You have just endured a terrible ordeal, and should be proud of your strength and courage. But there is no need for you to face your trauma alone. You are invited to discuss the tragedy with other victims this Friday evening at 7 p.m., Novoalekseevskaya Street, House 15, Apartment 36.
> Yours,
> Leslie Simonov
> *The Moscow Sparrow*

*

It took just twenty dollars to convince a local police commander to give her a list of the victims' names and addresses. Vitaly, Konstantin, Gleb, Mark—nearly half were men, Leslie noted; her heart fluttered at the prospect of seeing them with clean faces. She recruited Lara's daughters to help, and by the end of the day, they had slipped the flyer under twenty-eight apartment doors, following the route of the trolleybus north to the exhibition center and beyond, to a peaceful neighborhood where, as Ksenia pointed out, they could glimpse retired cosmonauts tending the gardens of their government-issued parcels of land.

Leslie was fortunate to live in a building that was Stalin—rather than Khrushchev-era, forged of sturdy brick and solid pipes; however, the apartments themselves were tiny. She had borrowed chairs from her downstairs neighbor, but she was unprepared when twenty-six of the twenty-eight bombing victims quietly streamed in beginning at 7:30, lining up their shoes in neat rows by the door. Now they faced her in the living room: men and women, mostly middle-aged, with a few pensioners and young people, holding cookies and sipping orange soda from paper cups. Some of them had bandages wrapped around wrists and knees; several wore hearing aids. A tall, blond man with a dimpled chin stood out from the crowd. Leaning against the wardrobe, he smiled at Leslie as if they shared some private joke.

Leslie glanced at Lara, who gave a deep nod.

After thanking the survivors for coming, Leslie explained that she herself was not on the bus when it exploded, but that the tragedy had affected her so deeply she felt as if she shared their pain. "You see, I'm an American, but I have Russian ancestors." She shook away a vision of Grandpa Serge thrashing the panty hose in the air. "I believe that as long as the terrorists are more united than we are, as long as we confront our trauma in isolation, it will be impossible for us to overcome this ordeal." Her guests nibbled their cookies with downcast eyes. "It's my privilege to give you a forum to speak to other survivors *po dusham*, tonight and in the future, with the goal of healing through conversation and friendship."

After a long stretch of silence, the tall man stepped forward. "I was wondering, that is, if it's not too crass to speak of," he said, coughing into his fist, "if anyone has gotten their compensation yet."

A murmur rose up, then subsided as a woman's voice filled the room. "I called City Hall today," she said, "and they told me we can pick it up at the general cashier's office on the first of the month."

There was some discussion of where the cashier's office was located, and much confusion and rustling of paper as the woman repeated the address three times. Leslie began copying it down for those who didn't have a pencil.

"Are they giving us all the same amount?" an old man asked.

"They told me I'd get a thousand dollars," said the tall man.

Everyone agreed that they, too, had been promised a thousand dollars.

"In rubles, I suppose," a woman sniffed.

The survivors began to discuss whether they might sue for a higher figure. Some felt litigation was futile, as the government presumably had not planted the bomb, though one man advanced the theory that Yeltsin's daughter had masterminded the explosions to stir up public support for the war.

"I saw some dark-skinned types on the street after I got on at Malomoskovskaya," an old woman said. "But I don't think I could identify them now—they all look the same to me."

Another man said he'd seen S.R. bragging on the news about planting the bomb.

His followers did it, a woman corrected.

"Leave it to the Germans to disguise one of our enemies!" an old man bellowed.

"I heard the rebels are buying their weapons from neo-Nazis in Berlin," someone said.

"Perhaps," Leslie said, raising her voice above the hubbub, "we should avoid assigning blame, and talk instead about how we might cope with the experience."

The tall man stepped forward again. "Have we decided we're satisfied with a thousand bucks each?"

The survivors looked at each other and shrugged.

"As long as they pay us," a woman said.

"I have my doubts," a man said darkly.

"Well, if it's agreed, then...." The tall man bowed at Leslie. "Thank you for the refreshments."

"Oh ... you're welcome, but don't you—" Her voice was drowned out by the scraping of chair legs. "You're welcome to stay," Leslie said to several people, but they only smiled.

When the front door closed, the tall man was gone. Just five of Leslie's guests were left: Lara and her two daughters, an old woman leaning on a cane, and a man of about forty who looked like the composite of the Russian men Leslie had met through her column. He had the same drooping eyes and brown moustache, the same eyeglass case tucked in the pocket of his short-sleeved shirt, the same gray slacks and tattered briefcase. He smiled at her sadly.

Leslie looked around the room at the empty cups and cookie crumbs. It was not the wide support network she had envisioned, but perhaps a small circle of confidantes would be more rewarding. Remembering the photograph of S.R. stuffed in her bureau drawer, she felt a burst of outrage, and her spirits rallied. Like the rebels, this group was small in number—but they were on the side of good, not evil.

*

The rebel leader began to appear in Leslie's dreams. One night he proposed marriage to her over dinner at a restaurant. When she tried to turn him down politely, he pulled a grenade out of his jacket and tossed it playfully at her sweater, where it stuck like a burr. Leslie went from table to table, asking each party in her most apologetic voice to help her remove the grenade, but they were all German skinheads, and they ignored her. A few nights later she dreamed that S.R. was holding her hand, guiding her through the rubble of the Chechen parliament building in Grozny on a warm summer night. "See what those people have done?" he said, his sunglasses reflecting the stars. "Do you understand now why their trolleybuses mean nothing to us?" She awoke from each dream in a daze, feeling for several minutes that she had gained some key insight into his character.

Then the sensation would fade, leaving her with a peculiar restlessness when she confronted his face, impenetrable and mocking, in the bureau drawer.

A few days later Leslie convened another meeting at her apartment. Lara and her daughters, the sad-faced man, and the old woman with the cane showed up within five minutes of each other, an hour late. There was no sign of the tall man or anyone else.

As Leslie ushered the small group to the kitchen table, Lara unveiled the name she had thought up for them: the Victims of the Second Moscow Trolleybus Bombing, or the ZhVMTV, as the acronym came out in Russian. She produced a bottle of wine and made a toast to mutual understanding among the victims of the world.

Leslie suggested they share their memories of the explosion. "It might be"—What was Russian for "empowering"?—"*upolnomochivayushchii*," she improvised.

"We picked ourselves up and rushed to the exit," Lara said, "but the door was stuck, so a man kicked it open. Was it you?" She frowned at Lev, the mustachioed man. He shook his head and looked down into his cup. "Well, some man did, anyway, and we helped each other out."

"We were choking, and our clothes were torn and smoky," said Vera, the old woman, in a whispery, excited voice. "None of us could hear a thing." She looked around the table, her eyes wide.

"Yes," Lara said. "That's what happened."

They all nodded gravely.

When Leslie urged them to explore their deeper emotions, Vera, her hands fluttering, protested that it depressed her to talk about the bombing. She suggested they choose a topic to discuss at each week's meeting, such as cooking or tennis or tips on economizing in a democracy.

"I'm sure there are plenty of such clubs in Moscow," Lara said. "But this one is intended to help us cope with the tragedies of the past."

Leslie looked down at her lap, trying to hide her excitement. Lara got it!

"Well then, I'll be off," Vera said. "I've got to be up early to collect bottles." She downed the rest of her wine, stood up with the aid of her cane, and patted Leslie's hand. "Much luck to you!"

"As traumatic as the bombing was," Lara said after the old woman had hobbled out the door, "it was not nearly as painful an experience as the loss of my lifelong dream." Glowering at Lev, she began to tell him about the rigorous training required of airport ground controllers. Then she described her own inability to tell right from left. Finally, directing the full force of her stare upon him, she hurled these two elements of her story together like comets colliding in outer space. As Lara replenished their glasses, Leslie looked around the room at her kitchen friends and felt herself growing warm and content. Lev glanced at all of them sidelong, like a cowering puppy. Leslie found his shyness endearing, and she let her hand brush against his sleeve as she pushed the plate of cookies closer to the group.

*

In the final days of July, bombs exploded in railway stations in the southern Russian cities of Astrakhan and Volgograd, wounding several people. S.R. emerged from his mountain hideout to claim responsibility for the latest attacks, and he vowed to continue fighting Chechnya's battle for independence by sabotaging the Russian rails.

"The survivors of the trolleybus bombing on Prospect Mira," Leslie wrote, "do not understand why Mr. R. refers to his terrorist activities as a 'rail war.' My friends do not consider themselves warriors. These ordinary Russian citizens would simply like to ride a bus or a train without fear of being blown to bits."

The ZhVMTV's next meeting began with Lara retelling the story of her life's major disappointment and ended with Lev dozing off with his head on the table. Leslie was pleased by the companionship they had so quickly established, and the saga of Lara's thwarted career in aviation was compelling. But she worried that Lara's fixation on the past was preventing them from discussing other concerns. Surely there were issues Lev would like to share with the group; he might even like to confide in Leslie privately. Leslie herself was looking forward to the cathartic moment when she would reveal the shameful history of her real family to her surrogate one.

With the goal of helping Lara through her pain once and for all, Leslie convened the next ZhVMTV meeting in the shadow of the Worker and Collective-Farm Girl monument at VDNKh, the All-Russia Exhibition of Economic Achievements. It was a hot Saturday morning, the sun bleeding through a paste of smog, and Lara blotted her forehead with a handkerchief as Leslie led them down the long quadrangle, past grand, antebellum-style buildings with names like CHEMISTRY and ANIMAL HUSBANDRY etched into their stone façades. Women in their summer finery promenaded arm in arm, while men staggered beneath huge cardboard boxes stamped with primitive depictions of microwave ovens and washing machines.

"Here we are," Leslie said, stopping in front of a building labeled TRANSPORT.

"Oi." Lara's jaw quivered, as did her hearing aid's plastic cord. Her daughters latched onto her arms. Lev retreated a step. Leslie smiled gently, and he fell back into line.

"Lara." Leslie clasped the woman's shoulders and locked both of Lara's laser-beam eyes with her gaze. "It upsets me that you are still haunted by the loss of your lifelong dream. I sense it's keeping you from moving forward. I brought you here to help you gain a sense of...*zakritiya*."

Perhaps Russians didn't typically use "closure" in a psychological sense, but Leslie had made herself clear. "I will try anything," Lara said, sounding almost meek.

Once filled with exhibits touting the unparalleled ability of the U.S.S.R. to shuttle its citizens to and fro, the Transport building was now divided into a warren of stalls, each crammed with imported household appliances and electronics. Shoppers shoved each other down the narrow aisles and pressed against glass display cases for the best views of American computers, German toaster ovens, and Japanese stereo receivers. Leslie found an open space for the ZhVMTV meeting at the back of the hall, near the garbage bins brimming with balled-up safety warnings printed in useless languages, and shashlik sticks sucked clean. Above the chaos, red and white tiles adhered stubbornly to Soviet glue, melding into a crude pointillism: ships steering firmly through the sea, trains snaking curvaceous mountains. Lara stared gloomily at the pockmarked jetliner overhead.

"Let's gather around," Leslie said, taking Lara's hand. The daughters linked up beside their mother. Lev closed the circle, one naked palm cupping Leslie's fingers, the other floating near the concave stretch of bronzed skin between Ksenia's low-hanging skirt and crop top. "Shut your eyes, please." Leslie peeked to make sure everyone complied. Lev's round face reddened, beading with oil like a bowl of borscht. "Now. I'd like us to imagine that we're passengers in an Aeroflot 747 that is descending into Moscow—all of us except Lara, who is below us on the ground, preparing to land the aircraft."

Lara let out a gasp and squeezed Leslie's hand.

"It's nighttime, and Lara is using lighted batons to guide the plane. The control tower is radioing directions into Lara's ears, and she is signaling right, then left, then straight ahead. She trusts her instincts—trusts her arms to go left, then right, then left again. The captain is at ease, knowing that his plane is in competent hands. He follows Lara's directions precisely: right, left, straight ahead." Lara's hand swung Leslie's in circles, looping the signals it had learned years ago. "The plane lands with a gentle bump and glides smoothly down the runway," Leslie said. "Lara breathes deeply and lowers her weary arms. She walks back to the airport, satisfied that she has executed her job perfectly."

Beside her, Lara was sobbing. Leslie and the two daughters enveloped her in a hug. After a moment, Lev joined the embrace. The shoppers elbowing by took no notice of the small huddled group.

*

Back at home, Leslie dashed off an account of the breakthrough. Inspired by Lara's bravery, Leslie told her readers, she planned to ask the group to help her confront her own demons. Next, shy Lev would have his turn.

When she turned in the column, Jason's mouth hung open for a long moment. "Maybe next week you could write about . . ." He appeared to be trying to grow a goatee, and the pale yellow tufts on his chin struck Leslie as somehow indecent. "About something else, you know, besides the trolleybus bombing and your, um . . . club?"

Riding home in a packed subway car redolent of sweat and pickled beets, Leslie fumed. Write about something else! Like what, the christening of a Dunkin' Donuts? Another noxious bus trek to Tchaikovsky's house museum? What could possibly hold more human interest than the survivors' attempts to navigate the tragedy? Nothing. Nothing, that is, except another bombing.

Leslie found herself gazing at an old man's dried-apple face, floating in the middle distance. The man's eyes fluttered shut; Leslie's followed suit. Her stomach dipped as the train rose, the tan summer sky lowering to meet them. A garnet star glided by. The train had become a monorail, riding the lip of the Kremlin wall. A bearded man in black sunglasses and a jaunty beret muscled through the standing throng and sidled up to Leslie with a backward shove. "What is wrong with you Russians?" S.R. whispered, his orange-scented exhalations tickling her eyelids. "Can't you see that all we want is to be left alone?" Leslie was paralyzed. "Next station: Black Cat Joint-Stock Company," a woman's voice intoned. S.R. pressed something into Leslie's hand and slipped away. Looking down, she found herself clutching a paper sack brimming with cookies.

Leslie's eyes snapped open. She gulped in air, shocked to find the train still screeching through the tunnel, her hands empty. The old man bobbed before her, working his lips, just another drunk held upright by the crowd.

*

"What's *he* doing here?" Lara cried as she filed into Leslie's kitchen with the rest of the ZhVMTV that night. She was scowling at the newspaper photo of S.R., which Leslie had attached with fast-food magnets to her steadily churning refrigerator. Before exposing her own vulnerabilities, Leslie had decided, she would assist the group in overcoming shared assumptions, ones perhaps as dangerous as those she had acquired from Grandpa Serge.

"That's a good question, Lara." Leslie poured a round of chilled kvass but left the Danish cake roll glistening uncut; she didn't want her audience floating on a sugar high during her revelation. There were already too many distractions in the room: Lev's sporty lime-green shirt, unzipped to reveal a thicket of auburn curls; Lara's naked right ear (her hearing aid had vanished); and the buttons pinned to Lara's and her daughters' chests, which read GET OUT NOW, ASK ME HOW. "I'd like us to think about that," Leslie said. "What *is* he doing here? Here in Moscow, that is."

"He's in *Moscow*?" Lara exchanged alarmed glances with her daughters and Lev.

"Oh, no. At least, I don't think so. What I mean is, why did he plant the bomb?"

"*He* didn't plant it," Ksenia corrected.

"His men, then," Leslie persisted. "What did he want, exactly?"

Kitchen Friends

The group showed less evidence of strain than the sweating cake roll. Above their heads, the wall clock flicked away seconds like a timer on a game show, or a bomb. "To—blow—us—up—into—tiny—pieces," Lara said finally, her eyes zooming inward, marbles on a collision course with Leslie's nose. "That's what he wanted."

"Yes, yes—but why?"

"To attract attention to himself?" Irina offered.

"To attract attention to his *cause*," Leslie said, wishing she didn't sound like an exasperated schoolmarm. "Their fight for independence. Today, on the subway, it struck me: S.R. is a victim, just like us."

"A victim!" Lara barked.

"Lara," said Leslie. "We may disapprove of S.R.'s methods, but we can still appreciate his dedication to his cause. Just think of how the Chechen people have suffered, yet still they continue their struggle. We, of all people, should understand." They looked at her glumly, bored history students. "Think of our own past," she hinted.

"Nineteen-ninety-one!" Lara shouted and slapped the table, beaming at her daughters like a matriarch on Russian *Family Feud*. Just the other day, while waiting for the nightly news, Leslie caught a snippet of the show. *What did we have shortages of ten years ago?* the pinstriped host had asked a family of five from Novosibirsk. *Cigarettes!* the teenage daughter shouted. *Sausages!* the son piped. But it was their mother, flushing with a survivor's proud certainty, who cried out the answer given by 68 of 100 randomly surveyed Russians: EVERYTHING!

"That's true," Leslie conceded. "But I was thinking of . . ." Blank stares all around. "Eighteen-sixty-one? The emancipation of the serfs?"

"I wasn't alive then," Lara said, folding her arms over her chest.

"Oh, I know that." Leslie took her seat. She looked down at her hands. "There's something I've been meaning to tell you." Her ears scanned for some sign of interest—a tabletop vibration, an intake of breath—but picked up nothing. "My own ancestors owned an estate." She looked up. The other four were staring wearily at the opposite wall, like subway passengers; Lev was even swaying slightly. "They owned people, too. Other Russians. They kept them like animals."

The vacant expressions on the ZhVMTV's faces jelled and solidified until they were all perfectly still, like posed figurines. The clock quieted, receding against the gold-braid wallpaper as if painted there. Beads of perspiration thickened atop the cake roll like drops of glue; even Leslie's rattletrap fridge shuddered to a halt. The entire kitchen felt as lifeless as a diorama in a museum. The horror of her disclosure must have stunned them into fossilization. Nothing and no one in the room would ever budge again.

But even as Leslie despaired, she detected something stirring in the room—a twitch, a tremor, at the edge of Lara's mouth. The tic spread to the other side, becoming a matched set. Leslie watched as Lara's lips, straining against some unseen force, began to rise, stretching upward at a glacial pace. In a final burst of effort, the lips separated, carving craggy dimples in Lara's cheeks, revealing tiny rows of teeth in a palette of fall colors, like Indian corn. This, Leslie sensed with a chill of deep foreboding, must be Lara's smile.

"It certainly has been a hot summer." Lara's voice had turned singsong and unnaturally high, like the female announcer's on the Metro when the tape spooled too quickly. On either side, the girls unleashed youthful versions of their mother's grin, accessorized with pearly teeth and lip-gloss shimmer. Lev rubbed his eyes with his fists and took a long swallow of kvass.

"Of course, Moscow is always hot in July, but this year!" Lara burbled. Above the Cheshire leer her eyes blinked like satellites, one pinned on Leslie, the other on Lev.

"That's absolutely true," Leslie said with fervor, hoping Lara was trying to change the subject out of tact. Did the ZhVMTV

Kitchen Friends

accept Leslie despite her family's ignominious past? "It's been terribly hot!"

"It makes you want to get away, the heat." The longer Lara's smile endured, the more painful it looked, as if engineered by unseen hooks and wires. "Don't you ever just want to get away? Say, to the great European capitals? Have you been to Paris? Rome? Istanbul?"

"Well...yes," Leslie confessed. "Of course, this time of year, it's just as ho—"

"What would you say, Lev," Lara interrupted as the eye that had been fastened on Leslie scurried to join its mate, "if I told you that in just a few months you could be running your own business, building financial security, and touring the world!"

Lev raised one eyebrow.

"Don't look so surprised! It's true!" Lara crowed. "With a little help from Travelife." She patted her button. "'Get out now, ask me how!' That's the Travelife motto."

"I don't understand," Leslie said. What did any of this have to do with her ancestors? "What are you selling, exactly, Lara?"

"Social advancement, you might call it. Access to the finer things, freedom to go and come as you please—or simply to *go* and never return, if that's your fancy." She winked. Lev blushed.

From her lap Lara produced a purple brochure, the Travelife logo branded on its outer fold in yellow letters. Lev opened the brochure as if it were a delicate undergarment worn by a trembling lover. In the blurry center photo, the Eiffel Tower leaned like the Tower of Pisa.

"A woman I work with is halfway to Europe," Lara said, "and she's only been in business a few months!"

"You haven't given anyone any money, have you, Lara?" Leslie said, trying to channel her frustration into constructive skepticism and wrest back control of the meeting. She hadn't told them yet about Bloody Wednesday, the infamous Simonov-led revolt!

"The initial investment is quite reasonable," Lara told Lev.

"It seems like such a sudden change in careers for you, Lara," Leslie persisted.

Lara's smile cracked as it swung over to Leslie. "As you might recall, I've always been interested in air travel."

Now Leslie was the slow pupil. "I see."

"On Tuesday, when Alyona from the bread counter approached me, I thought, It's a dream come true!" Lara pulled the plate with the cake roll toward her. "Soon the girls will have their own businesses, too. It's so simple, anyone can do it!" She aimed the cake knife at the refrigerator. "Even him!" S.R.'s half-raised hand signaled acceptance of the challenge.

Leslie jumped in. "Which brings me back to—"

"Maybe if he had his own business to occupy his time," Lara snarled, slipping back into her everyday voice as she sawed at the cake roll, "he wouldn't be so interested in blowing us up." The daughters doled out the plates; Lev took a bite with soundless gusto. "Give the bandits their freedom, I say."

"Really?" Leslie said.

"We've soiled our hands with their filthy lot long enough." Lara relaxed into a dreamy tone. "Murder's in their blood, after all."

"Lara! Surely you don't mean that."

"Of course I do." She brushed her hands together, raining tiny chocolate bullets onto the table. "In general, we Russians would be better off without all of these outsiders underfoot."

Leslie felt her neck stiffen. "I didn't know you felt that way, Lara."

"It's a well-known fact that people get along best with their own kind," said Lara. The daughters flashed wan smiles of assent. "Common traits bring you closer together. We Russians, for example. We like to improve our lives—but I know that's not for everyone. Take you, for example."

At the same instant she vowed to ignore the request, Leslie heard herself ask, "What about me?"

"There's a certain Americanness to your character, Leslie," Lara mused. "A nostalgic view of life, shall we say, an obsession with the past. We Russians don't have that luxury. We're people of the future."

"But Lara ... I *am* Russian," Leslie reminded her. "Russian-American."

"Russian-American, eh?" Lara said. "Like a dictionary?"

The daughters giggled. Lev smirked.

"But I am," Leslie pleaded. How could Lara question this essential fact? It was the seed of Leslie's presence here, from which all else was supposed to bloom. "Remember, at the hospital? You said I was like family!"

"I was sick then, and weak," Lara said. "I'm better now."

"I know! Because I—"

"Because you helped me?" Lara lifted an eyebrow. "I'm much obliged, but my family can take care of me from now on. My Russian family."

"But Lara, I'm Russian, too!" Leslie cried. "As Russian as you are!"

"We have to go now." Lara pushed back the table. "We've got a Travelife conference in the morning."

Leslie leaped to her feet and snatched S.R.'s photo from the refrigerator. Tiny plastic hamburgers and hotdogs rattled to the floor. "I'm as Russian as he is!"

Lara stopped in her tracks; the others bumped up against each other. "You call him Russian?" she roared. "Look at that skin of his! Look at those shifty eyes!"

Leslie shivered. How could Lara see S.R.'s eyes behind the reflective lenses?

"I'll say one thing for him," Lara continued. "He knows who he is. He doesn't try to be what he's not." She brushed past Leslie. The girls and Lev followed her into the hallway.

"Wait!" Leslie shouted. "My grandparents—half of my blood—"

"Half of her blood," Irina echoed.

"A half-breed," Ksenia whispered. "Like a mutt."

"But I'm not a mutt!" Leslie protested. "I come from aristocrats!"

"What kind of fool do you think I am?" Lara shouted. The others were slipping out the door. "American aristocrats?"

"No, no! Russian aristocrats!"

"Russian aristocrats, eh?" Lara stooped to tie her tennis shoes.

"They were!" Leslie wailed. "We were! I am, I am!"

"Don't you know they were exterminated a long time ago?" Lara jabbed at S.R.'s photo, which Leslie still brandished in her outstretched hand. "Just like your friend will be," she growled, venom in her terrible eyes. She spun on her heels.

"You'll never get rid of me!" Leslie cried after Lara's retreating figure. "I'm more Russian than you'll ever be!" At this, she crumpled the photo in her fist, stifling sobs of rage.

In the week following the meeting, Leslie left several phone messages for Lara and her daughters; Leslie had bought them an answering machine at VDNKh, after Lara admired it, as a sort of congratulatory gift. Leslie ached to apologize for her elitist outburst, but they did not return her calls. She stopped by Produkti and was told Lara had quit.

Leslie slept fitfully and spent her days alternately napping and staring at her computer's blinking cursor. Each night she watched the news. Battle statistics from the south varied widely; the grainy stills of the dead and wounded reminded her of antiquated tintypes. She missed one deadline, then another, and still Jason did not call to inquire about her column.

On a warm mid-August day, the Kremlin's new security chief called for a cease-fire in Chechnya and for peace negotiations to settle the conflict permanently. Apparently, the television commentators scoffed, the mighty Russian army had been brought to its knees by a raggedy gang of bandits. The next day marked the one-month anniversary of the second trolleybus explosion. Just before the time of the blast, Leslie pulled on some clothes and headed to the corner of Prospect Mira and Novoalekseevskaya Street.

At first she thought the small group hunched between the cars and pedestrians was a gathering of commuters waiting for the trolleybus. But as she crossed the street, Leslie realized she was approaching the other members of the ZhVMTV. All four bowed their heads as if in prayer. Ksenia clasped a bouquet of yellow roses. GET OUT NOW, ASK ME HOW buttons were fastened neatly to all four shirts and blouses.

"Hello," Leslie said, stopping at the edge of the circle.

"Oh," Lara said. The others watched her. "Hello there."

Lev and the daughters stepped aside, opening the circle like a gate. Leslie took a step forward and let her arm brush against Lev's. For more than a minute, the five of them stood squinting at each other's shoes. Then Ksenia tossed her bouquet onto the tracks.

"Maybe it would be better if the flowers were closer to the curb," Lev suggested. They all stared at him. He hadn't spoken since that first night, when he told them his name. "It would be a shame for them to be run over."

Ksenia retrieved the roses and dropped them at the curb.

"I'm surprised to see you all here," Leslie ventured.

"We wanted to make sure we had achieved ... how did you put it?" Lara asked. "'Closure.'" Her new, terrifying smile flickered across her face. "As we embark on our new lives."

"That's wonderful, Lara," Leslie said. She had helped this woman, whether Lara cared or not. That might have to be enough. But she had one hope left. "I want you to know, I'm very grateful to the ZhVMTV, for your friendship and ... Lev?"

She tried to catch his eye, but he was staring at Ksenia, who gazed stiffly over his shoulder as if she were about to be photographed. Leslie was dazzled by the girl's rare beauty: Ksenia was sphinx-like, with sun-burnished skin.

"Fate can surprise you sometimes." Lev shrugged. "That's all." A number 48 trolleybus was weaving toward them, and he followed it with his eyes, which then settled again on Ksenia. Gazing at Lev beneath fluttering eyelids, the girl rose up on her toes, extending her bare midriff like a telescope, entwining her slender arms above her head. She let out a low purr. "The cashier's office promised they would have our money today," Lev said.

"We'll go with you," Lara said.

Lev, Lara, Ksenia, and Irina waved at Leslie as they hurried toward the corner. Leslie watched them board, then stared after the trolleybus as it rattled down the street and melted into the haze of traffic. She looked at the flowers, wilting against the hot pavement. A film of grit already muted their garish yellow petals. Leslie felt she should do something to conclude the ceremony—cross herself, or dream up a secret wish. Finally she made a vague curtsy, looked quickly in both directions, and turned, hurrying toward home.

Copyright ©2003 by Katherine Shonk

How I Discovered America

Penny Newbury

*In nature's infinite book of secrecy
A little I can read.*
             —Antony and Cleopatra

It seems that at least once in this life I should be given credit for something. All right, I choose this. It was actually me who discovered the New World, more specifically, Groton, Connecticut, around 500 B.C. Or was it A.D. I forget. It was 500 something, and I've never repeated the experience, never come close, never so much as found fifty cents on the sidewalk, won a frozen pizza at a Grange Hall raffle, found a body in the woods. I always wanted to be involved in the headline HIKER FINDS BODY. But no. I have to settle for discovering America, and it seems that right about now, twenty-five years after the actual psychic event, I should try to cash in.

Background. And there's so much of it. Which to tell, which to consign to another life? Because any claim to greatness needs, in its defense, background. Even I know this, and I've never been great. See? There's proof right there, of instinct, of collective unconscious. Maryan says that's where I fished this discovery out of, the collective thingie, that we all are hooked up to. I don't know. She also says that my pathological fear of dirigibles stems from my past life as a passenger on the Hindenberg. Don't know that either.

I grew up in Groton. That is to say, I was a large, stringy-haired fourteen-year-old girl in Groton when the town was wild and magical, with abandoned mansions and unguarded river docks and brambled paths through swamp and thicket leading down through time, as all paths led in Groton back then. It seemed, to my sister Maryan and me, that Groton could be the cradle of civilization. It had Fort Griswold, Lantern Hill, bubbling and oozy Lake Gungywamp—all overgrown, all forgotten. If you were a kid in Groton it was your business to hack through to Lake Gungywamp until you could see the light on Lantern Hill that failed to warn the Americans that the British were coming, until you could smell the blood and shit of the soldiers hunched in the moats at the battle of Groton Heights—the only battle of the Revolution that the Americans lost—until you could hear in the stagnant quiet of Lake Gungywamp the giggling ghosts of Mohicans and Pequots.

So we started, as kids in Groton, back in time, and our childhood and adolescence was a race to catch up. Of all our haunts, Lantern Hill was the farthest away from our house. Actually it was in "Center Groton," or Ledyard, and we had to hitchhike to get there and climb the white silica-covered trail the mining mules used for a hundred years, pretending we were prospectors, pretending we were nowhere, and back then, I guess it was about 1974, you'd get to the top and you could see Uncle Bob Christie's dairy farm on Route 2, and Long Pond, and tiny Lantern Hill Pond, and later on the tiniest part of the roof of the bingo parlor on the reservation. Or off the reservation. But close. Close enough for jazz, Mike would say. Mike was one of our regular rides, from Route 184 halfway down Lantern Hill Road to the tiny cabin where he lived alone with his kitten. A few years later, when I hitched the road by myself, up to Northwest Corner Road where Tim the game warden lived, I would deliberately stop at Mike's cabin on the way back to see if he would give me a ride. I guess that's another story, the story of the reservation and its spooky, smoky rumors, and the silver

Quonset huts and the tippity shacks lining Long Pond where Mike, and Indians, lived. Not many. And not well. But they were there, nestled among the ledge and brambles like autumn leaves, and sometimes I would pray that I would not get a ride on Lantern Hill Road until I reached them. All the years hitchhiking Lantern Hill Road and I never reached them, only Mike, and only at night. Close enough for jazz, that's all they need to be. They? I would ask Mike. He had, after all, some tribal relatives in high places. "I'm not involved in that shit. I don't do drugs and I've never been to Providence." I had no idea what he meant. I wish I still didn't.

Who knows how it would have ended for Lantern Hill if the bingo parlor had not exploded into an emerald green casino, if the reservation and silica mine and Uncle Bob's farm and Long Pond and Lake of Isles and life itself had not been swallowed up by every evil private interest known to humans and animals and rocks, turning the easternmost tip of my childhood into something forever soiled and obscene?

Still, twenty-five years later, teenagers repeat the creepy legends of Gungywamp, and the ghosts chuckle in its soupy mud five miles away. Even the blood money of the casino backers isn't amulet enough, and last I checked, this sloshy section of Groton, on the edge of Gales Ferry, is still sticking its tongue out at the fat Foxwoods Resort.

It was our second favorite place to go, Gungywamp Lake, and you could find it only if you'd been to summer camp there, and fished for catfish in the evenings, as we had. You could find the little abandoned rowboat, hidden on the bank by overhanging willow and bittersweet and concord grape, and you could push or paddle out with a board or a shoe to the still middle, where you could scare the crap out of your sister and yourself at dusk with stories like "Monster with a Hook for a Hand," and "Green Penny," and "The Ghost of Gladys Tantaquidgin's Grandmother." When I was fourteen Gladys was about a hundred and forty, so Gramma had to have been born eons ago, but there she was, haunting Gungywamp still.

A couple of years ago I read an article in a pretty big magazine—*Harper's*, I think—about a group of people, not just from Connecticut but a regular little movement, who were interested in Gungywamp for some very suspicious reasons. The story ran under the heading "From Our Random Series of Strange Delusions." Fine, I thought, think that way, you buncha weenie editors—you're not the ones who discovered the New World...but why were these psychic sniffers prowling around my turf? It was, you see, all starting to fit together.

The Indian Museum in Old Mystic didn't get too many visitors but it had lots of cool things like arrowheads and pots and occasionally it had Gladys when she and her brother Harold weren't at the Pequotsepos Nature Center, near Gungywamp, another place that adulthood has made impossible for me to find my way back to. If you grew up in Groton or Mystic or Ledyard during the 60s and 70s, and probably the 50s, Pequotsepos was a mandatory field trip. I was eight when I had my trip, and something happened there that has affected my life ever since. In a way it was a prelude to my discovery of the New World, in a way it was nothing.

This is what I remember of Pequotsepos: Not much. A big tree. A dark longhouse. Gladys's brother Harold who did most of the talking. He had beautiful, soft, long gray hair. There were baskets on the walls. Everything was brown and shiny with age. I was comfortable there because it smelled like my grandmother and great-grandmother with whom I lived. The brother, after all, was no pup back then either. He took us out back to a dirt yard with a big flat stone that had a beautiful indentation in it. He told us that Native Americans used to grind corn on this stone with another smaller stone. He told us solemnly, "Everyone gets a chance to do this," as if it were the only thing we would possibly want to do there, and as soon as he said it, it was. For me, anyway.

So I don't know why I stole the turtle.

Of all the ignoble, disrespectful, meaningless things I've done in my life, I still view this with the most shame and regret. I had no money to buy anything, and there was a little gift shop at the Nature Center. Little dolls and tiny birchbark canoes. . . and a beanbag turtle. I saw it, I can see it now, on a shelf about eighteen inches off the floor, about the height of my knees then. I wanted it as I had wanted nothing before or since. Who knows why? It was probably the only thing not related to any type of Pequotsepos "theme," I don't even think anyone on the reservation made it. They could have. Who knows. It could have been calling to me, in its corduroy-turtle way, but why it couldn't have said *Save up your money and buy me*, I'll never know. I was not a dishonest girl. I had never stolen anything in my life. The notion just suddenly appeared, something about the dark longhouse, the voices and movements of the tired, slightly bored hosts, made me all of a sudden wild and devious, and after I had taken my turn at the grinding stone, I slipped back in the little brown room and scooped up that turtle and put it in my pocket. And immediately felt sick. Gladys did not take her eyes off me. She said nothing, but I sensed for the first time an interest. "This is my sister," her brother had said, pointing to her in a chair, for even back then she couldn't do much but sit and look like what Harold had said she was, a princess. I loved them both, he with his long hair, she with her buckskin slippers and pursed lips and royal bearing. From the moment I set tootsies in that nature center, I had wanted those two wrinkly denizens of my past to notice me, and they had not. And then the turtle. And then Gladys watching.

I can't remember how long I kept it but I never took it out, never played with it, never told anyone. I thought for years of Gladys and her brother. She continued to live, this princess, waiting, I used to think, for me to find the courage and nobility to return to Pequotsepos and come clean. At last she could take no more of Groton and the little dark room and her kind, bored brother and the museum of arrowheads, and so she died, and the small but then-valid members of the Pequot nation gave her a solemn, quiet funeral, and then I began to dream about the tunnels.

*

When did it start? I think it started with the rock.

    I lived in Groton Heights, in the Historic District, in one of the three oldest houses in the area. It wasn't elegant, and it wasn't worth much, it was just damned old. 1780, said the assessor when he came. Chestnut beams holding up the chestnut floor, valiantly but without much success now since the basement was dirt. My family had owned the house since about 1940; I have a photo of Aunt Emmy and Uncle Monk standing with Estella, my grandmother, and her sisters Vera and Cleone, in front of the newly purchased house. I have no idea how I know that this is why the photo was taken. The date and names and "House on Broad Street" are on the back, but I know that it is one of those "Just bought a house" photos. It still has its lovely white clapboard and red shutters, that came off when I was four and were replaced with asbestos siding. The photo was taken in winter or spring; the yard is bare, and the shrubs are miniscule, babies...for twenty years those women would slave in the gardens, importing boxwood and pheasant-eye narcissus and six kinds of roses and blue spruce and different types of grasses planted in patterns in the acre that was behind the house—circles of bluegrass with backgrounds of nearly yellow-green ryegrass. And then the vegetable garden that could feed an entire neighborhood. A jungle of iris. A field of poppies. Three rows of currants. Concord grapes hiding the chicken coops. And the chicken coops hiding the stone wall beyond. The coops were torn down when I was about twelve and the little chickweed began to grow around the glacier rock embedded in the corner of the yard. It was a magic and enormous yard, by Groton Heights standards. And as I grew older I learned every inch of it, and finally reached the back corner, where a long, smooth-as-glass gray rock lived, and in this rock was carved an arrow that to me looked like a prehistoric bird footprint, only it had a more or less perfect circle drilled into it where its point was, and this arrow fascinated me for reasons I could not understand then and do not understand now. I am sure, now, that it was an old, I mean a really old, survey marker, since it was in a corner of the property, but why it pointed in the direction it pointed, and why no adult could tell me what it was, I could not say. I thought it had something to tell me. I wanted to solve its mystery and yet I knew that the mystery of this particular arrow was not its relation to a property survey. Maybe it wasn't the arrow at all. Maybe something about the rock, the corner, the stones on the steep, steep wall that led up and over to the next property. Things were not on a level in Groton Heights. You had to climb up six or ten feet to get to another yard. And maybe that was it. Maybe the level of the yard there was what drew me, because the level of Slocum Terrace was the same thing, the same idea, and a different thing happened there, different but connected.

So with the arrow, I began to think that there was a secret in Groton. I did not know what it was. I was fourteen and miserable and Groton had something to tell me and I did not have the key, the Rosetta stone, to translate it.

*

My sister and I considered Fort Griswold ours. We spent most of our free time there; when we weren't roaming Thames Street looking for waterfront trouble, we were spying on older kids and adults who, if we were lucky, went there to make out. Mostly we wanted to just not get caught at something. It's not a big place and you can learn its paths and trenches and battlements quickly. It overlooks the mouth of the Thames River and so is elevated high above the six or seven parallel streets terracing down to the river. It is always windy. You can fly kites there. In front there is a stone entrance with a ten-foot high bronze plaque honoring all the dead of this battle, including Colonel William Ledyard, who upon surrendering asked to be killed by the British with his own sword. He got his wish, and his name's up there too, along with the name of the drummer boy, aged twelve.

Beyond the stone entrance and the cannons are the grassy battlements, which surround a small field connected to the lower part of the fort by a stone tunnel that always smelled of urine. Maybe twenty-five feet long, six feet high, and damp. Our favorite part of the fort. Not a tunnel, really, just a bermed overpass through the battlements. Maybe that's where I got the idea. I don't know. I only know that after a while of standing outside the fort on the cement that held up the cannons, looking through the gate and in, I became convinced that under my feet was another tunnel, hidden, and it led through the fort and down to the river. I would stamp my feet on the concrete and say to Maryan (and whoever else we could drag along) "It's hollow! Don't you hear?" I guess they didn't, or else they didn't care.

This conviction grew, daily, and more and more knowledge began to float into my head. Beside the fort and across the street from my elementary school was an enormous yellow stucco house that was owned by an elderly (and crazy, went the story) woman who lived alone with her dolls. One day I got the courage to knock on the door. Oh, it was a wonderful house. It had twenty-six rooms, and on the outside were gables and juttings and balconies; from Thames Street you could see the majestic river side of it—turrets, stained glass, tiled roofs, trumpet vines, stone water spouts in the shapes of demons. I do not remember what my excuse was going to be for knocking. I was fourteen. I think "I lost my dog" was what I was going to say. You had to pass through a tall gate bordered by a high stone wall. The front door, behind this wall and an odd, twisty porch, was hidden from the street, and it was open a crack. I peered in. I remember a shelf on the far side of a huge room. Mirrors. Blue glass. Bottles. Millions of bottles. And beside them, dolls. Light was coming in from somewhere. There was a thick, rose-colored carpet. It was silent as a tomb, except for the clock.

I could be making it up, that the woman called to me, "who is there?" I could have seen her, I could have never seen her. I used to have recurring dreams of that spot—not of the house, not of the blue glass room, but of walking to school, as an adult, coming back for a meeting, a reunion, an offer of work or study or permanence of some kind—and being stuck there and wanting to but never getting in.

It was at that moment, when I saw the room with the bottles, that I knew that the tunnel under the front of the fort was also on the side of this house, and led down to the river.

With every such discovery, though more of intuition than of evidence, there was a detailed accounting on my part, to anyone who would listen. I had no proof, except a carved arrow a quarter of a mile away, a hollow sound in front of an old fort, and a glimpse into the secret life of a spinster, but it seemed sound to me. I cannot fathom what my family thought. They thought I had a good imagination, is what they thought.

I also told Steve Guillermo, with whom I was in love at the time. Steve Guillermo was a dockboy, that's what they called them then. Even I was a kind of dockboy—a tomboy who hung around the dock where my father ran Spicer's Marina, in Noank. Actually there were many dockboys, but I loved only Steve Guillermo. He was twenty-one when I was twelve when I began to love him, and this continued, unrequited and somewhere in the back of my head, for maybe four years until I was sixteen and was "transferred" to Siberia—the Stonington Marina.

Steve Guillermo was soft. I mean, he looked as though he would be soft to touch, like a sweet animal. He was quiet and had brown almond eyes with long lashes; he wore wire rimmed glasses, and had wispy brown hair that even at twenty-one was beginning to thin. He did not walk, he glided, quietly and without a sound, arms at his sides as though he were balancing books on his head, a way of walking I tried to duplicate for at least a year until I gave up. He wore faded Levis and striped crew shirts and boat shoes. Everything about him was clean and gentle and well-worn. I think, besides my loving him, that it was this quality in him, this sense I had that there were parts of him that were somehow older than twenty-one, that made me tell him about the tunnels. He never treated me like a kid. He must have known I was infatuated with him and he had to put up with it every weekend when I worked there, and every day in the summer when I was out of school, and he was graceful and kind and loving, and he showed me all kinds of wonderful secret things, like *Mad Magazine*, and later *National Lampoon* when he'd graduated from *Mad*. If my father happened to scream at me for something, Steve would comfort me with a word or two, nothing much, just a gesture, a sympathetic voice. He taught me about the shore life of little animals and how to tie knots and where the sandworms lived and how to fish for snapper blues. He also taught me how to smoke a joint, and looking back I don't think this was a bad thing. It was a secret thing, a thing shared, like an older brother would do. We did it in the dank basement of the tackle shop and when we heard footsteps he threw the thing to the back of the room; when the coast was clear we hunted for it and finally found it in a can of varnish. We dried it out and finished it off and I was not, and still am not as far as I can tell, any the worse for it.

  He taught me how to use a sickle to cut grass, how to nail planks to a dock ramp, how to flush an outboard engine, how to break ice around pilings with a steel iceboat. I remember no extremely philosophical conversations we ever had though he talked to me a lot. I think, looking back, and I have thought about this from time to time, that Steve Guillermo was a simple soul, not an intellectual, a philosopher or an artist. He went to college for a semester and then dropped out. I do not remember what he studied.

  Five years after I stopped working for the marina and seven years after I had last seen Steve Guillermo, I was registering cars for beach passes and I met his wife, Rita, registering their car. With her was their son Frankie. I remember when Frankie was born because Steve Guillermo was engaged to Rita when I first met him. It seemed an obstacle, but not insurmountable if I just didn't think about it. Because when you're me and you're twelve, what exactly do you expect the people you love to do for you? Be kind to you. Hang out and talk. Listen to your foolishness. Comfort you. And he did. And I remember that day, when I registered Rita Guillermo's car, this wide, severe-looking woman who turned absolutely stony (if she could have gotten any stonier) when I recognized her name and her son's, and I gave a little cry of delight, because, well, give me credit: I'd snapped out of it a while ago and so now was just happy to make an old connection in whatever way I could to that part of my past that was tinged by so much kindness.

I remember her coldness: *Yes, she did remember me. Yes, she knew who I was. Yes, her son was seven now, she must be going. Come along Frankie. Slam.* And I sat there and looked out the window at the whitecaps around Pine Island and I thought *I caused her pain back then. I was talked about, back then, by him. I mattered, to him.* Who is to know, really, when one is being cared for? I want the list, the roadmap, to go back in time or at least back over the past, and seek out those places where I need to say "I know now what you were all about. I know now that you were a gift, and part of what was in my life that pushed me forward." I think people deserve to know that, no matter how belated, no matter the distance.

And so when I was fourteen I began to tell Steve about the tunnels, about how I knew where they were, about how I didn't know why they were there, only I knew they were there before the fort was there, and that they were under Slocum Terrace too, and that they were connected and that someday I would prove it. And I would say "Steve, oh Steve, you've got to believe me," and two years later when I was sixteen and seeing him less because I got shipped around to different marinas to work, Steve would grin that lovely grin, his sleepy eyes slitty and nearly closed, and say, "Are you still thinking about those tunnels?"

And my father, with the hearing of a fruit bat, always lurking behind some collection of Penn reels or dangling Christmas Tree rigs, would add, "And are you out of your bloody mind?" He used words like that, Pop did. I think he felt more comfortable talking like a British pirate on the high seas, because Pop was a little out of place too. Back from World War II as a merchant seaman having been in all the wrong places (Pearl Harbor, the Bering Sea) at all the wrong times, he never seemed to fit in Groton, the town like a shirt one size too small, its collar always choking. He had his little charter boat, he caught a shipload of bass, bluefish, cod and Pollack, he ruled Fisher's Island Sound...and it was just too damn small. Oh, there were tragedies, too, trailing after him like so many hungry, squawking gulls, but we won't go there. At least not now. We may want to yank a few out of the bag later, dust them off, see how they fit with my discovery, but wouldn't it be nice if I could discover America all on my own, not relying on the stuffed trousseau of Bizarre Home Life that every New England girl receives, that they start packing for you at birth?

At home, Pop called things by their nautical names too. "Hey, move out of the gangway, you two." "What is this shit all over the deck?" "Move aft to your rooms before I smack you loose-eared." Until I was sixteen Pop was an active drunk (I always liked that phrase, though it didn't fit him; all he ever did was sleep when he wasn't on the boat). The kitchen was a maze of bottles and bar implements. To cook anything we had to learn how many jiggers were in a cup. And at dinner, "Gimme another belt of milk, would ya?"

Words out of place, people out of time. We could practically smell the past, so close was it breathing at our backs in the stories told of my father, and Howard and Bob Christie—all three wild-eyed and drunk, back from the war; out racing cars at night on Lantern Hill Road; giving the C.O.s the slip, though since they were all hunters and didn't poach, the old C.O.s didn't care. I grew up with names in my head but no faces—Konow, Overturf, Whitman—until I started hanging out with the younger ones. Sons of wardens were now the wardens, wild in the woods when North Stonington and Ledyard were wild, given a map and a car and a shotgun and told to get lost for four months while they learned every back road, every trout stream, every browsing ground and jacking lot in the northeast.

How I Discovered America

That sense of being pushed back in time was almost suffocating because I couldn't quite touch it, couldn't quite get there, always stopping just short of that life of before, that life of my father and true woods, real wildness, the Groton and Ledyard of the game wardens, of my father's youth, of the handful of Pequots on Long Pond in their Quonset huts. It did not seem so odd, then, to be dreaming of tunnels at night and waking up at four in the morning, hearing the doves and looking out the screen door and needing to go to Fort Griswold, needing to sleep in the tall grass of the battlements. Needing to, and not understanding why. What was odd, given the track record of the nut cases of my youth, the minimum security sanitarium that was Groton in the 1970s, was everyone's refusal to take me seriously. Actually, I didn't take myself seriously either, and secretly thought, without much alarm, that I was out of my bloody mind.

*

Other magical things in Groton in the 70s: abandoned houses, old and creepy and Victorian, or earlier, out in the weeds, in plain sight in spindly neighborhoods—just begging to be broken into, or sashayed into, really. Some were full of furniture and some were full of boxes and some were haunted and some, like the big green house behind the Lambert's, were beginning to be worked on by hired contractors like Marvin Eichelberg. I adored Marvin, because he was a stranger, because he was older, because he had wispy hair and glasses and reminded me of Steve Guillermo, and because he was there, two houses away, tearing out plaster and puttying windows. Tony Lambert and I used to steal *Playboy* magazines for him from Poppe's General Store while we were waiting for Mr. Chernay to get together Tony's papers for his paper route. We'd smuggle them to Marvin Eichelberg, doing his unfathomable carpenter things in the big green house, and I would rummage around in the cellar while he echoed through the rooms upstairs. I was fourteen. For God's sake it seems as though I was fourteen forever. Maybe I was fifteen. Let me age a bit in this narrative.

In the basement, in corners, I found boxes of letters and envelopes with Masonic symbols on them and return addresses from the National Sojourners' Association. What's a sojourner? I'd asked Mrs. Lambert, though I have no idea why I asked Annie's mother and not my stepmother. Mrs. Lambert's name was Sophia. The family was Catholic, and you said this about the Lamberts in that lowered voice that people in Groton used to indicate the sort of separateness that Catholics had: they ate dinner at 4:30; they took baths every night; they wore things called "medals" which I thought were the coolest and wanted my own. There were six kids and a niece and a mother, Sophia, and a father, Michael. In other words there were a mess of 'em, because, well, they were Catholic. They were also, in retrospect, about the most fucked-up family I have ever known in my life. Kleptomania and vandalism and incest and pedophilia all rolled up into one nice little unit.

Annie Lambert was my best friend. We were the same age. I only hope she got out of that family intact because I couldn't see any of the rest of 'em making it into adulthood. I asked Sophia Lambert, a tired-looking woman who was lots younger than I am now, what was a sojourner? Of course she got a little prim when she saw the Masonic logo but that was nothing new to me, my family was stuffed with that hocus-pocus. She said, "Well, it's a kind of traveler, a wanderer. Why don't we just destroy all those envelopes and not go in the basement again?" Good advice I didn't take; I not only kept going back to the house, I went looking for Marvin in his ratty apartment below Slocum Terrace when he didn't come to the house anymore. One day I found him. He invited me up to the room he had and there were three other men. Marvin had a double-barreled shotgun and he had it pointed at me and I sat on the bed while the three men talked about me and what they should do to me. It was the oddest thing. Oh, they were drunk off their asses and they were of a sensibility to get quite crude about the whole thing. All I can remember is, them discussing should they tie me up or not, should they let me go or not, Marvin with his big glasses and broad sweaty drunk face, and didn't I realize it was not a good idea for little girls to go following construction workers around? They let me go, I believe, when I decided I'd had enough and wanted to go. "I called Tony Lambert," I told Sophia Lambert. "Well, why'd you go there?" was her response. Where was my family, that I didn't tell them? Hiding, most likely. Not the most active of drunks, no.

I saw those envelopes, those papers, hidden as they were in a strategic location not a hundred yards from the rock with the arrow, and I knew they were telling me that some secret society knew about the tunnels.

I began to take Annie exploring with me and my sister. In the summers my cousin Laura would visit from New Jersey and we became a loud gang of girls, walking deliberately by my old haunts—the fort, Slocum Terrace. Being unruly. I threw a bottle once, and it shattered on the road in front of an old woman's house. She had a red pump in the front yard. The house was dark and still. Slocum Terrace rose up from this road like a 200-foot green cliff, rising to a stone retaining wall as old as the fort and it was truly that steep. The glass crashed everywhere and the old woman came out. We got our best "screw you" attitudes ready and she smiled at us, especially me, and said, "Oh, I'm so glad you didn't cut yourselves. Now, why don't we pick up the glass and put it in this can here?" and I found myself walking over to her and doing what she said. "And here's some nice cool water to wash your hands" and she showed me how to use the hand pump and water spurted out and everyone disappeared. Just she and I stood there and she said, "There's magic here and you know it. Up on the terrace, in the walls. So many things to find!" Her house, soft and brown, sat in the shadow of Slocum Terrace. Her kind face. I never went back to see her. I wasn't that way then. I wish I could say that I was, that I followed up on things like that.

But I took Annie Lambert back to Slocum Terrace, and we dug into the recesses of the stone wall on the side opposite

Monument Street. We found jars of coppery paint, and rusty jewelry, and disintegrating embroidery, and I knew that here was another place, and I told her about the tunnels. I said the tunnels were here, too, they were connected right behind this wall. But she wasn't too interested, she just wanted to play with the paint and spy on Andy Kosloskey and his girlfriend Cathy when they came to the little park on the other side of the wall to make out.

So that was the map of the tunnels in my mind, put there by dreams and boredom and kind women and echoes and spaces behind things that I couldn't get to. From my house, somehow, to the fort, to the big yellow house down to the river, then snaking across Slocum Terrace Park and down to the river, crisscrossing back and forth—that's where I felt them, that's where they stayed. I would like to say I got reactions when I talked about them. I must have sounded like John the Baptist. But mostly I got silence, because what would you say, really, to this kind of kid?

*

I could attach a Lesson, the lesson being that there really are no coincidences, that eventually you do get everything you want, eventually you are right about everything, only it is never on your schedule, it's on the cosmos's schedule, and the cosmos is not some benign grandfather with a library and a fluffy couch and a box of chocolates, it is a malicious nasty little dancing elf. You do become wealthy and famous, only posthumously. You are reunited with your lost love, only to have him killed three months later. You do get to meet Jesus, only you are not aware of it until years later, years after he's gone. You do discover America, only twenty-five years after you've moved away and proclaimed you have no home and look with disdain on that cramped, backwoods place and the failure it always represented. And all the stuff we do whose significance we cannot gauge because we've already stumbled blindly onward, away? *Get it away from me, get it behind me, don't show it to me.*

How I Discovered America

*

Every New Year's Day the Groton Cycling Club has a sort of biking answer to the Polar Bear Swim. You meet at the little Norwichtown green and you go about thirty-two miles, which is pretty far considering you're probably a big fat cow since putting your bike away in October, or November. The pace is brisk; you grit your teeth and hope. This particular New Year's Day I was, what? Thirty-three? So it was, what, nineteen years later? I had moved from Groton, an hour farther north, and I had forgotten, completely, anything to do with the dismal past, and if I was not, at that moment, happy it was because of Other Themes I have no intention of touching upon in this story.

Wayne and I decided to go. Wayne and I had known each other for maybe ten years, part of a crowd of biking enthusiasts who later become good friends, sometimes marry each other, have children, and keep biking. He kept me company on those days when my boyfriend couldn't ride with us. It had been two months since my boyfriend and I had broken up though, so it was a good bet that from now on it would be just me and Wayne.

Wayne was a drummer in a jazz band. He called people "cats" and would ask you back to his "crib." He'd had a gig New Year's Eve so he was not in terribly great shape that morning and I biked ahead with many folks I didn't know. The weather was that oddball New England January weather that sometimes can get to fifty or sixty degrees. Mostly there were men—for some reason most women still don't much care for competitive cycling. I fell in with a stocky sort of guy, I remember he was kind of Aryan looking, kind of Navy-looking, as most men from that area tended to be, and pleasant enough, though our pace, not our conversation, kept us together. At the end of the ride, back at the Green, I discovered he'd parked his car next to my truck. And we got to chatting while I waited for Wayne and while he waited for some of his buddies. We spoke of where-are-you-from. Very quickly I found out he lived on Monument Street, in Mrs. Cruz's old house. I knew every family on that street. I knew every bush, every crack in the sidewalk; it was, after all, the road to my elementary school, the road to the fort, the road to the yellow house, the park above Slocum Terrace, the Bill Memorial Library with its private museum filled with dusty butterflies and mummies' hands. I told him this sadly, told him that I knew it a long time ago, though. "It's okay," he said. "My wife and I are, I guess you would call us, history buffs. We've been studying the area pretty, well, fanatically." The slightest pause, as he was cleaning his glasses. Then, "I suppose you know about the tunnels."

What is the line that should come after this part in the telling? That I stared? That I thought he had said it in a dream? That at first I didn't know what he meant?

Because, of course that isn't true. I knew. I think I said, Tell me about them. The Norwichtown Green was starting to spin.

"Well, like I said, we belong to this group of anthropologists that believe, from looking at records and stuff . . ." he mentioned maps and previous scholarship and I was just plain squinting at him now . . ." that there were pre-Celtic civilizations living in this area, long before the native Americans, like 500 years before, and they had this system of tunnels. As a matter of fact Dr . . . ." Damned if I remember what he said his name was, "found part of a tunnel, beside . . . well, you know the big house by the fort?" I said I was familiar with it, yes. "Well, going from there to the Thames River. See, his group, which has spoken with someone from the TV program *Nova*, has determined that there's a series of these tunnels, and they were getting ready to film an episode of *Nova* down by, um, you know Slocum Terrace?" Slightly, I said. "Well, they brought cameras and everything. But there's an old woman there who won't let anyone on the property. For godsake, it's an archaeological treasure!"

I began, slowly, to tell him about the tunnels. The tunnels of my dreams, written in survey markers and on old envelopes. He grinned at me slightly; he had no more faith that I'd ever thought of these things than I had that he was actually real and not some New Year's Day figment of my sweaty imagination.

Wayne creaked in. We did not exchange business cards, phone numbers or astrological signs, this man and I. I have a vague recollection of knowing his name. More beyond that, I did not want to know. I cannot possibly say why this was so.

What I'm thinking is, even if he was full of shit...where did it all come from, those years of that stuff living in my head? Maryan said, when I told her, that I must immediately find a psychic or a channeler, whatever the crap they are, and do a past life regression. I coulda been one of 'em.

Didn't do that either.

I suppose, after all, it is merely enough to have discovered a thing, free it up for others to discover it too. But part of me won't go back and look...why? What is it that Groton's got on me, that keeps me away from this?

What if I were to go back, go back to Slocum Terrace and find that fissure, that copper crack in the wall where the Druids squeezed through? Like Pequotsepos and Gungywamp it will be gone, gone, not replaced, just invisible. Because there were so few times in my life when I was exactly where I was supposed to be at that moment, and heaven opened up, and if I had known what to call it, or that it was possible, I would have called it *joy*, I would call it being given an amulet, a little compass with an arrow like a little bird print, that could point me back into the woods, back into possibility.

Delta Interval

Drew Johnson

On the first day, we cut the grass. In some places it is up to our shoulders, and in these places it is hot, heavy work. At first, Ray and I fight over the jimmy-blade, which is small and light and curves from its long handle, up and around like a half-finished question mark. Only it is sharp. With this blade, the grass falls in easy, simple motions—the arms kept straight and tensed. You can only do this for short stretches before the tendons begin to beg and muscles cramp up.

Ray and I have just met, and despite the fact that he is old enough to be my father, we find ourselves in a testing mood and do not break for an hour. It is this hour that is only half-lit, the mosquitoes are sleeping, and it is my favorite hour. No one is expected to speak, so the grass falls audibly with the sound of a heavy drunken whisper.

The man who does not have the jimmy blade is stuck with the kaiser blade. The kaiser is heavier, the handle more like an axe's than the jimmy's broom handle, weighing five pounds alone. The blade on the kaiser is short—an angry thickset German comma— and it is sharp too, but your arms move when you swing it and the rhythm is harder to find. You can force the kaiser's rhythm though, in a way the jimmy won't allow, using unformed strength to make the rise and fall. So the man with the kaiser blade will use it, well or forced, as long he can stand and then hold it out for the other man without a word. He will take the kaiser reluctantly and give up jimmy, striding through the fallen grass soaked with dew, cool and briefly clean until it meets and mixes with sweat.

As we move up the rise, small trees are growing and these are stubborn enough that they will only give way to the kaiser, which is now appreciated, sought after. Its heavy thuds signal the way for the first tentative conversations and my time is over.

*

This is the flattest place I don't have to imagine, the Mississippi Delta, the flattest place I know. All that rises here is man-made and we work bracketed by the mile-away levee at our backs and the strange curve of the centuries-old native mounds before us. There are dead men here and they huddle beneath us. We are here to dig them up. We will threaten and cajole with our shovels and trowels and they will tell us about themselves.

"Where were you on the night of Friday last, say, five hundred years ago?" Ray says, menacing the ground in his best backwoods sheriff swagger. We have given over our blades for shovels and are taking the tops of the mounds off, having trimmed them. Ray will play bad cop, I will play good cop.

Ray drinks half a fifth every night, and a whole on Saturday night, which is followed by no morning. It is always Jim Beam, which I smell on such mornings as there are, for he sweats, though we do not speak of it, and while the pit—hopefully a grave we are digging up—deepens, the air becomes close with sweat. At first nothing and the dirt comes away reluctantly; it is mostly clay and, sorry to say, it does not sift for shit.

Ray and I share a room in a hunting cabin on the wrong side of the levee and he sleeps opposite me and snores. The entire field crew sleeps here, but Ray and I share a space because I snore as well, a noisy enough duel with no one to hear it. If I am able to sleep. It is a summer of floods, a summer when Iowa and Missouri are wiped clean and the water this far south has been slowly rising. Each night I wonder if I will wake up wet and panicky, the water invisible in the dark.

Sometimes I dream of water and wake up with a start to stare at Ray and his open eyes. Ray sleeps with his eyes open, something I do not do and something that does not bother me, except when I am waking like this. Then it is like reaching the place where a limit of danger meets a limit of safety, only to be pushed back across. In the dreams I have suffered a great variety of injuries but the water is the worst. I dream that I have been lying in it, asleep but aware, and that a deep ache has set in as my flesh loosens—this a prelude to a deeper rot.

*

It is said that if you take a shovel out of a truck in Mississippi, Sam Holiday will hear it, and if you put it in the ground he'll know where you are. Ours is a passing interest, Ray's and mine, when Ray has gone back to his family and I to the rest of my life, leaving this place, this state, for good and for all. Holiday will still be considering the dirt, Holiday taciturn in the best way, not only in his bearing but in his mind. He does not share the cabin with the rest of us but, rising early, drives two hours up from below Clarksdale to meet us each morning by the mounds. Setting us in motion, he seems to appear only when we have found something and then is hardly surprised.

After four days of dirt we begin to find the fired clay that was a house. The clay was mixed with grass before it was fired and we break it up in chunks, sometimes finding seeds or their imprints, even once finding the curve of the chuff of a hand. We stare at this curving thumb, a reflection of this brick, which we may find farther below. The thumb will have darkened into the hard color of the brick. We map the ruins within inches, on paper, and go below them. These unnamed people were not quite the people who called themselves Chickasaw and Choctaw, neatly divided and so each fighting the other. These people buried themselves beneath their houses. So as we go through the floor we know we will find them, and we bite less deeply with our shovels.

While we do this, Ray tells me about his youth and how he was a truck driver, a soldier—a private, a corporal, a convict, and then a private again. He patiently explains that his father raises ostriches in Georgia, and that his grandfather makes moonshine. He tells me about his boys, eight and eleven. And he tells me all this while we work, and he tells me again when he is drunk, and I know the stories by rote and still I hear them again. He tells me past the point of my retelling them, until I have been brutalized into that most complacent listener. But I must not be that unwilling, for I have a favorite. Ray has told it until it's hidden in the shape of a joke, but, part by part, it's shot through with its own kind of darkness. It's a story about trucking, about driving a flat-bed of expertly rigged palm trees cross-country, about trucker's drugs and hallucinations of camels.

*

One late afternoon we are all out behind the cabin, watching the river slowly going by, taking an old unused dock into itself, as inexorably as a star comes apart. Ray is cleaning his pistol, in the cabin I alone am without one. Others drift up to look at the strange Czech automatic. He puts it back together, takes an empty fifth down to the piles, on what's left of the half-submerged dock, and sets it up. Another worker, carrying the oldest working revolver anyone has ever heard of and a garbage bag of empty beer bottles, wades in beside Ray and begins setting them up. The first bottle, Ray's fifth, glows almost white in the sun.

The shooting begins slowly, everyone rusty, no one wanting to mess it up too badly and have to hear about it for the rest of the dig. But even before he's warmed up, Ray is clearly best, and is soon one-handing shots in groups of twos and threes, working through the supply of empties, making a physical account of how much we've drunk. The hard tap and tinny ring and the skish of the bullets are loud enough, and new enough, that I can't help but jump a little. Ray seems not to notice, but coming back from the dock, having set up another round, his third, Ray hands his pistol to me. Everyone waits, smiling. Ray looks at me and says, "Shoot the bottles, not me, and we'll be fine." Ray grins and I try to get the feel and balance of this handgun. I have never really held a gun in my life and will not need to, so for me to aim awkwardly is almost right, it proves something, and my stance is the balance of the world at a remove, of reaching the end of your second decade without a gun in your hand, the unhappy mean of hours and hours of only the sense of television. I feel like some badly acted cop and I fool myself enough that when the gun fires I am confused when none of the five bottles bursts. The bullet makes a second's wound in the river and I hear small laughter behind me. Again I pull the trigger, and miss everything but the river. An open laugh from somewhere behind me. Ray makes a small instructor's gesture, a twist of thumb and wrist, mutters something. Still I miss.

"He's shootin' the river!" is Ray's giddy excuse. "Shoot the river boy!" and for the hell of it, I empty the rest of the magazine into the river. The flash and jerk and smell of it are heady in the damp air, and I'm a bit loose, easy and embarrassed—but not feeling it, like a drunk on the edge who can't get worried. Ray takes back his pistol and reloads it slowly, his hands weird with the motion of something learned to be done quick slowed down.

Mr. Holiday, the head of the dig, walks up, coming away from washing rocks to see what trouble we're playing at. Everyone talks

Delta Interval

guns with Holiday for a few minutes and the sun drops lower. The brown beer bottles are a glassy yellow, brighter now than the sun that lights them. They're there, on the rail, at attention, in their own sort of deference as Mr. Holiday begins to speak.

"Last week, I had to do what I have to do every year. Go before the State Legislature and justify Archives' budget to a bunch of men who were looking to cut and prune and pinch. Someone from every department does it and it is seldom very much fun."

Holiday starts slow and, out of our deference, we listen.

"So everyone catches it bad from someone and when I get in there for my turn, after I've sat down, after I've said hello, I can tell that I'm gonna get it from this one fella sitting way up and to the left. Found out later, he was the standard case, contractor, good family, could handle anything his little corner of the state offered, but was expected to keep going up. So he was elected almost as a way of getting him out, so other folks would have room to be important. He looked about that unhappy, not out of his depth so much as at it. Then people start asking questions, and though I keep my eye on him, he doesn't say much, doesn't seem to know when to break into the old hands' old monologues and so I go ahead and forget about him. Then, as we're coming round the corner and I've taken a mild dusting, not too bad, had worse, the man finally speaks up. He says, 'Sir, your department is the State Department of Archives and History?' And I say, yes it is. And he says 'Would you say that your department's job is to discover and catalog and record the history of the state of Mississippi?' And I said that that seemed a serviceable definition of what we do. And he said 'And your department has an annual budget of how many millions of dollars?' And I named a figure. And he gathers himself up for one more question and asks, 'And your department has been in existence since 1902?' I say back, 'So far as I know' and then I know it's coming by the way he grins, but for all of me I don't know what the 'it' is gonna be. Then him, sitting back like I'm beat, and me and everyone else wondering just how, 'Well in that case, sir, I must ask. Why aren't you done yet?'"

Holiday smiles through the late-afternoon laughter. He smiles with the same smile I will bear when I tell it. A good smile. But now Holiday takes the pistol again and for a moment sights down toward the dock, he seems to be weighing his chances—he will extend the story, spin both parts off in an endless *on the other hand*. He starts to speak again, then doesn't, then does, "My father skippered a submarine in the Pacific. He shipped out right after mobilization began. I was very young, and so the one time he came back, as old as I had got, I felt younger. But that one time he was back in time for my birthday. I got to have a rifle when he found I didn't have one already and as there was only a little time, he took me out to teach me that day. It was what you'd imagine— the pump-action .22 and he apologized when I told him that everyone I knew already had one and he teased me, 'It's because I leave you with all these women' by which he meant my mother and his sister.

"But we didn't go for squirrels. When I asked about it, he was very vague so that I stayed quiet while he drove us onto the base and down to the pier. We went down onto that funny narrowing deck a sub has, it makes you feel like you're trying to balance on a whale, and I wondered if he was going to teach me the difficult business of shooting fish outside of a barrel. Instead he pulled out a wooden box from my mother's kitchen, still dusted with flour. He reached into it and pulled out a handful of the little metal cups that you bake muffins or cupcakes in. He showed me how to stand, sight and then squeeze. Then he tossed a few down to float on the water and I had to put holes in them and then they'd fold up with the force of the bullet and settle down out of sight. I wasn't bad at it, but my father was still pretty quiet—only if I looked right at him would he smile sudden and very wide, and so, after a while, we drove home. The ship—the other ship—was called the Asagumo, a destroyer."

Holiday smiles another smile, this one by way of apology, hands the pistol back to Ray and walks up to the cabin. The rest of us follow him in. For another hour I can hear Ray working through the rest of the bottles, three at a time, four at a time. After his bullets run out, I hear him throwing the bottles against the dock, breathing hard and swearing in the near-dark. When he does come in, I am in bed. Before he follows suit, he glances back at me as if he has forgotten something, then speaks, "Goddamn Gooks."

*

The next day, at the bottom of the pit, I find the pieces of a boy. I am slipping thin layers of dirt off, as if I were taking the earth apart in existing pieces rather than making parts as I go. Descending slowly, the colors of the clay seem unconscious, are artistic, and they have the look of murals, and I try to read them but they are natural, and closed.

On the floor I see something brown and pale. A single fragment? Or is it what it seems to be, the pale crushed cheek of a dead man, suspended in the earth?

We begin to use the small mason's trowels in order to go deeper, sculpting and finding the ground's embrace, its hold on the bones. The articulated burial begins to form a kind of relief, the raised long bones lifting up out of darker soil, soil seething with the organic, its dark blush.

Small distances in the pelvis and face are measured and we put a number to the time that these bones existed, before they became bones in the sense of earth: seventeen years. Though his skull is crushed, it is complete, and the word *braincase* has always startled me, for it is seldom used save when it is empty. He is revealed. The names and numbers we can put to him become prismatic. For me at least, they accumulate but will not cohere.

The grainy bones come away from the earth and we look at how the long bones are strangely eaten at and twisted, gnarled in a way that resembles the gnawed beaver limbs embedded in creek beds. It becomes apparent that this is syphilis, that these marks are the tracks of the disease and its slow progression. I can see the disease's tracks more clearly than the boy who suffered them.

So I sit, during a break, my legs splayed, holding my hat and wondering at this ground bone-meal boy in front of me, who died in pain, and was buried here. Here, the suffering has been preserved as well as the sufferer. It is not enough though. It remains a chance encounter. A bump with a stranger. A pardon-me, sir. He is in my pit, or I am in his.

There is all kinds of water in the air today, but it is the rain we watch for. When it comes we'll have to cover the burial quickly, and we have already raised a little levee to guide the water around and past and down, back off this tiny rise into the flat expanse before us. We have the boy up on a bier of earth now. We are aware of his whole being, of all there is of him, and each way the bones are interlaced.

He is lying on his right side and his legs cross at the middle of the femur and the middle of the calve. His arms are huddled in against his collapsed rib cage and the fallen down skull is tipped back, the mandible aside and down among fragments of collarbone. One of his teeth has slipped out and lies in the no man's land between the palate and the jaw. A vast mouth, if you read it wrong.

I look up over the edge of the pit as the air thickens. Staring out of the pit, I can just see it. I call out—"Rain"—but everyone has seen it at the same time. We cover the pit, weighing the tarp down

Delta Interval

with pieces of the mound's masonry. There is nowhere to go and we stand, watching it coming. The flatness here allows you to see rain completely and far away, sometimes miles, advancing like a solid wall across the fields. It doesn't entirely make sense when you look at it, for a storm seems somehow more vast this way but also finite—a whole shape that can be described before it engulfs you.

I take five steps forward and five back, momentarily taken with the idea that there is nowhere to go. At five hundred yards we can see just how hard the rain is falling. I can see the force of the drops raising dust and then pressing it back down to mud. We are all silent and then the storm drinks the distance, a hundred yards at a time. In the long, last second, Ray lets out a high wail and I let my head fall back. In between, sweat-dry and soaked, I can feel the big drops smacking my body, making a loud flat noise. I am saturated then, and the rain slides off, its voice lowered. The water tears up the bare earth, and large rivulets rake down the face of the mound to pool around my boots. I can no longer pick out any one sound, there are only overlapping syllables, words missed in breath.

*

That night, Ray and I are sitting above the muddy grave. The storm has opened up and we can see the night here and there. It has been dry enough that I drift from discomfort into abstraction, trying to sort out the sky from the changing puzzle pieces—farther out, farther—in the end, I admit that I don't know the stars' patterns well enough to recognize them from only a part. That and Ray's drunken mumblings bring me back.

We're out on the mound tonight. By being here we're trying to outguess the pothunters. Everything's a god-awful muddy mess and since no one would reasonably want to be sitting out here, it would be a grand time to steal some pots. It's been a bad summer for it and it's ten grand and upwards that an unbroken pot will bring once it's vanished into those channels. So Ray and I are out here with his Czech pistol and a borrowed revolver. We don't really expect anything, the mud is unpleasant enough whether you're legal or not. My borrowed revolver sits beside me on the blue tarp.

Ray is at ease. His long grey hair is pulled back and his beard is browned with dribbled whiskey. He leans back in the night, his pistol and his fifth by his feet. He isn't smoking. The smell carries so far, but you can feel that there is no one out here but us. Ray sits up and speaks, but I can't understand. He tries again but it comes out in a series of choppy wet coughs. He gives up and takes a long drink from the fifth. He wipes his mouth, stands up, sticks the gun in his belt, and says, "Time to take a piss."

"Go take a piss."

"Time to take a piss."

He stumbles away with the chatter a drunk's system makes coming back to me out of the night. Then I can't hear him anymore and the night gets quiet, even the crickets are low.

I sit, for the moment watching my borrowed pistol. It's a whole thing and it makes more sense on its own than the dead boy behind me. I put my palm over the checked grip, cool enough at first, but, as my sweat runs along the grooves, it warms and I pick it up. I sight down the barrel into the dark. There is nothing to see. I place my hand and the pistol in it on my shoulder and rest my head against them. With my eyes shut, the sound of rushing blood in my ear fills the world, and there is no mistaking it for the sea. It is me.

Then there is a crash, and the ground to my right jumps. Little chunks of mud fly against me and my heart starts a pretty good clip. I shout Ray's name. I can hear him laughing out there and then the crash again as he fires. The ground on my left sprays me with loose dirt. I wipe it off frantically. *I can't move, I won't shift*

Delta Interval

my feet, the joke won't miss, he won't fuck up, I won't get shot. So I just stand there, trying to be an easy target to miss, for some reason holding the revolver as if I might shoot back. Ray keeps firing, nothing close as the first two, nothing close enough that I can even feel the air move, but I start shaking anyway. *Be a good target*, I think, *hold real still.*

Then Ray comes back out of the night, his belt still unbuckled, the pistol in his hand, a great grin on his face. He says nothing to me, but sits down facing his empty fifth, and in a little while he leans back and passes out. I am sitting now, trembling, and I shout his name from three feet away and get nothing. So I reach over, point at the bottle with a gesture so easy, a rhythm to this violence. Feeling the trigger give, I let the hammer fall in the dark, and make the loudest noise I have ever made. Ray's fifth leaps, scatters into pieces and comes down still. Pinpricks of glass stand in the mud and fragments, bright with whiskey, cover his boots and shins. Ray shifts, but does not wake.

*

Before the bones come out of the earth, we have mapped how they lay. We've measured it, and when I close my eyes I can see it, in stages, laid out in the earth. For everyone else, there is this picture, and I am in the pit for scale, laid out as straightforwardly as he is not—on my back, my feet together. I turn my head though to look him full in the face, but the pit is cramped and his head tipped back. Instead of his averted eyes I am staring through the gaping earthen mouth into the vertebrae, jumbled together like a train wreck. I move my eyes down, at his cuddled arms, the thicket of ribs. Picking out the trace of spine through this, my eyes follow it back up and rest on the skull. I wait for the shutter to snap, the earth impossibly cool beneath my cheek. I climb up and out.

That I climb into the bed of the pickup truck, ready to go, is not important. The treeline is as far as it is, the mounds are where they were—their dimensions more impressive than their motivations.

My sweat is just turned stale, the sun is off, the air cooling. I lie back in the truck bed and stay there while the truck starts and moves off the site. I watch the uniform sky and feel the slow rise of the truck over the levee, where I could sit up and see the site receding. There is no need to look. The time between turns is the only measure of where we are.

*

That night we are all drunk, but Ray is ahead of us still. He hands me another and it goes into me like nothing at all. I am past the point of feeling it and decide to make an announcement, "I am inebriated!" and there is sympathetic laughter.

I glance over to Ray, sitting alone on the couch, holding his beer in both hands and staring at it. I sit down next to him. He doesn't react. I reach over and tap his bottle with mine. A toast. At that small tap of glass upon glass, Ray reaches over and grips my arm, hard. He stares into my open eyes. When his words finally come, he speaks them in a heavy, drunken whisper.

"I want my boys to be just like you."

"Just like my boy?" This me, wondering.

"No. You like me. No. Me like them. Them like you."

Blooding

Chris Abani

We worship in different ways. With wine, the flow of worldly sweetness; with alligator pepper seeds, the hot and painful trials; with nzu, the sign of peace; with water, the blessing of the holy spirit; with blood, the essence of all life; with food, to fill the hunger of gods; with prayers, to allay the wrath of demons. But greatest of all this is the offering of kola in communion, the soul calling onto life.

AFIKPO. 1972

Elvis had no idea why his father had summoned him to the backyard, away from the toy fire engine he was playing with. He had no idea why he had been asked to strip down to his underwear, or why Uncle Joseph first strapped a grass skirt on him and then began to paint strange designs in red and white dye all over his body. He was five years old and had learned that not only did no one explain much to him, but that it was safest not to ask. Uncle Joseph had a habit of expressing his impatience in slaps.

His mother Beatrice stood in the shadows, leaning on a door frame for support. She was ill and had been for a while. Whatever was going on must be important, Elvis thought, if she had gotten out of bed for it. She had a sudden coughing bout and would have fallen over had Aunt Felicia not caught her and led her back in.

"Mommy! Mommy!" Elvis called struggling to get to her.

"Stand still," Sunday said pulling him roughly by the arm. Elvis stumbled, but steadied himself against his uncle. Near tears he watched Beatrice retreat into the house. He looked around for Oye, but she was nowhere to be found. Instead he saw his teenage cousins, Innocent and Godfrey, and a gaggle of other boys ranging from ten to nineteen. This group was made up of young men from the neighboring hamlets that had come to welcome Elvis on his first step to manhood as dictated by tradition, and as part of the ritual they would form a retinue of singers. The truth was they were only there because they hoped that they would all be treated to good food and plenty to drink. Sunday noticed Elvis's attention straying and realized that he was looking for his mother and grandmother.

"It is time to cut your apron strings," Sunday said to Elvis. "Dis is about being a man. No women allowed."

"Easy, Sunday," Joseph said.

"Easy what? Dis is why he has to learn early how to be a man, you know?"

"I know, but easy."

Elvis stood still throughout the exchange as Joseph continued to paint.

"Eh, Joseph, I have some White Horse whiskey, let me bring it?" said Sunday.

"You need to ask?" Joseph replied with a chuckle.

Sunday got up and went in the house to fetch the whiskey from his private hoard in his bedroom. From the house came the quiet protest of Elvis Presley's "Return To Sender" played at a low volume. As soon as Sunday was gone, Elvis started asking questions. "What is happening?"

"Today, Elvis, you are going to kill your first eagle."

"But I'm too little."

"Don't worry," Uncle Joseph said, laughing.

"But why must I kill the eagle?"

"It is de first step into manhood for you. When you are older,

Blooding

de next step is to kill a goat and den from dere we begin your manhood rites. But dis is de first step."

Sunday returned shortly with the whiskey and two shot glasses. He sat down with a grunt and opened the bottle. Holding it over the ground he poured a libation, while Joseph responded at appropriate moments. Joseph took the proffered shot glass and downed the whiskey in one gulp, snapping the empty glass out to his side, allowing any errant drops to water the ground. He grunted and grimaced.

"Ah Sunday, dat na good brew dere. Pour me another."

"Don't finish my good whiskey. Dis stuff is not kaikai."

When Joseph finished painting Elvis, he sent his son Godfrey out to summon the male elders. While he was gone, Joseph handed Elvis a small homemade bow with an arrow strung in it. On the end of the arrow, pierced through its side was a chick. It was still alive and it chirped sadly. There was a line of blood from its beak that ran into the yellow down around its neck. The blood was beginning to harden and stiffen the down into a red necktie.

"It is alive," Elvis said.

"Of course it is. You just shot it," Joseph replied.

"I didn't."

"You did," Sunday said.

"Is this an eagle chick?" Elvis asked.

Joseph laughed.

"Elvis you funny. No it is chicken, eagle is too expensive."

Elvis stood there holding the bow and arrow, with the helpless chick as far away him as possible. He did not want the blood touching him. He tried not to make eye contact with the dying bird. When the old men assembled, Sunday passed the whiskey around and the men took swigs straight from the bottle.

"Do we have a kill?" they asked in Igbo, all speaking as one.

"Yes, we have a kill," Joseph replied.

"Was it a good kill?" the old men asked.

"Yes," Sunday answered.

"The father cannot speak," the old men said.

"Yes," Joseph said.

"Where is the kill?"

Joseph pointed and Elvis stepped forward. The old men smiled and looked at each other.

"In our day it was a real eagle."

"Let's just get on with it," Sunday said.

The old men glowered at him. Then one by one they walked up to Elvis and blew chalk powder in his face. They anointed his head with oil and taking the bow and arrow from him and passing it to Joseph, they spat in his palms and muttered a blessing for him. Then they walked out of the compound.

Innocent, at fifteen, was Elvis's eldest cousin. Elvis knew that Innocent had been a boy soldier in the civil war that ended two years before and that when he slept over at Elvis's house, Innocent woke up in the middle of the night, screaming. Oye told him that Innocent screamed because the ghosts of those he had killed in the war were tormenting him, and if he, Elvis, didn't behave, Innocent's ghosts would torment him too. Other than the war story about Innocent, Innocent and Godfrey, who was thirteen, were virtually strangers to Elvis. He admired them from a distance with their towering afros and platform shoes, but as teenagers they didn't have much to do with him.

Innocent bent and lifted Elvis up onto his shoulders. He felt very grown-up sitting there, seeing the world from that high. Uncle Joseph handed the bow back to Elvis and they followed the old men out of the compound, accompanied by the group of young men who now joined the procession singing.

They followed the old men up the road, singing the praises of Elvis as a great warrior and hunter. The road headed away from the square towards the farms and ritual spaces. It was unpaved and

Blooding

lined by trees Elvis knew simply as bush mango trees. They grew in straight lines. He once asked Oye how come wild trees could grow in such a straight line.

"They don't, laddie," she said. "In tha olden days, criminals and murderers were buried alive, standing up. A flowering stake was driven through their heads and they became the trees. Tha's why tha fruit is so sweet."

She cackled at his horrified expression. Beatrice intervened. "Mama! He is only five."

"Children are never too young to hear tha truth. You know why tha criminals were killed tha' way? Redemption. In death they were given a chance to be useful, to feed fruit-bearing trees. Do you understand?"

Elvis shook his head.

"Don't worry, someday you will."

But Elvis could never walk past the trees without feeling the ghosts of the criminals reaching out to him, and neither could he eat the tasty fruit. High up on Innocent's shoulders, he felt the leaves brush his face like hungry fingers and he was really glad when the old men turned off the road and into the bush. They soon came upon a huge Iroko tree that served as the clan shrine. The old men stopped, and taking the bow and arrow from Elvis, approached the tree. They freed the chick, tying it upside down to a branch, next to others that were in several stages of decay, hanging like grotesque ornaments on a Christmas tree. The old men plucked a tail feather from the bird and stuck it in Elvis's hair. They cut the tree-bark and dipped their fingers in the sap, tracing patterns on his face. And then it was over. Sunday picked Elvis up and held him close to the decaying birds. Elvis turned away from the smell.

"Don't turn away from death. We must face it. We are men," Sunday said.

Elvis turned to him, tears brimming.

"But it stinks."

"So does life, boy. So does life," Joseph said. "Come, Sunday, leave your son to join his mates. He is a man now. Come, we still have to finish dat whiskey."

Sunday nodded. He looked at Elvis for a long moment before putting him down. Turning to Innocent and Godfrey, Sunday told them to watch over their cousin and then he left with Joseph. The group of singing boys followed them, intent on joining in on any festivities. Innocent picked Elvis up and carried him on his shoulders as they walked back to the house, stopping at a kiosk just outside the compound.

"Why are we stopping?' Godfrey asked.

"Ah, Elvis done taste him first blood, so as a man, he must drink with men," Innocent replied.

Ordering beers for himself and Godfrey, he opened up a cold bottle of Fanta for Elvis.

"How you dey?" Innocent asked him.

"I was afraid," Elvis replied.

"Dat's how dese things are. De trials of dis world things come as surprise so you must have a warrior's heart to withstand dem. Dat's why your papa no tell you about today. You understand?" Innocent said.

Elvis shook his head and took a sip from his soda.

"Leave him. He is a child," Godfrey said. "Dere is time for such talk later."

Innocent nodded and took a swig of beer. Sitting on the counter in his grass skirt, drinking his Fanta and watching Godfrey and Innocent tease the girl behind the counter, Elvis felt like a man.

Copyright © 2003 by Chris Abani.

Apocrypha

Dan O'Brien

When my father comes home from the war, he needs a job. He spends that year working for his father: together they're Doyle & Sons, and they're good at outdoor digs. My father does the digging, down in holes like graves, lifting buckets of mud and rocks and roots up over his head to his father—my grandfather, whom I'll never meet—who kneels at the excavation's edge.

"There comes a time," my father still says, "when you realize you don't want to spend the rest of your life up to your eyes in other people's shit."

So he quits, borrows his father's funeral suit without asking, sets out on foot for Town Hall where he applies for and receives a job as Scarsdale's first shrub-enforcement officer.

*

Section 294-1 of the Scarsdale Town Code prohibits visual obstructions of the vegetable kind. Other sections of the Code address violations of a man-made nature, such as fences, clubhouses, illegal additions to the domestic structure. Section 294-1 applies mainly to intersections, though the confluence of drive- and roadway is by no means out-of-bounds. Those first few years of work, my father—who's never considered himself an artist—makes this diagram on the reverse of thousands of letters:

From a point on the road seventy-five (75) feet behind the intersection, from a height of thirty (30) inches, the law requires a clear field of vision seventy-five (75) feet in either direction; any and all plant material residing within this highly theoretical zone must be cut to a height of no more than thirty (30) inches, or removed altogether, within a period of fifteen (15) days or said home-owner runs the risk of a $100 fine and/or thirty (30) days in jail.

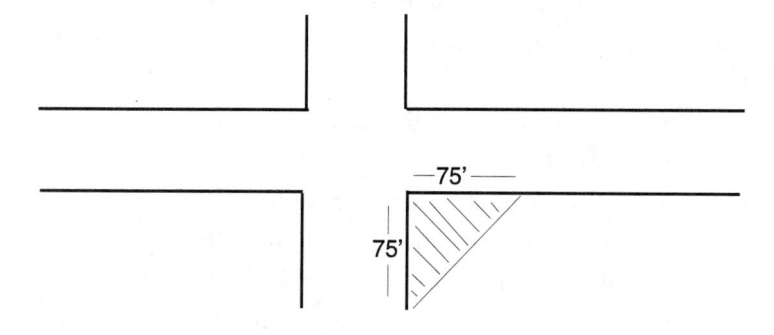

My father has been known to roll out under cover of night in a gray unmarked sedan and pour gallons of No-Gro into the roots of offending shrubs, should residents fail to take action in a timely fashion; by morning, the bush is always dead. No one's ever gone to jail for failure to comply with 294-1.

*

He falls in love with the names of bushes: prehistoric rhododendron with her reptile leaves; hardy privet, nature's barbed wire—used in trench warfare, or so my father says; the brilliant, luminous azalea. The azalea is my father's favorite bush. Though he's not much of a romantic (this is well before he meets my mother), he writes a free-verse poem on Town Hall stationery in which he describes the azalea as the sort of bush that might grow out of a lover's heart, could one's heart be full of dirt (and he considers it, in his own case, an apt metaphor).

And not just normal names, he loves the scientific as well: internally he recites the *Buxus sempirvirens, Berberis calliantha, Forsythia suspensai, Cotoneaster adpressus,* and they comfort him because they remind him of the Catholic Church of his youth.

And not just the common or the scientifically religious: my father's mouth delights in the euphonious *Winged Euonymus, Euphorbia Spurge;* the near-classical *Leycesteria* as well as the impossibly trite *Carefree Delight,* the ever-populist *Stardance,* the *Creeping Justice.* The vine called *Creeping Justice* thrills my father in a troubling way.

But he always returns to the azalea. Something in that burst of red: months of dormancy then springtime, flurries of pollen, a scattershot of deep pink—or crimson as he prefers; there's something deep in that red color, he thinks to himself without thinking, something like *déjà vu.* And one day, when he has a family of his own—and he does want a family, he wants that more than anything out of life—he'll plant azalea bushes all over the yard.

*

Now, it's true that the citizens of Scarsdale are significantly Jewish. Imagine their alarm when they receive these letters from the state—or town, anyway—threatening imprisonment with a cruciform sketch. World War II is recent history, and yet many irate residents, many of whom know (some of whom are) Holocaust survivors, make casual comparison to the Nazi regime in their letters of protest against my father and Section 294-1. Most comply begrudgingly: they martyr themselves, butchering robust shrubs down to the requisite height, until all that's left are stumps, shoots of green off bald black trunks. Everywhere one drives in these days of 1950s Scarsdale, bundles of limbs rot at curbside.

Some residents suspect my father of anti-Semitism, and while it's true he's grown up working-class and Irish, he has nothing against the Jews; in fact, he considers himself one of them: "A Wandering Jew," he'll call himself far into his later years, for reasons only he'll pretend to understand (he'll never leave Scarsdale behind, nor vacation outside the state). And of course there's the Jewish girl he'll marry soon, my mother; so it's fair to say his prejudice is more personal in nature.

One day he's out cruising in his gray unmarked sedan when he passes his house, the small house he grew up in on the outskirts of town where he still lives with his parents and the rest of his anonymous clan, and he realizes that the family hedge is in violation: why hadn't he noticed it before? And if my father is many things he is above all fair; he spends his entire Saturday cutting the family's privet down to thirty (30) inches, every stalk gripped at knee height in the hedge-clipper's hinge, sliced in one motion and the green wood tossed aside.

That night he dreams the heads of swans are growing up out of his front lawn. He walks from bird to bird, snaps their necks in his hands.

*

I tell these stories like this—words spoken, face to face—because I don't care for the confines of literature all that much. I don't like the page—don't trust it; I don't like to write things down. Because once you write it down you can't tear it up, change it—without revision. And even revision has to one day end. I don't care for endings.

I like to begin, again and again the same stories. At least in my most private moments of storytelling—late nights with friends, drunk with young women as I seek to test just how much of me they can take—I recount memories as mythology of the most personal kind. And I change a word here, or snip a word there, trim an incident down to its essence or lop a branch off altogether to bring my personality into focus. And I never worry very much whether I've told the truth exactly; because I never do. And who cares? It never makes sense, never entirely, this story of my family and what went wrong, because something did go wrong, something strange and mysterious happened in my family and specifically to my brother and nobody can figure out why.

It was a fine family to outside eyes. And most of my memories are, if not happy, boring; a few traumatic incidents punctuate years of protracted and mostly unjustified dread. We were all of us terrified, all the time, I don't know why; though to be fair my mother claimed we were nervous types from the moments of our births.

Some say judge a family by its fruit: six kids, not a single grandchild (that we know of); two drug-addicts, five alcoholics (there's overlap here); countless marriage and divorce and marriage again, and again; one paranoid schizophrenic, four manic-depressives, one bi-polar who also claims to be unhappily bisexual; a suicide (successful—who knows how many attempts?); and then there's me, your speaker, a storyteller.

Yes, it's true: I tell folk tales for a living. And lately I've begun to actually make one—a living. Not a good one, of course, but enough to keep me telling. There's an entire underground circuit supporting professional anachronists like me: expos, county fairs, symposia, cable TV, birthday parties for children of ethnographic filmmakers. The list goes on.

I'm partial to the Irish myths, in case you're wondering— *Cúchulainn, Fionn, Oisín*—and I've perfected a convincing brogue; so in a sense you could call me a sham. But through it all my aim has been true: tell the old stories again, and again, and again, and somehow make them new.

Before I became a traditional storyteller I ran a Psychic Supply store in Yonkers. And I made a habit of testing my own products whenever I could. This one time I bought a Do-It-Yourself Past-Life Regression tape for my VCR. The program was designed to hypnotize the viewer, to coax you deeper into your unconscious—deep enough (if you believe this sort of thing) so as to remember the last few moments of your most previous lifetime.

My most previous lifetime ends in World War I France. Like my father before me (or after me, depending on your take), I am a foot soldier. I'm German. The water in the trench is cold, up at my crotch. Rats flutter around my boots. An officer with a weasel face jams the barrel of a pistol up beneath my jaw and orders me to charge.

I scramble up out of the trench, my rifle and bayonet before me: ribbons of mud unfurl from knees and toes as I run the cratered battlefield—I come upon a privet hedge! My father's right: nature's barbed wire. But this hedge is immaculately groomed—geometric even—tall as a man it spans the horizon in both directions.

I stoop to peer through its prickly mesh. Behind me, weasel-face aims to shoot. I take a step back, close my eyes and leap.

Caught like a fish in a net: I'm shot through the neck. To this day I retain a birthmark here, the size and shape of a bullet hole.

*

What is it about shrubs? I think I know what they've come to mean in my life; but what still stumps me is what they mean to my father.

Though I haven't seen him in years, he's always been a neat man. He keeps his hair and mustache trim but not martial. Clothes are clean with sharp lines creased in leg and sleeve. Some might call him a tight-ass, or a curmudgeon, but his demeanor is more disengaged than disapproving. He resembles most of all a somewhat dandified barber.

In later years, of course, he moved on from his job as shrub-enforcement officer. But he never left Town Hall. He was the Water Commissioner, then Director of Public Works. I don't know if he's retired now, or even if he's alive or dead.

But no matter how his career changed, he always returned to his shrubs; on holidays and weekends—as a hobby, perhaps the only hobby he's ever had. He'd remove his neatly pressed shirt and drape it over the black iron handrail that climbs the four steps to our red front door. With his v-neck undershirt tucked tightly into belted slacks, he would take delicate hand-clippers to the roses, rhododendron and forsythia; long scissors-like cutters pruned back the evergreen and low hanging flowered branching of the dogwood tree; electric clippers, wielded at hip level like a machine gun, buzzed the privet to a near perfect right angle.

Whenever there was a problem in the family, and often there were problems, my father would lose his cool and his scant hair would fly amuss and he'd throw a piece of crockery, punch a table or wall—or sometimes one of us, though never past the point of bruising. And he'd cry afterwards, in private, as if we couldn't hear, as if we'd hurt his feelings so terribly much by making our childish mistakes; and he'd ask my mother in hushed, pathetic tones, How could we have let this grow so far out of control?

*

This is how my mother meets my father:

She's sitting in a sandbox, cross-legged, bouncing a baby on her thighs. She's eighteen, or thereabouts, wearing shorts with legs loose and high around her white, round thighs. Her chest is flat.

She's got hair like Dylan Thomas, but she's pretty. This baby's not her baby, but my father doesn't know that yet (she looks born to have kids), as he squats and says nothing articulate in greeting but offers a thick ex-plumber's hand, palm up for the baby to paw and slap. The baby's hands are chapped and pressed with grit. Its eyes widen as it looks from my father's hand to his face to his eyes, and it begins to cry. To wail. My father stands and turns because he thinks it's seen all the way to his heart, all the way to what he is.

My mother stands too and leaves the baby in the sand. "It's okay," she says. "It's just my sister."

*

My mother would remember it differently:

Her family's received this fascist letter in the mail from the Town of Scarsdale demanding they cut their shrubs to a height of thirty (30) inches or less or else. She thinks this is about as reasonable as *Kristallnacht*. Her father's not home. He's a businessman who rents office space near Penn Station and has white ladies gloves manufactured in the Far East, then shipped back to this country where they're sold at Macy's or Gimbel's at family prices. He's an aspiring tycoon, a closet Jew, and she hardly sees him.

Her mother is passed out in the living room in just her panties and a mink, rhapsodizing about some affair she may or may not have had with Kirk Douglas in Jamaica in 1936. (My mother looks nothing like Kirk Douglas.)

My mother's dropped out of state college to come home and care for her sisters, all four of them, but she doesn't care: she doesn't want school anymore anyway. What she wants is a family all her own. And she wants to make it right now, build it—her family. And she wants as many kids as her womb will bear, and she's going to be a great mother to them. A great mother the way Picasso is a great artist. This is her ambition, and it makes her feel self-righteous and sexy.

She's called the Town Hall on behalf of her parents-in-absentia, and demanded an on-site interview with this "J. Doyle" in Public Works who's terrorizing this town for no damn good reason at all, when who should pull up at the wheel of a gray unmarked sedan looking positively *film noir* but my father? Up the front lawn he climbs, this pale young Irishman in crisp slacks who's already a war veteran, his white shirt glowing in the noonday sun. He's got pimples on his chin, faint stubble on his cheeks. He can't be much older than she is.

The first thing he does is not to say hello, but to plant one knee in the sand and put his hand out to my mother's kid sister, who not only doesn't cry, but smiles.

*

As long as I've known him, my father never said a word about his childhood; hardly anything about his parents who were dead before I was born. Or his brothers (two, older) who we never heard from once.

He never mentioned Korea, either. Like the war itself, it just didn't happen. Not one word, not one story told, about those or the other years before our births. And to tell the truth, I'm happy. I'd rather imagine him the way I see him, according to my mood or to answer the bias of a day: rigging plumbing in camp, he's ribbed by the other soldiers for his studiously blue-collar nature; in an office somewhere with metal fans droning, he writes letters to parents of the deceased (agonizing over a word, the spreading branchwork of a sentence or paragraph, pen clutched like hand-clippers); a rifle at his hip and a rustle in the bushes—murder is not beyond him; nor are mistakes, as his boot brushes the tripwire like a guitar string.

Once, after we'd dug up a length of crushed sewage pipe in our own backyard, my father was changing out of his boots. Off came the boot and the wet sock with it and there I saw it: his naked foot for the very first time, pale and deformed in the outdoor light, toes missing, some partial or misshapen; only the thumb toe whole, curled like an unfolding white shoot.

*

When I was eleven, Scarsdale suffered a plague of raccoons. Packs of these dark-minded pests eviscerated our trash on a nightly basis. As the oldest of six children, I was expected to clean it up.

In the summers it was worst: larvae twisted in the sun, flies snarled the chicken carcass or peppered the feces the raccoons had left behind. When my siblings were babies—and there were always babies—there was the wreckage of the diapers to reclaim from the pachysandras. My mother believed there was a lesson to be learned in confronting what one found most repulsive (even if she hadn't spoken to her parents since her elopement many years before), and so I wore rubber gloves and breathed through my mouth when I had to breathe at all.

My father took pity on me, or maybe it was just the principle of the thing: "Let's fix this," he said one day.

He made the preparations, opened the kitchen window, removed the garbage lids outside. Past midnight he touched my shoulder, careful not to wake my younger brother as he slept across the room from me, peaceful and like a much younger child, as if he grew younger now as he slept.

At the kitchen window my father and I waited. And we watched as a caravan of raccoons came streaming through a gap in the backyard fence, humping along a dirt trail they'd worn in the grass through so many nightly incursions; and they swarmed over and into the open cans.

My father handed me his lighter. So this is what Korea was like! I sparked the light. My father waved the wick through the flame and dropped the M-80 out the window, down into the mouth of an open can.

A white, chemical pop, and then a thin high note: raccoons toppled out of the can like seals, some of their limbs paralyzed. We watched them crawl and flop in odd, confused patterns. They shook their heads comically from side to side.

"Don't," my father said, and I was ashamed to realize I had laughed. We heard footsteps above our heads. "Go to bed," he said.

The next morning my brother was up before me. He stood at the bedroom window, looking down at my father outside who cocked a baseball bat behind his head. A raccoon had survived the night, paralyzed by the M-80, and my father had to finish the deed as quietly as he could. I lifted my brother and carried him from the window.

Later, I helped my father bury it. I wore gloves, held the wheelbarrow steady as he lifted the carcass on his shovel. The flesh was already like mud but not mud, a living thing but uninhabited, like a mask discarded. I rolled the wheelbarrow to the hole my father had dug, and dumped the body in.

We covered it with dirt. Years later he planted an azalea bush nearby.

*

In another lifetime—before France and World War I—I was an Egyptian boy named Muhammad Ali al-Samman. I was out with my brother, who looked just like my younger brother looked around the time he killed himself, except of course in this lifetime we were Egyptian, both of us wearing beads and sandals and things. (It's quite common to be siblings with your siblings in a previous life; often you're born endlessly to the same family, though often in varying constellations. Who knows? Maybe one day I'll be my father's father: reincarnation as a kind of karmic revision.)

We are collecting *sabakh*, my brother and I, the soft soil for crops, trenching with crude spades in a sandy field: no vegetation, no shrubs as far as the eye can see. One of us, it doesn't matter which, strikes the stone of a buried tomb, and as we dig deeper we see the tomb is as big and wide as an outhouse or tool shed. I raise my spade to puncture the stone roof.

"No!" my brother cries and holds my hand fast. "A curse may reside within!"

"Foolish brother!" I laugh, because I am older than he and know so much more of the world. "There is gold in that tomb." And he relents at the mention of gold, because our poverty far outweighs our fear.

With one sharp blow the roof crumbles. Primitive bricks and desiccated clay tumble into darkness below, and I drop myself in too, landing shin-deep in a bed of powdery sand. I'm looking for gold: but the tomb is a single room, and in the dim light already I see it's empty; empty except for where the sunlight falls like a spotlight across a red azalea bush, absurdly in full, fiery bloom.

Disappointed that we haven't found gold, my brother and I dig up the bush and bring it home to our Egyptian mother for firewood. Within a week we're all dead of malaria.

*

Are you wondering why my brother doesn't have a name, in this lifetime or any other? You don't even know if the brother I've mentioned now several times is always the same brother (it is); all you know for sure is that he's one of several siblings, male and female, and that he'll eventually kill himself.

But what if I told you the real reason I won't give you his name is that he doesn't deserve one? He doesn't need one—he doesn't count. Not in this story. He's a casualty; a mistake or an accident but ultimately there's no story here because there's no reason, no satisfactory reason for what he does.

Because he doesn't leave a note. It's late winter, almost spring, it's late in the afternoon and there are islands of snow. No, it's dead of winter, and the grass is dormant under inches of ice and snow. No: it's morning. There isn't snow, it's all pale almost-white grass, and red azalea bushes bloom, pink and red, and I'm home from school halfway up the four front steps to our red front door when I notice crows up in the dogwood, so many crows hopping from branch to branch, cawing, sparrows shiver in the privet hedge, it's a day of slanting light in mid-February and the hedge is skeletal, empty now, snow, whatever snow there is, was, is melting. Azaleas are definitely not in bloom. Crows caw high up in the dogwood tree. It's dead quiet out here anyway. Overcast and dark—it's sunny, I find my brother around the side of the house. What's he doing here? Hiding? From what? One arm pinned behind his back. His back is flat on top of his leg. His leg bent back and his foot up beside a face like a mask. It takes me what seems like minutes to realize he's jumped.

I stand above him and wonder, what will I tell my family when they get home?

*

Recently, one late evening on Clear Island, a tiny fragment of cliff and mud off the coast of West Cork in Ireland, I was sitting in the company of perhaps a dozen storytellers just like me; it was a retreat of sorts, and I, in my so-called expertise and relative fame, was the retreat leader. I was to be paid a substantial fee. I'd spent the bank-holiday weekend teaching them memory-tricks, stories of *Cúchulainn* and *Fionn* and *Oisín*; I had my thick accent in high gear and a few drinks in me, and I'd just finished this story—the story you're hearing right now, more or less, about shrubs and raccoons, about wages of repression and the sins of the father and these various recollections of past lives, all culminating in a brother's senseless suicide—and someone spoke out clearly and simply as if solving a riddle: "Apocryhpha."

And I said, "I beg your pardon?"

And he said—he was a Welshman, clergy of some sort—"Apocryhpha is the hidden text. That's what you're searching for."

I had an image of my brothers and my sisters for an instant, all of us alive and well and sane, shovels in hands, in a field of overgrown shrubs, working soundlessly.

"But the thing about the apocryphal books of the Bible," continued the Welsh minister unbidden, speaking to all of us now as if he were the teacher and no longer the pupil, "is that they've often been not so much lost as excluded."

"Excluded?" I said, genuinely shocked. "For what reason?"

"For not being accurate."

"Accurate?" I repeated, even more shocked, and also because I was very drunk. "But why?"

"For being forgeries," he said. "You know: fakes."

"Are you accusing me," I asked, panicked now, slurring, trying my best to stand, "of lying to you all in some way?"

"Not at all!" he said, and the others tried to calm me. "I'm merely suggesting—I'm suggesting there may not be a hidden text at all, in your case. Sometimes in life there is no true story."

I sat down. "...then what?"

"Then what *what*?" asked the Welsh minister.

"If there is no true story—"

"You make one up."

He was sitting in a rocking chair by a low peat fire. A silver plate hung on the wall behind his head.

*

The story goes, my father plants azaleas in the front yard, one for each child born. They want a large, happy family, my mother and my father, and they raise their kids well and each of them grows happy and healthy to maturity. My parents are successful because they try so hard.

    I imagine him still out in the yard in summer or late spring, clipping back the bushes in his slacks and undershirt. He's an artist to me, the way he struggles in each season to make a pleasing shape out of what nature has given.

Movie Moguls Resurrect Gristlehead!

Richard Newman

How not expect, upon my resurrection,
me: half-starved, more than a little grumpy.
I sucked a few brains, they brought the tanks,
the helicopters, the heavy metal, a schoolbus
full of counselors begging me to get
in touch with my inner child. It's times like this
I wish I didn't live in times like these.

I've picketed my fence with human femurs.
My hut rests on a thousand fingerbones
if I need to let my fingers do the walking.
They can have their realistic, low-budget effects.
The future is nothing like it used to be.
The past is less and less like it ever was,
but the people sure tasted better back then.

Dr. King's Refrigerator

Charles Johnson

अन्नाद् भवन्ति भूतानि
Beings exist from food.
—Bhagavad-Gita,
Book 3, Chapter 14

In September, the year of Our Lord 1954, a gifted young minister from Atlanta named Martin Luther King Jr. accepted his first pastorate at the Dexter Avenue Baptist Church in Montgomery, Alabama. He was twenty-five years old and, in the language of the Academy he took his first job when he was ABD at Boston University's School of Theology—All But Dissertation—which is a common and necessary practice for scholars who have completed their coursework and have families to feed. If you are offered a job when still in graduate school, you snatch it and, if all goes well, you finish the thesis that first year of your employment when you are in the thick of things, trying mightily to prove—in Martin's case—to the staid, high-toned laity at Dexter that you really are worth the $4,800 salary they are paying you. He had, by the way, the highest-paying job of any minister in the city of Montgomery, and the expectations for his daily performance—as a pastor, husband, community leader, and the son of Daddy King—were equally high.

But what few people tell the eager ABD is how completing the doctorate from a distance means wall-to-wall work. There were always meetings with the local NAACP, ministers' organizations, and church committees; or, failing that, the budget and treasury to balance; or, failing that, the sick to visit in their homes, the ordination of deacons to preside over, and a new sermon to write every week. During that first year away from Boston, he delivered forty-six sermons to his congregation, and twenty sermons and lectures at other colleges and churches in the South. And, dutifully, he got up every morning at 5:30 to spend three hours composing the thesis in his parsonage, a white frame house with a railed-in front porch and two oak trees in the yard, after which he devoted another three hours to it late at night, in addition to spending sixteen hours each week on his Sunday sermons.

On the Wednesday night of December first, exactly one year before Rosa Parks refused to give up her bus seat, and after a long day of meetings, writing memos and letters, he sat entrenched behind a roll-top desk in his cluttered den at five minutes past midnight, smoking cigarettes and drinking black coffee, wearing an old fisherman's knit sweater, his desk barricaded in by books and piles of paperwork. Naturally, his in-progress dissertation, "A Comparison of the Conceptions of God in the Thinking of Paul Tillich and Henry Nelson Wieman," was itching at the edge of his mind, but what he really needed this night was a theme for his sermon on Sunday. Usually, by Tuesday Martin at least had a sketch, by Wednesday he had his research and citations—which ranged freely over five thousand years of Eastern and Western philosophy—compiled on note cards, and by Friday he was writing his text on a pad of lined, yellow paper. Put bluntly, he was two days behind schedule.

A few rooms away, his wife was sleeping under a blue corduroy bedspread. For an instant he thought of giving up work for the night and climbing into sheets warmed by her body, curling up beside this heartbreakingly beautiful and very understanding woman, a graduate of the New England Conservatory of Music, who had sacrificed her career back East in order to follow him into the Deep South. He remembered their wedding night on June 18th a year ago, in Perry County, Alabama, and how the insanity of segregation meant he and his new bride could not stay in a hotel operated by whites. Instead, they spent their wedding night at a black funeral home and had no honeymoon at all. Yes, he probably should join her in their bedroom. He wondered if she resented how his academic and theological duties took him away from her and their home (many an ABD's marriage ended before the dissertation was done)—work like that infernal, unwritten sermon, which hung over his head like the sword of Damocles.

Weary, feeling guilty, he pushed back from his desk, stretched out his stiff spine, and decided to get a midnight snack.

Now, he knew he shouldn't do that, of course. He often told friends that food was his greatest weakness. His ideal weight in college was 150 pounds, and he was aware that, at five feet, seven inches tall, he should not eat between meals. His bantam weight ballooned easily. Moreover, he'd read somewhere that the average American will in his (or her) lifetime eat 60,000 pounds of food. To Martin's ethical way of thinking, consuming that much tonnage was downright obscene, given the fact that there was so much famine and poverty throughout the rest of the world. He made himself a promise—a small prayer—to eat just a little, only enough tonight to replenish his tissues.

He made his way cautiously through the dark, seven-room house, his footsteps echoing on the hardwood floors like he was in a swimming pool, scuffing from the smoke-filled den to the living room, where he circled round the baby grand piano his wife practiced on for church recitals, then past her choices in decorations—two African masks on one wall and West Indian gourds on the mantle above the fireplace—to the kitchen. There, he clicked on the overhead light, and drew open the door to their refrigerator.

Scratching his stomach, he gazed—and gazed—at four, well-stocked shelves of food. He saw a Florida grapefruit and a California orange. On one of the middle shelves he saw corn and squash, both native to North America, and introduced by Indians to Europe in the fifteenth century through Columbus. To the right of that, his eyes tracked bright yellow slices of pineapple from Hawaii, truffles from England and a half-eaten Mexican tortilla. Martin took a step back, cocking his head to one side, less hungry now than curious about what his wife had found at public market and stacked inside their refrigerator without telling him.

He began to empty the refrigerator and heavily-packed food cabinets, placing everything on the table and kitchen counter and, when those were filled, on the flower-printed linoleum floor, taking things out slowly at first, his eyes squinted, scrutinizing each item like an old woman on a fixed budget at the bargain table in a grocery store. Then he worked quickly, bewitched, chuckling to himself as he tore apart his wife's tidy, well-scrubbed, Christian kitchen. He removed all the beryline olives from a thick, glass jar and held each one up to the light, as if perhaps he'd never really seen an olive before, or seen one so clearly. Of one thing he was sure: no two olives were the same. Within fifteen minutes, Martin stood surrounded by a galaxy of food.

From one corner of the kitchen floor to the other, there were popular American items such as pumpkin pie and hotdogs, but also heavy, sour-sweet dishes like German sauerkraut and schnitzel right beside Tibetan rice, one of the staples of the Far East, all sorts of spices, and the macaroni, spaghetti, and ravioli favored by Italians. There were bricks of cheese and wine from French vineyards, coffee from Brazil, and from China and India black and green teas that probably had been carried from fields to far away markets on the heads of women, or the backs of donkeys, horses and mules.

Dr. King's Refrigerator

All of human culture, history and civilization scrolled at his feet, and he had only to step into his kitchen to discover it. No one people or tribe, living in one place on this planet, could produce the endless riches for the palate that he'd just pulled from his refrigerator. He looked around the disheveled room, and he saw in each succulent fruit, each loaf of bread, and each grain of rice a fragile, inescapable network of mutuality in which all earthly creatures were co-dependent, integrated, and tied in a single garment of destiny. He recalled Exodus 25:30, and realized all this before him was showbread. From the floor Martin picked up a Golden Delicious apple, took a bite from it, and instantly he pretended the haze of heat from summers past, the roots of the tree from which the fruit was taken, the cycles of sun and rain and seasons, the earth and even those who tended the orchard. Then he slowly put the apple down, feeling not so much hunger now as a profound indebtedness and thanksgiving—to everyone and everything in Creation. For was not he, too, the product of infinite causes and the full, miraculous orchestration of Being stretching back to the beginning of time?

At that moment his wife came into the disaster area that was their kitchen, half-asleep, wearing blue slippers and an old housecoat over her nightgown. When she saw what her philosopher husband had done, she said, Oh! And promptly disappeared from the room. A moment later, she was back, having composed herself, though her voice was barely above a whisper: "Are you all right?"

"Of course, I am! I've never felt better!" he said. "The whole universe is inside our refrigerator!"

She blinked. "Really? You don't mean that, do you? Honey, have you been drinking? I've told you time and again that orange juice and vodka you like so much isn't good for you, and if anyone at church smells it on your breath. . . ."

"If you must know, I was hard at work on my thesis an hour ago. I didn't drink a drop of anything—except coffee."

"Well, that explains," she said.

"No, you don't understand! I was trying to write my speech for Sunday, but—but—I couldn't think of anything, and I got hungry...."

She stared at food heaped on the floor. "This hungry?"

"Well, no." His mouth wobbled, and now he was no longer thinking about the metaphysics of food but instead how the mess he'd made must look through her eyes. And, more importantly, how he must look through her eyes. "I think I've got my sermon, or at least something I might use later. It's so obvious to me now!" He could tell by the tilt of her head and twitching of her nose that she didn't think any of this was obvious at all. "When we get up in the morning, we go into the bathroom where we reach for a sponge provided for us by a Pacific Islander. We reach for soap created by a Frenchman. The towel is provided by a Turk. Before we leave for our jobs, we are beholden to more than half the world."

"Yes, dear." She sighed. "I can see that, but what about my kitchen? You know I'm hosting the Ladies Prayer Circle today at eight o'clock. That's seven hours from now. Please tell me you're going to clean up everything before you go to bed."

"But I have a sermon to write! What I'm saying—trying to say—is that whatever affects one directly, affects all indirectly!"

"Oh, yes, I'm sure all this is going to have a remarkable affect on the Ladies Prayer Circle...."

"Sweetheart..." he held up a grapefruit and a head of lettuce, "I had a revelation tonight. Do you know how rare that is? Those things don't come easy. Just ask Meister Eckhart or Martin Luther—you know Luther experienced enlightenment on the toilet, don't you? Ministers only get, maybe one or two revelations in a lifetime. But you made it possible for me to have a vision when I opened the refrigerator." All at once, he had a discomforting thought. "How much did you spend for groceries last week?"

"I bought extra things for the Ladies Prayer Circle," she said. "Don't ask how much and I won't ask why you've turned the kitchen inside-out." Gracefully, like an angel, or the perfect wife in the Book of Proverbs, she stepped toward him over cans and containers, plates of leftovers and bowls of chili. She placed her hand on his cheek, like a mother might do with her gifted and exasperating child, a prodigy who had just torched his bedroom in a scientific experiment. Then she wrapped her arms around him, slipped her hands under his sweater, and gave him a kiss. Stepping back, she touched the tip of his nose with her finger, and turned to leave. "Don't stay up too late," she said. "Put everything back before it spoils. And come to bed—I'll be waiting."

Martin watched her leave and said, "Yes, dear," still holding a very spiritually understood grapefruit in one hand and an ontologically clarified head of lettuce in the other. He started putting back everything on the shelves, deciding as he did so that while his sermon could wait until morning, his new wife definitely should not.

San Diego Dreams

Keith Lee Morris

It's photo day for coaches' pitch, and the coaches—straight from their day jobs at the saw mill or the real estate office—are hustling the kids in their bright shirts and caps and hustling the photographers, too, trying to get it over quick so they can work in a little batting practice before the rain.

"Keep in line there, Devon," Coach Reynolds says to my seven-year-old son. "You're next. You got your order form and your check?"

Devon holds the form up for Reynolds to see, and Reynolds nods and leans down and tucks Devon's shirt in the way he wants it. Number half-an-eight, my son's shirt reads in the back now. He's the smallest kid on the team, and his shirt is at least a size too big. "Your dad sign that check?"

Reynolds is a loan officer at the bank downtown, and he thinks people can't take care of stuff like that without his help. Devon looks at the check like it says something in Chinese.

"It's OK, Devon," I say. "You just give it to the photographer." My hands feel funny in my pants pockets, like they should have something else to do. Reynolds shoots me a look, but I don't even bother to meet his eye.

The photographer finishes with the kid in front of Devon, and Reynolds shuffles him, the kid, off to Diamond #2. "You guys toss some grounders to each other," he says. "Stay in front of the ball."

Stay in front of it. Keep your eye on the ball. Keep your shoulders square to the plate. Such is Reynolds' vast knowledge of baseball, but I guess it'll do for coaches' pitch. Devon seems to like him. "What's the most important thing we did today?" Reynolds says at the end of every game. "Had fun!" the kids shout. "That's right," Reynolds says. "Group hug." And they fall all over themselves like a bunch of clowns. It's total bullshit. What's most important to Reynolds is that his team of first-graders wins, and he doesn't like Devon much because he's not strong enough to hit the ball out of the infield. They taught Reynolds all that group hug crap at the organizers' meeting. Like kids have to be told baseball is fun. Devon's been playing since he was three.

The clouds aren't screwing around now. It's pretty early in the year for thunderstorms in north Idaho, but these clouds aren't kidding. We're talking thirty minutes, tops. They look like big dirty sheep rumbling toward the pine trees.

Devon's got a bat and he's striking his pose, but the photographer steps out from behind the tripod. He tilts Devon's cap up and messes with his elbow. "Keep your elbow up," he says. "That's right." But that's not Devon's natural stance. He doesn't swing level unless he starts the bat low. He looks over at me with a nervous grin on his face. I shrug, telling him it's OK. It's only for the picture.

Click. There it is, caught for posterity, Devon's skinny arms and narrow shoulders, a grin with one tooth missing. Back when I was a kid, you got one picture, which was a team shot. I remember I played for the local A&W Root Beer, and there was a kid in the picture named Jeff who wore his glove on the wrong hand for laughs and another kid named Todd who got caught picking his nose. Me, I looked very serious, standing smack dab in the center. But now they get a group shot and individual 8x10s and 5x7s and trading cards to boot.

So we're off to Diamond #2, me and Devon. I walk along with him, my hand on his cap. "Looks like rain," I say.

"Will I have time to bat?" he says.

"I hope so."

One thing about Devon, he's ready to get a bat in his hands. He can't hit his way out of a wet paper bag, but he's got itchy palms, and that earns a certain amount of respect, even from Reynolds. And I like the way he charges the ball in the field, too. Even when they get good enough to really start zipping the thing around, I don't think Devon will show any fear.

At Diamond #2 they toss the ball back and forth, more or less like Reynolds told them to. The other moms and dads are in the bleachers, but I stay down on the field behind the first base line so I don't have to talk to anyone. That's what I do all day now, talk—head of team sales for a regional sporting goods store. I talk to coaches and athletic directors and youth league organizers and tell them that they need our new Riddell helmets and our new Nike basketball shoes and our new Spalding pitching machines. Eastern Washington and north Idaho and western Montana. Spokane and Deer Park and Bonners Ferry and Whitefish and Libby. And here, Sandpoint, my hometown.

I used to throw a baseball. I threw it hard and a little too straight. Maybe I never had enough dip and slide to make it in the big leagues, I'll never know. I threw it hard and straight.

But I got my start here on Diamond #2. Threw my first shutout here in Little League. Hit my first home run right over that outfield fence, right over the billboard that says "Bob's Super Drug."

Reynolds comes up with the last of the kids—#11. They get their pictures taken in numerical order. Reynolds has his hand on the kid's shoulder. Reynolds's got his baseball cap cocked at an angle that simulates someone who could actually play.

San Diego Dreams

Me, I could play. Little League, Pony League, Babe Ruth, American Legion. I could hit and I could field and I could run and most of all I could pitch. I pitched my way to a full ride at Washington State and a promise from the San Diego Padres that they would draft me after my freshman year if I proved I could step up to the next level. After all, I hadn't seen much competition in north Idaho, which isn't exactly a hotbed for baseball. Like I say, I might not have had the stuff—I was working my way toward ninety-plus on the fastball, but my curve was more like a wrinkle. It remained to be seen. But my fastball had what's called "pop" and "sizzle." Batters told me they could hear it coming from the time it left my hand.

One Saturday at the end of my senior year I was bored and I drove by the high school just to see what was happening. They had a pick-up basketball game going in the gym, a few of my friends and some older town guys I knew. I was bored, and I wanted to play, but I was wearing flip-flops, those old sandals you bought for a buck that lasted you a summer. One of the town guys happened to have an extra pair of shoes. We played and we played, nothing special, just killing an afternoon, and I didn't even care that the guy's shoes were rubbing me raw. That night I had ugly red blisters, and my next start in Legion was just two days away.

Just throwing warm-ups I could tell I was in trouble. I could feel the blisters filling again. By the end of the first inning they'd already popped. I didn't tell my coach. Tough it out, play with pain—that's what you learn in sports. That's what they do in the big leagues. Every inning the pain got worse, but I found that if I shortened my stride to the plate when I threw it wasn't quite as bad. I lost a little control, but still pitched well enough to go the whole nine, and we won 5-2. By the time I got the last out I could hardly walk. I waited till I got home to take off my cleats, and my socks were a bloody mess. And for some reason my shoulder throbbed and burned.

I got blood poisoning from the blisters and ended up in the county hospital. I was sick enough to miss two starts, and I probably should have skipped a third. It was my senior year, though, and I was busting everybody's ass, and getting ready to pitch for WSU the next spring and be drafted by the Padres. So I got back out there with my tender feet. Same thing—the blisters again, the shortened stride, and now the throbbing in my shoulder even while I pitched. At the time, I was more concerned about my feet. But it was my shoulder that hurt for the rest of the season, even after I'd gone back to my regular throwing motion.

In the fall I went to WSU, and that whole first year of college I fooled myself that everything was OK. I'd open a door and my shoulder would twinge. What did I think? How is it that you can't see things coming when you're eighteen?

*

Reynolds still has them playing catch. He better get a move on if he wants anyone to bat.

Devon chucks the ball to the kid across from him and it goes wide and the kid has to chase it down. My son glances up at me, wanting to know how he's doing. I give him a firm nod and clap my hands quietly, more like a pantomime of hand clapping. "Gotta get the glove all the way down," I say. I bend my knees and hold an imaginary glove in front of me. "Can't stop it if you don't get down to it." Devon nods and bends his knees and gets his glove down on the ground. He's missed two grounders.

"That's right, Devon," Reynolds says, looking over at him for the first time. "Way to look alive."

The kid throws Devon a grounder and it dribbles past the side of Devon's glove. "Gotta move on those, Devon," Reynolds shouts, and claps his hands. "Move, move, move!" he says, scooting sideways like a fat crab. It makes you wonder what kind of qualifications they have for who coaches these teams. If he could move, there wouldn't be a problem. He knows to move. He's slow. That's the problem.

I don't usually get to see Devon's games and practices, because my work takes me out of town. But this afternoon I get to because we were together at our "Future Superstars' Most Valuable Moms" promotion, a cheap advertising scheme that our owner, Ben Finley, thought up to tie in with Mother's Day of all things. There was some argument as to whether Devon's entry was valid, since he was the child of an employee. I finally had to stop by Finley's office and work on him for a few minutes before he said it was OK. They judged the entries anonymously was the main reason. And I told him, too, that it would mean a lot to my son, who was kind of awkward at other things.

The contest is: Explain in twenty-five words or less why your mom is "most valuable," and Devon's was chosen out of all the first grade baseball players' in the school district. *My mom is beautiful and caring*, it said. *She is generous and she loves me and my sister Annie. I love her and my dad more than anything on earth.* Twenty-eight words, but what the hell. It was that "and my dad" that put him over.

The judges were our company secretaries, and one of them, Nancy Wheeler, when she found out it was my son, told me that it made her cry. That's how Devon is, a sensitive kid. He tries so hard, and sometimes makes me feel like crying, too.

I was never much with words. He gets it from his mother. Janine was an English major at WSU, whereas I was business management. Most of the athletes were business majors so that's what I signed up for, and after I bombed at baseball I never had the wherewithal to switch to something that interested me. To tell the truth, I only stayed in school to be with Janine, whom I dated from freshman year. There was nothing I ever wanted to do besides play baseball. My whole life I wanted to play baseball.

That's the hard part now, not playing—just driving from place to place and talking and selling things to other people who don't play anymore, either. It's no good watching some guy fill out a purchase order for team uniforms when you can't wear one yourself.

I lost my uniform pretty quick. We started practice at WSU in February, and it was fucking cold, and I couldn't have busted a plate glass window. Absolutely nothing on my fastball. My shoulder hurt every time I threw.

One day Coach stopped practice and came out to me on the mound. "You all right?" he asked me.

"Sure," I said.

"You hurt anywhere?"

"No." I wasn't telling. Back then, surgeries weren't as successful. You didn't have shoulder surgery at nineteen and go on to pitch in the big leagues.

"Then what's wrong?" he said.

"I don't know," I said. "Too cold, maybe?"

He nodded, went over to talk to an assistant coach. They came back out to the mound. "You know how to throw anything else?" Coach asked. "You got a change up?"

I looked away and didn't say anything. The shortstop and third baseman stood together talking and watching, their gloves on their hips. The left fielder jumped up and down, trying to keep warm.

"Knuckle ball?" the assistant coach said, and then I got to stand there on the mound and watch them grip the ball with their fingernails and argue about how to throw one. It was a pretty half-hearted argument, their eyes and the tone of their voices telling the real story, that they knew they'd wasted a scholarship. I looked around at the other players, and pretty much said goodbye. I thought about something I'd had in my head for a while, how the San Diego streets were lined with palm trees, and how I wasn't going to see them.

San Diego Dreams

It hurts on days like this, rainy days, my shoulder. I suppose that's an old cliché, but my shoulder doesn't seem to know that and goes on hurting anyway.

So all this week I've been traveling to city parks and meeting with coaches and moms and kids to offer them free pizza and give them laminated copies of the kids' entries and tell them how much our sporting goods store is proud of excellent mothers and fine young athletic boys and girls who love them so. Today was Sandpoint, and with Janine and Devon and Annie there, and other people I knew, I dropped all but the most necessary bullshit. Devon was proud, and Janine and I were proud, too.

Grove Dooley calls to me from the bleachers—"Donnie! How you been?"

"Fine. You?"

"Good. Looks like rain."

It's warmer out too than it's supposed to be. Strange for north Idaho in May. You can hear thunder for sure now coming from the black bottoms of the clouds. Ten minutes, maybe.

Reynolds has got them scattered across the field all out of position. He's stroking grounders to each kid in turn, and surprisingly enough he's getting them to the right place more often than not. Maybe he did play a little baseball way back when.

He's got Devon playing some sort of first base/second base/right field hybrid, squeezed between the three positions so he's really got no territory to call his own. The first baseman is a big kid, anxious and aggressive, and when it's Devon's turn, Reynolds lays down a soft grounder and the kid at first moves in and cuts it off.

"That one's yours, Devon," Reynolds says, as if Devon's somehow to blame. But Devon does the right thing, exactly what I would have told him. When he sees the other kid is going to make the play, he runs to cover first base. That's how Devon is, a smart kid.

He knows. If you're going to get the batter out, somebody's got to be on the base. Even Reynolds knows this, and he sees what Devon's up to and decides to play along, dropping his bat and trotting down the line like he's trying to beat the throw.

But when the kid fields the ball, he stands up straight and gets ready to toss it back to the empty home plate. "Throw to first!" I say.

I'm an adult, and in north Idaho kids are still taught to respect adults, and so he turns automatically, looks at Devon, and fires it hard right on the money. Devon gets his glove up in time, but he closes instead of opens it. The ball glances off the leather and catches him on the chin.

Devon drops to a knee, and I start forward, but Reynolds is already there. Devon stands and slaps his glove against his leg while Reynolds kneels in front of him. "I'm fine," Devon says. "I'm OK." He looks over at me and I nod and do the pantomime of clapping again.

"Good job," I say softly. The corner of his mouth turns up and he looks at the ground and I can see he's almost crying. "Good job," I say. "That's the right play. Way to go. You OK?" But he doesn't say anything. I feel the people in the stands watching me.

At "Future Superstars' Most Valuable Moms," in the middle of all the balloons and crepe paper ribbons, Devon sat there looking at the words he wrote to Janine, not paying much attention to the other kids and sipping on his Coke. The secretaries had written the misspelled words over in red ink, evidently thinking the mothers wouldn't figure out what their kids were trying to say. Devon looked at the mistakes he'd made, holding the straw in his mouth, not even knowing it was there. Janine was talking to one of the other moms about PTA. I was pretending to listen, a slight smile and a steady nod. Devon looked at his words—ginurous, buetiful, karing—and I knew what he was thinking, that he wouldn't make those same mistakes again.

And yet he closes his glove instead of opening it. How? What message in his hand and his brain? He closes his glove, and I love him more than anything on earth, but an ugly feeling rises in my chest, a sense of—what—disbelief? The ball comes to you, you open your glove and catch it.

We had a kid on my Little League team named Allen Dinkovich. As if that wasn't bad enough, he played like he was retarded. He sat down in right field and searched for four-leaf clovers. Our coach was ex-military. "Stand up, Dinkovich!" he'd shout. When Allen Dinkovich was at the plate, he hunched into himself. When the ball came, he dropped the bat at it with utter hopelessness. Just dropped the bat from his shoulder.

During summer, we'd get the neighborhood kids together to play Wiffle ball in someone's yard. "I'm Allen Dinkovich!" we'd say, dropping the bat into the grass like it was made of lead, like we were falling asleep. Some smartass would sit down in the grass. "Stand up, Dinkovich!"

Reynolds calls them in one by one for batting practice. I swear to God it should already be raining. The clouds are thick as mud. But still the thunder comes from a distance. I want Devon to get to the plate. He's better at the plate, won't have to go home thinking about the muff at first base if he can just get a couple of swings.

It seems like it takes forever. The kids miss and miss. Devon's a contact hitter. He can't hit it hard, but he can hit it. I watch the clouds and fiddle with my tie, jingle the change in my pockets. Finally it's Devon's turn.

"Keep your elbow up," Reynolds says to him when he takes his stance. Great coach, taking tips from the photographer. Devon puts up the wrong elbow. "Here," Reynolds say. He drops the ball on the mound and moves in to supposedly help. By the time Reynolds gets done with him, Devon looks like a puppet with tangled strings. He glances over at me, and I shrug and wince and clap again.

Reynolds tosses him the ball, soft and underhand. Softer than with the other kids, I think. Devon swoops down at it with the bat, like he's beating a rug with a broom. The older kid Reynolds has convinced to stand behind home plate throws the ball back to the mound. They do this over and over again, like they're playing catch. Each swing of Devon's is jerkier, more desperate. The third baseman tosses pebbles at the shortstop. I can see Devon blink back tears.

Hate. Love. I feel them both standing here. I hate the elbow he can't keep up. I hate the arms and legs that won't work the way they should. I hate that he'll be the kid who gets shoved on the playground at school, and that he'll fight back, because that's the way Devon is, and that it won't do him any good. I hate that he'll have to learn to grow up weak. I feel like yelling.

And sometimes I do, sometimes at home. Sometimes I do yell at Devon. He spills things. He knocks over the chairs. I yell sometimes because I can't stand it anymore. I was a pitcher, a pretty good one. I threw the ball hard and straight.

And at night, after I've yelled, after Devon has gone to sleep, I look at him in his bed where his awkward arms and legs tangle the sheets, and tears come to my eyes, and I step out the front door and stand in the cold and stare at the night and wonder what kind of person I've come to be. Sometimes I close my eyes and dream of San Diego.

But I love Devon. I love him in a way I won't ever be able to love Annie, who grows up strong and straight, who can outrun Devon already even though she's only five years old. Me and Annie will share things. I love Devon in the way you love what can't be shared.

Reynolds is badgering him again, messing with his elbow. "Maybe you'd like me to pitch!" I shout. "Let me throw and you stand there and do what you think you have to do."

It's come out too loud, too angry, and I force a smile to compensate. I feel something on my sleeve, and I look down, and raindrops quiver in the grass next to me. On the highway, I can hear a logging truck rattle and blat, emptied of its load and gearing down and turning on the road for home. I look back up at Reynolds. He smiles a tight smile. Yeah, his eyes say. Sure. Dad's going to pitch. We'll have a group hug afterwards.

I get a ball and take the mound. I can hear them in the bleachers—a little hum, a little buzz. Those who know me are explaining to those who don't. I am, after all, still the only kid in this Idaho town who ever got a call from the big leagues.

Reynolds is looking at me, looking at the crowd, his face showing confusion. He knows me from the sporting goods store, but he didn't grow up here. I'm just the guy who sells him bats and catcher's gear, gives the league what he thinks is a pretty good discount. That's my job. Don't let them know the markup. "OK," Reynolds says. "Let's get the elbow like so." He nudges at Devon's tiny arm.

Our family doctor says it might change. We were at the office for Devon's chicken pox. He was wearing his Padres hat. "What do you want to be when you grow up?" the doctor said, checking out the red marks. "Tony Gwynn," Devon said. Then Janine and Devon and Annie went to the waiting room so I could talk to the doctor. "It may change," he said. "Sometimes kids just have a long awkward stage." But it's not the truth. Kids sort out who's who and what's what and everything they think they'll ever need to know about the world right here on Diamond #2.

I nod at Devon. I say, "You just take your regular swing." He relaxes. "That's right," I say. "Just like we do at home." He brings his bat down. A smile takes shape on his face, and I smile a little back at him. Just bring the bat through on a level plane. Reynolds hovers, unsure. I start my arm back.

I think of that cold February at WSU. I think of the unease, the embarrassment. Not for me, but for the others. The others who had come there to play, who could still play, wondering what had happened to me. I call on that, that lonely feeling, that feeling of can't instead of can. It's the part of me that can't that makes my bond with Devon.

My arm goes back and there's that slight twinge in my shoulder, even underhand. I'll toss it soft just like Reynolds. Toss it soft, that's my pact with Devon, the trading card between him and me. And Devon will hit the ball this time, wait and see.

But as my arm comes forward I close my eyes. The rain is slanting down, and the warm air feels like some other place. The kids behind me aren't kids anymore, the tiny bleachers and the sparse crowd and the rutted basepaths not the same ones here in Idaho. It's not Devon at the plate, but someone up there with something bigger in mind. A foe, someone to test myself against. My arm hits the bottom of its arc, slow and careful, my arm knowing Devon is there, knowing it can't come too fast, knowing that if there's any hero left in me it has to come in being gentle, has to come in doing what I can to help with what he lacks while he moves on ahead of me in other things. But behind my eyes it all happens differently. It's Reynolds there in the box, a better version of Reynolds, strong and whip-fast, his elbow cocked perfectly. I feel my hand opening in slow release, but behind my eyes I'm letting one go hard and high and tight, and Reynolds doesn't know whether to stand in or get away. He can hear it coming, my fastball. He can hear the stitches sizzle like the rain.

Hillary Falls

Steve Almond

Lashed to the final ridge, Hillary breathes in ratchets. He looks like a billygoat in his ice-beard and sinewy wool—lungscraped, bloody-toed in crampons. This is the glamour of not being dead. But listen: him and that Sherpa, Sherpa Tenzing, they aren't just holding on for dear life as the winds of Asia whip scarves around them. No, they're whooping it up, hugging, kissing each other on the chappy mouth, dancing the cancan and man, that's when it happens—Hillary falls. Tenzing too. Over the edge and all the down way, tobaganning the South Col and greasy Western Cwm, hauling ass over crevasses that plunge blue for miles. He's all smiles. So's Tenzing. Hell, they can breathe again, the air like rich pudding and sun spinning frostbite into steam. They blush and giggle and tangle themselves in rope.

I know. I know what the papers say. But that's just what happened, just men and their panting truth. Hillary is still here, outside Katmandu, a great white leopard who bakes pastry. Tenzing keeps him as a lover. At night, they walk the path of candles around the temple and they say: Remember this? Remember that? Remember when it was just two of us and clouds? Whose idea was that anyway, Hillary says, and Tenzing purrs: Come here loverboy, give us a hug, draw us a bath, let's wash the ambition from our human skin and nestle in a bed of feathers, warm, like chickens or angels.

Rumors Of Myself

Steve Almond

In Nebraska I met a man, or possibly further north, and left him for his wife to find. His sedan drove well and I don't know honestly why I abandoned it outside Pierre—there was something in the air I liked, an apple stillness that reminded me of fall.

Daytona was nothing like I'd imagined. They drove slowly there, beaches stained yellow with rain. I met a waitress who showed good mileage. She seemed to agree with my habits and went easily along. I doubt a cigarette would have saved her but found I had to ask; her hips hung red with indecision.

In winter I circled the southwest, where truckstop lights showed scorpions scattered across the sand. A professor took me to bed among them, a sticky pile of pictures, his wife and children in his wallet.

Up north the rains blur everywhere and trees loan us the impression of a time less hindered by travel. A man with a reliable car found me coiled by the side of the road. I didn't ask for him to stop or to open his door. He told me of his years on the police force bopping niggers on the head and doted on a doberman he nursed himself by hand.

I stumbled down Mississippi looped in the loose arms of cloverleafs and sometimes slept against concrete. An insurance man in Beaumont funneled me pills as smooth as skin. He wanted to be trusted. He said I should lie still and wait till I felt the ocean.

My own mother never asked for an accounting of me. She knew love was nothing more than a failure to discern.

And so my young quarry, limp with sleep, I shall ignore the roadmap of peril tattooed along your belly. Let us lie here yet awhile and sift the radio for rumors of myself and, as the day turns tender, watch the clock of clouds blink red. The past will only keep swallowing the present, but often that's okay. Catch me on the right day and this car of yours becomes a painted bow and the gift of your faith plucks me inside. And I can assure you without hesitation that my fingers have never misunderstood flesh, not once, have arrived in the province of death at the invitation of sorrow.

There is no sorrow in your dreams my dear girl, my dear sweet young girl. And so I am incapable of harm. I am blameless, translucent.

Mr. Albert's Remedy

Steve Almond

A true story

Back in 1953, down in Wynot, Mississippi, a white man by the name of Blake walked onto the property of Mr. Albert, the man who, years later, would marry my mother. The intruder, Blake, was drunk, listing in the wind, and he was carrying a shotgun.

Blake raised the gun and killed Mr. Albert's two roan mules, which represented the entire fortune of his life, three decades of labor at cropping. The man made a point of staging this execution in plain sight of Mr. Albert. So close, in fact, that Mr. Albert heard the thud of his animals hitting the dirt.

With the loss of his mules, Mr. Albert lost his farm, and was forced to scrape out a living selling greens from his garden. He carted these greens up and down Route 133, Wynot's central artery, in a wood-wheeled wagon.

Many years later, returning from town, Mr. Albert stepped on a nail.

He ignored the wound, which grew infected with tetanus, consenting to see a doctor only when his ankle began turning green. The doctor felt he would lose his foot, and put him on antibiotics. Mr. Albert called my mother from the hospital and asked to say hello to me. I was home from college, grudgingly tending his mustard greens, bored out of my skull.

What I want you to do, he said, *is take that plank, the one out by the hog pen, near the bucket of nails, and nail it into a fresh young pine. You do that*, he said, *and I do believe this cut on my foot will heal up.*

It did.

A few years later, Mr. Albert mentioned to me that, while he was in the hospital, he'd seen the man who shot his mules forty years earlier. Blake had been shot by his own son, who found Blake beating the boy's mother. Although his injuries did not seem serious, he died on the operating table, in the room right next to where they put Mr. Albert.

Mr. Albert expressed no joy in this news, only somber affirmation.

I do believe that is because he shot my mules, Mr. Albert said calmly.

He turned to his son, the boy he'd had with my mother, who was himself back from college, and pointed to the plot out back, where his greens rose in neat rows.

I'm going to need help with that, he said.

When his son complained, Mr. Albert said: *The only reason you're rubbing your head on them college walls is because of those greens, boy.*

Again, his tone was not angry. But it expressed the tolls of his belief, which had allowed him to withstand a life he did not want his son to suffer. The boy headed out back, and I did too, and Mr. Albert sat on the back porch, on his rocker, and watched us crouching and piling greens in his wagon; he touched his foot gingerly and occasionally nodded.

Mississippi Story

Jeffery Renard Allen

> It
> is my history and
> it
> is my autobiography
> when he sings
> > —Sterling Plumpp
> > "Mississippi Griot"

The driver takes a quick and cautious glance at me in the rear view mirror, then returns his calm but vigilant gaze to the highway and says, "A little town in East Texas. I doubt if you've heard of it." Though there's no traffic, he keeps the mini-van at a crawl, both hands on the steering wheel, his foot pushing into the hum of the engine. His hair is short and neat, slightly longer than a boot-camp cut. He is a long-limbed fellow, slim and strong in a long-sleeve cotton shirt, his skin smooth and bright, milky innocence.

"No. I don't think I have." I lean forward a bit on the wide seat to hear him better, the joints of my shoulders sore from the plane ride.

"Well, I had never heard of the University back home."

"No?" says Dr. Hallard, the crown of his head rising above the seat cushion in front of me, bald and pointy as a chess bishop, a few remnants of hair here and there on his brown wrinkling scalp.

"Not where I'm from," the driver says. "It's kind of isolated. I think my mom had been there once. She and my step-dad are driving up next weekend to help me build a shed for one of my professors."

Dr. Hallard is a professor back East, specializing in Russian history, if I heard him correctly. He rocks about in his seat, trying to make himself comfortable. We're both long in the leg, the mini-van much smaller than it seems, plush cushions fostering the illusion of space. What we both must be thinking: a white boy chauffeuring two black men down a Mississippi highway.

"You keep busy," Dr. Hallard says to him.

"Yes. I've had to since I lost my scholarship."

"Do you still train?"

"I try to find the time."

"You really must. Sixteen feet." Dr. Hallard sighs in astonishment.

"Yes. My best jump."

"Wow."

"There were a couple of other guys back home who could make that jump. One went out to California. One went to New York. He made the American team. I came here and had a good first year, but then I seemed to fall off. I don't know what happened. I was training hard, as hard as I ever had, as hard as I could."

"Yeah, well—" Dr. Hallard shakes his head, the same way he had earlier at the airport, accepting the mishap of his luggage with cheerful resignation.

"So, have you been on any digs?" I ask the driver.

"Yes, several. We have quite a few sites right here in Mississippi."

Bleak sunshine, the shuddering windows project heavy foliage under an overcast early spring afternoon. Vertical trunks and tightly-positioned leaves chart our progress toward the town.

Dr. Hallard says, "There are many Civil War battle sites throughout this area."

"Yes, I know. Several big companies have been constructing strip malls on many of the old battlefields," the driver tells us.

"You don't say."

"Yes."

"Such a shame."

"Quite a few people have been trying to stop them."

"That's good. A railroad used to run right along here." Dr. Hallard points to the grassy roadside beside the opposing lane. I take a long and thorough look. Think I see the ghostly outline of railroad tracks. He adds, "They would run their transports up and down here."

"Yes."

"So there were always plenty of raids and acts of sabotage, not to mention actual battles. Oh, man. I can't even name all of the battles that happened down here. Let me see." Dr. Hallard taps his fingers on his scalp, sorting through a mental index. "There was Holly Springs, and Cornith. Shiloh, of course. And Tupelo—"

"That's where my family is from," I say.

"Oh yeah?" the driver says. "That's about forty miles east of here."

"Well, not exactly. They're actually from Fulton. Houston."

"So you've been down here before?" Dr. Hallard asks.

"Used to come all the time when I was a kid to visit my great aunt. That's been what, thirty years. Then again, I was here ten, twelve years ago for her funeral."

"You might want to drive over while you're here," the driver says.

"Perhaps. That really is surprising. All this time, I never knew the University was so close to where she lived."

"Less than an hour's drive. Most students hang out and party in Tupelo."

"Rather than Memphis?"

"Yes."

"Why?"

"Tupelo is not quite as far."

Dr. Hallard asks him, "You've been to the battlefield at Tupelo?"

"No. We do mostly Indian sites."

"Ah. There were many tribes in this area."

"We have several sites only a few miles from the University," the driver tells him.

"Any interesting finds?"

"Always. I can't begin to tell you."

"There must be so much to see."

"Yes."

"So, how do you know where to dig? I mean, how do you narrow down to one spot?"

"Glad you asked," he says. "Let me tell you. We put an infrared camera on a huge helium blimp. Now, this blimp is the size of a basketball court. Bigger. The robotic camera travels along it and pinpoints places where you might find some artifacts. It's quite amazing."

"Wow."

"A blimp, huh?" Me, Hatch, the skeptic.

"Yes."

I think about it, uncertain if I'm impressed. *You have made me glad. At the works of your hands I sing for joy.*

We ride in silence for a while, tires measuring out time. The highway seems inconsequential in this landscape, like a jackknife that can be folded back into its handle. Disappear. An occasional car or truck creeps down the road like a steel and glass insect. Breaks here and there in the tree-jammed roadside, elbow room for squat houses with compact driveways. No garages. Every now and then some ragged suggestion of a farm. Cow or horse or chicken or pond or crop—one fact among many in this terrain of the hidden and the seen.

"What kind of winters do you all get down here?" Dr. Hallard asks the driver.

"Oh, mostly rain. Every once in awhile we'll get some snow. Two or three inches hit the ground and everything shuts down," he tells him.

"That figures. You probably aren't prepared for it the way we are up north. No plows or salt."

"I guess not. The roads get really slippery, dangerous."

Many trees at the margins of the highway are stooped over in fascination at whitening earth, twistings of vine and branch like so many whorls on a fingertip.

"Hey, what do you call that stuff?" Dr. Hallard asks.

"Oh, that's kudzu," the driver tells him.

"So that's what kudzu looks like."

"Yes. They imported it many many years ago."

"From Japan?"

"I think so. They brought it over to control the spread of rank weed and briar. But it grows like crazy. A month from now it'll cover everything."

I press out the image, all of Mississippi wrapped in a kudzu shawl. Justice.

The road gradually rises to a crest I can't see beyond, then flattens out again. White letters on green metal inform us that the town is two miles ahead.

"One thing you might want to know," the driver says. "Tonight is our big night here. You'll find a lot happening."

"Thursday?"

"Right. I don't know why, but Thursday is our Saturday."

"Okay."

"And you should also know that your hotel is a short walk from the town square. Five minutes. You'll find many stores there and plenty of restaurants."

"What do you recommend?"

"Benjy's is pretty good," he tells us. "Try their catfish in red wine sauce."

"Okay. We'll keep it in mind."

Off in the distance I see what appears to be a courthouse with a small yard in front where a colossal marble pedestal rises some fifty feet above the ground, a bronze soldier mounted there, facing the road, looking across heights of air to confront all who approach. Closer now, I see a human figure leaning against the pedestal, sharply outlined in gray coat and black pants and shouldering a confederate flag, black stars patterned into a cross against a dark blue-gray background. The rude eyes of witness reveal a black Confederate soldier.

"What the . . . Motherfucker," I say, unmindful of the crude edges of my words.

"Yes. He's caused some controversy," the driver tells us.

I say nothing, for anything I might say would be so much less than what I feel.

The black Confederate is fitted in a full-length gray coat with a cloak-like attachment, a small, short-brimmed hat, the crown folded over toward his forehead like a scorpion's stinger, and black jeans and black gym shoes. His flag is attached to a pole no thicker than a broom handle, certainly not military standard or issue. An old rusty boy-scout canteen crosses his chest and waist. His skin is so dark that his fingernails glow like tracer bullets.

The driver says, "Next month we will be voting on a referendum to remove the flag from the state capital and all state buildings. He wants them to keep it up."

"Now I've seen it all," Dr. Hallard says.

"Some kind of joke?" I ask.

"I don't know. All I can say for sure is that he's caused quite a bit of controversy."

The driver circles the square, circles the courthouse, circles the bronze statue. I can't chance a good view of the reb's face, but he moves his head in our direction, peeps us, and raises the flag higher. Somehow, I feel that we are on display, the three of us in the mini-van like some rare species behind glass.

Moments later, we exit the mini-van in the hotel's driveway. I search through my wallet, slide free a five, the biggest tip I can spare, a full two dollars more than what I would normally give.

*

The town is fighting to keep Applebee's, Banana Republic, Old Navy, Wal Mart, and Circuit City out of the courthouse square where uniform two-story brick and wood buildings with verandas perched on ten foot high posts house expensive shops and services, bars and boutiques, restaurants and cafes. On Friday nights, book clubs cram into the confined spaces of these shops. The town prides itself on being a hyperliterary community and boasts more reading groups than any other municipality in Mississippi. Homes in the immediate radius of the square—rehabbed antebellum structures and their modern imitations—hold the market at a million dollars or more. A national magazine recently honored the town with a high distinction, calling it the third best retirement community in America.

In a small garden left of the entryway to the red brick cement-lined library, a Faulkner bronze, dressed in hat, suit and tie is seated at the far end of a glazed green-gray park bench, both taller and larger than Faulkner actually was in life. His legs are crossed at the knees with his left hand resting on them, right arm across the top of the bench back so that he is seated at an angle, turned slightly toward you, smoking pipe in hand—a man both relaxed and dignified, inviting you to sit down and join him. Dull metal clothing and skin are set against a fresh, bright cropping of red tulips and various hues of perennials directly behind him. A small slim-trunked tree is planted ninety degrees to his right, the leaves either the palest of green or dried and crumpled to a brown autumn tint. And

Mississippi Story

bronze and bench are positioned in the left extremity of a mosaic arc, alternating bands of rectangular red stone and curved green slab.

Continue on to the square's center where a small group of white reporters have flocked around the black Confederate, cameras swooping about, pens pecking words onto their notepads, microphones perched in air. From the tone of his voice, I can tell that he is taking a firm stand on the issues, gesturing emphasis and keeping tabs with his fingers. I take a moment to lock his physical details into memory. The small gray hat has a thin black belt across the front, a tiny gold buckle dead center above the short, black visor. The small hat with its folded-over crown reminds me of an old ice bag. My aunt would unscrew the lid, drop a few perfectly square cubes into the pouch, twist the lid tight, then place the pouch cold and hard on a lump. The ice bag reb is a man in his early to mid-thirties with pronounced cheekbones that form a thick V under each deep-set eye, a nose so compact and modest you might overlook it, and lips no wider than a nickel. He gives me an offhand glance, the camera finds him. He actually stops talking and poses for me, left foot on the curb, left hand positioned on left knee, eyes looking slightly to his right, off-camera, flag across his right shoulder. The flag hand also holds a small black disc, a portable CD player, the headphones draped about his red-shirted neck. The shutter moves and emblazons him in celluloid. His damn fool twin distant and small on a light-catching strip.

*

Bent at the waist, a man my age and build prepares to enter his compact Japanese car. He looks up, sees me, and straightens himself, keys in hand.

"How are you?"

"Fine. How about you?"

"Never been better." He approaches me. "Can I ask you something?"

"Sure." I'm expecting some mundane question about weather or directions.

"Hey, did you talk to that guy?"

"Not really."

"Did you hear what he was saying?"

"I really wasn't listening. I mean, I wasn't even trying to hear what he had to say. I figured he was crazy, that's all."

"He ain't crazy. No, sir. I knew that guy way back in high school. He may be tricky. Ain't crazy though. He been tellin all these reporters that he's got a wife over in London and a brother in Germany and that he's got a degree from this college and a plaque from this organization. All kinds of stuff. He's got a whole lotta them supporting him."

"Uh huh. So you think he fakin it? Hustlin' them?"

"I'll put it to you like this. He don't care nothing 'bout no white folks."

From *The Daily*
The University Police Department states the following incidents have been reported between Wednesday, March 14, and Tuesday, March 20:

SUSPICIOUS PERSONS

*Monday, March 19, 3:31 P.M. UPD received a report of a suspicious person in the J. D. Williams Library. The person was described as a black male, no facial hair, and in his mid 20s. Negative contact was made with the person by UPD.

*Friday, March 16, 9:52 A.M. UPD received a report of a suspicious person in the lobby area of Carrier Hall. He was described as a black male, approximately 5'6"–5'7" tall, 160–175 pounds, short hair, clean shaven and dark complexion. He entered an office where he asked to use the phone and also asked if there was any food in the building.

Mississippi Story

*

Dr. Hallard and I are the first guests to arrive for the cocktail party at an antebellum mansion, a white two-story structure with six green slat-backed wooden rocking chairs positioned across a long wide porch.

"Isn't this something?" he says.

"True that. Sure we should go in? We might not get out."

He laughs.

We enter the house and go right to the bar, discreet, taking little notice of our grand surroundings. Dr. Hallard is taller than I am, and I have come to learn that he is a jocular man. He tells me how much he likes my work, that I'm the real deal, how he can't wait to read more.

"Well," I say, "I learned everything I know from you." I give him a playful slap on his blazer-covered back. I've never read him.

"Oh no." He laughs. "I'm just an historian trying my hand at new things in my old age."

"That's where we're at home. I try my hand too."

Sharply dressed, a middle-aged woman approaches us. She has a long face and a protruding mouth like a sea horse's. "Hi, I'm Mrs. Jason. I'm with the University."

"Glad to meet you."

"You're—"

"Yes. And this is Dr. William Hallard."

"Of course, I recognized you both. So glad you could join us."

"Glad to be here."

"You folks enjoying yourselves?"

"Most definitely."

"Good."

"This is some house."

"Have you had a look around?"

"No."

"Please do."

I set off in one direction, Dr. Hallard in another. Wander through odd-shaped rooms which open one out into another. Let my gaze wander over gaudy Victorian settees and sofas, four-footed mahogany bookcases with scrolled cupboard doors, cylinder-topped bureaus on bowlegs and bun feet, peg-calved corner tables, inlaid *bonheurs du jour*, etched display cabinets, heavy curtains like mounds of hardened lava, narrow-shouldered grandfather clocks like genetically altered men. Every inch of the papered walls blocked with paintings—equestrians, seascapes, landscapes, and portraits—tree, sail, saddle, and cheek textured in age-thickened curls of oil.

The house quickly fills. People casual in conversation. Tilted heads and raised glances. Tinkling ice. Quiet sips. I make many introductions, names and professional descriptions which I quickly forget. I make my way back to the bar, where the bartender is hard at work, his hands circling a small table with a neat arrangement of tonic and seltzer water, vodka and soda, wine and whisky, lime and lemon. He wears a white shirt, black bowtie crossed at the throat, and black slacks. He speaks in a high light cadence, like a rock skipping over water. He hands me my gin and tonic in a plastic cup.

"Would you know the story behind this house?" I take a sip. Just right.

"Yes. It's a miracle it's still standing. They burned everything else." His face reveals no emotion, shark gaze, eyes black and blank. "It was owned by a doctor who treated both sides during the war."

"I see."

"The University purchased it a few years ago."

"Well, thanks for enlightening me."

"My pleasure."

"Yes." I watch him work, words stirring inside me. I take my drink and hurry off to the dining room. Various guests gathered around a cloth-covered mahogany table crowded with plates, pots and utensils. Some fishy substance—life feeds on life—in rectangular pans kept warm by flaming canned heat. Dinner rolls like bare baby butts cradled in a wicker basket. Salad growing in glass bowls. Dressed like checkerboard squares—white shirt, black pants, white apron, black shoes—bustling attendants enter and exit the room, trays at the ready.

"Is that crayfish?" I ask one of them.

"Crawfish," she says.

"Okay. That's how we say it where I'm from."

"And where's that?"

I tell her.

"I have family up north."

"Do you."

"Enjoy your food."

"I will."

I eat till I am stuffed. Clean my hands on a cloth napkin and toss it on a waiter's shouldered platter. Then I travel down a long hall with a polished floor like a wooden runway which leads to the roped-off upper story, oak banister and rail gleaming like a wet tongue. I take a seat on the carpeted stairway, red rope inches above my head. I down my drink, neck craned back and plastic cup covering my mouth muzzle-like. Sight along liquored edge and see a woman smiling down at me. A saloned blonde in her early to midforties, pure East Coast elegance in a black party dress with perfectly matched jewelry. Her skin is puffy, rebellious, refuses to stay flat.

"Did you try the crawfish?"

I lower my cup. "Yes. Delicious."

"Do stay. Dessert should be ready soon."

"I can't wait."

"So, how do you like our town?"

"Fine so far."

"Your first time here?"

"Yes. Well, not exactly. My folks come from these parts. Houston."

"Oh, that's only about forty miles west of here."

"So I've been told. I used to visit my great aunt every summer when I was a kid."

"Well, enjoy your stay."

"I plan to."

"I think you'll find the people in town are more than friendly. They'll go out of their way to help you. Anything you need, just ask."

"I will."

"And you know, before you leave, you should go down to Benjy's and try their shrimp and grits dinner. It's an absolute delicacy."

"I will." I make my way back to the bar and discover Dr. Hallard, drink in hand, keeping the interest of a circle of listeners. (Perhaps he will hold them seven nights with seven hundred tales.) I follow the path of duty to the sitting room where a squadron of eaters and talkers are sprawled about in high-backed armchairs. I talk to this person and that but soon run out of things to say. Conversation congeals into polite patterns. Attentive gazes and curious glances recede into fatigue or boredom. Faces go lax from alcohol. I scan the room for fresh skin. Survey the mansion one last time. Have another drink or two. End up back where I started. Voices pelt me, bang and run rough. I could attack. I could trot like a bull through every room of this fucking mansion, charge my enemies head on, bumping and butting those who refuse to give way. Stomp down ugly. Instead, I escape to the porch and scoot into a rocking chair. I am tiny inside it, a baby in a high seat. Notice a huge oak just left of the house wide as three men. Stare out at the road, a dark screen of trees behind it. And I listen. Steady insect hum like incoming missiles.

I rise from the chair and set out for the hotel. The night rises and falls before me, trees shimmering in the lamped dark. Hot blots of light where moths and gnats and winged anonymous others stick and burn, their wings like flaming shrouds. I can hear their panic.

Mississippi Story

If I am attentive, if I incline my ear, these woods will tell me great secrets.

*

In mythical geography, sacred space is essentially real space, for in the archaic world the myth alone is real. It tells of manifestations of the only indubitable reality–the sacred.

*

My oldest cousin and I catch a flight to Memphis, rent a car at the airport, and just outside Fulton find a cheap motel owned and operated by Indians from India. We sit in silence, he on his bed and I on mine, staring down at the dark lake of floor between us, hoping to draw up memories from forgotten deeps. The next day we help lower our aunt's coffin into a freshly dug grave, fist by fist. I feel the rope tug and pull, the red dirt shift under my feet, feel myself being yanked forward, snatched down into the open box of earth.

*

"Wasn't that in Jackson?" The receiver tight against my ear, wedged between my shoulder and cheek.

"No," my mother says. "Tupelo."

"Tupelo?"

"Yes."

I am looking at a watercolored landscape, broad pastures and fields rimmed in a cheap metal frame.

"The Klan headquarters were right there, downtown. I think they still are. The only place in the world where I've ever seen one."

"That's what I was wondering." I unfold a map of Mississippi and spread it across the bed. "Because somebody at the party said that Jackson is south of here. And all this time I thought we took the bus from Memphis through Jackson to Tupelo."

"No way."

"Now I know."

All this time, these many years, I've had the geography wrong. I've told people that my family comes from the Delta. But the Delta is a five or six hour drive south of here. Or is it? I'm starting to learn that Mississippi is larger than I ever imagined. Its boundaries have slowly grown since I was a child. The state busting its seams, moving out into space, ragged at its edges like an ink blot on paper.

"What do they have scheduled for tomorrow?"

"Nothing important. In fact, I don't plan to attend any of the morning events."

"Won't they be expecting you?"

"They might be. I plan on having a look at the Faulkner estate. It's supposed to be a short walk from here."

"Do you think that's a good idea?"

"I don't believe they'll—"

"Wouldn't do too much walking around down there if I were you."

*

Ruled in one corner of the cemetery, the Faulkner family plot is surrounded by a low concrete wall with the family name chiseled on a limestone carved in the form of a columned Greek arch three to four feet in height. Faulkner and his wife are buried inside parallel tombs, their place of final resting memorialized by two marble plates, each six feet in length and four in width, surfaces almost metallic in the sun. Trees cast a dark mass of shadow over the graves, a jutting peninsula in the shape of a black branch, and jagged leaves like toothy-edged archipelagoes. I'd heard that the cemetery keeps a bottle of Jack Daniels whiskey at the plot for visitors to take a sip in Faulkner's honor, a libation of sorts. I see the remnants of a bottle, a handful of knuckle-sized chunks of glass and square fragments with weather-faded labels. Jack Daniels? Faulkner's dog has earned burial rights in a parallel plot:

Mississippi Story

> E.T.
> AN OLD
> FAMILY
> FRIEND
> WHO CAME
> HOME
> TO REST
> WITH US

I set the camera's self-timer and kneel beside the Greek arch.

*

I had hoped to visit the Heritage Museum which has a collection of over fifty battle flags, but then I learn that the flags are too fragile to be displayed. I turn down an invitation to attend church and on aimless feet head out of town on one of the main roads. A cat lies sprawled in a ditch, its pink tongue curling stiffly to the ground, stretched like bubble gum. Just a ways up, a priest stands on the wide cement walk outside his church—a modern structure with a sleek frame, airy doors and windows, a roof boldly tinted like the blood of sacrament, and a cross carved with an artist's keen and distinctive touch—and fellowships with wafer-skinned members of his parish. Smiling, talking, laughing, shaking hands, patting backs, kissing babies and pinching cheeks. His skin is a shade or two lighter than his black cloak. (Black absorbs everything, even cast off sin.) He seems much older than his parishioners, well-groomed go-getters in their twenties and thirties who sport designer dress and drive luxury cars. (The parking lot jammed full.) He is balding, the last of his hair putting up a good fight, a tight black band clinging to the back and sides of his head, a bat with wings clamped. His jaw is lined and twisted, head screwed into his white collar. (White repels. May starched collar keep the devil away from soft throat.) And the expression on his face is by turns sympathetic, pensive or joyful. In ear distance, I can just make out the words, "We can kneel down together or alone anytime anywhere and ask for God's help."

I want to say something to knock the wind out of him. Does he whiff toe-jam at the foot of the cross? Does Lazarus have nightmares about the shunned grave? I bite my tongue. Men are made from the earth and shall return to it. No match for Holy Ghost power.

I concentrate on my footwork, leather rhythm. (During the Civil War, popular consciousness developed a theory to explain the tremendous endurance of men in battle. Called the "theory of the conversion of force," it postulated that every shock was absorbed into the body and stored in the form of energy.) Clean-framed homes with aluminum siding give way to weeded lots spotted with rusty metal milk cans like hollowed-out bombshells, hitching posts covered in ghostly mold, shriveled up sheds sinking into the earth. Long abandoned antebellum dwellings decaying there, wood indented with the teethmarks of storms. Lumber imploding to wild angles. Rooms sheared away. Porch and plank constricted in snakelike brambles. Unhinged trellises curling away from structure like suspended high wire acrobats. Architectural achievements reduced to antiquated puzzles of oak and timber.

Sun straggles yellow then red across the sky. Trees hold their formation, kudzu laced through trunks and leaves. At one point I must appear lost—a dark fugitive—because a white man pulls his car over to the graveled shoulder, steps out of it, and asks if I need assistance. No, I tell him. He offers me a ride. I like to walk, I tell him.

"Well, you have a good day now."

"The same to you."

A mile or two later, an old black man comes rolling down the road on a golf cart, shouting pronouncements through a bullhorn. I later discover that he is the only black mayor in the county. He quiets down for a moment to greet me. Rolls on. A welcome introduction to geographical extremes, communities dotting the forest like dice flung and let be. Mississippi is still the poorest state in the Union, but black people have owned land in this part of the state since the days immediately following the war's end. No shotgun shacks here. Native sons and daughters live in six-bedroom trailer homes with working fireplaces and bubbling jacuzzis.

Nothing like my aunt's home in Fulton—Mississippi continually spoils my recollection of things—a range house with one door which opened both into her living room and onto the front lawn, and a second door, which took you through the kitchen to a cement overhang and patio paved all the way down to the noisy gravel driveway. She would dress in men's overalls and rubber boots and go hunt for heavy watermelons—yellow meat inside—that grew wild in the wooded decline behind her house which everyone called "the snake pit."

Sweat spills, a river inside me. My feet cramped, confined in shoes too stubborn to break. Murder each step. Hot water rising in my chest, I draw in fire, expel ash. Drop down in roadside dirt. Shut my eyes and try to picture my aunt's face.

*

That night in my hotel room, I attempt to write her a letter. Words reverberate in the air like hummingbirds. I can see it all taking shape. (Sound the trumpets.) I lie back on the bed, hands cupped behind my neck, dirty shoes extended over mattress edge. I stare at the white ceiling until I can see through to the bone, down to the collagen, reflective substance that reveals.

*

At the complimentary breakfast buffet, I nurse a cup of gritty coffee and munch on wedges of cool watermelon while Dr. Hallard, between hearty crunches of toast and bacon and forkfuls of scrambled eggs, gives me the lowdown on a story he read in the morning paper. Tongue red with strawberry jam, he tells me about a black woman in some remote Florida town who draped her baby's carriage in a confederate flag, then camped out before the courthouse. Handcuffed, she is reported as saying, "It's our history too."

*

I leave the hotel to a cyclone of embraces. Promises to call or write. Visit. At the airport, I find a cool seat in a wedge of shadow and wait to board the plane. Dressed in identical outfits (white blouses, red vests, and black skirts), three ticket agents—a white woman sandwiched between two black women—power-walk the long lobby, elbows working frantically like clipped bird wings, chattering through labored breaths. The woman closest to me carries a half-empty bottle of water, liquid which they presumably all share. *All of us are being transformed into the same image from one degree of glory to another.* They reach the lobby's end, then circle back the way they came. Five minutes later, they reach the lobby's end and circle back.

*

"They kept giving me a hard time. Then somehow it came out that I was a student at the University. You should have seen the looks on their faces. They had a truck bring it all the way from Memphis to Mississippi and everything. Even gave me a discount."

"Wow."

"People love that school down here."

"The Harvard of the South."

"I'd rather be at Harvard."

"So, did they throw in a free wadermeln?"

"Watermelon. I'm going to break you out of your country ways."

"Who's country? I'm not country. You country."

"I'm not country."

"You the one from Memphis."

"Everybody from Memphis is not country."

"Okay. Whatever you say."

"Everybody down here doesn't talk like you."

"That's my Mississippi roots."

"Don't blame it on Mississippi."

"You've made your point."

"So you should start—"

"I need to ask you a favor."

"What?"

"A favor. That's the main reason I called. Think you could drive over to Fulton and take a few photographs of my aunt's house?"

"Fulton? I don't know anything about Fulton."

"Didn't say you did. But it's not that far from you. You must know somebody who knows."

"Perhaps."

"Come on."

"How do you even know the house is still there?"

"It might not be."

*

Several years ago, fish farmers brought Asian carps to the Mississippi River to harvest them after flooding had severely reduced the number of catfish and other local species. On their own, these carp learned to defy their environment. They jump out of the water three to four feet into the air like dolphin and bang into the side of casino ships or fall onto the hook- and worm-crowded decks of low-sided boats. These carp weigh six pounds now but will weigh twenty pounds a year from now. Of course, there is no market for fish that fly.

Pearls to Swine

N.S. Köenings

Spa, Belgium—Summer 1980

A weaker person than myself might have been changed by so much rudeness, or by what happened in the garden. But I am still the same. I will not frustrate the hungry child or snub the thirsty man. With proper guests, a visit would be smooth. Our home and grounds are gracious. I have not given up. I do still like the sound of silverware on dishes, and I like raspberry jam, ferocious in a jar. A bedsheet turned down by the pillow, a good, clean towel folded on a chair. But you know, *on ne sait jamais*. Think twice, I say. Be careful. Because once you've given them a washcloth and a bed, nothing can protect you. Not your sweetness, not your natural desire to involve an honored stranger in your life, and not even—here's the worst—not even your good taste.

And yet, how pleased I was at first. Before telling Gustave my idea, I went into the tower rooms one after the other and gazed onto the grounds. Just look at those big fields, the pine trees in the distance! See how pale and blue the town, the bathhouses, the spires, so small from our fine heights! And closer in, how promising the urns looked on the patio—filled with snow just then, but already I could fathom them abubble with petunias. And beyond the berry hedge, the real curiosity, the animals Gustave has fashioned from the bushes. Now that's something to look at! A camel, a horse, an egret, and a pony. Yes, we have a world unto ourselves. Filling my eyes with grass, pines, and sky, I practiced what I'd say when I went up to his office: Gustave, I'd say, in a bright, loud voice so he would have to pay attention, it's time we had some guests.

It isn't that we're lonely or have nothing to do. Gustave has many things to occupy his time. There's that big collection of clay potsherds and celadon, and beads made out of glass, which he has gotten through his work—we have crossed the world on lecture tours and digs—and he has other hobbies. A person in Bulgaria, to whom Gustave pays large sums, mails butterflies and moths. Gustave frames the specimens, and hangs them in the hallway. Those butterflies alone could give an afternoon of pleasure! And, as I've already mentioned, there's that very special zoo: the topiary, as Gustave likes to say.

Every other Tuesday in the summer, people come from town to see, though Gustave worries for the beasts. He fears the children will strew carbonated drinks and ice creams in the flowers. But I called *l'Hôtel de Ville* especially, to say when they could come. Better twice a month when you expect it than at any time they please, I said. And so they come, but when they do, Gustave goes upstairs. To date, which you would notice on your own if you were to come out on a tour, and as I've already said, Gustave has a horse, an egret, a camel and a pony. He's begun a tortoise, too, but it is taking him a little longer to complete, which I for my part think, ha-ha, is not a big surprise.

I myself am always busy. I could have my hands full, for example, with just the correspondence. If Gustave had his way, no one would write us more than once. I keep in touch with all the people we have met, though we've not traveled in some time. Why, just three days before the first arrival I wrote another letter to Morocco's Minister of Culture, and I told him, as I always do, that I will never let myself forget how kind he was to us, how nice the ride on the Corniche so very long ago, and how much we did appreciate that very sweet mint tea. And of course, I cook, I pickle things, I read.

I make preserves for us when the berries come in summer. I like to tease Gustave and say that both of us excel at keeping things just so: you dig, I say, I pickle and conserve. We're both proud of how we label things—Gustave says precision with a label separates the shoddy from the great. In fact he had just typed up a card for a new butterfly, and was pinning the blue thing onto a heavy cotton sheet when I went to his office. I said, to see if he would soften up, that those gauzy little wings were the color of our winter sky, but he did not answer me. He started talking about labels, and I had to interrupt. That may well be, I said, about the labels, but what we need here is guests. Some visitors, I said. All those foreigners we've met, they've been so generous with us. It's our turn now to push into the world the kindness we've received.

Gustave was thinking of the bushes, I am sure. "I don't want strangers tramping on the grounds," he said. He looked up with a pin between his lips. I told him I would never ask into our home a person or any pair of persons who would be capable of tramping. *Tramping.* We ought to send some invitations for the summer, when everything is best, I said. We have so much to give.

"Do what you like, Celeste," he said, and because he couldn't open wide for fear the pin would fall, his voice came out a blur. I did do what I liked, of course, although I wish sometimes looking back that Gustave had put his foot down. Afterwards, he said it could have been predicted. That mixing comes about through hard, unpleasant business: if you find a Chinese plate with a plain old East Coast pot, you'll know there was a war. He even said, "It's fortunate that they're long-dead and we won't see it for ourselves." Well, that may be fine reasoning or poor when it comes to pots and beads, and I'm no judge of that. But he doesn't understand the world of living beings like I do, that we need company, and gentle conversation. Gustave even said, this morning, "At least they didn't hurt the bushes." The bushes!

So I sent out my invitations, one to my old friend Sylvie, who now lives in New York, U.S.A., and the other one to Liège, which

Pearls to Swine

although it is not very far from here you might think another country. I wrote to La Maison des Jeunes Femmes Abandonnées, which has a well-known program for the girls they like to help. From New York Sylvie wrote to say it would be wonderful if Petra came to see us. The House in Liège was also very gracious. They said they'd send us an unmarried girl who had fallen into difficulty but would by then be on the mend, and to whom we would surely do a proper world of good. I had brightly colored dreams in which the two became great friends. It was exciting to envision—one girl come from Liège, another from America, not a thing in common but their girlhood and the grounds.

We've been all over Europe and the best places in North Africa, but never to New York. I think it would be charming. I know some feel the U.S.A. is poor in taste, from the Rodeos to that big Statue and *le foot americaine*. Yvette said so herself when I told her where Petra would be coming from, and she was wrapping me a nice half-kilo of *pâté*. She said, "Don't buy too much of this, then. Hamburgers, that's all they like to eat." Well, I took my half-kilo as I always do, and didn't pay attention. I'm sure I don't agree. Where would we be now without Americans, I always like to say.

When I told Yvette the girl Therese would be coming from the House, she threw back her broad head and gave a hard snort through her nose. Her view of human nature is nothing to be proud of. "She'll steal the sheets from under you," she said. I thanked her very nicely and snuck a sample of salami while she was counting out the change. I can get along with people of all kinds. Don't I send my flowers to the abbey when the beds come into bloom? I was sure Therese would be well-mannered, and that Sylvie's girl would bring me some interesting presents from New York.

*

Petra came three days before Therese. Our place was blooming with spring-time! We had sparrows shaking in the trees, and the bees, though it hadn't quite got warm, were spying on the ivy. It was morning. I had just made a fat loaf of *pain gris*, and was having a *verveine* in the library upstairs, where Gustave has shelved my novels. I was wearing blue. Gustave was standing by the window with a cup of Chinese tea, looking out at nothing as he sometimes does, and he called out to me, nodding at the glass. "It must be Sylvie's girl," he said. I went to stand beside him, and as I pulled the curtain to the side I caught a whiff of his tobacco. I straightened up my slip beneath my skirt and set my toes right in the bottom of my shoes. I held my head up high. Here we are, I thought, the hosts. And what a couple we still make. I stood beside my husband, and I looked down at the girl.

She had traveled from the station in a taxi. Her driver was a fat man, panting with the case he'd just extracted from the trunk of the Maria. He'd left the engine running, I could see the steam rise from the cab. The girl was dangling a velvet purse from one long bony arm, and fumbling with the money. Her hair was dark and thick. I thought Gustave must be wrong, that it had to be the other one, the unfortunate from Liège, come a few days early. When she bent to gather up the coins she'd scattered in the stones, her spine showed through her dress. It can't be, I told him. That's got to be Therese, I said. That cotton dress had seen some better days, and her white socks were bunched up at the ankles over a pair of buckled shoes. She must have got the days confused, I said, moving closer to my husband. The girl was nodding-bobbing at the driver as though he were a king.

"No, don't you see?" he said. "She looks just like her father." All I could make out was that her dark-haired head was large and the rest of her was thin. The fat man raised his empty hand up to his face and moved it in an arc out from his brow like a person tipping a good hat. The girl was easily amused, I saw. Then the driver popped back into his cab and barrelled down the drive. Strange, those cars take people on fine trips now, and we don't think about it twice. Used to be a Black Maria meant the S.S. were taking stock. Well, the girl had no idea. As she said later, she feels like an American, doesn't know a thing about it, not Marias, not potato cakes, not hiding in a basement, and she's never heard of chicory.

Anyway she must have felt us looking at her, or perhaps a bird flew by, or there was a rustle in our ivy. Because she lifted up her chin and I saw exactly what she was. My god-daughter, what a sight. Gustave was right, she did look like her father—an Antwerp face with dusky, caterpillar eyebrows, like something in a cabaret. Though it was clear she was a girl, and it's true she was attractive in a serious sort of way, with a big and heavy head—a Hannah, or a Ruth, if you can get my meaning. Then I looked hard at her hemline and at those awful crumpled socks, and caught sight of her knees. She did have stunning calves. That one time Sylvie came to Tunis with her husband, I do remember thinking Hermann's shapely legs were wasted on a man.

She didn't have the sense to come knocking on the door, just stood there, holding to the suitcase with both hands, that old purse drooping to the ground on a sorry knotted string. She stood frowning at the ivy, biting at her lips. A baby! Sylvie said she was sending a grown daughter and instead we got a baby. I thought, it's a good thing Gustave heard the car come in the first place, or she'd have stood there until lunchtime and we'd not have known a thing.

Downstairs, Gustave took her case away and she tried to shake his hand but instead he put his arm around her shoulders and brought her in himself. I was quite surprised at him, although you will agree Gustave can be disarming when he remembers where he is. Petra looked as if no man had ever put his hands on her before, arching her long neck like a far-sighted person at a bug that's landed on their chest. What a cardigan! I thought. A thing the color of pea soup that slid all over her and by the time she'd come into the foyer it had fallen off her shoulders and was bunched around her elbows. I squinted, then I opened my eyes wide, to convince myself again that this was the delinquent girl instead, but it was not to be.

At that moment I was so distracted by her looks I couldn't think what her name was. Gustave—bless him, he always knows what things are called—must have sensed what I was thinking. "Petra," he said (to help me, I believe), "this is your god-mother, Celeste." When she looked at me and smiled, she was exactly like her mother and it took my breath away. Here is what was strange: she had her father's lips, full and wide from top to bottom, but quite short side to side, yes, Persian-like, you know, but when she smiled and brought out dimples, I could see old Sylvie laugh. What a combination. Dear God, I thought. Out loud I said, that settles it. Petra. God-daughter-of-mine. Gustave rolled his eyes, but I think he was amused. I kissed Petra on both cheeks and while I was leaning in she took my hands with both of hers and held them very tight. She kissed me back with her eyes closed. I smelled milk and eucalyptus on her. She's not a woman yet, I thought, no, she's just like a sick child.

I told Petra I'd have lunch for her quite soon, that she should bathe and change her clothes. She didn't speak but turned pink. Sylvie's smile and that dark hair, I never did get used to it. Gustave took her to the tower room, which I thought would be very pleasant for her since you can see the chamomile and from the other window on clear days the bathhouses in Spa. I wanted her to understand how nice it is here, and to make sure Sylvie knew it, too.

She spent a very long time upstairs, I thought, and she used a lot of water. When she came down, her hair was even blacker, and tied up in a rag. She'd changed into some trousers. I myself don't wear them, but women these days will, and she looked a little better than she first had in that dress. Brown trousers with a periwinkle blouse, and the pea-soup cardigan again. I thought she looked Polish. Or Italian.

For lunch we had *salade frisée* and eggs and some nice slices of roast beef I'd got in town from Chez Yvette. I asked Petra if she had ever eaten this before and Petra said that yes, her mother made it here and there, but the lettuce she was used to was not so nice as this. That bath must have done her good because she wasn't shy at lunch. She finished off the salad and asked for more meat twice. She clutched the fork in her right hand and barely used the knife, which I forgave her at the time, because they left when she was three.

Petra's French was not too bad. She didn't have an accent when she spoke, and although later I kept hoping that the girl would make mistakes, she didn't. But she thought hard about what words to choose, and sometimes she'd wait with her mouth open in an 'o' until the right thing came. *Son séjour améliorera peut-être son français*, her mother'd written, hoping we could get the language streaming through her daughter's blood again. *Elle n'a personne avec qui parler*. Well, Petra had two people now to speak it with, and I impressed the fact upon her. We'll talk a lot together, you and me, I told her. I have a lot of novels. Petra nodded carefully across her empty plate. She was quiet for a moment. I wondered if she was imagining the two of us together on the terrace, companionable, sipping our *cassis*.

As it turned out she spent very little time with me, even early on. Instead, she worked it up to say that she was very enthusiastic about walking by herself, and that she would like to see the grounds alone. Like a mental convalescent, I thought then (she did sometimes seem gloomy). "*J'marche vite*," she said. And I thought of telling her that I, too, in my time, could keep up a fine pace, but she smiled like Sylvie does, and I felt warmly towards her, yes I did. I thought, she is a good child.

Gustave, who is not a hearty eater, was already drinking coffee. He said to Petra that if she was going to be looking at the topiary could she please not touch the animals, as he liked to be meticulous with the shaping and the binding of the boughs. He should put up a sign, I sometimes say—Don't Feed The Animals!—and see what people think. I did feel he was somewhat harsh with her.

After lunch, Petra followed me right into the kitchen and I almost fell over with the shock of it when I turned around and saw her with our three plates and our cutlery stacked up in her arms. The cardigan had slipped right off her back again. "Can I help you?" she asked me. I thought of telling her that we don't stroll into strange kitchens and drop dishes into other people's sinks—that's rude even in Morocco. But I didn't, no, I slapped those words right back down my throat and said, not today, dear. You sit down and start behaving like a guest. She handed me the plates and then her mouth closed and she shuffled back without another word. She was not stupid, no. I think she understood.

Gustave left the table, as he does, and while I was rinsing plates I heard him say to Petra that he was going to frame a something-*polyxena*, and how it's also called 'Cassandra,' would she like to see it? She said thank you very much for now, perhaps some other time. When I came out again Gustave was gone and she was standing by the window. She thanked me for the lunch, and said she'd like to take a walk if that was fine with me. I told her yes it was, enjoy yourself. It struck me then that she did not know how to please, but surely she did want to.

*

You know I'm always up at five to make the bread. I love this place the best at dawn, when the sky gets sharp with that strange blue before the light, the same blue that comes between the sunset and the night. I had an aunt who used to say that blue meant it was *l'heure des loups*, when wolves can see but people can't. Though my eyes are pretty sharp, I tell you. For those first three days I made *cramique*, with raisins and lump sugar, which I save for special times, and I'd set the table fresh with cloths we got in Egypt. Damascene, they call it. And arrange the fruit jars in the center of the table:

gooseberry, blackberry, and a clever marmalade I do with winter oranges from Spain.

Then I'd pull the heavy curtains up so I could feel the light change. I'd put coffee on the stove, and then I'd sit down by the window in the dining room to wait. Coffee in the morning is something Gustave picked up in his travels, before he married me; I like *mon petit café* at ten o'clock, with a novel on the patio. But Petra liked her coffee, too, I found out on the first day. At first she got up early. And she dressed for breakfast, not like Americans we see in films who wear their bedclothes to the table. But she drank more coffee than Gustave ever does, three cups one after the other as if it were grenadine in August. From then on I made sure there was enough for Gustave, too, when he came down at eight.

After breakfast Petra would go off and walk. She didn't think to ask me if I'd like to sit with her, or if I had a book she could read. I suppose she didn't show much interest in us, but it seemed all right at first. She's just a child, I'd tell myself, and she was raised abroad.

We'd have a lunch at noon, and then a nap for Petra and Gustave while I sorted out the dishes and planned the next day's meals. *Chicons* and veal on the first day, then *quiche lorraine* with mushrooms from the woods, which we still had for dinner on the third because I made enough to last. *Reibekuchen* with salami for our dinner on the second (because there was no need for Petra to imagine we were fancy all the time), and on the third for lunch a *filet de sole* with asparagus besides, and for a dessert, *crème brûlée*.

Just the day before, the nuns had called from Liège to say that everything was set and they were putting the poor girl on the train at seven in the morning. We could expect her here by lunchtime if she caught the omnibus, and earlier if the train was an express. But we ate the sole and *les asperges*, the three of us, alone. Gustave very wisely said, "She'll get here when she gets here," and there was nothing to be done. Afterwards Petra said that after all she would like to see those butterflies if Gustave was going to be free. He raised his eyebrows very high as though he couldn't see her well, and shut his mouth quite tightly as though thinking. Then he held his elbow out so she would have something to hold, and they went up the stairs with Petra asking him if he strolled the mountains with a net and caught them all himself. "No," he said, with quite a throaty voice, I thought. "My beauties come to me." She laughed. I suppose Gustave was paying her a compliment, trying to be kind. I stayed right there at the table. I do like a dessert.

Later I went out to the patio and sat down with my novel. A story by Françoise Sagan, it was, in which a young Parisian girl fools her student-suitor with his worldly sailor uncle. It's silly but I even wondered, not seriously, you know, if Petra had a boy at home and now was upstairs eyeing Gilbert and the butterflies as this girl was doing with the uncle while the wife stitched napkins in the garden. It was a lovely afternoon with lemon-colored sunlight—cool enough to wear a wrap, and the geraniums in their pots were brilliant, just giving up new flowers. I wondered where Therese was. As it turned out, she was on the way, almost as expected.

It was Petra came across her on her walk, which she took after Gustave had shown her all his frames. She called me from inside, through the window in the dining room, which looks out on the urns. Once the two of them were in the house and I was getting my mind around the look of the new girl, Petra told me how it was. She'd gone into the woods, she said, and she was heading for the abbey when she saw a stranger on the path, struggling with a suitcase. "I asked her where she was going, and, imagine, she was coming here!" Petra looked—although I didn't like to think it—like a dog that's found an old shoe in the grass. Her color was quite high. Some strands of her thick hair were loose and springing like fresh parsley. That French was really flowing in her veins again, and hotly too, to look at her, I thought.

"*N'est-ce pas merveilleux?* At first I thought she must be wrong." I'm not sure what's marvelous in meeting with a plump girl sweating through the woods and finding out that she is going where you've come from when you know that she's expected, but I will give Petra credit for at least being surprised that we would knowingly invite a girl like that into our home.

Therese was not at all as I'd imagined. What did I expect, you ask? Someone thinner, first of all. Worn by care, and bony. Before she came I could already see myself scooping squares of butter from the loaf and slipping them into her soup while she looked the other way. Someone pale, whom I could fatten up. I'd thought she might be gaunt, and tired. The sisters wrote, back when I arranged the thing, that by the summer she would have had a child and a nice home be found for it. They were especially pleased about our home, the head sister had written, because "it will soothe Therese to recover in the country." The letter had made much of the fact that just beyond our woods there is an abbey. "She will be close to God," they said. Oh, it's silly, perhaps. We ourselves don't go to church, because Gustave won't allow it. But I expected someone just a little saintly, someone who'd been wronged. Someone I could look over and think, as Gustave does when he contemplates his potsherds and the dullest of the moths, her kind will inherit the earth.

Well, there was nothing saintly about her. Nothing. Just as Petra did not look like her mother, Therese was nothing like I'd thought. She was like an abbot, not a saint, the kind of abbot in a Brueghel painting you can almost hear. A loud one, yelling about pigs, and belching in between. There was something oily about her, a greasy glow about her nose and lips, a thickness to her. Her hair was dark and just as oily, rather thin, and falling on her face so she was always peering through the strands. Her eyes were very narrow, and blue like morning glories, which I do admit surprised me. She had heavy forearms and thick hands, with two pink plastic rings on her big fingers, the kind with a false jewel glued on.

Welcome to Spa, Therese, I said, anyhow. Her dress was the color of blood oranges, very raw and sunny. It was far too small for her. She was quite a fat girl and it was clear she didn't know how to make herself look smaller. Her waist was done up very tightly with a yellow plastic belt that somehow matched her dress. I thought, she looks like an actress in a vaudeville. But I remembered she had had a baby, and maybe that's why she was fat, and perhaps that dress would fit her in another month or so. That's right, I told myself she was too poor to buy herself loose clothes. I even felt that when she knew me better I could reach out to her forehead with my hand and rearrange her hair, tuck it back behind her ears.

But then she spoke—with what a voice, I tell you, low and even like a man's. "Madame," she said, looking me directly in the eyes. Nothing shy about her blue ones, sharp, they were, like mine. Her look gave me a broiling feeling from my head across my chest. Petra was in the kitchen making tea, which she had never done before. I sat down with Therese at the table and asked about her trip. We expected you at noon, I said. Honestly I didn't mean to chide her, but she did take it that way.

"Forgive me, I had things to do," she said. She began to pluck the brambles from the sleeves of her bright dress. I watched her pressing them onto the table in a line, and I thought that even with her crumpled socks, Petra looked more saintly. *This* girl wore high heels—dancer shoes that matched the belt, with ankle straps that bit into her feet. I thought, no wonder she'd been sweating in the woods.

What things? I asked, then, conversationally, so she could see I'd be her friend. I scooted closer to her, leaning forward in my chair. I smiled, I did. "Things." She put her elbows on the table and started pulling at her cuffs. She crossed her legs and swung one heeled foot back and forth at me. What she said next to me with that low voice I still can't quite believe. "Private things, if you have to know." The look she gave me would have got a rise out of a man. I know I sat up tall. With those narrow eyes still on me, she took one of her hands (black beneath the nails, I saw) and scooped the brambles up into a pile before she brushed them all at once to scatter on the floor. All this without so much as a blink, and then she propped her chin up with her fist and gave me a thick smile.

I knew then that she had tricked the sisters, and tricked me. She hadn't come here to recover, and she hadn't come to be near God. I didn't like to think what private things she meant but I had some good ideas. Petra came in with a tall pot of *verveine* and three good coffee cups, looking quite excited. I was too unsettled at the time to tell her that's not really how it's done—there's a cupboard full of lovely china meant for tea in the next room. Therese dropped five cubes of sugar in her cup and stirred her tea quite noisily, I thought. Petra sat across from me and beamed. Petra was behaving as though this girl were a queen—really she was doing all she could to please her, that's how it looked to me that day, right at the beginning. It wasn't really a warm day, but I felt peculiar, let me say.

Therese said in her man's voice, "The pony's nice, though. Who would take the time to make a pony out of bushes? Really nice!" I was about to answer her, thinking, at least she's found something considerate to say, but I could see that she was saying it to Petra. Petra nodded smoothly, as though she'd lived with us for years, and said, "That's Gustave who did it." She gave me that smile of hers and poured me out some tea. I was going to say something about the china. But I couldn't. You understand me, don't you? It would have been silly then to talk about the cups.

*

Here's what it was like in our house after the bawdy girl arrived: loud, dangerous, and strange. Gustave liked her! In fact, while I was telling myself all the time to feel good things about Petra, who couldn't help where she'd been raised or looking so much like her father, Gustave, when he paid attention, behaved as though Therese was a something-*polyxena*. It must have come from that digging in the earth he does, which I've always thought unhealthful. "For buried treasures, *ma jolie* Celestine," he's often said to me, "you must put your hands in muck." Well that may be fine for broken pots, I've no right to speak of those, or muck. But it's another thing for girls.

Her lipstick! I'd say to him. She came down to meals with her mouth painted red like a balloon, the kind of red that looks like day-old blood and accidents there's no pleasure in recalling. Her paint would mark my things: the forks she used, my crystal glasses, the napkins that we'd bought in Egypt. And no matter what we're meant to think of napkins, that they're for making stains on you'd rather not see on your clothes, I know whoever said it hasn't washed white Damascene by hand. Once I asked her, not to make a fuss, but I was curious, do the sisters allow you girls to wear make-up out at the Maison? My voice was very cool, as though it weren't important, just a friendly question. "Am I at the sisters' now, Madame?" She looked right back at me and she took such a bite of mashed potatoes I heard her teeth scrape on the spoon.

All Gustave could say, weakly, absent-mindedly, as though I were asking him about the curtains, was "She's pretty, Celestine." Once he looked up from some clay bits he had set out on his desk and put his hand on mine. "We've had nothing bright in this house for so long!" As though I'm not pretty. I have three shades of coral pink I wear if it's been nice out and I'm going into town. But when Therese came and put her shiny mouth on everything it hit me that maybe Gustave's never noticed. Not for a long time.

She's rude, I'd say. "No, no," he'd say, as though he spent any time with her to judge. "She's spirited, that's all. C'est la joie de vivre." Joy, is it? I would think. At dinner that first night the girl asked me straight out how much I'd bought my blouse for—the ruffled silk one I had made in Liège, you've seen it, light blue with long sleeves. Then she said why spend more than several hundred francs on something you were just going to take off. The way she looked at Petra then it made me wonder what she thought one did exactly after taking off a blouse. And Petra! Petra's sunken little cheeks looked so flushed to me just then I asked myself if she was taking up the face-paint, too.

Next Therese turned to Gustave and asked how much he thought our old house could be worth. "Expensive keeping this house up," she ventured, talking with her mouth full. "You could make a great hotel here, really *quelque chose*, and bring some German tourists." Germans! Thankfully, Gustave didn't hear her right. He just looked at her over his glass of *vin de table* and let out a little "Hmm." He looked at her so much you'd think he'd never seen a girl.

At breakfast she dropped jam across the tablecloth because she'd talk and shake her knife before the berries could get safely from the pot onto her toast. When she saw the coffee cups she said, "Oh, *moi j'bois du chocolat*." I brought her cocoa in a cup and, looking through her oily hair she said, "Celeste, you don't have any bowls?" It gave me a shiver, that, to hear her use my name.

To top it off, she sang. I'd hear her from downstairs sometimes, bellowing up there, and not nice songs, either, not *Les Cloches de la Vallée* or something like *La Vie en Rose*, that I could sing along to but ditties she must have learned from sailors, or the father of that child the sisters said she'd had and given up. And there'd be Petra laughing up there, too. My god-daughter, laughing. That was the worst of it, I think, that Therese had Petra eating from her hand. I felt extraordinarily alone.

*

The last time I'd seen Petra she was no bigger than a bread loaf and she was swaddled up in white. It was me who held her while the priest splashed water on that powdered baby head. I'll witness this new child come waking to the world, I said to Hermann and Sylvie. I'll care for her if anything should happen. I shudder now to think it. Long life to Hermann and to Sylvie, I say each time I pour out a *cassis*, if I catch myself in time: *à la bonne vôtre*, I say. Though I did try to be nice to her, I did. I offered to go with her to the topiary several times, because now and then on a hot day I do like to walk among the beasts, and get some shade under the camel. But each time I asked Petra, she said, "Not yet, not yet," measuring her answer like salt into a spoon. "I want to wait until I can't bear not to go." Whatever that means. I was hurt, that's the truth. But I kept trying with her.

I never let her do the dishes, and insisted that she leave the tablecloth for me. I like to brush the crumbs together first, then shake the cloth outside—for birds, you see—and Petra wouldn't have, I know, thought of such a thing. But I did everything I could for her. I made sure she had coffee, food enough. I filled the refrigerator with fine roast beef for her and with two kinds of Edam. I did my part, and it's a shame that she couldn't see it.

I barely saw the pair after breakfast. They would disappear upstairs, saying "Thank you for the *petit déjeuner!*" and I'd hear nothing from them until noon. Sometimes I'd see them walking through the kitchen, coming from outside, and I didn't even know they'd gone—no, I'd spend whole mornings in the house, thinking they were in the library, finding things to read, or talking, only to discover they'd been playing in the woods. Unsettling, it was. Sometimes it made me wonder if I even knew where I myself had been. Well, I was feeling strange already, but it's the topiary did it, that first Friday morning. That's when I knew for certain that the whole thing was a mistake.

I had come in from the patio and picked up Gustave's demitasse and saucer from the table. I was standing at the sink, as I often do, looking out the window just above the taps. The day was green, we had a dim and chalky sky, and it was definitely damp. It was the kind of day we soon forget about if it's been sunny and there has been a breeze. When the sky has come back blue, you think how lucky we must be to live in this region of the world. From the kitchen window I can see a nice expanse of chamomile, and when it's dim outside, it all looks very soft. The chamomile had got quite high already and all the stalks were bursting with those sturdy little flowers. When the wind blows, it's got quite a smell to it, like a steeping cup of tea. Just beyond it I can see to where Gustave's bushes are.

The sweetest one, I think, is Gustave's little pony. Gustave read up on breeds before he did it, and this little bush is now a perfect Shetland Small, feasting on the grass. From the kitchen I could see the pony, and the egret, too, although it's smaller, and that big old bucking horse. Gustave is proud of that one, too, which took seven years to build. And, like the Shetland, it's a special breed. A Lipinzaner, if you want to know, with flaring hoofs and hairy ankles, up on its rear legs.

Well, at first I thought I'd seen a bird. We do get gulls out here, though we're far out from the sea. A flash of white, it was. But then it passed again and I thought it was a flag. I got out my wolf eyes. I put down the cup I had been washing, and took some steps outside to see what I could see.

The white thing was no kind of bird at all, but Therese's blouse afloat above her head. She was running back and forth between the pony and the Lipinzaner, skipping now and then—just like a horse would, I dare say. She wasn't wearing the blouse anymore, of course, and she was bouncing, you know what I mean. Once I got out there I could hear that she was yelling something, too, or laughing. Is she out there alone? I asked myself. Much later when I finally told Gustave about it I assured him that my first thought was for the bushes, because I knew he'd be concerned, but really I wanted to make sure I'd seen what I had seen. That loose girl from the sisters' with her bosoms all revealed.

When I got a little farther down the hill, I crouched down in the flowers because I didn't want the girl to see me. I slipped my shoes off so I could tuck my feet under my skirt, and I rolled up my sleeves so I could get down on my elbows. It was a hot day, remember, despite how grey it was, and I felt very damp. I could feel some nettles on my legs, but a person will put up with pain if there's something dreadful happening. Tell me, I thought, this time out loud—as though the flowers could have helped me—that she's out there alone.

In vain, it was. Next I saw Petra shooting out from underneath the horse, laughing just as loud. She had kept her blouse on, that was good, but it hurt to see her chuckling with that girl. Petra's parsley hair was loose and she waved her purple scarf around to match Therese's flag. Petra got down on all fours and pranced over to the pony and then she huddled underneath it. I thought, they are playing hide and seek.

Therese was not a handsome girl, not really, and she had just had, supposedly, a child. So she had little business taking off her skirt, but that's exactly what she did. She was standing right in front of Petra and she let the brown thing drop down to her feet and she stepped out of it, still hollering. Something like, "Oh! cruel cavaliers!" if my memory is right. Her thighs were wobbly just like my preserves are when they've come out clear and right. Even from where I was lying I could see how at the knee and along the plump insides they were just a little red. Chafed. Then she started leaping.

On the down, she'd crouch and dig her fists into the grass and pull some up in clumps. On the up, she'd raise her hands into the air and let the grass clumps go, so the blades would scatter wildly. Up. Down. Up. Down. With my eyesight I could see that some of the loose grass got stuck on her, although from where I was and with the greenish light the blades looked black, like tiny eels, pasted to her limbs. Petra pretended to be frightened. She turned her head away and then I saw her arms come up around the pony, from below, like the strap that holds a saddle to a horse. But she must still have been laughing.

Next Therese sang another song for Petra. I couldn't make out all of it, but I did hear Petra's name, "Petra *ma belle*, Petra *ma jolie*." My hair started to prickle then, from heat, and I felt sweat come pooling in my eyes. I wanted them to stop, but—it's terrible to say, and here's what it can come to when you bring the wrong girls home—Therese made me afraid. On my own land I was too frightened to go down there myself and order them to stop. Laughter can really harm a person, don't you think? I went back to the kitchen on my knees, because I thought if I got up they might come chasing after me. Petra had been ruined. I took one look back just as I got close to the kitchen and the last thing that I saw before I pulled myself onto the tiles and locked the door behind me was Therese, in a pair of yellow panties, raising up a leg in a very loose and ribald way as if to mount the pony's back.

I knew I couldn't tell Gustave. He might have fainted, or had a heart attack, and I would have had to ask that big girl for help. And while, God forgive me, it would have been poetic justice to have her cause her own host's death through all that foolishness of hers, of course, I couldn't tell him. And perhaps they hadn't done the bushes any damage. But I was damaged, I can tell you that. The nettles were the least of it.

*

That night Gustave was in good spirits with a call that had come through for him from Egypt. It must have rung while I was shoeless in the chamomile. I'm usually the one to fetch the phone, and I enjoy it, especially when it's a foreign scholar. North Africans, they are, professors. They're always so polite it makes my toes curl in my shoes. It made me even angrier with that big girl that I'd missed my call because of them.

A year ago it was a man calling from Khartoum, asking if Gustave would be their guest and give a talk, as they'd found something new out there. Of course we couldn't go, and Gustave later said that they hadn't any money, something about the Sudanese professors all being kicked out of their schools and how the man I'd talked to was a fraud. But still, he'd been so nice to me I felt I should remind the man that I was someone's wife. In any case this call from Alexandria had Gustave very pleased, and he opened up a bottle of Sancerre, which I do like very much, though I felt that it was wasted on the girls. Petra drank it like she drinks her coffee, as if it were water, and Therese drank hers very slowly. She sat circling the mouth of her wide wineglass with a finger, which as you know will coax a humming sound. That's the way to make a crystal glass explode, I thought, but I couldn't bring myself to say so.

I can't shake the feeling, either, that that night after the scene among the bushes there was something new with us, sitting at the table. The two of them looked different, somehow. Petra didn't talk. She hadn't worn her cardigan to dinner. She'd put on a black blouse without sleeves that had a pointed collar buttoned at the neck. Perhaps it was my headache, but it seemed to me her arms glowed, as though she'd rubbed them down with vinegar, or lard. She was drinking like a fountain.

I made a point of asking her what she'd done all day to see what she would say. She looked up very coyly and couldn't keep my gaze. Her eyelashes were so very wild and long they looked like those tarantulas Gustave has a picture of. Gets those lashes from her father, I thought, or maybe that Liège girl had lent her some mascara. Petra couldn't keep her eyes on me, and she only nodded at Gustave, who was explaining how the two of us might take a trip in winter. "To Alexandria," he said, "where the world's finest books once were." Petra said "A trip is nice," and Therese gave out a smothered little laugh, as though she had in mind a journey of her own.

But all in all, she was quiet, too, after her performance with the pony. Now and then she made a show of listening to Gustave's every word, blinking her blue eyes at him like the wings on a still butterfly that's sucking at a flower. I was still upset. I chewed a bit of anchovy from the salad for a long and salty time, and then I took another. Though thinking about Alexandria did make me feel better. Not so dirty, and not so—oh, I hate to say it—old.

I asked Therese if she would do the dishes, please, and told them all that I was going to bed. She must have been accustomed at the sisters' to doing work around the place, because she said she didn't mind. She got up from the table, drained her wine glass in one gulp and strode into the kitchen before I had folded up my napkin. She even looked relieved. I peeked into the kitchen then before going up the stairs, and it was true, Therese knew how to care for china: she was very careful with the plates, put spoons with spoons and knives with knives. My head hurt and once I got to bed I wished Gustave would hurry up and lie beside me. One likes a man's warmth, now and then.

*

I know they say if you are on the trail of evil, evil you will find. And when you've brought it in yourself, well in some ways it's your fault. But the worst was yet to come. I've said already how I like to get up early, how the house is mine then, in the hour of the wolves. I got up extra early for the whole of that next week, to get myself together. At four o'clock, or so. I was shaken up by everything I'd seen.

The first night I thought I should stay in bed a little longer and try to get some warmth out of Gustave, who if he's sleeping deeply doesn't mind it if I curl myself around him. But my eyes were open wide, and you know it's wearing to be wide awake beside a man who sleeps just like the dead. So I made myself get up. The sky was black, still, not even heading up to blue, and I felt good. As though I could surprise an evil thing if it came to trouble us.

I took to walking through the whole of our big house, corridor by corridor, up each and every hallway, as though I were on patrol. Our bedroom is *au deuxième*, something Petra found amusing. For her it was always the 'first floor,' and downstairs was 'the ground.' Anyway, I'd walk first to the third floor, where we've closed up the rooms. I'd take a candle with me, and try not to think too hard about how the house could use a thorough dusting. It was draughty, too, and even in my housecoat I was chilled. But the cold will do you good, I always say, cold will keep you sharp.

I'd walk all the way past the central staircase and to the far one that goes up into the tower, and then down again, in stone. I always leave my slippers at the bottom of the steps to have them in the morning, so the spiral stairs were cold. But it made me feel just like a girl, wandering in that house with nothing on my feet, awake while everybody slept.

They were in the tower—that's where I had put them, one room across the landing from the other, Petra's looking out to Spa over the pines, and Therese's, come to think of it, with a nice view of the chamomile and of my husband's zoo. Maybe she'd planned her little ride from the beginning, the first time she set eyes on that stallion from the top. I'd put gardenias in their rooms the day each of them came, and I'd given them replacement flowers to take up on the Thursday, just before the show. I liked to tell myself that I could smell the petals in the stairwell—a cool smell, that, so white.

The first few times I made my rounds the girls' doors were both closed. Shut very tight against me, that's what it felt like. I'd move to each in turn, and listen. I hoped that they were sleeping well, honestly I did. I wished each of them good dreams. The best ones come at dawn, they say, and that's what I think, too. One morning I tried to think of Petra as a baby, how she'd looked when I held her up to that old Brussels priest so he'd toss some water at her. When we walked out onto the Sablon she didn't make a sound, not even when we passed the antique vendors, and you know how startling they can be.

Like I said, I'd make the rounds, and then go on as usual, as though I hadn't slept a little less than a person really should. I'd make the bread and coffee, set the jams out in a row and put out fresh napkins. Once Therese arrived, Petra stopped coming down so early, and I'd read in the dining room until Gustave had come for coffee and to tell me what he was tackling that day. The girls came down so late I left them to it, and I'd take my book onto the patio. It was as if we had no guests at all, just a presence, and even— when Therese took to washing up the breakfast dishes—as though we had a maid. And I thought, well, all right. I tried to be forgiving.

With all of my patrolling, I'd get tired in the afternoons and I would go to sleep. And the truth is you can't keep watch with your eyes closed. I'd go onto the patio in the afternoon and in spite of all my fears I always fell asleep and when I woke up it was six. I'd wake up very cold and need to go upstairs to get a cardigan, then race into the kitchen to start cooking for the evening.

It's because I fell asleep that those girls got so free. If they'd told me they had dreams of going into town, I would have taken them, I would. I would have pointed out the extra bicycles we keep in the garage beside Gustave's old Morris. And I would have remembered how the sisters had advised me not to let Therese wander alone. That she needed supervision. But I think now that several times they looked as though they'd done some things in secret—something hot about their hair, and the way they'd come down from the tower, sometimes holding hands.

When I discovered I was missing money, I can't say I was surprised. It must have been Therese. Because although Petra had a slight look of the cabaret about her, she wasn't cheap, like Therese was. And if Petra knew of it, or if she had had a hand, well, she would not have done it all alone. Sylvie may have gotten married to Hermann, but that does not mean she was dishonest. It was after dinner that I found my wallet short. After I'd made them all a quiche with which I'd served a plate of carrot soup and sweet creamed radish greens. Gustave was in his study and I couldn't go to him. He'd have told me to be more careful with my things, how precaution and precision are welded at the hip. As though my jams aren't labeled nicely with a date on every pot.

It was one thing, going to the tower rooms while the girls were fast asleep, but quite another to go up when I thought I'd find them wide awake and talking. I waited. I'd go to them in the dawn. Maybe Therese would be dreaming thickly and so dead to our world that I could look through the girl's luggage and find my thousand francs.

Well, it didn't turn out that way, in the end. The last day was a Monday, I remember, because I thought that after I had gotten breakfast I'd bring the mower out to straighten up the lawn for when the townsfolk came on Tuesday. And because I often make some tartelettes or bigger pies and set them on a table for the children, I also thought as I was walking down the hallway in the dark that I could choose the apricots and pit a bucketful by noon.

I heard her, first. I was just coming to the landing, and something told me I should blow the candle out. I set it down just near the door, and I was feeling everything so sharply I noticed how the air was warm above the wick and there was smoke around my ankles, which made the rest of me feel cold. It was a kind of shuffling that I heard, the kind of noises thieves must make at night. It wasn't even four yet, so I thought, what could she be doing? I thought for sure it was Therese, since she'd already stolen from my purse. It stood to reason she'd be up this time of night, doing something of which I could be afraid. But it wasn't. And she wasn't by herself.

Petra's door was open. I could tell because there was a moon. The light was shining through her window, and it would have glowed right through my dressing gown and revealed me if I hadn't slipped myself very smartly flat against the wall. At first I thought maybe Petra had a fever. She was making little sounds like children do when they're asleep and in the clutches of a cold. I thought I'd go to her and ask if she was well. I think I would have liked that: when you haven't any children of your own you think sometimes how nice it would be to help them when they're sick. I could bring a cool cloth for her forehead. But it was the moon that stopped me, how it glinted off a gold thing on the dresser before I looked closely at the bed. I'd got quite near now, had my fingers on the lintel, and like I said, I see quite well at night.

The gold thing was Therese's vinyl purse, unzipped at the mouth. And next to it—I saw, because I sidled to the doorway and I squinted both my eyes—was a pile of Petra's things, her *Illustrated*

Guide to Belgium, Lichtenstein and Luxembourg, and a vial of *L'Air du Temps*. In the corner—which gave me quite a start—was Petra's purple case and right beside it, Therese's yellow one, pointing straight out from the wall, like a pair of Gustave's shoes. On the chair there were some clothes, and it was another shock to see that old skirt tangled up with Petra's long-sleeved cardigan, thrown one over the other. What's the use of making up two extra rooms if your guests are going to go behind your back and share a single one? I didn't like to think about the two of them so close, their things mixed up like that.

Of course, it wasn't just their things that were pressed up together. Petra wasn't there alone. There was a lump beneath the blankets with her. I couldn't see her face, but Therese was a lot bigger than Petra, so I knew that lump was her. There was that shuffling again, hands tight on the sheets, a sort of night-time cooing, which sometimes Gustave makes. I must have caused a sound, because they suddenly went still. Well, I went still myself. All my breath went sailing out of me and into that warm room. I was like Lot's wife, I was, rooted to the ground.

I wondered how long they'd been together in one room—if on the other days when both the doors were closed I was missing something all along. You can't know what goes on behind a door, not really, even if your eyes would pierce the wood. My eyes were smarting in the dark, and it wasn't from the smoke. I looked over at the desk again to where that purse was gleaming and I thought, that's where my thousand francs are. I wanted to walk right in and past the bed and take my money back, but my feet were stuck like leeches on wet skin. So what if they know that I'm right here, I thought? They ought to be ashamed. The covers moved then, and that's what set my legs free, but I couldn't go inside. I reached out and shut the door, and then I ran downstairs so fast that I was panting in the kitchen. I went directly to the *chambre froide* where we keep all the apricots and berries and sat down against the door.

I couldn't have the girls here any longer. Not like this, not mashed together in one room making plans against me. What would you have done? I didn't bake the bread that morning. I pulled out the heel from Sunday and had a cup of tea, which calmed me, made me think of England. They'd make the coffee on their own, I thought. I'd forget about the money if both of them would go.

*

In the end, Petra did it for me. She came down in that old dress of hers, arms bare, her hair all wild and loose, and found me in the kitchen. "No coffee?" she asked me. And when I pointed to the maragogype in the glass jar on the counter, she set to making it herself. I'd been crying, but I'm sure it didn't show. If it had, Petra would at least have kissed me on the cheek, or told me to sit down.

"Listen, *marraine*," she said, very friendly, as though nothing wrong had happened. In fact more talkative than she had ever been. "We'd like to go to Liège, to spend a few days there, is that all right with you?" She turned the gas on with the lighter and then walked into the dining room. "I thought, you know, that since this is my first summer in Europe, *on irait même à Knokke*. That's where the beach is, isn't it? Have you ever gone?" Well I guess that 'we' was Petra and Therese, though if she'd told me from the start, I could have gotten used to the idea and we would have gone together. I've been to Knokke once or twice. Blue sea, Italian ice creams, and a pretty little wind. I could have planned it for her if she'd told me. But it was clear she meant Therese. I told her she could do exactly as she liked. I didn't tell her that Therese was not allowed to go off by herself, or that I'd promised Sylvie I'd take good care of her daughter. I walked right past her to the breadbox, and cut myself some heel.

They must have agreed to act as though I hadn't seen them in the night, as if I didn't know that they had turned into a force. I couldn't bring it up to Petra. Not to Sylvie's little girl. She watched me chewing and I had to put the bread down. I didn't like her eyes on me. I told her I was going to go upstairs to change.

On the way, I got my courage up. If I couldn't tell my goddaughter exactly what I thought of her, I'd say something to the other girl. That's right, I thought. I'll talk to this Therese. Petra's door was open, and Therese was in the room, which I guess she had come to think of as her own, and she was looking in the mirror. She was putting on her lipstick, mouth tight and open like a fish. "Celeste," she said, her voice peculiar because of how she held her mouth. Then she told me to come in with a tip of her big head. I saw her bags were packed, and I felt the wind go out of me again. I sat down on the bed. It's crazy, isn't it? I'd gone up to tell the girl to go, that I'd be calling to the sisters to expect her, but when I saw she'd beaten me to everything, it almost made me sad. I hadn't thought that things would go so fast.

You're leaving? I asked her. Today? I looked at my own hands along the crocheted spread for a moment, and though I didn't mean it, I was tatting at the blanket like a child. Therese was putting on her belt. She breathed in very hard to make her waist as small as it could be before fastening the buckle. All trussed up, she let her breath out, and then she said, very softly, which was not her usual tone, "Ah, *non. Merde!*" I looked to see what she was doing. She was frowning, looking down. It's not pleasant to say but I think there was a stain on the girl's bodice. She reached onto the bureau for a handkerchief, which she pressed into her dress. My mouth went very dry.

When she looked into the glass again, she smiled at me, as though a leak in your own breast were nothing to be shocked about, not something to conceal. She put a hairpin in her mouth and started combing her brown hair. Rather a lot of it came out into the teeth, I saw. For a girl who cared so much about her looks, I thought, she isn't very lucky. When she spoke she sounded sorry.

N.S. Köenings

"*C'est pas grave*," she said, "It doesn't matter," and I wasn't sure what she was saying. She went on, "Petra wants to see the coast. And a rest would do me good." Her hands moved very slowly. She put the comb down, and she blinked. "All of that nice wind."

I was looking at her eyes. Very blue, they were. I looked into the mirror at myself to see if my own were that blue, too. I even wondered if her baby's eyes were the same color. It didn't bother me at first that she was looking at me, or that we get winds right here, and as I said, now and then some gulls. But it did make my jaws hurt, that they were leaving me before I could order them to go.

Then she did a thing that made me jump. "It's not so bad, Celeste," she said, and then she winked at me. That wink felt like a slap, you know, the way you feel when you've held out a piece of cake to someone and she keeps talking and doesn't take it though your hand is plain as day. The plump girl winked at me just like an actress would, as though we had a secret. But that wink helped me pull myself together. I smoothed the blanket down. I do not balk at hardship.

I said, you'll be out before lunch, then, and she looked a bit surprised, and I think I was pleased. I didn't feel like unwrapping any meat for them or cracking any eggs. I made myself get up from the bed and I went to see Gustave who was in the study. He was clacking at the typewriter, and he didn't hear me when I pushed open the door.

The girls are leaving us, I said. And though sometimes I sneak up very close, and quietly sit down on the free arm of his big chair, I couldn't make myself go in. "That's strange," he said. "So sudden." And he kept clacking at the keys. "Both of them?" Both of them, I said. He didn't look up once from the machine.

*

I made myself very small. I waited in the tower staircase at the bottom, while I heard them up the stairs, packing their last things. I heard Petra go across to Gustave's room to say goodbye, and I'll give her this much, she sounded awfully polite. Her French had gotten better. Then she came bouncing down in that pale dress of hers, the one she'd worn on the first day, her cardigan pulled tight around her bony little waist. I asked if she wanted me to call a car for her, but she kissed me on the cheek and said they'd walk their luggage down the hill. "Don't worry about us," she said. "I'll write you." Did she think I'd gone to all the trouble of inviting her out here for the summer so she could run off to the beach with a cheap girl who'd given up a child? I guess she did. I guess that is exactly what she did. We never did get presents from New York. From the start, she'd had no idea what we'd wanted from her. She'd never smelled like milk, or eucalyptus. That's what I thought about while she stood waiting in the hall.

Therese came down with her yellow case, and I noticed that her posture was not bad. She was far more able with her suitcase than Petra was with hers, what with her broad arms. Therese stopped in front of me and she looked right into my eyes. She'd put some hairpins in, and they looked very neat. I could look at her whole face. "Écoute," she said. "*Tu vas quand même pas leur dire?*" She was asking me quite underhandedly not to call the sisters to tell them she was gone. She'd also given up on *vous*, and maybe if she hadn't, I'd have made a different answer. Of course I am, I said. I will telephone the very moment you are gone. Don't think you'll get far. I don't think Petra knew a thing about it, that's how sly Therese was. I opened the front door for them myself, and then I stepped aside.

At first while they were walking, I imagined calling up the sisters and telling them precisely what I thought of their large, abandoned girl. And how I'd done my best for her, but when someone hasn't any manners nothing's going to suit them. And how she'd damaged me. At the same time, and I can't tell you why it is, I also felt the way a person does after they have made a lovely meal and the guests are getting up to go. You wish that they would stay so you could do it all again.

I watched them. It was another green, dull day, and the girls stood out quite sharply. When they reached the very end of our long driveway Petra turned around and waved at me, with that strange smile on her face which was both Hermann's and Sylvie's. Though just then it didn't look quite like her mother's or her father's, and it wasn't Persian, either. Therese only turned her head over her shoulder, and maybe she smiled at me, too. I didn't wave at them, exactly, but I did curl my fingers in my pocket. I suppose I made a fist. Petra shrugged, Therese leaned on her arm, and the two of them walked off.

From far away, you know, they looked like two ordinary girls. Nothing special. Certainly not horrible, not at a distance like that, when they were growing smaller and I could hear their footsteps echo in the gravel, their cases dragging on the ground. You wouldn't have known to see her from a long way as I did that Therese had had a child, or that it had been taken off to someone else, or that she was the kind of girl who'd drop her skirt so easy. She was having a hard time with her dancing shoes and swollen feet, but I supposed once they found the blacktop she would be just fine.

When I went back inside, Gustave was sitting at the table with his demitasse, and a magazine on pharaohs. "They're gone, then," he said. And I said yes, they were. Then he said the coffee didn't taste quite right, and I can't help it but that made me feel a little better. I went into the kitchen to get the apricots. Tomorrow's Tuesday, I told him. There's a topiary tour. He groaned. "I wish you hadn't said that was all right," he said. "It's like throwing pearls to swine."

I stuck my head out and I looked at my own husband. Pearls to swine. There he was, the famous archaeologist, telling me about giving pearls to swine. I left him at the table and went in to make the pies. I must have gotten very busy with them, and that's why I never made the call. In fact it was already afternoon when I remembered. And once it came to me that I'd forgotten, well, it seemed a little late. I did tell Gustave I had called, so he'd be relieved that I am not a person to be fooled with. I even told him that the nuns were informing the police and would make them bring her back. He just nodded at me once, then went back up the stairs.

Already I could smell the apricots getting warm and softening in the oven. I went into the hall and pulled the cloths out for the tables. I could iron them and get them nice before the pies were done. Then I set the tables in a place that could be seen from the horse's bucking and the pony. Later on I'd clean the two rooms in the tower, make them neat again.

The pies came out quite well. I made a circle with them on the kitchen table and I covered them with cloth. Then I went out onto the patio with a glass of bitters and some ice, and a novel I had longed to read but never had. The sun came out. The geraniums and petunias were as bright as I had hoped they'd be when I'd watched the urns in winter. I could smell the chamomile, and very slightly, too, the pies. I do like those second Tuesdays. I opened up my book and before I started reading I thought how nice it would be if lots of children came to look at Gustave's zoo. If they would finish off the pies, say thank you, and promise to come back.

Viewpoints
by
Christy Karpinski

"I have always been interested in how children see the world. Searching out their vantage point, I have discovered not their viewpoint, but my own. Curious about the mystery and strangeness of the space we first inhabit, I have begun to explore this intimate world.

These images are from an ongoing project begun in the winter of 2003."

CHRISTY KARPINSKI's photography has been exhibited at the Hokin Gallery in Chicago, the Salon Studio's National Juried Exhibition 2002, and the Main Photographic Workshops Gallery. It has also been featured in *Shots Magazine*, *Feline Magazine* and the *Photographers' Forum 2002 Best of Photography Annual*. Currently an MFA student at Columbia College in Chicago, Christy grew up and studied in Arizona where she received a degree in Women's Studies.

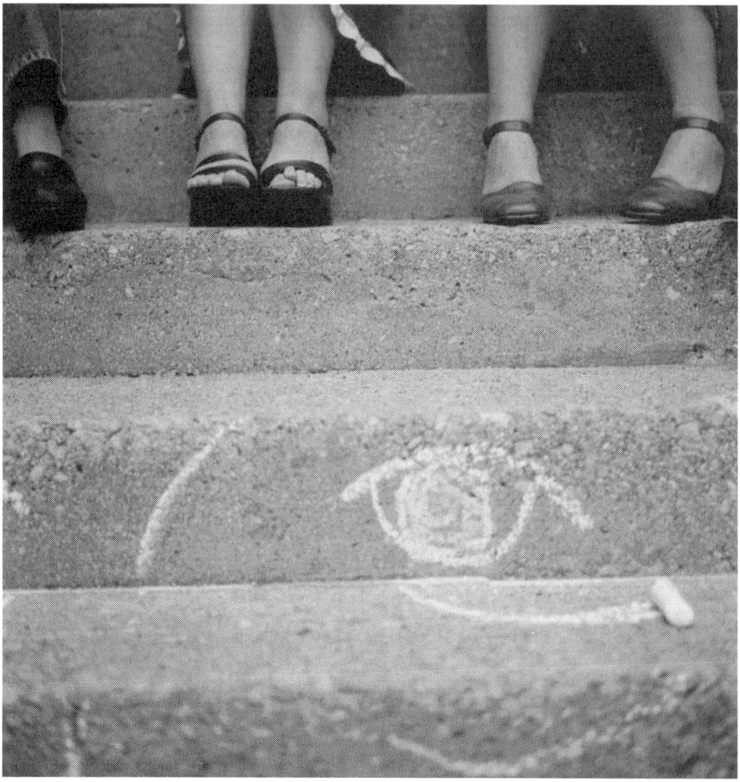

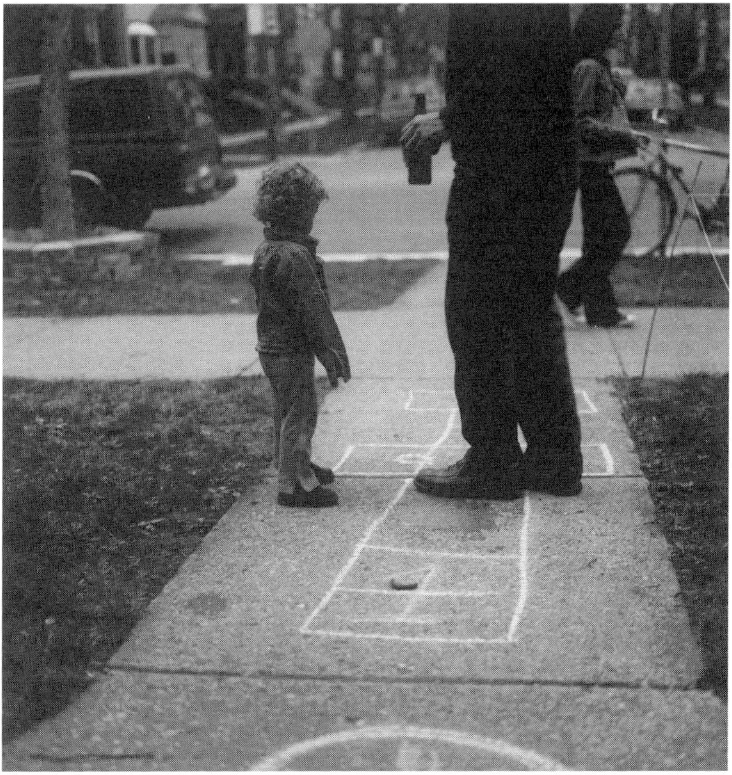

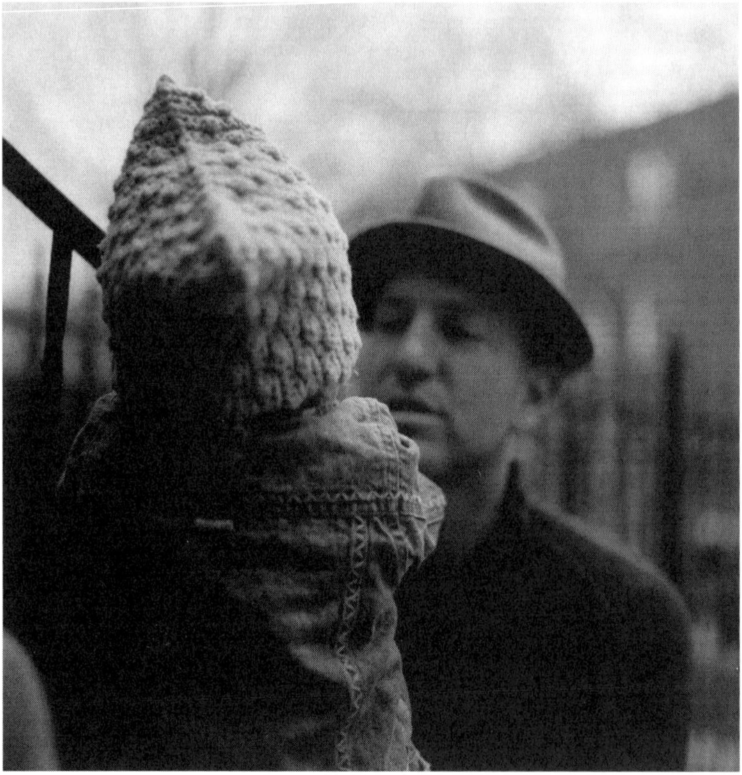

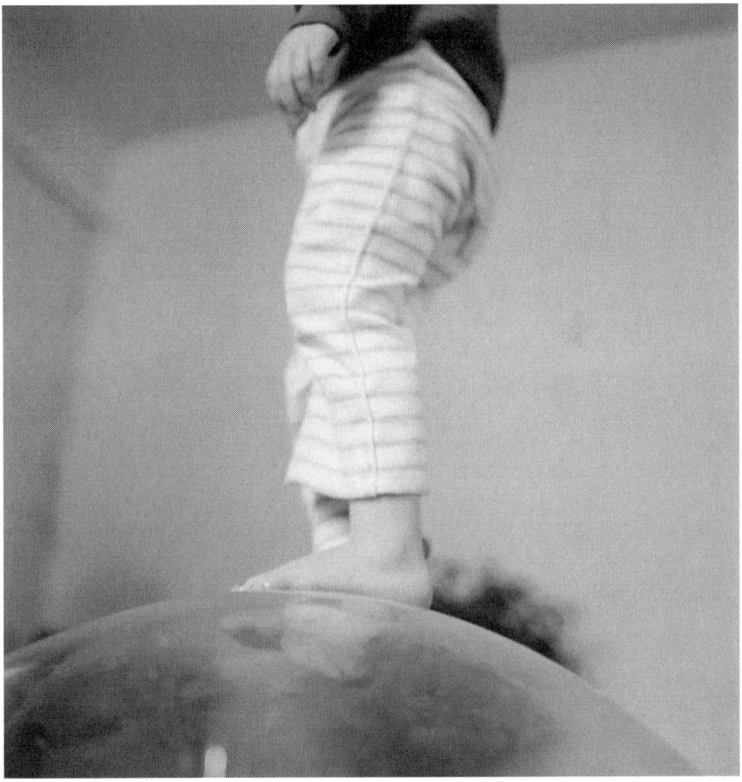

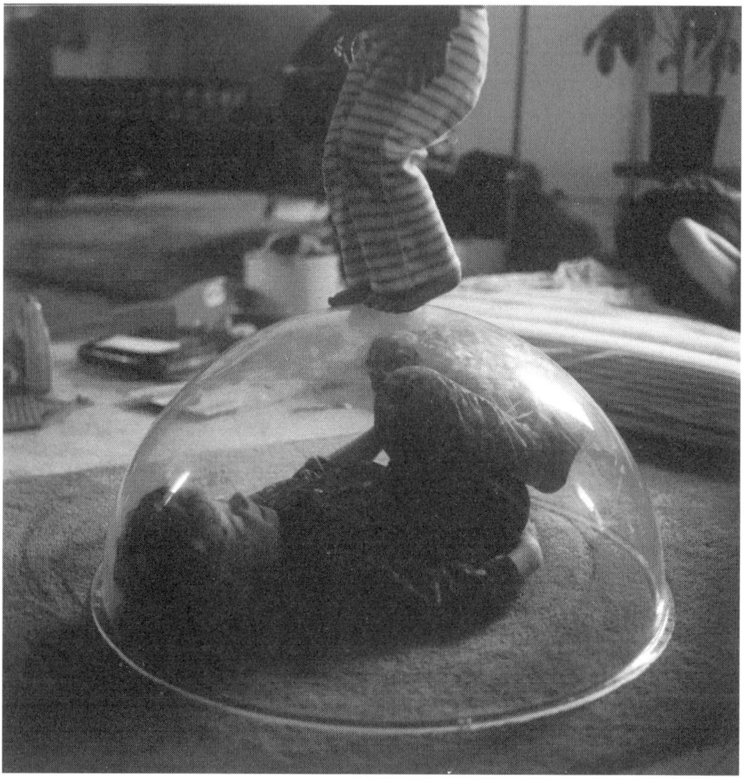

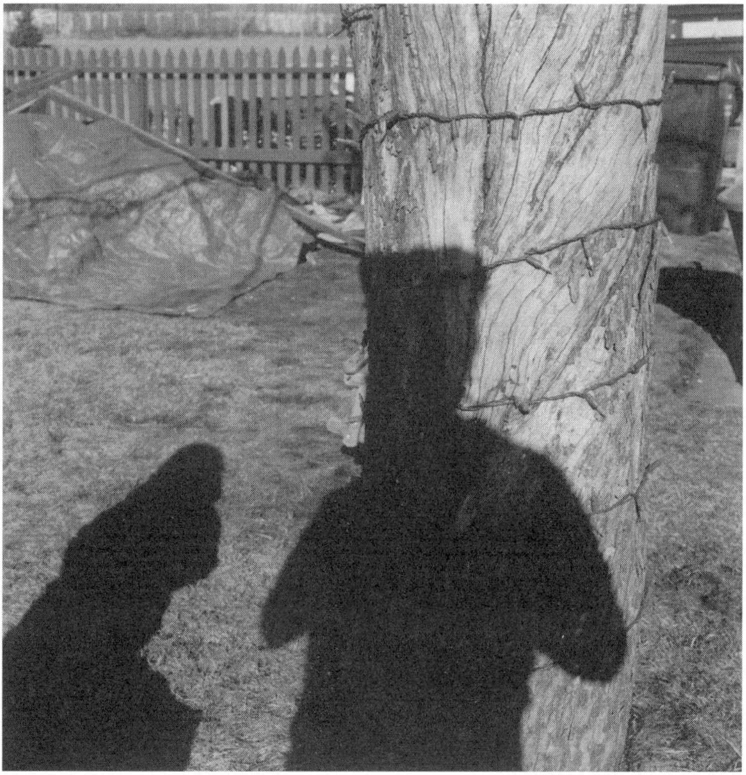

John Casey

JOHN CASEY is the author of *Spartina*, which won the National Book Award, of *The Half-Life of Happiness*, and other books of fiction. His fiction and essays have appeared in *The New Yorker, Sports Illustrated, Harper's, Shenandoah, Ploughshares*, and other magazines and anthologies. He has translated two Italian novels: *You're An Animal, Viskovitz* by A. Boffa, and *Enchantments* by Linda Ferri. Casey teaches at the University of Virginia. His essay "What's Funny?" was presented at the Sewanee Writers' Conference, Sewanee, Tennessee.

What's Funny?

John Casey

My earliest memory of what's funny is that it meant trouble. Someone had done or was doing something indecorous, insubordinate or inappropriate. Inappropriate. "Johnny, that is inappropriate behavior! And don't you laugh either, Tommy Flynn." Inappropriate. What a scolding, pecksniffian, thin-lipped, cold-blooded, brittle, airless, nasal Aunt-Polly-taking-Tom-Sawyer-by-the-ear word. It is Malvolio telling the roistering Sir Toby Belch that he should MEND HIS WAYS. So I cheer for Sir Toby's boozy answer: "Dost think because thou'rt virtuous, there shall be no more cakes and ale?"

That was my first idea—that laughter is on the side of the bad boys—a small portion of relief for those under the thumbs of Sister Margaret Mary, drill sergeants, customs officials, *maitre d*'s at French restaurants. It is encouragement for sassy counterattack by those accused of being inappropriate.

A half-dozen ideas buzzed in. I looked for help from psychological and philosophical experts, ancient and modern. I discovered that the subject of humor has a vast bibliography, almost none of which is useful as how-to advice. I went to a lecture and heard some Freud. None of the jokes that Freud gives as examples of humor are at all funny. Someone said they were funnier in German and people laughed.

What's Funny?

I was happier with a book called *Laughter (Le Rire)* by Henri Bergson, and it's worthwhile, partly because once in a while his examples of humor are funny and partly because he directly contradicts my first notion that we laugh to cheer up the misfits. Bergson thinks that laughter is a way to bring the misfits in line. He believes in society in a wonderfully optimistic way; he believes that there is a shared social consciousness that punishes crime with legal penalties and lesser asocial behaviour with laughter. "Our laughter is always the laughter of a group... However spontaneous it seems, laughter always implies a kind of freemasonry or even complicity with other laughers, real or imaginary." "Laughter is a kind of social 'ragging,' a method of 'breaking in' people to the forms and conventions of society, a way of curbing eccentricity and unsociability in their early stages." (*Encyclopedia*)

This idea is a more democratic version of a line of thought I'd heard at the lecture. For the Ancients (Aristotle, Cicero, Quintillian, et al.), comedy was satire, a reproval of vices, and Renaissance followers of this line—for example, Hobbes and Castiglione—thought laughter was chiefly used as a way of putting people in their place, of maintaining hierarchy against upstarts. Of the philosophers and social theorists mentioned, only Spinoza goes for *joie de vivre* as a cause of laughter. Later on he was joined by Henry Fielding, the only writer mentioned so far who actually made readers laugh.

To continue with Bergson. Laughter is not in sympathy with the aberrant person. "Try for a moment to become interested in everything that is being said and done; act in imagination with those who act, and feel with those who feel...." No laughter. "Now step aside, look upon life as a disinterested spectator: many a drama will turn into comedy. It is enough for us to stop our ears to the sound of music in a room where dancing is going on for the dancers at once to appear ridiculous." (Berg, p 10).

A shorter version of this lack-of-sympathy theory is a remark by Mel Brooks: "Comedy is when you get eaten by a lion. Tragedy is when I cut myself shaving."

This notion is borne out by the experience of an actor friend of mine. He had to take a pratfall on stage. When he fell far upstage, everyone laughed. When he fell halfway downstage, everyone laughed except the first two rows. When he fell right on the lip of the stage, nobody laughed. Several people in the front row, who'd heard the thump of his hipbone, said, "Ow!" This actor's experience may put to rest the facile theory of humor as malice, that we laugh at someone slipping on a banana peel because we're mean. We're not mean—we say "Ow," at least if we're close. As we get farther away we become cartoon watchers.

It turned out that what Bergson thinks laughter is reproving isn't roister-doister, isn't social misfits because they're misfits *per se*—what laughter is reproving is *inelasticity*. One way he begins to make this clear is by pointing out that most tragedies are named for the principal character. *Andromacque, Phèdre, Le Cid*. It's true for Shakespeare as well as for Racine & Corniellle. *Hamlet, Macbeth, Othello*. Molière's comedies are called *The Would-be Gentleman, The Miser, Les Précieuses Ridicules, The Hypochondriac*. They are named for a vice or a pretension. In the tragedies the main character has more than one quality, is pulled back and forth between qualities. In comedies the main character is a marionette, and all the strings attach to one quality, often one that the character is blind to. The tragic characters are more or less aware of their qualities, but in any case they are trying to adapt. The comic characters are not; they are operating in mechanical obedience to their obsessive quality. They are inorganic, and Bergson's idea of good social life is that it is organic, always in a process of vital adjustment.

A variation on a character who is comic because controlled mechanically by one quality is a character who believes that things are happening mechanically when they are not. Bergson cites a passage in *Tartarin sur les Alpes* in which "Bompard makes Tartarin... accept the idea of a Switzerland chock-full of machinery, like the basement of the Opera House, and run by a company which maintains a series of waterfalls, glaciers and artificial crevasses." (This may have been a funnier idea before the late 20th century invention of theme parks—now it might just be scary.)

A friend of mine owns a hundred-ton Newfoundland schooner. One summer Martin Scorcese was making a movie of the novel *The Age of Innocence*. There's a scene in which the hero is looking at the heroine who is standing by the sea. He says to himself something like this: *If that schooner passes the lighthouse before she turns around, it's all over.* Winona Ryder was hired to play the part of the heroine; my friend's schooner was hired to play the part of the schooner. An assistant director was buzzing back and forth in a speedboat, talking to Mr Scorcese by walkie-talkie, and to the schooner by bullhorn. He yelled through his bullhorn, "Action" and the crew weighed anchor and hoisted the sails. The assistant director yelled, "Go past the lighthouse!" The sails filled, the bow wave began to gurgle. A minute later, the assistant director listened intently to his walkie-talkie and then yelled through his bullhorn, "Hold it right there! . . . Now back it up a few feet!" then added as an afterthought, "Winona sneezed."

The repeated Bergsonian formula for the comic is "the mechanical encrusted on the living" and the living schooner and the mechanically-minded assistant director fit neatly.

So far so good. But there are a few quibbles. According to Bergson, repetition or duplication inevitably suggest the mechanical. If we see two people on stage doing exactly the same thing we laugh. The more the merrier. Yes—sometimes. But are the Rockettes funny? It's not entirely a rhetorical question. By themselves they're impressive and kind of sexy. What might make the mechanical aspect more apparent and therefore comic is the kind of thing we've

JOHN CASEY

seen in a score of movies—the heroine or hero gets mixed up in the Rockettes or their equivalent—she faces the wrong way, her face is in anxious movement, in contrast to the fixed smiles of the Rockettes—perhaps she almost gets kicked. She's like Charlie Chaplin, caught in the huge cogs of the machinery in *Modern Times*. But that we have to make an adjustment points to a crack in the veneer of the shiny theory.

A stronger quibble is with the idea that the mechanization of the human body is funny *per se*. Frankenstein's monster isn't funny. We could make him funny: Abbot and Costello meet Frankenstein....

Before picking on Bergson some more, I'd like to say that his book does belong on the short shelf of works helpful to writers—alongside Stanislavsky's *An Actor Prepares*, Aristotle's *Poetics* and Vladimir Nabokov's *Speak, Memory*. Of these, only the Nabokov is a work of art. The others are uphill going, but the view is worth the climb.

As ingenious and sometimes fruitful as the encrustation-of-the-mechanical-on-the-living theory is, there are other ways to explain the same funny event. The passage from Bergson that put me in mind of the schooner story is this: "... when reading the newspaper I came across a specimen of the comic...a large steamer was wrecked off the coast of Dieppe. With considerable difficulty some of the passengers were rescued in a boat. A few customs-house officers, who had courageously rushed to their assistance, began by asking them 'if they had anything to declare.'"

Bergson isn't very good at telling a funny story. There are two weak points. One is the phrase "some of the passengers were rescued in a boat." This implied to me, for a moment at least, that other passengers drowned, and I became sympathetically alarmed. More awkwardnesses arise in the next over-elaborate compound sentence. "A few of the customs-house officers, who had courageously rushed to their assistance...." Their rushing to the rescue is a piece of action better put in its proper chronological order and in its own sentence—after the wreck but before they all gather on shore. It is also odd that "a few customs-house officers ... began by asking them ...." Were the officers speaking in chorus? Clarity, clarity, clarity. And then the punchline loses immediacy by being in indirect speech rather than direct—"Have you anything to declare?"

I'd also like to see the passengers, just a glimpse. Probably missing various articles of clothing, wouldn't you think? Water pouring out of the pockets of the men's frock coats. The women's ringlets clinging to their cheeks like strands of a wet mop.

A good exercise for someone interested in comic scenes would be to rewrite the incident. Where to start? What point of view? How to have the shipwreck frightening, but not mortal? Everything true enough, so that the customs officer's question is wildly incongruous.

Incongruous. Out of proportion. Is it just the officer's mechanical response that is comic? I think we also need the largeness of the large steamer, and, although Bergson doesn't bring it up, it might help if there were some enormous waves rolling in from a North Atlantic storm. If this whole affair were about a rowboat that overturned while crossing the Rhine on its way to a customs house in Strasbourg, there might still be some contrast between an emergency and being asked a silly question, but not the contrast between the force of the sea, which has just tossed around a ship the size of a shopping mall, and the suddenly pipsqueak voice of human regulation.

Incongruity comes in different modes. One thing doesn't fit with another because it is too big or too small. A small child wearing her father's overcoat. A three-hundred pound man wearing a thong bikini. Or they're the wrong shape: a square peg in a round hole, or a long sofa being carried up a two-turn stairway. Or of incompatible textures—something that's flaccid when it should be stiff: Trying to use a wet noodle as a pipe cleaner, is what came to my mind.

Incongruity, like the encrusted mechanical, isn't necessarily funny but it is often an auxilary or a catalyst to a comic scene.

Topsy-Turvy

Reversal of fortune is Aristotle's favorite tragic plot. But in tragedy it comes after a long struggle, and we are as sympathetically aware of the inner turmoil of the main character as we are of the objective events. The doom is an inevitable consequence of the relation between the internal and the external. Topsy-turvy also is a reversal, but with a banana-peel oops-a-daisy swoop of suddenness. The primal form of topsy-turvy is jouncing a baby on your knee. "This is the way the ladies ride—trot, trot," and then the gentlemen canter, the huntsmen gallop, until "Here comes the country boy" and you swoop the kid into space from one side to the other saying, "Hobbledehoy! Hobbledehoy!" Or the New England variant: "Trot trot to Boston, trot trot to Lynn. Look out, Maud, you're going to . . . *fall in!*"

If it gets a laugh, it's because of the gasp of weightlessness, and then it's all right again. But there has been, in the midst of the usual gravity, a sudden alternative.

Oscar Wilde's wit thrives on the sudden unexpected alternative. When he was on tour in America, he was taken to Niagara Falls. His escort said, "Will you look at that. Isn't it amazin?"

Wilde said, "It would be amazing...if it went up."

The reason Wilde was on tour, by the way, is that Gilbert & Sullivan had had a great success in England with their show *Patience, or Bunthorne's Bride*. The main character of fun is a poet who swans around in a lovely velvet jacket with a lily in his hand. Gilbert & Sullivan wanted to put the show on in America, but they were afraid Americans wouldn't get the joke, so they secretly funded Wilde's tour and sent their play along in his footsteps.

Back to Niagara Falls. "Oh come now, Mr. Wilde," one of the white-gloved matrons said. "It is such an inspiring sight that couples come here on their honeymoon."

Wilde said, "Then it must be the second biggest disappointment in a young bride's life."

What's Funny?

In *The Importance of Being Earnest* a lot of the comedy is topsy-turvy, particularly in its turning the English caste system on its ear.

> ACT ONE, SCENE ONE.
> Morning-room in ALGERNON'S flat.... The room is luxuriously and artistically furnished. The sound of a piano is heard in the adjoining room. LANE [the butler] is arranging afternoon tea on the table, and, after the music has ceased, ALGERNON enters.
>
> ALGERNON: Did you hear what I was playing, Lane?
> LANE: I didn't think it polite to listen, sir.

After some to-and-fro about the servants drinking the champagne and Algernon asking Lane about Lane's married state, Algernon abruptly but languidly says, "I don't know that I am much interested in your family life, Lane."

> LANE: No, sir; it is not a very interesting subject. I
> never think of it myself.

A bit later, Algernon, aside: "Lane's views on marriage seem somewhat lax. Really, if the lower orders don't set us a good example, what on earth is the use of them?"

Each one of the men, while remaining in their apparently undisruptable master-servant relation, catches the other off-balance and executes a verbal judo throw. Algernon's enthusiasm for his own piano playing is met not with direct contradiction but with a side-step and a foot-sweep of wicked politeness. Algernon's dismissal of Lane's family life is met with such total agreement that it is as if Lane fell on his back and flipped Algernon up and over. But Algernon lands on his feet, and, with a comic turn of his own, twists the conventional wisdom, about the correspondence of the social and moral order, upside down.

And now he's ready for Jack, Lady Bracknell, Gwendolen, Cecily, Miss Prism and the Reverend Doctor Chasuble.

Cecily and Gwendolen also flip each other, but sometimes each achieves a sudden weightlessness on her own. In the following passage Gwendolen and Cecily are quarrelling with exquisite correctness. The Ernest in question is of course both Algernon and Jack.

> GWENDOLEN (quite politely rising): My darling Cecily, I think there must be some slight error. Mr. Ernest Worthington is engaged to me. The announcement will appear in the Morning Post on Saturday at the latest.
>
> CECILY (very politely rising): I am afraid you must be under some misconception. Ernest proposed to me exactly ten minutes ago. (Shows diary).
>
> GWENDOLEN (examines diary through her lorgnette carefully): It is very curious, for he asked me to be his wife yesterday afternoon at 5:30. If you would care to verify the incident, pray do so. (Produces diary of her own.) I never travel without my diary. One should always have something sensational to read in the train....

Riffs go on.

> CECILY (thoughtfully and sadly): Whatever unfortunate entanglement my dear boy may have gotten into, I will never reproach him with it after we are married.
>
> GWENDOLEN: Do you allude to me, Miss Cardew, as an entanglement? You are presumptuous. On an occasion of this kind it becomes more than a moral duty to speak one's mind. It becomes a pleasure.

Neither Mr. Wilde nor we are laughing at the innocently intent maidens in order to reprove their faults. On the contrary, we

What's Funny?

are happy to see them wafting lightly upwards into the realm where pleasure is more than moral duty and narcissism is just one of many sweet odors to be savored.

There is an additional comic skill at work here, perhaps not readily apparent in extracted passages. The broad comedy of masquerade and deception—Algernon and Jack both pretending to be Ernest, the mystery of Jack's parentage, Lady Bracknell's snobbism capsized—is an old but worthy tune played on the A string of Wilde's violin. What produces the sense of life being lighter than air is that Wilde is simultaneously trilling on the E string, double-bowing hemi-demi-semi quavers. The trills wouldn't be as good without that tune.

Wilde's light-hearted nimble bad-boy reflexes unfortunately did him in. When he sued the Marquis of Queensbury for libel—the Marquis had referred to Wilde as a sodomite—Sir Edward Carson was the lawyer for the defense. When Wilde was in the witness box, Carson hammered away at him about his having entertained a stableboy.

> "Did you invite him to dinner?"
> "Did you give him wine?"
> "Did you... did you... did you..."
> "Did you kiss him?"

Wilde said, "No."

Carson paused. This pause has become famous among trial lawyers. The Carson pause.

Wilde said, "He was far too ugly."

*

Sir Edward Carson went on to become an Ulster Unionist leader. Oscar Fingal O'Flahertie Wills Wilde lost his civil case, was then prosecuted criminally, and went to jail. He wrote *De Profundis* there,

The Ballad of Reading Gaol shortly thereafter, and died in exile three years later. I don't know but hope that it is true that Wilde's last words in a run-down hotel room in France were these: "Either that wallpaper goes, or I do."

To return to our own land and the subject of the comic as a function of abrupt inversion—there is this report from Volume II of Shelby Foote's history of the Civil War: General Bragg, having been driven east through most of Tennessee and on past Chattanooga, won the battle of Chickamauga for the South. Longstreet and Polk urged him to follow through and destroy Rosencran's Northern army completely. Bragg wasn't sure the northerners were in such utter retreat, in spite of the loud cheers of his own troops. "...a Confederate private, who had been captured the previous day, escaped and made his way back to his outfit. When he told his captain what he had seen across the way—for instance that the Unionists were abandoning their wounded as they slogged northward...he was taken at once to repeat his story, first to his regimental and brigade commanders, then to Bragg himself. The stern-faced general heard him out, but was doubtful, if not of the soldier's capacity for accurate description, then at any rate of his judgement on such a complicated matter. 'Do you know what a retreat looks like?' he asked.

'I ought to, General,' the private said. 'I've been with you during your whole campaign.'"

Who laughed then?

To laugh at a private getting the better of a general, you have to be a civilian, or have the soul of a civilian under your gold braid. Do you also have to be at least momentarily unaware of what was outside and less than a mile from Bragg's tent, which was ten-thousand dead? Shelby Foote writes, "...the butcher's bill (of dead and wounded) North and South, came to 16,170 and 18,454 respectively. The combined total of 34,624 was exceeded only by the three-day slaughter at Gettysburg..."

What's Funny?

In Bragg's tent, who laughed?

We can't know. Shelby Foote doesn't tell us. Can you imagine who might have laughed then? An attendant brigadier, colonel, major, or captain? And if he'd come to the tent through the field of dead, what would you think of his laughter? Would you think it inappropriate? Or would you see it as relief, a short, earned leave from service at the front? I can imagine laughter as a reaction to horror or grief, but how much better if there is something comic to accommodate it.

Shelby Foote does tell us this: "(What the private said) endeared him to his comrades, then and thereafter, when it was repeated, as it often was, around campfires and at future gatherings of veterans." I laughed when I read what the private said. In Shelby Foote's book it comes before the listing of the dead and wounded. It is on a printed page, here and now, not then and there.

*

Another sudden inversion. Giorgio Bassani's novel, *The Garden of the Finzi-Continis* is about a Jewish family in Italy during the 1930s and World War II. The Italian Fascists didn't systematically kill Jews, but they treated them in a way that made it possible for the Nazis to ship them to concentration camps after the collapse of the Italian government. However the opening chapter of the novel includes a scene that takes place after the war. A family and friends drive to Cerveteri to have a picnic among the Etruscan tombs, a usual and popular Roman outing. On the ride back to Rome the narrator is enjoying the view of the sea through the pine trees. They're all happy—except the little girl. The narrator asks her what's wrong.

"It was sad."

"What was sad?"

"The Etruscans."

"But, Lucia, they died, oh, three-thousand years ago."

"What difference does that make?"

A sudden alternative, an upending of complacency. It's certainly not comic. Does the topsy-turvy theory therefore fail? I think not, but it needs help. Perhaps none of the factors—neither distance, nor encrustation of the mechanical, nor incongruity, nor topsy-turvy—works in isolation. And, more importantly, if one of the factors is at odds with the others, the comic effect becomes something else. What the girl said put us at a distance from the picnic party, but it also removed the distance of three-thousand years. Either by reason of ignorance or innocence or simply standing outside of time, she didn't think of the Etruscans as far away. More importantly, for the narrator riding beside her in the open car under the pines, what she said also removed whatever distance he had managed to put between himself and the deportation of the Finzi-Continis, between himself and their unfindable graves.

Precision & Immediacy

We noticed that Bergson, in re-telling the story of the large steamer and the customs-officer, made his point, but also made the telling somewhat awkward and as flightless as a dodo. There was a need for order, precision, and direct, immediate speech. I also suggested more details, and that suggestion may be a problem. Details can either make a story more immediately visible or slow the pace. A lot of the art of storytelling, not just funny storytelling, is in the balance between detail and pace. Both are necessary to immediacy—it's sort of like being able to believe in the particle theory of light and the wave theory simultaneously.

If you are putting a comedy on stage, the two oldest rules in the book are pace and bright light. You don't want shadows or sight lines into darkness. But what is this bright light to someone putting prose on a page? I think the translation is precision.

What's Funny?

A by-the-way piece of circumstantial evidence: any fiction writer who gives a public reading is often surprised when the audience laughs at a passage the writer thought was just simple clear description. But, coupled with the good will of the audience and the slight nervous tension in the room, simple clear description has the effect of sudden illumination. And bright light or its equivalent has another happy effect: you realize that you are going to be shown things so clearly that you aren't going to have to think.

Precision is a component of wit, which is sometimes comic and sometimes just a bit different. It must be precise, perhaps even more precise, but sometimes it makes you think and that detour between words and the blossoming of them in the inner senses, that detour by way of thinking, produces a pleasure that is too slow to trigger the physical response of laughter.

The Duke of LaRochefoucauld wrote relatively few pages, but he worked his maxims over and over. It is true that he spent a great deal of time making love and war, but once he settled down, he wrote and rewrote, polishing his brief remarks until they became, at their best, as spare as haiku: "We all have enough strength to endure the misfortunes of others."

LaRochefoucauld was careful not to use either obsolete or out-of-the-way words, or words that he thought were not likely to survive. There are no references to the military equipment of the Seventeenth Century, nor to customs, dress or architecture. In his ambition to leave a text that would not require footnotes, he has been successful. This is an exercise that the French have greatly admired, and also two professors at Duke University who have written a style manual called *Clear and Simple as the Truth*, an awkward but finally justified title. LaRochefoucauld is their chief icon of classic style, and their initial quotation of his work is a description of a lady:

> *Mme de Chevreuse avait beaucoup d'esprit, d'ambition*
> *et de beauté; elle était galante, vie, hardie, entre-*

prenante; elle se servait de tous ses charmes pour réussir dans ses desseins, et elle a presque toujours porté malheur aux personnes qu'elle y a engagées.

translation I
Madame de Chevreuse had wit, ambition and beauty; she was flirtatious, lively, sure of herself and enterprising; she used all her charms to further her plans, and to anyone she involved in them, she almost always brought disaster.

translation II
Madam de Chevreuse had sparkling intelligence, ambition and beauty in plenty. She was flirtatious, lively, bold and enterprising. She used all her charms to push her projects to success, and she almost always brought disaster to those she encountered on her way.

Neither translation really sews it up. The problem is partly the particle y, which serves many purposes in French: it can mean there, thereto or thereby, or in, for, to or about, me, you, he, she, it, us, them. But it can be inserted neatly, like the tip of a finger on the first half-hitch of a knot so that the final bit of tying will end up taut. The two translations handle the y problem differently, but the more important difference is that the older translation (no. II) is lengthened with modifiers—"sparkling intelligence," "in plenty"— and the final phrase "to those she encountered on her way" is a modifying subordinate clause that dribbles off the end.

To modify, to improve exactness or to leave spare? One answer to that question is this parenthetical remark from an Adam Mars-Jones story in which a man has just been convicted of murder at the Old Bailey. The judge comes in with the bit of black cloth on his head that means bad news. The omniscient narrator comments, "The phrase 'I sentence you to death,' like the phrase 'I love you,' is better left unadorned."

That quoted passage could serve as an Occam's Razor for anyone trying to write precisely.

The polar opposite of the spare and ageless precision of the LaRochefoucauld is precision through abundance. Here are two footnotes from David Foster Wallace's narrative of his Caribbean cruise on a luxury liner. The title is "A Supposedly Fun Thing I'll Never Do Again."

38 This is the reason why even a really beautiful ingenious powerful ad (of which there are a lot) can never be any kind of real art: an ad has no status as gift, i.e. it's never really for the person it's directed at.

40 This is related to the phenomenon of the Professional Smile, a national pandemic in the service industry; and no place, in my experience, have I been on the receiving end of as many Professional Smiles as I am on the (S.S.) Nadir: *maitre d's*, Chief Stewards, Hotel Manager's minions, Cruise Directors—their P.S.s all come on like switches at my approach. But also back on land at banks, restaurants, airline ticket counters, on and on. You know this smile—the strenuous contraction of circumoral fascia with incomplete zygomatic involvement—the smile that doesn't quite reach the smiler's eyes and that signifies nothing more than a calculated attempt to advance the smiler's own interests by pretending to like the smilee. Why do employers and supervisors force professional people to broadcast the Professional Smile? Am I the only customer in whom high doses

of such a smile produce despair? Am I the only person who's sure that the growing number of cases in which totally average-looking people suddenly open up with automatic weapons in shopping malls and insurance offices and medical complexes and McDonald'ses is somehow causally related to the fact that these venues are well-known dissemination-loci of the Professional Smile?

Who do they think is fooled by the Professional Smile?

And yet the Professional Smile's absence now also causes despair. Anybody who's ever bought a pack of gum in a Manhattan cigar store or asked for something to be stamped FRAGILE at a Chicago Post Office, or tried to obtain a glass of water from a South Boston waitress, knows well the soul-crushing effect of a service worker's scowl, i.e. the humiliation and resentment of being denied the Professional Smile. And the Professional Smile has by now skewed even my resentment at the dreaded Professional Scowl: I walk away from the Manhattan [cigar store] resenting not the counterman's character or absence of goodwill but his lack of professionalism in denying me the Smile. What a fucking mess.

This passage is a cascade, a torrential rant. But within the wave the particles are particular. There is, for example, the high-falutin' anatomical terminology: the circumoral fascia and the incomplete zygomatic involvement. (I finally looked it up—"pertaining to the zygóma." Okay. At least it's on the same page. "Zygóma: the bony arch on each side of the skull in vertebrates, consisting of the malar or jugal bone [cheek bone] and its connections, and forming a junction between the cranial and facial bones; the zygomatic arch.")

This is mildly funny—the guy is in such high dudgeon about these smiles that he obsesses to the point of lunatic, but accurate, research. He immediately zags back from his zig into second-year med school jargon and puts it in plain language: "...the smile that doesn't quite reach the smiler's eyes."

The next time he reverses field it's from the smile to the scowl, i.e. denial of smile. And now he's moving faster—Manhattan, Chicago, South Boston—all quick cuts but with immediately recognizable detail fragments. By the end he's moving so fast, and with such accumulated weight and friction, that he just melts.

So there's another, and last factor in this catalog of comic effects: the melting or collapsing of an elaboration. I think the rule is that the labor in the elaboration has to be honest labor. The writer has to take part as whole-heartedly in the construction as in the collapse. David Foster Wallace is serious about the Professional Smile; he builds a case that is eerily logical and rhetorically well made. At the same time he shoots himself off like a rocket with a loose fin.

A sub-corollary to the honest-labor-in-elaboration theorem. I have heard from others and noticed in my own work that when a writer wants to let a character have a ridiculous, a preposterously bad idea, if the idea is concocted, made out of a kit for bad ideas, there is little comic effect. If, on the other hand, the idea is a notion that I have once believed and held dear and only finally got over, then that idea planted in a character is more likely to have enough life to it to be truly funny.

Somewhere in the midst of Gibbon's *Decline and Fall of the Roman Empire*, Gibbon quotes a French historian who says, "Nothing is beautiful if it's not true." That applies to what's funny too.

Guess Who
Was At The Party?

Kate Hill Cantrill

She didn't look a thing like his girlfriend. This alone should have been a sign that she was just a fling, a diversion from what he had known for the past five years. She began to think of his girlfriend as *Guess Who*. Guess Who was at the opening? people would say. Guess Who *RSVP*ed yes for the party? Guess Who was wearing a half-shirt and showing her midriff? Guess Who got a dye job?

The city had never been smaller. Everywhere she went she saw him, saw her, or worse, saw them together. They looked wrong together, that was obvious to everyone, but still, when she saw them and when she would look down and pretend not to, it made her stomach wrench. Guess Who was small, terribly small, small like illness which, she thinks, is all part of the reason why he felt he should stay. Guess Who looked like she might just fall over at any minute. Sometimes she thought of flicking her, just walking up to her and flicking her shoulder with her long pointer finger and Guess Who would go toppling forward, knocking her teeth out on the sidewalk.

He was solid, too solid probably, more like thick. He had some bad points, which she tried to focus on. Grooming was an issue, although sometimes it was sweet—the little tufts of nose hairs that crept out in a laugh, the way his hair stuck up like enthusiasm—but certainly this sweetness would pass and she would be left with him, disheveled and thick. Although, after five years, Guess Who didn't seem to mind, or at least, didn't seem to think that they were points important enough to let him go over. Maybe she even liked his faults. Maybe they kept him with her. Maybe he looked in the mirror sometimes and thought, *No one else would have me.* Insecurity can make you feel safe sometimes.

Guess Who would have him, though—faults and all.

She liked how he was tall, like her, not like other men who just kept shrinking. No, he was tall (it was all in his legs, but even so), and when they walked hand in hand she didn't feel at all like she was walking a dog, stopping to allow him to keep up. They had the same rhythm, and sometimes, after coffee, they both got crazy and laughed and bounced down the street and talked about things that last forever—houses, kids, friendship. That's how it started, see, with a friendship, that was how she was able to get so close without Guess Who getting territorial. She wasn't trying to mess things up, she just heard how sad he sounded whenever he'd say, *I have to go home now.*

He is confused, however. He still calls sometimes and just says, *hey*. It is a small city, after all, and so it happens quite often that he sees her. Mostly she is walking alone and quickly because she has things to do, many many things. She keeps herself very busy which he admires. Guess Who doesn't have a job. Guess Who used to bake but worked somewhere where termites fell from the ceiling into her cakes and so she quit. *Lame.* Guess Who couldn't cut it.

She bakes too. He used to love her baking because it always flopped but tasted like heaven. He told her every cake should fall apart and every pie should sink, otherwise they're just too pretty to eat. Guess Who makes beautiful cakes.

The last she heard through the network of friends involved in the matter was that he's not with Guess Who anymore. (Not that that is any matter anymore for *her*. She dropped out. She said, Have him, and walked away—she was tired). Fantastic, she thought, just what I need. After all the back and forth and back again, now that he was forth, she wanted him to stay that way—just to keep her sane. Didn't he at least owe her that, a little bit of sane?

She was going to a party, it was one that she had every right to attend. Unfortunately, it was also one that Guess Who had every right to attend. It was a party of the mutual friend. She got her hair cut. She bought a new shirt. She wore the shoes that she sometimes felt bad about, the shoes being so fancy but in the back of her closet. She put sparkles on her eyelids and gloss on her lips. She had a good smile and was going to use it that night. She practiced at home telling jokes to her sister's iguana. You guana go too? I guana have a shot of Jack before I leave.

At the door, she rang the bell and Guess Who just happened to walk up behind her. Guess Who said *Hi*, like she meant it. *Funny*, she thought and mumbled something. All things considered, they shouldn't be talking. All things included the fact that she slept with Guess Whose man and she fell for him and she waited—not so patiently—for him to choose her, which he didn't. Guess Who was well aware of the facts, but was friendly as fire, there at the door. Guess Who said, He's not coming. I haven't talked to him, have you? But she just grumbled and then ran inside the door as fast as she could. Guess Who yelled behind her, I like your shoes!

She immediately drank enough to feel comfortable and then alternated a drink with water so as not to lose her edge completely—she felt somewhat on the defensive lately. She noticed Guess Who drank quite a lot. She was a little afraid that Guess Who would become the life of the party and so she kept an eye on her. She tried to laugh a little bit more and a little bit louder. She laughed at a guy who looked like 'Where's Waldo' and who explained to her that he liked natural women. By this he meant hairy and so she was out of the picture. She also laughed at a man who was visiting from Cali, as he called it, and said her aura was all flipped out. Come to Cali, he said. We have yard sales.

She left him and headed for Mutual Friend when Guess Who appeared at about the level of her navel. Guess Who said, *Hey* and *What's up* and other oddly bothersome things. Again she grumbled and tried to talk to Mutual Friend, whose frightened eyes grew wide when he saw her standing next to Guess Who. She could never tell whom Mutual Friend sided with more, which made her a bit uneasy. She'd like to be able to talk about Guess Who when the subject came up. She would like to say something like, I had a dream that I was carrying a beautiful old carpet bag and when I opened it Guess Who was inside and so I closed it up and sold it at a vintage store, but she didn't. She would like to say (mostly when she saw him and Guess Who walking all out of sync holding hands) that she could eat *two* Guess Whos and still not be full, but she didn't. Instead, she tried to walk away from the situation but Guess Who followed her. She walked away quickly and sat on the floor, which was a mistake because then Guess Who had a better vantage point to talk to her face. What do you want? she finally said. Guess Who just smiled.

She is an artist and is known for putting stickers on people at parties—kind of like walking, talking public art. Some said 'THIS SIDE UP' and everyone got a kick out of finding them on their pants pockets, shirt sleeves and shoe tops. One man took it off of his shirt and put it on his groin. He just wanted a reason to point there, she thought, men like that sort of thing. She was just about to begin to have a good time when she noticed Guess Who following her again. Your hair looks good—Guess Who said that? I dyed mine; can you tell? Guess Who's eyes were droopy and she looked like she'd be even easier to topple over. She thought maybe if she just blew in her general direction, Guess Who might fall over, even jam her eye on a corner of the table. This was the kind of thing she thought but didn't say out loud. She felt someone touching her back and she turned and Guess Who was there. What are you doing? she asked the little illness, but Guess Who just laughed. A few minutes later, Mutual Friend walked over and risked the appearance of taking sides by telling her that her back was covered with stickers that said, THIS SIDE UP. Who did it? she asked, although she already knew—guess who, asked Mutual Friend, guess who?

She went into the bathroom and took off her shirt to remove the stickers. One was flattering, meant you were a part of things; many were humiliating. She looked in the mirror and decided that she still looked good and went back into the party. Guess Who was outside the door. She was leaning on the wall and looking like she might fall over all by herself. Guess Who said, I haven't talked to him have you? and started to cry. She said nothing and tried to walk away but Guess Who grabbed her and pulled her down to her face. She's trying to kiss me, she thought and she pulled back fast. Guess Who fell down. Mutual Friend came over and gave her an evil look. She tried to *kiss* me, she said, and then, realizing that would never be believed said, she tried to *hit* me. Mutual Friend arranged to have someone take Guess Who home. Someone was short and stocky and put Guess Who's arm over his shoulder and walked her out. She looked like a child—her feet weren't quite working like they should. She felt bad for her and yelled up that no, she hadn't talked to him either. Guess Who just lifted her head and looked at her and smiled.

Smash and Grab

Michael Knight

At the last house on the left, the one with no security system signs staked on the lawn, no dog in the backyard, Cashdollar elbowed out a pane of glass in the kitchen door and reached through to unlock it from the inside. Though he was ninety-nine percent certain that the house was empty—he'd watched the owners leave himself—he paused a moment just across the threshold, listened carefully, heard nothing. Satisfied, he padded through an archway into the dining room where he found a chest of silverware and emptied its contents into the pillowcase he'd brought. He was headed down the hall, looking for the master bedroom, hoping that, in the rush to make some New Year's Eve soirée, the lady of the house had left her jewelry in plain sight, when he saw a flash of white and his head snapped back on his neck, the bones in his face suddenly aflame. He wobbled, dropped to his knees. Then a girlish grunt and another burst of pain and all he knew was darkness.

He came-to with his wrists and ankles bound with duct tape to the arms and legs of a ladderback chair. His cheeks throbbed. His nose felt huge with ache. Opposite him, in an identical chair, a teenage girl was blowing lightly on the fingers of her left hand. There was a porcelain toilet tank lid, flecked with blood, across her lap. On it was arrayed a pair of cuticle scissors, a bottle of clear polish, cotton balls and a nail file. The girl glanced up at him now and he would have sworn she was pleased to find him awake.

"How's your face?" she said.

She was long-limbed, lean but not skinny, wearing a sweatshirt with the words *Saint Bridget's Volleyball* across the front in pastel plaids. Her hair was pulled into pigtails. She wore flannel boxers and pink wool socks.

"It hurts like hell." His nostrils were plugged with blood, his voice buzzing like bad wiring in his head.

The girl did a sympathetic wince.

"I didn't think anyone was home," he said.

"I guess you cased the house?" she said. "Is that the word—cased?"

Cashdollar nodded and she gave him a look, like she was sorry for spoiling his plans.

"I'm at boarding school. I just flew in this afternoon."

"I didn't see a light," he said.

"I keep foil over the windows," she said. "I need total darkness when I sleep. There's weather-stripping under the door and everything."

"Have you called the police?"

"Right after I knocked you out. You scared me so bad I practically just shouted my address into the phone and hung up. I was afraid you'd wake up and kill me. That's why the tape. I'll call again if they aren't here soon." This last she delivered as if she regretted having to make him wait. She waggled her fingers at him. "I was on my right pinky when I heard the window break."

Cashdollar estimated at least ten minutes for the girl to drag him down the hall and truss him up, which meant that the police would be arriving momentarily. He had robbed houses in seven states, had surprised his share of homeowners, but he'd never once had a run-in with the law. He was too fast on his feet for that, strictly smash and grab, never got greedy, never resorted to violence.

Smash and Grab

Neither, however, had a teenage girl ever bashed him unconscious with a toilet lid and duct-taped him to a chair.

"This boarding school," he said. "They don't send you home for Christmas?"

"I do Christmas with my mom."

Cashdollar waited a moment for her to elaborate but she was quiet and he wondered if he hadn't hit on the beginnings of an angle here, wondered if he had time enough to work it. When it was clear that she wasn't going to continue, he prompted her. "Divorce is hard," he said.

The girl shrugged. "Everybody's divorced."

"So the woman I saw before—" He let words trail into a question.

"My father's girlfriend," she said. "One of." She rolled her eyes. Her eyes were a curious, almost fluorescent shade of green. "My father is the last of the big time swingers."

"Do you like her? Is she nice?"

"I hardly know her. She's a nurse. She works for him." She waved her hand before her face as if swiping at an insect. "I think it's tacky if you want to know the truth."

They were in the dining room, though Cashdollar hadn't bothered to take it in when he was loading up the silverware. He saw crown molding. He saw paintings on the walls, dogs and dead birds done in oils, expensive but without resale value. This was a doctor's house, he thought. It made him angry that he'd misread the presence of the woman, angrier even than the fact that he'd let himself get caught. He was thirty-six years old. That seemed to him just then like a long time to be alive.

"I'm surprised you don't have a date tonight," he said. "Pretty girl like you home alone on New Year's Eve."

He had his doubts about flattery—the girl seemed too sharp for that—but she took his remark in stride.

"Like I said, I just got in today and I'm away at school most of the year. Plus, I spend more time with my mother in California than my father so I don't really know anybody here."

"What's your name?"

The girl hesitated. "I'm not sure I should tell you that."

"I just figured if you told me your name and I told you mine then you'd know somebody here."

"I don't think so."

Cashdollar closed his eyes. He was glad that he wasn't wearing some kind of burglar costume, the black sweatsuit, the ski mask. He felt less obvious in street clothes. Tonight, he'd chosen a hunter green car coat, a navy turtleneck, khaki pants and boat shoes. He didn't bother wearing gloves. He wasn't so scary-looking this way, he thought, and when he asked the question that was on his mind, it might seem like one regular person asking a favor of another.

"Listen, I'm just going to come right out and say this, OK. I'm wondering what are the chances you'd consider letting me go?" The girl opened her mouth but Cashdollar pressed ahead before she could refuse and she settled back into her chair to let him finish. "Because the police will be here soon and I don't want to go to prison and I promise, if you let me, I'll leave the way I came in and vanish from your life forever."

The girl was quiet for a moment, her face patient and composed, as if waiting to be sure he'd said his peace. He could hear the refrigerator humming in the kitchen. A moth plinked against the chandelier over their heads. He wondered if it hadn't slipped in through the broken pane. The girl capped the bottle of nail polish, lifted the toilet lid from her lap without disturbing the contents and set it on the floor beside her chair.

"I'm sorry," she said. "I really am but you did break into the house and you put my father's silverware in your pillowcase and I'm sure you would have taken other things if I hadn't hit you on the head. If you want, I'll tell the police that you've been very nice, but I don't think it's right for me to let you go."

In spite—or because—of her genial demeanor, Cashdollar was beginning to feel like his heart was on the blink; it felt as thick and rubbery as a hot water bottle in his chest. He held his breath and strained against his bonds, hard enough to hop his chair, once, twice, but the tape held fast. He sat there, panting.

The girl said, "Let me ask you something. Let's say I was asleep or watching TV or whatever and I didn't hear the window break. Let's say you saw me first—what would you have done?"

He didn't have to think about his reply. "I would have turned around and left the house. I've never hurt anyone in my whole life."

The girl stared at him for a long moment then dropped her eyes and fanned her fingers, studied her handiwork. She didn't look altogether pleased. To the backs of her hands, she said, "I believe you."

As if to punctuate her sentence, the doorbell rang, followed by four sharp knocks, announcing the arrival of the police.

*

While he waited, Cashdollar thought about prison. The possibility of incarceration loomed forever on the periphery of his life but he'd never allowed himself to waste a lot of time considering the specifics. He told himself that at least he wasn't leaving anyone behind, wasn't ruining anyone else's life, though even as he filled his head with reassurances, he understood that they were false and his pulse was roaring in his ears, his lungs constricting. He remembered this one break-in down in Pensacola when some sound he made—a rusty hinge, a creaking floorboard—startled the owner of the house from sleep. The bedroom was dark and the man couldn't see Cashdollar standing at the door. "Joyce?" he said. "Please. Is that you, Joyce?"

There was such sadness, such longing in his voice that Cashdollar knew Joyce was never coming back. He pitied the man, of course, but at the same time, he felt as if he was watching him through a window, felt outside the world looking in rather than in the middle of things with the world pressing down around him. He crept out of the house feeling sorry for himself. He hadn't thought about that man in years. Now, he could hear voices in the next room but he couldn't make out what they were saying. It struck him that they were taking too long and he wondered if this wasn't what people meant when they described time bogging down at desperate moments.

The girl rounded the corner into the dining room trailing a pair of uniformed police officers, the first a white guy, straight out of central casting, big and pudgy, his tunic crumpled into his slacks, his belt slung low under his belly; the second, a black woman, small with broad shoulders, her hair twisted into braids under her cap. "My friend—" The girl paused, shot a significant look at Cashdollar. "—Patrick, surprised him in the dining room and the burglar hit him with the toilet thingy and taped him up. Patrick, these are Officers Hildebran and Pruitt." She tipped her head right, then left to indicate the man and the woman respectively.

Officer Pruitt circled around behind Cashdollar's chair.

"What was the burglar doing with a toilet lid?"

"That's a mystery," the girl said.

"Why haven't you cut him loose?"

"We didn't know what to do for sure," the girl said. "He didn't seem to be hurt too bad and we didn't want to disturb the crime scene. On TV, they always make a big deal out of leaving everything just so."

"I see," said Officer Pruitt, exactly as if she didn't see at all. "And you did your nails to pass the time?" She pointed at the manicure paraphernalia.

The girl made a goofy, self-deprecating face, all eyebrows and lips, twirled her finger in the air beside her ear. Officer Hildebran wandered over to the window. Without facing the room, he said, "I'll be completely honest with you, Miss Schnell—"

"Daphne," the girl said and Cashdollar had the sense that her interjection was meant for him.

Officer Hildebran turned, smiled. "I'll be honest, Daphne, we sometimes recover some of the stolen property—"

"He didn't take anything," the girl said.

Officer Hildebran raised his eyebrows. "No?"

"He must have panicked," Daphne said.

Cashdollar wondered what had become of his pillowcase, figured it was still in the hall where the girl had ambushed him, hoped the police didn't decide to poke around back there. Officer Pruitt crouched at his knees to take a closer look at the duct tape.

"You all right?" she said.

He nodded, cleared his throat.

"Where'd the tape come from?"

"I don't know," he said. "I was out cold."

"Regardless," Officer Hildebran was saying to Daphne, "unless there's a reliable eyewitness—"

Officer Pruitt sighed. "There is an eyewitness." She raised her eyes, regarded Cashdollar's battered face.

"Oh," Officer Hildebran said. "Right. You think you could pick him out of a line-up?"

"It all happened pretty fast," Cashdollar said.

And so it went, as strange and vivid as a fever dream, their questions, his answers, their questions, Daphne's answers—he supposed that she was not the kind of girl likely to arouse suspicion, not the kind of girl people were inclined to disbelieve—until Officers Hildebran and Pruitt were satisfied, more or less. They seemed placated by the fact that his injuries weren't severe and that nothing had actually been stolen. Officer Pruitt cut the tape with a utility knife and Cashdollar walked them to the door like he was welcome in this house. He invented contact information, assured them that he'd be down in the morning to look at mugshots. He didn't know what had changed Daphne's mind and, watching the police make their way down the sidewalk and out of his life, he didn't care. He shut the door and said, "Is Daphne your real name?" He was just turning to face her when she clubbed him with the toilet lid again.

Once more, he woke in the ladderback chair, wrists and ankles bound, but this time Daphne was seated cross-legged on the floor, leaned back, her weight on her hands. He saw her as if through a haze, as if looking through a smudgy lens, noticed her long neck, the smooth skin on the insides of her thighs.

"Yes," Daphne said.

"What?"

"Yes, my name is Daphne."

"Oh." His skull felt full of sand.

"I'm sorry for conking you again," she said. "I don't know what happened. I mean, it was such a snap decision to lie to the police and then that woman cut the tape and I realized I don't know the first thing about you and I freaked." She paused. "What's your name?"

Cashdollar felt as if he was being lowered back into himself from a great height, gradually remembering how it was to live in his body. Before he was fully aware of what he was saying, he'd given her an honest answer.

"Leonard," he said.

Daphne laughed. "I wasn't expecting that," she said. "I didn't think anybody named anybody Leonard anymore."

"I'm much older than you."

"You're not so old. What are you, forty?"

"Thirty-six."

"Oops."

"I think I have a concussion."

Daphne wrinkled her nose apologetically and pushed to her feet and brushed her hands together. "Be right back," she said. She ducked into the kitchen, returned with a highball glass, which she held under his chin. He smelled scotch, let her bring it to his mouth. It tasted expensive.

"Better?" Daphne said.

Cashdollar didn't answer. He'd been inclined to feel grateful but hadn't the vaguest idea where this was going now. She sat on the floor and he watched her sip from the glass. She made a retching face, shuddered, regrouped.

"At school one time, I drank two entire bottles of Robitussin cough syrup. I hallucinated that my Klimt poster was coming to life. It was very sexual. My roommate called the paramedics."

"Is that right?" Cashdollar said.

"My father was in Aruba when it happened," she said. "He was with an AMA rep named Farina Hoyle. I mean, what kind of a name is Farina Hoyle? He left her there and flew all the way back to make sure I was all right."

"That's nice, I guess," Cashdollar said.

Daphne nodded and smiled, half-sly, half-something else. Cashdollar couldn't put his finger on what he was seeing in her face. "It isn't true," she said. "Farina Hoyle's true. Aruba's true."

"What are you going to do with me?" Cashdollar said.

Daphne peered into the glass.

"I don't know," she said.

They were quiet for a minute. Daphne swirled the whisky. Cashdollar's back itched and he rubbed it on the chair. When Daphne saw what he was doing, she moved behind the chair to scratch it for him and he tipped forward to give her better access. Her touch raised goosebumps, made his skin jump like horseflesh.

"Are you married?" she said.

"No."

"Divorced?"

He shook his head. Her hand went still between his shoulder blades. He heard her teeth click on the glass.

"You poor thing," she said. "Haven't you ever been in love?"

"I think you should cut me loose," Cashdollar said.

Daphne came around the chair and sat on his knee, draped her arm over his shoulder.

"How often do you do this? Rob houses, I mean."

"I do it when I need the money," he said.

"When was the last time?" Her face was close enough that he could smell the liquor on her breath.

"A while ago," he said. "Could I have another sip of that?" She helped him with the glass. He felt the scotch behind his eyes. "It's been a coupla months," he said. The truth was he'd done an apartment house last week, waited at the door for somebody to buzz him up, then broke the locks on the places where no one was home. He was in and out in less than an hour. Just now, however, he didn't see the percentage in the truth. He said, "I did this mansion over by the country club. I only ever do rich people and I give half my take to Jerry's Kids."

Daphne socked him in the chest.

"Ha, ha," she said.

"Isn't that what you want to hear?" he said. "Right? You're looking for a reason to let me go?"

"I don't know," she said.

He shrugged. "Who's to say it isn't true?"

"Jerry's Kids," she said.

She was smiling and he smiled back. He couldn't help liking her. He liked that she was smart and that she wasn't too afraid of him. He liked that she had the guts to bullshit the police.

"Ha, ha," he said.

Daphne knocked back the last of the scotch, then skated her socks over the hardwood floor, headed for the bay window.

"Do you have a car?" she said, parting the curtains. "I don't see a car."

"I'm around the block," he said.

"What do you drive?"

"Honda Civic."

Daphne raised her eyebrows.

"It's inconspicuous," he said.

She skated back over to his chair and slipped her hand into his pocket and rooted for his keys. Cashdollar flinched. There were only two keys on the ring, his car and his apartment. For some reason, this embarrassed him.

"It really is a Honda," Daphne said.

*

There was a grandfather clock in the corner but it had died at half past eight who knew how long ago and his watch was out of sight beneath the duct tape and Cashdollar was beginning to worry about the time. He guessed Daphne had been gone for twenty minutes, figured he was safe until after midnight, figured her father and his lady friend would at least ring in the new year before calling it a night. He put the hour around 11:00 but he couldn't be sure and for all he knew, Daphne was out there joyriding in his car and you couldn't tell what might happen at a party on New Year's Eve. Somebody might get angry. Somebody might have too much to drink. Somebody might be so crushed with love they can't wait another minute to get home. He went on thinking like this until he heard what sounded like a garage door rumbling open and his mind went blank and every ounce of his perception funneled down into his ears. For a minute, he heard nothing—he wasn't going to mistake silence for safety a second time—then a door opened in the kitchen and Daphne breezed into the room.

"Took me a while to find your car," she said. She had changed clothes for her foray into the world. Now, she was wearing an electric blue parka with fur inside the hood and white leggings and knee-high alpine boots.

"What time is it?" he said.

But she passed through without stopping, disappeared into the next room.

"You need to let me go," he said.

When she reappeared, she was carrying a large stereo speaker. He watched her carry it into the kitchen. She returned a minute later without the speaker, took the parka off and draped it on a chair. She braced her hands on the table, waited for her wind to come back. "That was a mistake," she said. "I should've started small."

He looked at her. "I don't understand."

"It's a good thing you've got a hatchback," Daphne said.

For the next half hour, she shuttled between the house and the garage, bearing valuables each trip, first the rest of the stereo, then the TV and the VCR, then his pillowcase of silverware, then an armload of expensive-looking suits and on and on until Cashdollar was certain that his car would hold no more. Still she kept it up. Barbells, golf clubs, a calfskin luggage set. A pair of antique pistols. A dusty classical guitar. A baseball signed by someone dead and famous. With each passing minute, Cashdollar could feel his stomach tightening and it was all he could do to keep his mouth shut but he had the sense that he should leave her be, that this didn't have anything to do with him. He pictured his little Honda bulging with the accumulated property of another man's life, flashed to his apartment in his mind, unmade bed, lawn chairs in the living room, coffee mug in the sink. He made a point of never holding on to anything anybody else might want to steal. There was not a single thing in his apartment that it would hurt to lose, nothing he couldn't live without. Daphne swung back into the room, looking frazzled. She huffed at a wisp of stray hair that had fallen across her eyes.

"There," she said.

"You're crazy," Cashdollar said.

Daphne dismissed him with a wave. "You're out of touch," she said. "I'm your average sophomore."

"What'll you tell the cops?"

"I like Stockholm Syndrome but I think they're more likely to believe you made me lie under threat of death." She lifted the hem of her sweatshirt to wipe her face, exposing her belly, the curve of her ribs, pressed it first against her right eye, then her left as if dabbing tears.

"Ha, ha," he said.

Daphne said, "I'll get the scissors."

She went out again, came back again. The tape fell away like something dead. Cashdollar rubbed his wrists a second, pushed to his feet and they stood there looking at each other. Her eyes, he decided, were the color of a jade pendant he had stolen years ago. That pendant pawned for $700. It flicked through his mind that he should kiss her and that she would let him but he restrained himself. He had no business kissing teenage girls. Then, as if she could read his thoughts, Daphne slapped him across the face. Cashdollar palmed his cheek, blinked the sting away, watched her doing a girlish bob and weave, her thumbs tucked inside her fists.

"Let me have it," she said.

"Quit," he said.

"Wimp," she said. "I dropped you twice."

"I'm gone," he said.

Right then, she poked him in the nose. It wouldn't have hurt so much if she hadn't already hit him with the toilet lid but as it was, his eyes watered up, his vision filled with tiny sparkles. Without thinking, he balled his hand and punched her in the mouth, not too hard, a reflex, just enough to sit her down, but right away he felt sick at what he'd done. He held his palms out, like he was trying to stop traffic.

"I didn't mean that," he said. "That was an accident. I've never hit a girl. I've never hurt anyone in my whole life."

Daphne touched her bottom lip, smudging her fingertip with blood.

"This will break his heart," she said.

She smiled at Cashdollar and he could see blood in the spaces between her teeth. The sight of her dizzied him with sadness. He thought how closely linked were love and pain. Daphne extended a hand, limp-wristed, ladylike. Her nails were perfect.

"Now tape me to the chair," she said.

The Minor Wars

Kaui Hart Hemmings

The sun is shining, mynah birds are hopping, palm trees are swaying, so what. I sit in the easy chair I've brought from home and pick up the spoon from my lunch tray. I'd like to fling it into the air, catch it in my mouth and say, "Look at that, Boots." Boots is my wife, although I haven't called her that since the early seventies when she used to wear these orange knee-high boots in eighty-six degree weather. She'd top my utensil act by using a fork or a steak knife. Her real name is Joanie, and she's barefoot. She's in a coma. Dying the slowest of deaths. Or perhaps I'm wrong. Perhaps she has never felt more alive.

"Shut this crap off," I tell Scottie. She's my ten-year old daughter. Her real name is Scottie. She turns off the television with the remote.

"No," I point to the stuff in the window—the sun and the trees. "I mean this."

Scottie slides the curtain across the window, shutting all of it out. "This curtain is sure heavy," she says.

She needs a haircut or a brushing. There are small tumbleweeds of hair rolling over the back of her head. She is one of those kids who always seems to need a haircut. I'm grateful that she isn't pretty, but I realize this could change.

"It's like the bib I have to wear at the dentist when he needs X-rays of my gums," Scottie says. She knocks on the hard curtain. "I wish we were at the dentist."

"Me too," I say, and it's true. A root canal would be a blast compared to this. Life has been strange without Joanie's voice commanding it. I have to cook now and clean and give Scottie orders. That's been weird. I've never been that full-time parent, supervising the children on weekdays, setting schedules and boundaries. Now I see Scottie before school and right after school, and I'm basically with her until she goes to bed. She's a funny kid.

The visitor on my wife's bed looks at Scottie standing by the shaded window and frowns, then turns on a light with a remote control and goes back to work on Joanie's face. My wife is in a coma and this woman is applying make-up to her lips. I have to admit that Joanie would appreciate this. She enjoys being beautiful, and she likes to look good whether she's canoeing across the Molokai channel or getting tossed from an offshore powerboat. She likes to look *luminous* and *ravishing*—her own words. Good luck, I always tell her. Good luck with your goals. I don't love my wife as I'm supposed to, but I love her in my own way. To my knowledge, she doesn't adore me either, but we are content with our individual schedules and our lives together, and proud of our odd system.

We tried for a while to love each other normally, urged by her brother to subject ourselves to counseling as a decent couple would. Barry, her brother, is a man of the couch, a believer in therapy, affirmations and pulse points. Once, he tried to show us exercises he'd been doing in session with his new woman friend. He instructed us to trade reasons, abstract or specific, for why we stayed with one another. I started off by saying that she would get really drunk and pretend I was someone else and do this really neat thing with her tongue. Joanie said tax breaks. Barry cried. Openly. Joanie and Barry's parents are divorced and Barry's second wife recently left him for a guy who understood that a man didn't do volunteer work. Barry wanted us to reflect on bonds and promises and love and such. He was tired of things breaking apart. Tired of people resigning so easily. We tried for Barry, but our marriage seemed to work only when we didn't try at all.

The lady with the make-up (Tia? Tara? Someone who modeled with Joanie?) stops her dabbing and looks at Scottie. The light hits this woman's face giving me opportunity to see that she should perhaps be working on her own make-up. The color of her face, a manila envelope. Specks of white in her eyebrows. Concealer not concealing. I can tell my daughter doesn't know what to do with the woman's stare.

"What?" Scottie asks.

"I think your mother was enjoying the view," Tia, or Tara, says.

I jump in to protect my silent daughter.

"Listen here, T. Her mother was not enjoying the view. Her mother is in a coma."

"My name is not T," T says. "My name is Allison."

"Okay then, listen here, Ali. Don't confuse my daughter."

"I'm turning into a remarkable young lady," Scottie says.

"Damn straight," I say.

This Ali person gets back to business. Scottie turns on the television again. Another dating show.

I'm running out of toys. I can usually find a toy in anything. A spoon, a sugar packet, a quarter. Our first week here, I made up this game: who could get the most slices of banana stuck to the ceiling. You had to put a piece on a napkin and then try to trampoline it up there. Scottie loved it. Nurses got involved. Even the neurologist gave it a go. But now, nearing the end of our fourth week here, I'm running out of tricks. The neurologist says my wife's scores are lower on the various coma scales. The nurse says things, uses language I don't understand, and yet I understand her—I know what she's telling me.

"Last time you were the one on the bed," Scottie says.

"Yup."

"Last time you lied to me."

"I know, Scottie. Forgive me." My motorcycling accident. I had insisted I was okay, that I wasn't going to go to the hospital. Scottie had issued me these little tests to show my unreliability. Joanie participated. They played bad cop, worse cop.

"How many fingers?" Scottie had asked, holding up what I thought was a pinky and a thumb: a *shaka*.

"Balls," I had said, not wanting to be tested that way.

"Answer her," Joanie had said.

"Two?"

"Okay," Scottie said warily. "Close your eyes and touch your nose and stand on one foot."

"Balls, Scottie. I can't do that regardless, and you're treating me like a drunk driver."

"Do what she says," Joanie yelled.

I had stood still in protest. I knew something was wrong with me, but I didn't want to go to the hospital. I wanted to let what was wrong with my body run its course. I was curious. I was having trouble holding up my head.

"Look at yourself," Joanie said. "You can't even see straight."

"How am I supposed to look at myself, then?"

"Shut up, Matthew. Get in the car."

I had damaged my fourth nerve, a nerve that connects your eyes to your brain, which explained why things had been out of focus.

"You could have died," Scottie says. She's watching Allison brush color onto Joanie's cheeks.

"No way," I say. "A fourth nerve? Who needs it?"

"You lied. You said you were okay. You said you could see my fingers."

"I didn't lie. I guessed correctly. Plus, for a while there I got to have twins. Two Scotties."

Scottie nods. "Well. Okay."

I'm wondering what my accident has to do with anything. Lately, she's been pointing out my flaws, my tricks and lies. She's interviewing me. I'm the back-up candidate, the dad. I remember when I was in the hospital Joanie put vodka into my Jell-O. She wore my eye patch and teased me and stayed with me. It was very nice.

Scottie touches her mother's hair, which looks slippery. It looks the way it did when she gave birth to Scottie and our other daughter, Alexandra. Allison is now looking at me as if I'm disturbed. "You have an odd way of speaking to children," she says.

"Parents shouldn't have to compromise their personalities," Scottie says.

It's something I've heard Joanie say. I catch a glimpse of my wife's face. She looks so lovely. Not ravishing, but simply lovely. Her freckles rise through the blush, her closed eyes fastened by dark, dramatic lashes. These lashes are the only strong feature left on her face. Everything has been softened. She looks pretty, but perhaps too divine; too bone-china white, as if she's underwater or cased in glass. Oddly, the effect makes me like all the things I usually don't like about her. I like that she forgets to wash the lettuce and our salads are always pebbly. Or sometimes we go to this restaurant that's touristy, but the fish is great, and without fail she ends up at the bar with these Floridian spring-break sorts for a drink or ten and I'm left at the table all alone. I usually don't enjoy this, but now I don't mind so much. I like her magnetism. I like her courage and ego. But maybe I only like these things because she may not wake up again. It's confusing.

The manager of that restaurant once thanked me. He said that she always livened up the place and made people want to drink. I'm sure if she died, he'd put her picture up because it's that kind of restaurant—pictures of local legends and dead patrons haunting the walls. I feel sad that she has to die for her picture to go up on the wall, or for me to really love everything about her.

"Allison," I say. "Thank you. I'm sure Joanie is so pleased."

"She's not pleased. She's in a coma," Allison says.

I'm speechless.

"Oh my god," Allison says and starts to cry. "I can't believe I said that. I was just trying to get you back."

She leaves the room with her beauty tools.

"Oh mercy," I say. "I need to change some habits. I'm an ass."

"You're my dad," Scottie says.

"Yes," I say. "Yes."

"You're a dad-ass. Like a bad-ass but older."

"Mercy," I say.

Scottie wants me to step into the waiting room with her. She has something to tell me. It's a routine we have. She's afraid of speaking to her mother. She's embarrassed of her life. A ten-year-old, worried that her life isn't interesting enough. She thinks that if she speaks to her mother, she should have something incredible to say. I always urge her to talk about school or the dogs, but Scottie says that this would be boring, and she wouldn't want her mother to think she was a walking yawn. For the past few weeks or so, Scottie has been trying to have these worthy experiences after school at our beach club.

"Ok, Scottie," I say. "Today's the day. You're going to talk to Mom. You can read an article, you can sing a song, or tell her what you learned in school. Right-o?"

"Okay, but I have a story."

"Talk to me."

She smiles. "Okay, pretend you're Mom. Close your eyes."

I close my eyes.

"Hi, Mom. Yesterday I explored the reef in front of the public beach by myself. I have tons of friends, but I felt like being alone. I've seen this really cute guy who works the beach stand there. His eyes look like giraffe eyes."

I'm trying not to smile.

"The tide was low. I could see all sorts of things. In one place the coral was a really cool dark color, but then I looked closer and it wasn't the coral. It was an eel. A moray. I almost died. There were millions of sea urchins and a few sea cucumbers. I even picked one up and squeezed him."

"This is good, Scottie. Let's go back in. Mom will love this."

"I'm not done."

"Oh." I close my eyes again.

"I was squatting on the reef and lost my balance and fell back on my hands. One of my hands landed on an urchin and it put its spines in me. My hand looked like a pincushion."

I grab her hands, hold them up to my face. The roots of urchin spines have locked in and expanded under the skin of her left palm. They look like tiny black starfish that plan on making this hand their home forever. I notice more stars on her fingertips. "Why didn't you tell me you were hurt? Why didn't you say something?"

"I'm okay. I handled it. I didn't really fall."

"What do you mean? Are these pen marks?"

"Yes."

I look closer. I feel her palm and press on the marks.

"Ow," she says and pulls her hand back. "Just kidding," she says. "They're real. But I didn't really fall. I did it on purpose. I slammed my hand into an urchin. But I'm not telling Mom that part."

"What?" I can't imagine Scottie feeling such terrible pain. "Why would you do this? Scottie?"

"For a story, I guess."

"But Christ, didn't it hurt?"

"Yes."

"Balls, Scottie. I'm floored right now. Completely floored."

"Do you want to hear the rest?" she asks.

I push my short fingernails into my palm just to try to get a taste of the sting she felt. I shake my head. "I guess. Go on."

"Okay. Pretend you're Mom. You can't interrupt."

"I can't believe you'd do that."

"You can't speak! Be quiet or you won't hear the rest."

Scottie talks about the blood, the needles jutting from her hand, how she climbed back on to the rock pier like a crab with a missing claw. Before she returned to shore, Scottie describes how she looked out across the ocean and watched the swimmers do laps around the catamarans. She says that the ones with white swimming caps looked like runaway buoys.

Of course, she didn't see any of this. Pain makes you focused. She probably ran right to the club's medic. She's making up the details, making a better story for her mother, to get some attention from Joanie. Or perhaps to take attention away from Joanie.

"Because of Dad's boring ocean lectures, I knew these weren't needles in my hand but more like sharp bones—calcitic plates, which vinegar would help dissolve."

I smile. *Good girl*, I think.

"Dad, this isn't boring, is it?"

"Boring is not the word I'd use."

"Okay. You're Mom again. So I thought of going to the club's first-aid."

"Good girl."

"Shh," she says. "But instead, I went to the cute boy and asked him to pee on my hand."

"Excuse me?"

"Yes, Mom. That's exactly what I said to him. Excuse me, I told him, I hurt myself. He said, Uh-oh. You okay? Like I was an eight-year-old. He didn't understand so I placed my hand on the counter. He said a bunch of swear words then told me to go to the hospital or something. Or are you a member of that club? he asked. He told me he'd take me there, which was really nice of him. He went out through the back of his stand and I went around to meet him. I told him what he needed to do and he blinked a thousand times and used curse words in all sorts of combinations. He wondered if you were supposed to suck out the poison after you pulled out the needles, and if I was going to go into seizures. He told me he wasn't trained for this, and that there was no way he'd pee on my hand, but I told him what you always tell Dad when you want him to do something he doesn't want to do. I said, Stop being a pussy, and it did the trick. He told me not to look and to say something, or whistle."

"Scottie," I say. "Tell me you've made this up."

"I'm almost done," she whines. "So I talked about the records you had beaten in your boat. And that you were a model, but you weren't all prissy, and that every guy at the club was in love with you but you only love Dad because he's easy, like the easy chair he sits on all the time."

"Scottie. I have to use the bathroom." I feel sick.

"Okay," she says. "Wasn't that a hilarious story? Was it too long?"

"Yes and no. I have to go to the bathroom. Tell your mom what you told me. Go talk to her." She can't hear you anyway, I think. I hope.

Joanie would think that story was hilarious. This bothers me. The story bothers me. Scottie shouldn't have to create these dramas. Scottie shouldn't have to be pissed on. She's reminding me of her sister, someone I don't ever want her to become. Alex. Seventeen. She's like a special effect. It wows you. It alarms you, but then it gets tiresome and you forget about it. I need to call Alex and update her. She's at boarding school on another island, not too far away but far enough. The last time I called, I asked her what was wrong and she said, "The price of cocaine." I laughed, asked "Seriously, what else?" "Is there anything else?" she said.

She's very well known over at Hawaii's Board of Tourism. At fifteen, she did calendars and work for Isle Cards whose captions said things like *Life's a Damn Hot Beach*. One-pieces became string bikinis. String bikinis became thongs and then just shells and granules of sand strategically placed on her body. The rest of her antics are so outrageous and absurd, it's boring to think about. In her struggle to be unique, she has become common: the rebellious, privileged teen. Car chase, explosion, gone and forgotten.

Despite everything, her childishness, her utter wrongness, Alex makes me feel so guilty. Guilty because I catch myself believing that if Joanie were to die, we'd all make it. We'd flourish. We'd trust and love each other. Alex could come home. We used to love each other so much. I don't call her even though I need to tell her to fly down tomorrow. I can't bear to hear any accidental pitch of joy or release that may slink into her voice or my own.

*

Scottie sits on the bed. Joanie looks like Sleeping Beauty.

"Did you tell her?" I ask.

"I'm going to work on it some more," Scottie says. "Because if Mom thinks it's funny, what will she do? What if the laugh circulates around in her lungs or in her brain somewhere since it can't come out? What if it kills her?"

"It doesn't work that way," although I have no idea how it works.

"Yes, but I just thought I'd make it more tragic, that way she'll feel the need to come back."

"It shouldn't be this complicated, Scottie." I say this sternly. I sit on the bed and put my ear to where Joanie's heart is. I bury my face in her gown. This is the most intimate I've been with her in a long time. My wife, the speedboat record holder. My wife, the motorcyclist, the model, the long-distance paddler, the tri-athlete. *What drives you Joanie?* I say into her chest. I realize I've copied one of her hobbies and wonder what drives me as well. I don't even like motorcycles. I hate the sound they make.

"I miss Mom's sneezes," Scottie says.

I laugh. I shake with laughter. I laugh so hard it's soundless and this makes Scottie laugh. Whenever Joanie sneezes, she farts. She can't help it. This is why we are hysterical. A nurse comes in and opens the curtain. She smiles at us. "You two," she says. She urges us to go outside and enjoy the rest of the day.

Scottie agrees. She looks at her wristwatch and immediately settles down. "Crap, Dad. We need to go. I need a new story."

Because the nurse is in the room I say, "Watch your language."

*

At the beach club, the shrubs are covered with surfboards. There has been a south swell, but the waves are blown out from the strong wind. I follow Scottie into the dining room. She tells me that she can't leave until something amusing or tragic happens to her. I tell her I'm skipping paddling practice and am not letting her out of my sight. This infuriates her. I tell her I'll stay out of her way, but I'm not going to practice. Pretend I'm not there.

"Fine, then sit over there." She points to tables on the perimeter of the dining room. A few ladies are playing cards at one of these tables. I like these ladies. They're around eighty years old and they wear tennis skirts even though I can't imagine they still play tennis. I wish Joanie liked to play cards and sit around.

Scottie heads to the bar. The bartender, Jerry, nods at me. I watch Scottie climb onto a barstool and Jerry makes her a virgin daiquiri, then lets her try out a few of his own concoctions. "The guava one is divine," I hear her say, "but lime makes me feverish."

I pretend to read the paper that I borrowed from one of the ladies and move to a table that's a little closer to the bar so I can listen and watch.

"How's your mom?" Jerry asks.

"Still sleeping." Scottie twists atop her barstool. Her legs don't reach the metal footrest so she crosses them on the seat and balances.

"Well, You tell her I say hi. You tell her we're all waiting for her."

I watch Scottie as she considers this. She stares at her lap. "I don't talk to her," she says to Jerry, though she doesn't look at him.

Jerry sprays a swirl of whipped cream into her drink. She takes a gulp of her daiquiri then rubs her head. She does it again. She spins around on the barstool. And then she begins to speak in a manner that troubles me. She is yelling as if there's some sort of din in the room that she needs to overcome.

"Everybody loves me, but my husband hates me, guess I'll have to eat the worm. Give me a shot of Cuervo Gold, Jerry baby."

Jerry cleans the bottles of liquor, trying to make noise.

How often did Joanie say this? Was it her standard way of asking for tequila? It makes me wonder how we managed to spend so much time at this place and never see each other at all.

"Give me two of everything," Scottie yells, caught in her fantasy. I want to relieve Jerry of his obvious discomfort, but then I see Troy walking towards the bar. Big, magnanimous, golden Troy. I quickly hide behind my newspaper. My daughter is suddenly silent. Troy has killed her buzz. I'm sure he hesitated when he saw her, but it's too late to turn around.

"Hey, Scottie," I hear him say. "Look at you."

"Look at you," she says, and her voice sounds strange. Almost unrecognizable. "You look awake," she says.

"Uh, thanks, Scottie."

Uh, thanks, Scottie. Troy is so slow. His great grandfather invented the shopping cart and this has left little for Troy to do except sleep with lots of women and put my wife in a coma. Of course, it's not his fault, but he wasn't hurt. He was the driver and Joanie was the throttle-man because Troy insisted he wanted to drive this time. Rounding a mile marker, their boat launched off a wave, spun out and Joanie was ejected. When Troy came in from the race alone he kept saying, "Lots of chop and holes. Lots of chop and holes."

"Have you visited her?" Scottie asks.

"Yes I have, Scottie. Your dad was there."

"What did you say to her?"

"I told her the boat was in good shape. I said it was ready for her."

What a Neanderthal.

"Her hand moved, Scottie. I really think she heard me. I really think she's going to be okay."

Troy isn't wearing a shirt. The man has muscles I didn't even know existed. I wonder if Joanie has slept with him. Of course she has. His eyes are the color of swimming pools. I'm about to lower the paper so he'll stop talking to Scottie until I hear her say, "The body has natural reactions. When you cut off a chicken's head, its body runs around, but it's still a dead chicken."

I hear either Troy or Jerry coughing.

"Don't give up, Scottie," Jerry says.

Golden Troy is saying something about life and lemons and bootstraps. He is probably placing one of his massive tan paws on Scottie's shoulder.

I see Scottie leaving the dining room. I follow her. She runs to the beach wall and I catch her before she jumps off of it. Tears are brewing in her eyes. She looks up to keep them from falling, but they fall anyway.

"I didn't mean to say dead chicken," she cries.

"Let's go home," I say.

"Why is everyone so into sports here? You and Mom and Troy think you're so cool. Everyone here does. Why don't you join a book club? Why can't Mom just relax at home?"

I hold her and she lets me. I try to think if I have any friends in a book club. I realize I don't know anyone, man or woman, who isn't a member of this club. I don't know a man who doesn't surf, kayak or paddleboard. I don't know a woman who doesn't jog, sail or canoe paddle, although Joanie is the only woman I know racing bikes and boats.

"I don't want Mom to die," Scottie says.

"Of course you don't." I push her away from me and bend down to look in her freckled brown eyes. "Of course."

"I don't want her to die like this," Scottie says. "Racing or competing or doing something marvelous. I've heard her say, 'I'm going out with a bang.' Well, I hope she goes out choking on a kernel of corn or slipping on a piece of toilet paper."

"Christ, Scottie. How old are you? Where do you get this shit? Let's go home," I say. "You don't mean any of this. You need to rest." I imagine my wife peaceful on her bed. I wonder what she was thinking as she flew off the boat. If she knew it was over. I wonder how long it took Troy to notice she wasn't there beside him. Scottie's face is puffy. Her hair is greasy. It needs to be washed. She has this look of disgust on her face. It's a very adult look.

"Your mother thinks you're so great," I say. "She thinks you're the prettiest, smartest, silliest girl in town."

"She thinks I'm a coward."

"No she doesn't. Why would she think that?"

"I didn't want to go on the boat with her and she said I was a scaredy cat like you."

"She was just joking. She thinks you're the bravest girl in town. She told me it scared her how brave you were."

"Really?"

"Damn straight." It's a lie. Joanie often said that we're raising two little scaredy cats, but of all the lies I tell, this one is necessary. I don't want Scottie to hate her mother as Alexandra once did, and maybe still does. It will consume her and age her. It will make her fear the world. It will make her too shy and too nervous to ever say exactly what she means.

"I'm going swimming," Scottie says.

"No," I say. "We've had enough."

"Dad, please." She pulls me down by my neck and whispers, "I don't want people to see I've been crying. Let me get in the water."

"Fine. I'll be here." She strips off her clothes and throws them at me, then jumps off the wall to the beach below and charges towards the water. She dives in and breaks surface after what seems like a minute. She dives. She splashes. She plays. I sit on the coral wall and watch her and the other kids and their mothers and nannies. To my left is a small reef. I can see black urchins settled in the fractures. I still can't believe Scottie did such a thing.

The outside dining terrace is filling up with people and their pink and red and white icy drinks. An old man is walking out of the ocean with a one-man canoe held over his head, a tired yet elated smile quivering on his face as if he's just returned from some kind of battle in the deep sea.

The torches are being lit on the terrace and on the rock pier. The soaring sun has turned into a wavy blob above the horizon. It's almost green flash time. Not quite yet, but soon. When the sun disappears behind the horizon, sometimes there's a green flash of light that sparkles seemingly out of the sea. It's a communal activity around here, waiting for this green flash, hoping to catch it.

Children are coming out of the water.

I hear a mother's voice drifting off the ocean. It's far away yet loud. "Get in here, little girl. They're everywhere."

Scottie is the only child still swimming. I jump off the wall. "Scottie!" I yell. "Scottie get in here right now!"

"There are Portuguese man-o-wars out there," a woman says to me. "The swell must have pushed them in. Is she yours?" The woman points to Scottie who is swimming in from the catamarans.

"Yes," I say.

My daughter comes in. She's holding a tiny man-of-war—the clot of its body and the clear blue bubble on her hand, its dark blue string tail wrapped around her wrist.

"What have you done? Why are you doing this?" I take the man-of-war off of her with a stick; pop its bubble so that it won't hurt anybody. My daughter's arm is marked with a red line. I tell her to rinse her arm off with seawater. She says it's not just her arm that's hurt—she was swimming amongst a mass of them.

"Why would you stay out there, Scottie? How could you tolerate that?" I've been stung by them hundreds of times; it's not so bad, but kids are supposed to cry when they get stung. It's something you can always count on.

"I thought it would be funny to say I was attacked by a herd of minor wars."

"It's not minor war. You know that, don't you?" When she was little I would point out sea creatures to her but I'd give them the wrong names. I called them minor wars because they were like tiny soldiers with impressive weapons—the gaseous bubble, the whip-like tail, the toxic tentacles, advancing in swarms. I called a blowfish a blow-pop; an urchin, an ocean porcupine, and sea turtles were saltwater hard-hats. I thought it was funny, but now I'm worried that she doesn't know the truth about things.

"Of course, I know," Scottie says. "They're man-o-wars, but it's our joke. Mom will like it."

"It's not man-o-war either. It's man-of-war. Portuguese man-of-war. That's the proper name."

"Oh," she says.

She scratches herself. More lines form on her chest and legs. I tell her I'm not happy and that we need to get home and put some ointments and ice on the stings. "Vinegar will make it worse, so if you thought giraffe boy could pee on you, you're out of luck."

She agrees as if she was prepared for this—the punishment, the medication, the swelling, the pain that hurts her now and the pain that will hurt her later. But she's happy to deal with my disapproval. She's gotten her story, and she's beginning to see how much easier physical pain is to tolerate. I'm unhappy that she's learning this at ten years old.

We walk up the sandy slope towards the dining terrace. I see Troy sitting at a table with some people I know. I look at Scottie to see if she sees him and she is giving him the middle finger. The dining terrace gasps, but I realize it's because of the sunset and the green flash. We missed it. The flash flashed. The sun is gone. The sky is pink and violent like arguing little girls. I reach to grab the offending hand, but instead I correct her gesture.

"Here, Scottie. Don't let that finger stand by itself like that. Bring up the other fingers just a little bit. There you go."

Troy stares at us and smiles a bit, looking completely confused.

"All right, that's enough," I say, suddenly feeling sorry for Troy. He may really love Joanie. There is that chance. I place my hand on Scottie's back to guide her away. She flinches and I remove my hand, remembering that she's hurt all over.

*

We are at the hospital again even though it's late at night. Scottie insisted on it. She practically had a tantrum. "I'll forget the exact sensations that I need to tell Mom!" she had screamed.

She still hasn't showered. I wanted the salt water to stay on her. It's good for the wounds. She cried on the way over here, cried and scratched at herself. Her stings are now raised red lesions. A nurse gave them attention. She gave her some antibiotics as well. Scottie has a runny nose; she's dizzy and nauseous though she won't admit it's from swimming with poisonous invertebrates. She's miserable, but I have a feeling she won't do anything like this again. The nurse shaved her legs to get rid of any remaining nematocyst. Now Scottie is admiring her smooth, woman legs.

"I'm going to start doing this all the time," she says. "It'll be such a hassle."

"No, you're not," I say. I say it loudly, surprising both of us. "You're not ready." She smiles, uncomfortable with my authority. So this is what it's like.

We're going to stay the night. I'm sitting on the end of the bed putting eye drops in my eyes. We don't even look like visitors. We look like patients, defeated, exhausted from the world outside. We came in for shelter and care and a little rest, the staff here being so kind and lenient. It's nine-o-clock in the ICU. We walked in unannounced and Scottie received free medical attention. This can't be standard practice. It means it's over. Their indulgence is because they have no hope for us, or they've been advised by Dr. Johnston to scratch hope off of their charts. People become so kind right before and after someone dies.

Scottie opens the curtain and lets the night in—dark palm trees and the lights of other buildings. She asks me if she hurt the urchin as much as the urchin hurt her. She asks me why everyone else calls them man-o-wars. I tell her I don't know, in reply to the first question. I don't know how that works. For the second question I answer, "Words get abbreviated and we forget the origins of things."

"Or fathers lie," she says, "about the real names."

"That too."

She climbs up on the bed and we look at Joanie in the half-moon light. Scottie leans back against my chest, her forehead beneath my chin. I move my head around and nuzzle her. I don't talk about what we need to talk about.

"Why is it called a jellyfish?" Scottie asks. "It's not a fish and it's not jelly."

I say that a man-of-war isn't a jellyfish. I don't answer the question, but I tell her that she asks good questions. "You're getting too smart for me, Scottie."

I can feel her smiling. Even Joanie seems to be smiling, slightly. I feel happy, though I'm not supposed to, I guess. But the room feels good. It feels peaceful.

"Water," I say. "And blankets." I leave the room to get water and blankets.

When I come back towards the room, I hear Scottie say, "I have a remarkable eye." I stop in the doorway. Scottie is talking to her mother. I watch.

She is curled into her mother's side and has maneuvered Joanie's arm so that it's around her. "It's on the ceiling," I hear her say. "The most beautiful nest. It's very golden and soft-looking and warm, of course."

I see it too, except it isn't a nest. It's a browning banana, the remnant of our old game still stuck to the ceiling.

Scottie props herself onto an elbow, then leans in and kisses her mother on the lips, checks her face, then kisses her again. She does this over and over; this exquisite version of mouth to mouth, each kiss expectant, almost medicinal.

I let her go on with this fantasy, this belief in magical endings, this belief that love can bring someone to life. I let her try. For a long time, I watch her effort. I root for her even, but after awhile I know that it's time. I need to step in. I tap lightly on the door. I don't want to startle her too badly.

Sinners

Joan Corwin

To the surprise of everyone who knew of his condition in the months after the Great Wisconsin Fire of 1871, the Reverend Michael Chaston lived to a very old age. Those who became his neighbors after the event credited his recovery to the care he was given by the daughter he had saved from that terrible conflagration. Amy Chaston, they said, was fortunate to have been disfigured hardly at all by the fire: most of her hair grew back, and women of her own age observed that where it did not, the knot of pink tissue could have been disguised with some effort. But she never tried, even though she was pretty and men were always interested in her, drawn by her quiet devotion to her father. She limped clumsily, it was true, from something the cold had done to her in the water where her father had fought his pain to hold her for five and a half hours while the village of Peshtigo, on both sides of the river, burned to the ground. If she was in pain, she never complained, though Michael Chaston required her constant attendance.

The two were never seen to speak together, but appeared always to have a perfect understanding, and they must have been, people said, a great comfort to each other, for they had lost a dear wife and mother, Mariah, in the fire.

*

The air had been smoldering for weeks. Mostly the ash was too fine to really see, but sometimes it fell in flakes like snow, and the irony of this was not lost on the residents of Peshtigo, who had stopped scouring the cloudless sky and resolutely went about their days with set faces. Spot fires had erupted close to the town for a few days before October 8th, and the villagers were proud of the way they extinguished these fires with water from barrels and tubs placed at street corners; they even patrolled the swampy area to the west of town, where the peat smoldered as much as three feet below the surface and underbrush seemed to leap up to meet the occasional falling sparks brought on by gusts of wind from the southwest forests, which had been burning since mid-September.

So while the mood in town was tense and sometimes depressed, there was a generally held faith in the ingenuity of mankind, a vague confidence that with such efforts as those of the company men and the householders, this season of danger would pass without molesting Peshtigo's inhabitants. The explosive growth of the mill in the years since the war had encouraged an attitude of prideful optimism almost everywhere. An exception was the Reverend Michael Chaston's household, where the silent doom-saying of the Reverend's cold glare quashed all hopes, even those inspired by a recent forecast of coming rains.

Earlier that September, when the air had started to taste of char, the Reverend began reading Milton to his wife Mariah and twelve-year-old daughter Amy—the verses on Satan's humiliation. He read them over and over as though Amy and her mother were resisting him. He read them while Amy's mother grew weary and until Amy began to worry that the poet's meaning must be more subtle than it appeared and that she was too stupid or too compromised to understand. But just when she began to be really anxious for her soul, the close hot air, the desiccating taste of it, wore out even her father. He subjected them to the poem more and more listlessly and less and less frequently. By October 8th the readings had stopped.

Only a few townspeople besides those who were members of her father's congregation saw the hand of God in the local forest fires. Amy envied those who were without sin and—though she knew this was wrong—those who were benighted in the heresy of other faiths or in faithlessness itself. They did not suffer, as she did, as her father exhorted his congregation to suffer, the guilt of one's own complicity in the drought and the fires. This was nothing new: a sense of sin had attended her for most of her twelve years. It was always associated with her father and his omniscience in such matters. Amy believed that her father knew all her sins, but it was also her belief—based on his disdainful refusal to discuss them with her—that he expected her to recognize them herself. He had not actually said so, but he implied, whether he was excoriating his flock or leading Amy and her mother in grace before their undeserved bounty, that not to detect her own sin was to ensure her captivity to it.

Amy's father had turned thirty-eight that year. He was brittle and thin and had icy blue eyes that snapped, like ill-tempered dogs, with disapproval. Widowed Grandmother Chaston, who had lived with them until her heart stopped in 1868, had often told how even as a boy in Boston, as little as three and four years old, the Reverend would snap his eyes at other children and at those adults whose jolly mannerisms offended him. Grandmother Chaston told a story about a family friend, a Mr. Burling, an importer who had come drunk for dinner one evening to the Boston house, where wine was never served, and could not be dissuaded from sharing improper and gossipy stories which he found so amusing himself that he shook the water glasses with his laughter. Awakened from his bed by this guest's hilarity, seven-year-old Michael Chaston entered the dining room to witness the businessman erupting with red and humid face, a spectacle which elicited such a snap of the boy's cold blue eyes that Burling was immediately deflated and made his departure in a state of cringing apology.

For some few years before she was able to detect the self-congratulation in her grandmother's account of Mr. Burling's defeat, Amy naively imagined herself into the scene, where she would leave the Chaston table hand-in-hand with their jovial guest, accompanying him to his home, a comfortable home, she assumed, with a fire always made up, and port and cordials for gentleman and lady visitors respectively, and brandied fruits in footed glasses for the children—things her mother had described to her from a different kind of childhood. She would choose from a variety of candies which she had never tasted but had glimpsed in shops and in the hands of other children, and sit on the hearthrug warmly attentive while Mr. Burling, whom she saw in her mind as fat and plush, finished his funny stories. She did not know how to snap her eyes, which like her mother's were a golden hazel and turned down at the outer corners, giving her a constant air of sympathy. So, confident that she could not embarrass him as her father had, Amy imagined herself gazing fondly on Mr. Burling, touching his fat hand with her own baby one, kindling more and more of the warm humor that animated him.

But before she was six years old, Amy sensed that her fantasy was a voluptuous self-indulgence, and she felt she shared the shame with that ebullient guest who had been so effectively humbled by the juvenile Reverend. From that moment, Amy was continuously haunted by her sense of sin.

It was not this particular sin—her yearning for the jovial man's company, for his rich and careless life—which had ignited the forest fires, she was sure. It was not any of the small sins (as she was acute enough to rate them) in which she had indulged, or it might be more accurate to say, into which she had slipped, since her awakening to guilt. Even an accumulation of these, even the times she had shared something with her mother from which her father was by nature excluded, something sweet or gay, a touch, an idea, a joke, for a fraction of a moment—all of these together were not serious enough to warrant a plague out of Egypt as her father described the stifling smoke, the pestilential fires. Small treacheries they were, of God and Reverend, but they were not hot, not searing as real sin.

Amy might never have found out how she caused the Peshtigo fire if the big man Daniel Spence had not come to town that October afternoon.

There had been signs that something was going to happen. Infant fires blazed and died or were smothered by townspeople armed with wet blankets on the roads leading to and in the environs of the town. A haze of smoke hovered permanently along the streets. Open windows invited a layer of ash to settle like a dirty sheet over furniture and floors. Some young children became confused in the altered streets and alleys and temporarily lost their way. Then at last, where the Oconto Road entered the town from the southwest, smoke began accumulating like a thick fog, obscuring the traffic. Amy, though privately anxious, accompanied the neighbor children to the edge of town to watch the atmosphere thicken. They held hands in a line so that not one would be lost. Spanning the street like a chain of paper lanterns, they saw Daniel Spence emerging from the smoke—a *jinn* from a cloud.

Travelers were arriving in a steady stream, many from farms and cabins in the woodlands from which the persistent fires had finally driven them to the village for refuge. Most of these, men and women both, had wrapped kerchiefs and shawls around their faces, and the children lay low in the wagons with their arms around their heads, and still they could be heard choking. But Daniel Spence merely breathed in and out, making smoke eddies whirl around his nostrils. Ash clung to his auburn hair and beard. Very tall and broad and full, he was flushed and perspiring heavily as he strode forward, and when he wiped the sleeve of his coarse red shirt across his steaming face, he left streaks of black ash. He seemed like the very source of fire, like a radiant iron oven spewing smoke. All of the children dropped hands and gaped at him. Even some bowed and harassed adult inhabitants paused curiously. The big man looked hot enough to burn the hand of anyone who touched him.

Confronted with the broken chain of stupefied children, Daniel Spence exploded in laughter. They scattered, terrified, leaving only Amy, inside of whom the man's mirth had urged a small warmth, an embrous glow just reminiscent of the blaze of Mr. Burling's enjoyment. She smiled back. The big man opened bloodshot eyes very wide as he pushed toward her and lifted her off her feet in an embrace.

"You. I'd never know which was you if you had not made them golden eyes to shine."

It alarmed Amy to meet Daniel Spence for the first time in this way, and she might have struggled, she might have kicked the big man until he let her go, thereby changing the history of Peshtigo and her family, but before she could make any move at all, Daniel Spence did something that dissolved her. He buried his nose in her neck and cooed, "Let me breathe you in. Just let me breathe you in," inhaling deeply. "Yes," he murmured, "Mariah's girl."

With that, the flame in Amy changed to something, not wholly unfamiliar, but rare and intensely pleasing, so that when Daniel Spence pulled back to look at her eyes again, she clung to him tightly and he could not put her down.

His own eyes were liquid brown, and red-rimmed with heat.

For Daniel Spence, whom Amy loved immediately, she delivered a message to her mother without her father's knowledge. The big man had asked her that specifically—not to tell her father, the

Reverend Michael Chaston, either that Daniel Spence was in town, or that he was sending a message to her mother.

*

She came on them arguing in the Reverend's study. Mariah Chaston was standing with a hand resting lightly on the door-handle, her eyes slightly averted. Nor did the Reverend look directly at his wife, but he stood, rather than sitting, at his desk, with a finger poised on that part of his reading where he had left off at the interruption. They appeared to be talking past one another—to other invisible and formal associates at opposite corners of the same room.

They argued quietly. The Reverend never raised his voice, but Amy's mother spoke with so little passion that an outsider would have thought she lacked conviction and that it was Amy's father who won. And it was almost always true that Mariah would pray when the Reverend said pray, and be silent when he wished it, but the same argument, quiet and steady and unaltered in its rhythm and progress would arise again as though the idea had never been discussed between them. It made him tired, said her father. Her mother would fall silent and wait until the identical quarrel could be coaxed from circumstance again.

This was an old argument, and petty. It concerned the Reverend's collar, which was always stiffly starched and raised a rash around his neck. The only time the Chastons' quarrels had ever approached violence was when Amy's mother referred to the collar as the Reverend's cross, his attempt to emulate Jesus. Then he had flushed, a phenomenon never witnessed before by Amy. In fact, until that moment she had not thought of her father as containing blood. Could it be that she had never seen him bleed? Not even once when he had shaved to the faint blue line of his jaw? No, he never bled, and no veins pulsed in him that she could discern, and he was pale as a dead man, even in summer, since he shunned the enthusiasm of the sunny day. It was only in this moment of anger that suddenly he appeared to her as something other than the Reverend. Her mother fell back a step and apologized, but even young Amy sensed that her father had lost something in the moment when his color changed.

At this time during the fires, with the extreme heat of the air, the Reverend felt compelled to change his collar several times in a day, in spite of the increasing discomfort of freshly starched linen against skin. He could not bear to have it sag limp and sensual, against his neck. "It must be cool and firm," was his stern pronouncement, and as soon as one was discarded and replaced, it was sent directly to the laundress to be restored to the cleanliness and rigidity he demanded. For the past several days the collars had been stimulating a thick angry welt like a noose burn around the Reverend's neck. The eighth being Sunday, with no one at work, Mariah had supposed that once he ran through his stock of collars, he would have to be satisfied. But she had just discovered a store of crisp new collars, which he had laid in for the Sabbath earlier that week.

So now the argument resumed, though Amy's mother was careful with her words.

The Reverend was for propriety. "I will not be thought slovenly for the sake of my own comfort," he insisted tensely, through his teeth. The welt, a sign of his unflinching standards, was also proof of his capacity for suffering. "It is an example to my congregation."

"It is a reproof to your laundress," retorted Amy's mother, but quietly, as she moved from the room, so that the flush which had alarmed her daughter and herself would not reappear. The Reverend reacted little, but watched his wife narrowly and obliquely as she left him, followed by his daughter. His lips made a thin and horizontal line.

Amy was relieved at his self-restraint: she did not wish to see her father's blood rise to his pallid face when she knew she had a message to deliver to her mother that was a secret from him.

It was a measure of Mariah's dissatisfaction with her husband that, although it was the Sabbath and a sin to perform labor, she had gone directly from his study to her sewing-room to pick stitches from a worn dress which she was dismembering for scraps. The room, situated as it was over the kitchen, was stifling, but still she had had to light the lamp and pull it close to her because so few rays of the afternoon sun were able to penetrate the ash-laden air outside her window. She sat at the treadle-table with the dress in her lap. Her hair drooped from its pins and hung limply in places, and since leaving her husband's study she had unhooked her collar buttons. Her lips were slightly parted as she worked, and tiny rivulets of perspiration made tracks down her temples. She looked up when Amy entered, and absently rubbed her neck.

*

At that evening hour when she should have been renewing in prayer her covenant with God, Amy met Daniel Spence where she had left him, at the very spot of their embrace on the edge of town. It was harder to find than before. There were only a few people feeling their way in the searing air, and they were becoming difficult to distinguish.

When he had read the note, Daniel Spence threw his arms out wide and his head back and howled, "Oh, yes, and oh, yes, and oh, yes, my darling!"

She wanted him to hold her again, but he took a match from his breast pocket and struck it against his shoe. When the letter caught, a passerby clucked her tongue at this display of carelessness. He dropped the burning paper and waited until it was consumed before stamping and scattering the ashes. Then he took her hand.

"I got some time to kill, Amy Chaston, and I want you with me."

They ran across the charred south firebreak toward the forest. The ground was hot. There were only a few stumps, but the smoldering roots sent smoke into the air. For a month now, it had been hard to tell when the sun was setting, an event that had been losing its visual drama as the increasing smoke softened the contrast between day and night. The haze must have lifted this night and the time must have been earlier than she thought, because there was still a glow in the west, enough to make each other out dimly as they skipped among the embers. Now and then Daniel Spence would pick Amy up and crush her to him. Once she said, "Let me breathe you in!"

"All right then." He held her tightly. She closed her eyes and breathed deeply, pushing her body against him as though she could not get close enough. She thought she heard him moan, and suddenly something happened, some hot eruption inside her, and as it did, Daniel Spence dropped her, gaping at the rosy treeline. The moaning was rising to a howl—it was the sound of the wind in the distant trees. "My God."

A huge ball of fire was jumping from treetop to treetop in the wood. Behind it, the glow which they had taken for the setting sun was growing brighter as they watched. The fireball was igniting trees with the sound of an explosion as it bounced along. Then it was joined by another.

"Christ almighty! Run, for God's sake! Run to the village!"

He had to shout above the now roaring wind. A scorching gust threw her to the ground. Daniel Spence grabbed her arm and pulled her up, and her legs dragged on burnt stubble, so that there were tears in her skirts and stockings and bloody rakings on her shins. He swung her up over one shoulder, and struggling to remain on his feet against the violent intermittent blasts, he stumbled toward the town, not stopping at the edge as he had the last time but blundering into the dark and shrouded streets.

A loud whooshing passed overhead, followed by an explosion as an unseen building burst into flames. A woman screamed. Father Pernin's bell at the still unfinished Catholic church began pealing loudly on this side of the village; and then more distantly the Congregationalists' bell could be heard in its steeple on the east side across the river; and finally thinly, tinnily, in comparison with the other two, came chiming the bell of the Reverend Michael Chaston. People began to materialize in the streets carrying children and belongings, calling for missing family. They were lit grotesquely by the proliferating fires.

"Where?" demanded Daniel, turning around wildly. He dropped her on her feet. "Where do you live from here?"

Amy tried to distinguish her father's signal from the other, fuller tollings as she peered around her. Her eyes smarted and through the dense smoke she could only make out scattered fires and a few looming shapes of untouched buildings. When a team of frightened horses pulling a wagonload of furniture and a family shuddered crazily close to them, Daniel Spence lifted her into a doorway.

She made note of the large glass globe of green liquid suspended over the street before them just as it cracked and shattered in the heat. They were standing at the door to Alpertson's Apotheca, where her mother sent her when the hired girl had the toothache.

"I know where we are, Daniel Spence."

"Good."

She started out into the street again. He drew her back.

"No—along the buildings. Don't lose the buildings unless we have to cross a street."

They held hands, running when they could see clearly enough where to put their feet, slowing when they could only feel their way. Amy had to stop often and check for signs to orient herself; she had learned to examine the entranceways: here was the Branwen Feed Store, with the freakish double ox-jawbone hanging from its lintel; here was Jorgeson's Dry Goods entrance hung with saws and files like instruments of torture; and she knew a tavern or a flop house from the drunken lumbermen and rail laborers who lay unconscious on the plank sidewalk or in the sawdust streets.

They collided with people fleeing or searching for one another; many of them Amy knew. Some of them spoke to her, but she ignored them, pulling Daniel Spence with her. Where the smoke was thickest, a face would appear and withdraw suddenly, eerily, like a ghost. She knew she was near home when she heard Mrs. Hautemann screaming for her twin sons. Then they almost stumbled over Tommy Schwarzhoff crouched with his arm around his little sister at the foot of old Miss Penny's trellised front porch; Jemma Schwarzhoff was crying with her face in her skirt and her brother's eyes were filled with hopeless terror. After that, Amy wouldn't look at people at all.

The fires were still restricted to clusters of structures which had been ignited by the sparks that flew unpredictably, but these outriders on the frontier of the coming conflagration, fueled by the wind, were making relentless progress toward the northeast, crawling along like bright stains in the night. Now and then a fireball exploded as it struck a building.

At the end of a row of detached houses, Amy saw the outline of her father's pineboard church, gaunt and stolid, silhouetted by fires burning beyond it, and she tugged Daniel Spence desperately in that direction. As they drew closer, they could make out the figure of a young girl that might have been Amy herself swaying and stumbling in front of the church. It was Agnes Meyer, one of the children in the chain who had watched Daniel Spence emerge from the cloud. Agnes was alone, but she was talking rapidly to herself as she picked goose-down from a pillow she had clasped to her chest. Overcome with dread, Amy faltered and pressed against Daniel Spence. When Agnes saw them, she dropped the pillow. Then she reached out her arm and pointed, wailing.

"Amy! Amy Chaston! Amy!"

The church exploded behind Agnes, and sparks showered down on her. She went up suddenly, like a match; she was a small human bonfire, reduced in seconds to a tarred and twisted little body. Amy screamed. Daniel Spence picked her up and carried her past the smoking thing to where he had spotted Mariah Chaston on the porch of the Reverend's house. The house was burning on every level.

Daniel Spence threw an arm around Amy's mother and, cradling Amy in the other, swept them away from the Reverend's house.

"Michael went to look for Amy!" Mariah Chaston shouted as she ran.

Daniel Spence said nothing, but made his way toward the remaining undamaged section of town. More girls and women, their skirts attracting the devouring fire like more paper or floss, were lighting up the foggy darkness like human candles. Amy dug her fists into her eyes so she wouldn't see them. She kept thinking how naked Agnes had been when the fire had burned down to her bones.

When it became apparent that the fire had outrun them, Daniel Spence stopped.

"The mill sits almost in the river!" shouted Amy's mother.

"It's a mill, Mariah. It's bound to go."

"It's in the river, Daniel!"

He looked around wildly, pulling his hair.

"All right. We'll go…wait!" He began to rip the skirts from the waistband of her mother's dress. Then he tore off Amy's skirts as well. He grabbed Amy and let Mariah lead them.

Amy was so hot all over she thought she would burst into flame in Daniel Spence's arms and then ignite them all so that they would burn like Agnes Meyer. The heat was even inside her, a pressure behind her stinging eyes, and her throat felt blistered when she breathed.

They found themselves caught up in a crowd as they approached the bridge. The mill was still standing, and many people had had the same idea as Mariah. Daniel Spence stopped to take in the scene. He looked doubtful.

They were standing by a well. Several of the houses even this close to the river had their own wells, not dug very deep, and it was a measure of the drought that as the river sank, the wells had gone dry one after another from the other end of town to this. Daniel Spence dropped a stone, and when it hit, it sounded a muddy bottom. He lifted Amy into the well, letting her hands slide down gripping along his arms and wrists while he lay on his stomach over the edge. The shaft was narrow, and when her feet touched down, something on the bottom felt like a wet cushion. It was a dead dog in a shallow pool of water—she knew from touching it when she sat down. Amy began to cry. She could see the outline of Daniel Spence's head above her.

"Amy! I'm taking your mother to the mill. I'll be back for you." Amy heard her mother screaming her name and Daniel Spence shouting at the same time.

"There's no room down there for more than one, Mariah! And there won't be enough air for two when the time comes. She'll be safer there 'til we're certain."

Daniel's head appeared again.

"If you have trouble breathing, keep your head down low as you can. If there's no air at all, hold your breath for as long as you can."

"Daniel Spence," said Amy, hugging her knees. "Daniel Spence." The air in the well was sour, but not smoky. The dog must have just been thrown or fallen in. It didn't smell like anything but a wet dog. When she was sure Daniel Spence was gone, she squirmed in the close well space until she was curled up and could press her face against the dog's side. She didn't know how long she had been waiting when she heard a man's violent coughing above her.

"Daniel Spence!" she called to him joyfully. A burned and blackened face appeared above in a haze of weirdly illuminated smoke. The eyeballs shone stark white against the blistered skin, and all of the hair was gone from the charred skull. Wordlessly, the man reached down and stuck the muzzle of a rifle at her. She closed her eyes, but he didn't shoot.

"Take it," he said hoarsely.

She was afraid to disobey, and with this, he pulled her out. It was her father.

She could not speak to the grotesque apparition before her. Michael Chaston must have been in terrible pain: his nose and ears were gone; the skin on his upper lip curled away toward one cheek, and the rest of his face was a weeping sore. His pale eyes took in her exposed body in an icy rage. "Where are they?" he croaked, grasping the rifle tightly. She stared. "Do you know what you've done, you bitch? Where are they?"

Amy pointed to the mill. Michael Chaston clutched his daughter's wrist and dragged her toward the building. His hand was sticky with burns. She could see that the bridge was already overloaded with masses of fleeing forms, pressing on the crowds at the building's entrance. Then a terrible sound arose behind her, and she turned to see a wind of fire, a roaring whirling column which bore down on the riverbank in a fury. Her father was shouting, but she couldn't hear him. Others around her had their mouths open in screams, but she only heard the blast of the burning wind like a giant hell's engine. Her father dropped the gun and changed direction, clawing at both her arms as he pulled her down the bank and into the river.

She could not take her eyes from the flaming column as it raced across the bridge to the mill. There was a moment before the heat without engulfed the building and the windows burst inward. Then the entire structure collapsed in flames.

"Daniel Spence!" Amy screamed. There was an explosion from the burning mill, and flaming timbers flew like splinters and rained around them. Michael Chaston pushed his daughter's head under the water.

She spent the night in the Peshtigo River without her skirts, her father forcing her below the surface when the heat became too intense, or the sparks too close. They had to beware of cattle and timbers taken by the current—bodies, too, many of them partially burned, many of them small, animals and people bobbing along in a hideous burlesque. As the fire died down, the river grew icy, and Amy knew she would never be warm again.

They crawled from the water around two o'clock in the morning, and then Michael Chaston's real agony began. Amy herself could not walk on her numb legs, but lay by her father, listening to his screams, on the smoking bank where the mill workers from Menominee found them. They were taken up gently and laid in a tent until they could be carried to the Dunlap House temporary hospital in Marinette.

*

The Chastons, like many families, saved nothing from the fire. The church board, realizing the girl could not go out to work with her father to nurse and expecting Michael not to survive for long, made them a handsome annual pension. With it, the Chastons left their old neighborhood and settled on the opposite side of the river among new people who knew their story and watched out for them, cared for them from a distance.

For the most part they were left alone. For Michael Chaston was hard to look at, and the two of them seemed to need no one, but were sufficient unto themselves. When people did visit, they marveled afterward, at the wordless way the two communicated, at the lively snap of his lidless eyes which the weak old man could still manage when his beloved daughter entered the room, at the perfect patience of the lovely woman who grew old serving him, her heart's god. When they were both aged, newcomers mistook them for a married couple. The neighbors laughed and said there was no marriage as perfect as their affinity, for it was obvious how much the two had sacrificed for each other and how secure a place they had made for themselves in Heaven.

Jesus and Magdalene As Children

J. T. Barbarese

Maddy was dirty.

She had always been dirty. As a child her hair was filled with lice and wood chips from Yussel's shop where she used to hang at the door, long strands of it in her mouth. She would suck on her hair because she was hungry. The bottom of her loose-belted top was filled with mud or manure, and her face was as dark as a slab of burnt bread. Sometimes there was blood on her from fights in which she would beat up the boys who tried to take advantage of her and the bullies who tried to take advantage of the same boys. It was never her blood.

When Jesus first met her he was eight, she just seven. She stood in the sunny opening of the shop, turning something over in her fingers. He could not see what it was or make out her face because of all the light behind her and she standing inside it like a blue-fringed black cut-out. When he got close enough for her to touch him, she reached out and dropped a beetle on his shoulder and ran away, laughing.

It was instant love. He did not chase her. He didn't have to.

She was the one who found the strange things in the ground. Yussel saw them playing together by the side of the shop with the objects and the jar the objects came in. He brought them inside and thought about taking them to the *rebbe* in town. A small comb, a jar with something long and paperish inside, thin as dried wings, and a long thin white wand that might have been a bone, or a stick for writing—or a wand. Jesus was using it as a wand and waving it over Maddy, who was using the comb on her filthy hair and tossing the filth at Jesus, saying *Catch, Jesse*, and giggling. She had found the things because she was always looking, always poking and probing. His mother said, *I'm not surprised. Her face is always on the ground.*

The morning that Maddy found them she brought them right to him. *Jesse*, she hissed. He was in the shop, sweeping, and he shrugged and waved around him at the work he had to do. Yussel could not work in a clutter. Maddy walked up to the door, stuck her head in and hissed his name again.

You will have to wait, he said. *You know my father.*

Why do you call him that? she asked. *You know you don't have to call him that.*

Shut up, Maddy, he said.

Don't say shut up. I won't show you what I have if you say shut up to me again.

Then shut up.

She threw a handful of muddy chips at him and stood there giving him a hard steady look.

More for me to sweep.

Then don't, she said.

He turned his back and swept the muddy chips into his larger pile. She kept her position by the door of the shop. When Yussel appeared—he was always nice to Maddy—he placed one hand on her head and picked her up. *No kiss for you*, he said to Maddy. *No kiss for you*, she said back.

Then he kissed her on the cheek and she made to wipe it off.

She showed Jesus her discovery and he was changed forever. The objects were ordinary-looking but in some way not. They were clearly very old. Marks on them looked like writing but not in the script he was learning. He saw human marks, but not those of Romans or Jews. The two children sat alone in the middle of the road, playing with trash from the looks of it, and yet he knew then that this was an extraordinary day in his life. *Someone has been here before,* he thought. Not a year or a lifetime, longer than that. When Yussel saw the objects he grew very quiet and still and handled them carefully. Especially the wand. He lifted it to the light and ran his finger down the smooth shank. He held it to the light and placed it gently close to his nose so that the wand nearly touched his upper lip. He smelled it and said, *It takes a long time to skin a body.*

Then Yussel hid the object in the loft of the shop. Maddy stood there the whole time, silent and leaning against the wall of the shop, big eyes fixed on Jesus, twirling her hair. When Yussel told them to go back she did not move but stood there staring at Jesus. When she made up her mind, there was no changing it, so Yussel let her stay.

Jesus knew what she was thinking. Then she took his hand, even then larger than hers, and walked him into the sunshine and into the road. They walked a short bit and she would not give up his hand. Then she said, we'll go back later on. He thinks it's a secret. She described a spot in the loft where she said she had seen his father hiding things before. Jesus squinted at her.

How do you know about that, he said.

She dropped her eyes. I know things.

He went to sleep thinking of the things Maddy knew and the things Maddy had found. The comb was maybe for sheep carding, but there was Maddy using it, still caked with road filth, to comb her hair. Maybe a man had combed ticks from his dog or had combed his lower parts, a soldier maybe, months in the field, not having bathed, combing fleas from his loins. And there was Maddie combing her hair with it. The broken jar looked like any jar, but a jar found in the earth and covered with strange writing is no typical jar. Someone had owned it. Someone's hair or beast had been combed with that comb. Someone had used or known how to use the other things, the long stick or wand or bone and the stalk of bound papyrus. The bone of an arm.

People before me. He felt this as revelation, yet he also felt that it was ordinary wisdom. He had always known it. The ignorant religious folk in town could not think beyond the Foundation of the World and the Six Days. They were like his simple grandmother, Anne. Nothing happened that long ago because they had no way to measure time except in lifetimes. No monuments, no ruins. They had built nothing except a temple and what was mentioned in Torah. The Egyptians, they were builders. The stories of their tombs and the big sprawling sphinx fascinated him. People spat when they said the name Egyptian but he respected them. He respected any human achievement that gave history a concrete shape, that gave time extension and weight. Human beings lived. Even the Romans. Those stories too, of Rome, the coliseum, the senate, the aqueducts. What did they have?

He looked around him. A small town under a high empty sky. Yussel's shop in the foreground, the blonde walls brilliant, the crosstree of a fishing boat. They had their God and their families, their children and their teachings, and usually each other. They had The Law and the Law was eternal.

But they had no buildings.

He knew better. He knew that Yussel knew too, thought he hid his knowing as he hid the objects in the jar. Yussel was good at hiding things. Maddy seemed to know things too, but very different things. Maddy had a finger in her nose and her filthy hair in her mouth, hair that his mother Mary was always threatening to wash. Magdalene, Mary would say, let me bathe you, sweety, and Maddy would lower her eyes and take Jesus' hand and say Let's go, Jesse. She was filthy and silent when she was not chatting about nothing. Her family was still essentially homeless, always getting thrown out of one place or another. They had slept in the open, in cattle yards, in stables, up on Laundry Hill where they had wrapped themselves in Mary's snapping linens one day. He remembered it clearly: Maddy running away from his mother and down the hill, her finger in her mouth, one of his blankets over her shoulder, then stopping to turn back and stare at him. They had come right up to her but she still wouldn't surrender the blanket until Mary had said, in her gentlest voice, Do you have a blanket of your own?

When Jesus thought of nomads he thought of Maddy's family. Her father was always working and earning nothing, her mother always drunk and nearly immobile because of a stroke after Maddy's older brother was killed by Herod's son in one of the son's typical mad moments. They were the kinds of rulers who walked into people's homes and said, Here, I'm buying that. It did not matter what it was. A chair, a wall, a person. They would buy it. So they had taken her older brother and simply killed him, according to Maddy's mother, who simply got crazier and more intoxicated as time went by. There were no other children in the house and Maddy was easily bored until she met him that day on Laundry Hill. She looked at him and her mind was made up. It was instant love.

She was not good at much except following Jesus around.

His only fear was that some day he would find a reason to dislike her.

Angeles Mastretta

Amy Schildhouse Greenberg

When I lived in Mexico City in the late 1980s, I traveled frequently to the city of Puebla, two hours southeast of my smog-choked, adopted megalopolis. How could one not? Puebla was everything the Federal District wasn't: quaint, provincial, filled with aromas of chocolatey *mole Poblano* and redolent of times past, even near the end of the twentieth century. In fact, it was remarkably like the Puebla of stories in Women With Big Eyes. I walked among the señoras in the bustling open-air markets and behind señoritas down shaded streets in the late afternoons, listening to their chatter. Like 'aunts' in Mastretta's stories, women whose conversations I overheard seemed to lead lives as complicated and intrigue-filled as their supposedly more sophisticated counterparts in the Capital. Perhaps it was longing to revisit those charming streets and their fascinating women that drew me to translate Women With Big Eyes.

I admire the women Mastretta created in these stories. To me, they are strong, determined and passionate. They pursue their dreams, yet remain deeply involved in their close circles of families and friends. Mastretta refers to them warmly as 'aunts,' and that is how I too came to see them. She captured their lives with humor, affection and insight, using their unique local references and colorful expressions. I tried to mirror her expressive Spanish faithfully in English. This chance to return to Puebla and Pueblan women—albeit via translation—rewarded me with a delightful challenge.

Angeles Mastretta lives in Mexico where her 1990 book, *Mujeres de Ojos Grandes*, was a best-seller.

Tía Eloísa

Angeles Mastretta

Desde muy joven la tía Eloísa tuvo a bien declararse atea. No le fue fácil dar con un marido que estuviera de acuerdo con ella, pero buscando, encontró un hombre de sentimientos nobles y maneras suaves, al que nadie le había amenazado la infancia con asuntos como el temor a Dios.

Ambos crecieron a sus hijos sin religión, bautismo ni escapularios. Y los hijos crecieron sanos, hermosos y valientes, a pesar de no tener detrás la tranquilidad que otorga saberse protegido por la Santísima Trinidad.

Sólo una de las hijas creyó necesitar del auxilio divino y durante los años de su tardía adolescencia buscó auxilio en la iglesia anglicana. Cuando supo de aquel Dios y de los himnos que otros le entonaban, la muchacha quiso convencer a la tía Eloísa de cuán bella y necesaria podía ser aquella fe.

—Ay, hija —le contestó su madre, acariciándola mientras hablaba—, si no he podido creer en la verdadera religión ¿cómo se te ocurre que voy a creer en una falsa?

Aunt Eloisa

Angeles Mastretta
  Translated by
  Amy Schildhouse Greenberg

At a young age, Aunt Eloísa thought it wise to declare herself an atheist. It was not easy to find a husband who agreed with her, but by searching she found a man of noble feelings and gentle manners, whose childhood no one had threatened with such things as the fear of God.

They both raised their children without religion, baptisms or scapulars. And the children grew up healthy, handsome and brave, despite their not having inside them the tranquility granted by knowing themselves to be protected by the Most Holy Trinity.

Only one of the daughters believed in the need for divine assistance, and during the years of her belated adolescence she sought help in the Anglican Church. When she learned of their God and of the hymns that others sang, the girl wanted to convince Aunt Eloísa of how beautiful and necessary that faith could be.

"Ay, daughter," her mother answered, caressing her as she spoke. "If I have not been able to believe in the true religion, how do you think I am going to believe in a false one?"

Tía Mónica

Angeles Mastretta

A veces la tía Mónica quería con todas sus ganas no ser ella. Detestaba su pelo y su barriga, su manera de caminar, sus pestañas lacias y su necesidad de otras cosas aparte de la paz escondida en las macetas, del tiempo yéndose con trabajos y tan aprisa que apenas dejaba pasar algo más importante que el bautizo de algún sobrino o el extraño descubrimiento de un sabor nuevo en la cocina.

La tía Mónica hubiera querido ser un globo de esos que los niños dejan ir al cielo, para después llorarlos como si hubieran puesto algún cuidado en no perderlos. La tía Mónica hubiera querido montar a caballo hasta caerse alguna tarde y perder la mitad de la cabeza, hubiera querido viajar por países exóticos o recorrer los pueblos de México con la misma curiosidad de una antropóloga francesa, hubiera querido enamorarse de un lanchero en Acapulco, ser la esposa del primer aviador, la novia de un poeta suicida, la mamá de un cantante de ópera. Hubiera querido tocar el piano como Chopin y que alguien como Chopin la tocara como si fuera un piano.

La tía Mónica quería que en Puebla lloviera como en Tabasco quería que las noches fueran más largas y más accidentadas, quería meterse al mar de madrugada y beberse los rayos de la luna como si fueran té de manzanilla. Quería dormir una noche en el Palace de Madrid y bañarse sin brasier en la fuente de Trevi o de perdida en la de San Miguel.

Aunt Mónica

Angeles Mastretta
  Translated by
  Amy Schildhouse Greenberg

Sometimes Aunt Mónica wanted desperately not to be herself. She detested her hair and her belly, her way of walking, her limp lashes and her need for things besides the peace hidden in flowerpots or the time passing with busyness, and so quickly that it scarcely allowed anything more important to happen than the baptism of some nephew, or the strange discovery of a new flavor in the kitchen.

Aunt Mónica might have liked to be one of those balloons that children release to the sky, to cry over later as though they'd taken some care not to lose it. Aunt Mónica might have liked to ride horseback until she fell off some afternoon and lost half her head; she might have liked to travel to exotic countries or visit the towns of Mexico with the same curiosity as a French anthropologist; she might have liked to fall in love with a boatman in Acapulco, to be the bride of the first aviator, the girlfriend of a suicidal poet, or the mother of an opera singer. She might have liked to play piano like Chopin and have someone like Chopin play her as though she were a piano.

Aunt Mónica wanted it to rain in Puebla like it did in Tabasco; she wanted the nights to be longer and more irregular, she wanted to swim in the sea at dawn and drink the moon rays like chamomile tea. She wanted to sleep one night in the Palace in Madrid and bathe without a brassiere in the Trevi Fountain, or at least in the Fountain of San Miguel.

Tía Mónica

Nadie entendió nunca por qué ella no se estaba quieta más de cinco minutos. Tenía que moverse porque de otro modo se le encimaban las fantasías. Y ella sabía muy bien que se castigan, que desde que las empieza uno a cometer llega el castigo, porque no hay peor castigo que la clara sensación de que uno está soñando con placeres prohibidos.

Por eso ella puso tanto empeño en hacerse de una casa con tres patios, por eso inventó ponerle dos fuentes y convertir la parte de atrás en casa de huéspedes, por eso tenía una máquina de coser en la que pedaleaba hasta que todas sus sobrinas podían estrenar vestidos iguales los domingos, por eso en invierno tejía gorros y bufandas para cada miembro respetable o no de su familia, por eso una tarde ella misma se cortó el pelo que le llegaba a la cintura y que tanto le gustaba a su amoroso marido. Tan amoroso que para mantenerla trabajaba hasta volver en las noches con los ojos hartos y una beatífica pero inservible sonrisa de hombre que cumple con su deber.

Nadie ha hecho jamás tantas y tan deliciosas galletas de queso como la tía Mónica. Eran chiquitas y largas, pasaba horas amasándo, luego las horneaba a fuego lento. Cuando por fin estaban listas las cubría de azúcar y tras contemplarlas medio segundo se las comía todas de una sentada.

—Lo malo —confesó una vez— es que cuando me las acabo todavía tengo lugar para alguna barbaridad y me voy a la coma con ella. Cierro los ojos para ver si se escapa, pero no. Entonces hablo con Dios: "Tú me la dejaste, te consta que he soportado todo el día de lucha. Esta va a ganarme y a ver si mañana me quieres perdonar".

Luego se dormía con la tentación entre los ojos, como una santa.

No one ever understood, because she was never still for more than five minutes. She had to keep moving, because otherwise her fantasies would overtake her. And she knew very well that one is punished for them, that from the moment one begins to act them out, the punishment arrives, because there is no worse punishment than the clear sensation that one is dreaming of prohibited pleasures.

For this reason, she very determinedly had a house built with three patios; for this reason she thought to put in two fountains and convert the back area into a guesthouse; for this reason she had a sewing machine that she pedaled until all her nieces could show up dressed alike on Sundays; for this reason she knitted caps and mufflers in winter for every family member, respectable or not; for this reason one afternoon she cut her own waist-length hair, which her loving husband so liked. So loving was he that to maintain her he worked well into the night, to return home with sick and tired eyes and the beatific but useless smile of a man who upholds his responsibilities.

No one has ever made as many or as delicious cheese biscuits as Aunt Mónica. They were tiny and big; she spent hours kneading them, then baked them over a slow fire. When they were finally done, she covered them with sugar and, after contemplating them for half a second, ate all of them at one sitting.

"The bad thing," she once confessed, "is that when I finish them I still have room for an unfulfilled fantasy and I go to sleep with it. I shut my eyes to see if I can escape it, but no. So I speak with God: 'You left it with me, I swear to you that I've put up with a whole day of fighting. This one is going to beat me, and let's see if tomorrow you'll want to forgive me.'"

Then she went to sleep with temptation still between her eyes, like a saint.

Tía Amalia

Angeles Mastretta

Amalia Ruiz encontró la pasión de su vida en el cuerpo y la voz de un hombre prohibido.Durante más de un año lo vio llegar febril hasta el borde de su falda que salía volando tras un abrazo. No hablaban demasiado, se conocían como si hubieran nacido en el mismo cuarto, se provocaban temblores y dichas con sólo tocarse los abrigos Lo demás salía de sus cuerpos afortunados con tanta facilidad que al poco rato de estar juntos el cuarto de sus amores sonaba como la Sinfonía Pastoral y olía a perfume como si lo hubiera inventado Coco Chanel.

Aquella gloria mantenía sus vidas en vilo y convertía sus muertes en imposible. Por eso eran hermosos como un hechizo y promisorios como una fantasía.

Hasta que una noche de octubre el amante de tía Meli llegó a la cita tarde y hablando de negocios. Ella se dejó besar sin arrebato y sintió el aliento de la costumbre devastarle al boca. Se guardó los reproches, pero salió corriendo hasta su casa y no quiso volver a saber más de aquel amor.

—Cuando lo imposible se quiere volver rutina, hay que dejarlo —le explicó a su hermana, que no era capaz de entender una actitud tan radical—. Uno no puede meterse en el lío de ambicionar algo prohibido, de poseerlo a veces como una benedición, de quererlo más que a nada por eso, por imposible, por desesperado, y de buenas a primeras convertirse en el anexo de una oficina. No me lo puedo permitir, no me lo voy a permitir. Sea por Dios que algo tiene de prohibido y por eso está bendito.

Aunt Amalia

Angeles Mastretta
   Translated by
   Amy Schildhouse Greenberg

Amalia Ruiz found her life's passion in the body and voice of a forbidden man. For more than a year, she watched him come feverishly as far as the hem of her skirt, which billowed beneath their embrace. They didn't speak much; they knew each other as though they had been born in the same room, and they provoked trembling and happiness in each other merely by touching each other's overcoat. Their passion came out of their fortunate bodies with such ease that after a short while of being together, their love room sounded like the Pastoral Symphony and smelled of perfume as if it had been invented by Coco Chanel.

Their glory kept their lives uncertain and turned their deaths into an impossibility. For this reason they were as beautiful as an enchantment and as promising as a fantasy.

Until one October night when Aunt Meli's lover arrived late to their assignation, talking about business. She let him kiss her without putting up a fuss, and she felt his breath devastate her mouth as it always did. She held back her reproaches, but then took off running to her house and no longer wanted to know anything of love.

"When the impossible becomes routine, it is time to give it up," she explained to her sister, who was unable to understand so radical an attitude. "One cannot get involved in the mess of loving something prohibited, feeling it at times like a blessing, wanting it above all else—because it's impossible, because it's hopeless—and then turning oneself into the annex of an office. I can't allow myself to do it, I am not going to let myself do it. If in the name of God something is forbidden, for that reason it is blessed."

Tía Pilar & Tía Marta

Angeles Mastretta

Tía Pilar y tía Marta se encontraron una tarde varios años, hijos y hombres después de terminar la escuela primaria. Y se pusieron a conversar como si el día anterior les hubieran dado el último diploma de niñas aplicadas.

La misma gente les había trasmitido las mismas manías, el mismo valor, los mismos miedos. Cada una a su modo había hecho con todo eso algo distinto. Las dos de sólo verse descubrieron el tamaño de su valor y la calidad de sus manías, dieron todo eso por sabido y entraron a contarse lo que habían hecho con sus miedos.

La tía Pilar tenía los mismos ojos transparentes con que miraba el mundo a los once años, pero la tía Marta encontró en ellos el ímpetu que dura hasta la muerte en la mirada de quienes han pasado por un montón de líos y no se han detenido a llorar una pena sin buscarle remedio.

Pensó que su amiga era preciosa y se lo dijo. Se lo dijo por si no lo había oído suficiente, por las veces en que lo había dudado y porque era cierto. Después se acomodó en el sillón, agradecida porque las mujeres tienen el privilegio de elogiarse sin escandalizar. Le provocaba una ternura del diablo aquella mujer con tres niños y dos maridos que había convertido su cocina en empresa

Aunt Pilar & Aunt Marta

Angeles Mastretta
  Translated by
  Amy Schildhouse Greenberg

Aunt Pilar and Aunt Marta came across each other some years, children, and husbands after finishing elementary school. And they set about conversing as though they'd received their diplomas just the day before.

The same people had transmitted to each of them the same habits, the same values, and the same fears. Each in her own way had made something different out of all this. Merely by seeing each other, the two discovered the size of their worth and the quality of their manias; they took all this for granted and began recounting what they had done with their fears. Aunt Pilar had the same transparent eyes through which she had looked at the world when she was eleven, but Aunt Marta found in them the lifelong vigor of those who have undergone a great many troubles yet not stopped to bemoan a problem, but rather looked for its solution.

Aunt Marta thought her friend was beautiful, and told her so. She told her so because she had not heard it enough, because of the time she had doubted it, and because it was true. Then she sat down in an armchair, thankful that women have the privilege of praising each other without offending. That the woman with three children and two husbands, who had turned her kitchen into a business to free herself from the husbands and stay with the children,

para librarse de los maridos y quedarse con los niños, aquella señora de casi cuarenta años que ella no podía dejar de ver como a una niña de doce: su amiga Pilar Cid.

—¿Todavía operan lagartijas tus hermanos? —preguntó Marta Weber. Se había dedicado a cantar. Tenía una voz irónica y ardiente con la que se hizo de fama en la radio y dolores en la cabeza. Cantar había sido siempre su descanso y su juego. Cuando lo convirtió en trabajo, empezó a dolerle todo.

Se lo contó a su amiga Pilar. Le contó también cuánto quería a un señor y cuánto a otro, cuánto a sus hijos, cuánto a su destino.

Entonces la tía Pilar miró su pelo en desorden, sus ojos como recién asombrados, y le hizo un cariño en la cabeza:

—No tienes idea del bien que me haces. Temí que me abrumaras con el júbilo del poder y la gloria. ¿Te imaginas? Lo aburrido que hubiera sido.

Se abrazaron. Tía Marta sintió el olor de los doce años entre su cuerpo.

that this lady of nearly forty whom she could not stop seeing as a girl of twelve, was her friend Pilar Cid, provoked a devilish tenderness in her.

"Do your brothers still 'operate' on lizards?" asked Marta Weber. She had dedicated herself to singing. She had an ironic, passionate voice that garnered her fame on the radio and aches in the head. Singing had always been her relief and her play. When she turned it into work, everything began to hurt her.

She told her friend Pilar about this. She told her also how much she loved this man and how much that one, how much she loved her children, how much her destiny.

Then Aunt Pilar looked at Marta's wild hair, at her eyes like those of someone recently frightened, and she touched her affectionately on the head:

"You have no idea how much good you have done me. I feared that you might have overwhelmed me with the joy of power and glory. Can you imagine? How boring that would have been."

They embraced. Aunt Marta felt in her body the aroma of being twelve.

Blue Boy

Ramu Nagappan

When the baby cries, I put my thick finger on his forehead, and he hushes. In the third week of his life, I am sitting in his room, and I cannot help but notice everything he does: the way his fingers tremble, the way his tongue rolls, the way his body curls. Hands and feet, a round mouth, a sound most of all, he is not much yet.

He has not grown, and he does not eat. The doctor has seen him and smiled and said he is a rare one. I smile too and ask, "In what way rare? Do you mean sick?"

"Oh, you misunderstand. He's perfectly healthy, sir. There's no need to worry."

So I have brought him home again, and he lies in the crib, looking up at the yellow stars and sunny faces painted on the ceiling. There is the cry, and there is the way he stares and stares, his face all wrinkled. And in the crying, he suddenly refuses to breathe; for a moment I think he won't make it. Then he draws air again.

The clock shows ten forty-five. I slip out to the kitchen to fix some dinner. The brief rattling of the refrigerator door wakes him, brings another cry. The finger to the forehead, and the boy is out again. At eleven I am sipping a cream soup. On the table, a magazine is open to the same article I have been reading for a long time. I leave the empty bowl and take the magazine out to the deck where the night air has turned newly crisp and forgiving. A slight fog has crept into the hills where the house is perched, but I can still make out the water's edge, and beyond that, the lights of the city. The pine trees shiver noiselessly. I stand, shivering too, magazine dropped at my feet, and all I do is feel the air.

At midnight, I am on the phone again, the one in my bedroom, whispering harshly into a cupped receiver. The woman does not understand at first because the pulsing thread across continents is a weak one. I begin to shout. "I'm sorry to bother you again." I ask what I have asked before. There is a resentful muttering at the other end. "Yes, I will try them, too," I say. I try all the numbers I have. The baby must hear me but he does not cry this late. He is settled, glum, and there will be no disturbing him now. At twelve-thirty I put down the phone and give up for the night. In five minutes I am asleep too, lying diagonally across the bed, still in my clothes, in khakis and a white shirt, now grossly wrinkled.

*

The day he utters his first word is the day I name him. Naked, struggling with a green monster in the middle of the living room floor, he says, "Ma." He says it a second time, and a third, exultantly. The fingers tense around the monster. He is squeezing, astonished by his own voice. He is shouting, "Ma," looking about. It is instinct, I tell myself. The stuffing pops out one of the blue monster eyes and the eye dribbles across the rug as the boy skips. "No," I tell him.

He offers me the monster and kisses my hand lightly. He runs and falls, runs.

That night, I let him sleep in my bed, but he does not come too close. I tell a story about birds and flying children, and he will not take his eyes off me when I am done. Then I tell him a different story, something less frightening. He cries out nonsense, and in the middle of crying he begins to nod off. He sleeps at the far edge, and he mumbles something. He is between snoring and speaking. I am awake a long time. I decide to call him Neal from now on because that is what she wanted. She held the pink, crinkly body between her hands—unnamed, a four-day-old child. He cried in staccato bursts and she frowned, saying, "God! Look at it. Listen to that sound. You're supposed to love it right away, aren't you?" She shook her head. "How about Neal?" she asked.

    I said I wasn't sure.

    She said I wasn't ever sure. She said I was frozen whenever there was a decision to be made. She said a great many things. Then she spoke the name again and again. "I think it's perfect," she said.

    The boy mumbles in my bed. I reach over, very carefully, and put my finger on his lips. I tell Neal to dream quietly now, and he does.

*

I decide to give up on the numbers for good. I have called them all a dozen times, then crumpled the phone bills with their incredible international tolls. No one will speak to me.

    They are fed up. Her eldest cousin tells me I don't really want to find her. She laughs, this cousin of hers, saying I am fooling myself. Her voice swells. I imagine her whole body swelling with indignation. She may explode while on the phone. Then there is the shrinking, the way she seems to get smaller and nearer to me in space, the way the cousin whispers to tell me I have to give up now. I explain that we were together for three years, that the boy needs his mother. The voice grows shaky. I am a good man, she insists, but an unfortunate husband.

    Then she admits she knows where my wife went first. "She won't be there anymore," the cousin says.

    "She was in India then."

    "At first." She gives me an address.

    I write the same letter over and over. First in my head, later on scraps of paper, finally on the good stationery. Then I throw everything away, and rewrite, thinking I will say everything differently. It comes out the same every time. It is short, a page, about Neal mostly. I mention a few other things. I ask her to think about coming back. I ask her to worry about us.

I tell myself I am doing the right thing. I copy the final version of the letter several times. I put the copies into envelopes and write her name on each, then send one to each of these addresses: the school in New Jersey where my wife once taught English; her closest friend from college; the house where her parents once lived, a colonial that burned down and was rebuilt; the address in India my cousin gave me; her bitter grandmother, also in India, who is said to be the cruelest woman in her village.

*

I begin to notice peculiar things in the boy. The doctor with the glasses says Neal is unusual, and the doctor without glasses nods in agreement. They have run the tests, and the thing is proven. Something in the brain, a misalignment, a miswiring, something not easily detectable. But they say he might grow up normal after all. The doctor with the glasses takes them off and crosses his arms. "Neal's bright for his age, but his progress will be limited." He gives me the name of a center, a place where they will be kind to my boy.

When we get home Neal asks for a cat. "Blue kitty," he says. I tell him there are not many blue cats to be had. "Blue," he says. So the next day I go to the animal shelter, and there are indeed cats that they call blue, though they are actually an animal shade of gray. I find a fearless one and bring her home—a kitten with a kink in her tail. Neal kicks the thing and calls it a name. Two days later he is hugging it and chasing it and calling it Blue Boy. "It's a girl," I explain. But it does not matter, and the name sticks. They do not stop moving. Late in the night I hear them running, and I decide to do nothing to prevent it. I lie awake, happy for them. I never knew that Neal could run like that, and I never believed I would let him tear around the house breaking things with impunity. I am a softy.

Neal and the cat are inseparable. They go to the Center together where they play for seven hours until I pick them up. Neal shields the cat from the other children. "They hurt us," he whimpers. "But they hurt her better." Blue Boy and Neal eat together. Both on the floor. They prowl in tandem, and the teachers say they are beginning to sound somewhat alike.

One evening, two women from the Center come to talk to me. One old and one much younger. "This is a special visit," the young one says. "We don't do this very often, but we're quite concerned about Neal."

They sit and I offer them tea, and cookies from a tin, and I linger in front of them without sitting. "Don't be too alarmed," the young one says.

There is small talk, and there is counsel. The old one asks when I came to this country.

I tell them I was born here.

"Do you ever speak any Indian to Neal?"

"Tamil."

"You do?"

"Sometimes."

"You know, he doesn't even look Indian." The one looks at the other. "I mean, he doesn't look so much like you."

The old one asks about his mother and I explain.

"It must be hard," the young one says.

"It's not your fault." The old one crosses her legs.

They think I ought to take Neal to India where he can have more of a family. They say he needs a home. They say he needs other attention. They think he is a sad child.

"Really?" I ask. "He's pretty happy at home. We make a decent family, just the two of us." I call Neal to the room.

Neal comes in, swinging his arms, and he stands by my side. He grins at the women from the Center. There is chocolate at the corners of his mouth and I try to wipe it away. "Say hello," I tell him.

He does not. Blue Boy is at his heels, mewing. Then she runs at the women's feet and dances, pouncing at their shoes as they laugh hysterically. They say the cat is a great character at the Center.

They've made costumes for her. They dress her up as a bird, a ghost, a dog, a dead cat.

They praise Neal endlessly. Later, at the door they tell me I have a beautiful house. Near their car, when they think I cannot hear, the young one tells the other, "He's so well off."

"And he's only a young teacher."

"But a big man. A University position and all."

I am watching at the door. Neal has climbed up onto the counter and is staring at the women from the kitchen window. He is humming, smiling privately.

*

He is five, and they say in the new books that he needs something to challenge him. They say he needs something beautiful in his life. I buy him a violin, a tiny one that squeaks and whines and sometimes jumps to ecstatic notes. There are lessons every week. I don't have to make him practice. He pumps away at all hours.

At the Center they think that I am pushing him too hard, that I want a genius boy, that I believe there is a prodigy stuck inside the shell of an idiot. And at the Center they grimace when Neal tells them he played "Mary Had a Little Lamb" exactly forty-nine times Thursday night.

"Oh, and you are counting so well," the teacher tells him.

Neal has me make a tape of his playing and insists I listen to it in the car when I drive to the University. After a while, the repetition drives me mad. But I keep the tapes, and the violin teacher encourages him. She explains elaborately that he is really improving for such a boy.

Before Christmas there is a recital in a cramped school auditorium. The place buzzes with couples in fine clothes and children swinging their cases, grinning artlessly. We all sit very close to the stage, and I leave one seat open next to me. Eventually, I put my coat there. The program is quite short. I sit and clap more loudly than anyone for Neal, who goes first. During the reception, there are drinks and cookies, and Neal stays by my side, refusing to talk to the other children or their parents. He looks needlessly disappointed and shakes his head when they tell him he did a wonderful job. They call him a virtuoso, but he frowns.

Later he tells me I should have brought the cat to the recital. Seeing the cat would have helped him play better, he says.

*

Neal has green eyes. I notice this for the very first time when he comes running home with a bloody nose. Some older kid knocked him with an elbow. Nothing is broken, but there is quite a bit of blood. He stands there in the doorway, the women from the Center behind him, and he just looks at me. I notice the green eyes. "He's okay," the older one says.

"There was a fight," the younger tells me. They do not stay.

Blue Boy approaches Neal slowly, suspiciously, and the smell of blood must be something awful but delicious to her. Neal won't stop looking at me. He has a terribly small mouth, one that seems too tiny for the long and mournful cry that escapes the lips suddenly. He closes his eyes before touching the bloody nose. "I not able to smell ever again," he whispers. "They said."

"Who?"

"The boy with a mommy is a nurse, and the other one, the girl who stays up late to watch the doctor TV show."

"I don't think they're right."

"It hurts."

I get him some ice, and he watches television. He watches for hours, saying that this is what sick people do. So I let him, but I keep the volume down and make him sit far back from the screen. The shows are not half bad.

She would not have liked it at all. There was no TV in the house when she was here. "They're just loud and unbelievably repugnant," she said once when I suggested getting one. "And why would you of all people want such a thing anyway?"

But then after she left I got one and set it up prominently in the living room. When he was just walking, Neal began to plant himself there, awake late into the night while I was asleep on the sofa.

Now he watches intently, and the blood trickles from his nose for a long time. It stops, then it runs again. For days, it goes on, and Neal will not leave the house. The Center calls. The other boy, the violent one, has been removed from the program. I take Neal to the doctor, who tells us that it is normal, really, as long as it's just a little blood. The doctor tells me I'm an appalling worrier.

So he is stuck in front of the television, even when I am gone. A baby-sitter comes during the day and speaks delicately, but Neal will have nothing to do with him. The sitter is a tall, graying man, sixtyish. He mentions that he has five grown children and eight grandchildren; he mentions that he loves kids but the house is empty now. The neighbors recommended him, saying you can't trust anybody these days but you can trust this old man who loves everybody to death. He dislikes Neal though, and the feeling is mutual. After the first day, they hardly talk. The boy plugs his nostrils with two fingers and yanks them out, laughing at the red on his fingertips. "Doesn't hurt," he says.

Blue Boy sits in his lap and hisses at the sitter. The cat gets more determined every day. She opens the lower cabinets in the kitchen and rattles the pots and pans. She has managed to do some paintings a foot high up the walls: muddy prints, smeared food. She is an artist, a daredevil, a clown. She has become a grandiose and willful being. She will speak one day, I am convinced. She will give the orders. Throw us out.

She won't come near me except on rare occasions. I watch from a distance. She sweeps through the house, knocking over the plants and the neat piles of books, and then she hides. Neal laughs and swats her crooked tail. One evening I come home and the sitter is at the table, arms crossed. Blue Boy has dragged two sparrows into the living room and propped them up next to the TV. There is a thin trail of blood and feathers across the floor.

"She's a monster," I mutter.

"It's 'stinct," Neal says.

"Instinct?"

"Uh-huh."

After three weeks, he goes back to the Center. The cat, too. After dinner, instead of TV, the three of us go to the park up the street. Neal runs, Blue Boy hides from the big dogs, and I talk to the parents. Up on the grass we sit watching the sunset. The first time we go to the park, our neighbor, a middle-aged mother, tells me I'm a brave man. It seems that she knows our story. I shrug and say that her teenage daughter is getting more beautiful every day. Neal drops into my lap while I am talking to her, and then the cat draws near and gives her a slow pink yawn.

"You bring your cat to the park?" she asks.

Neal giggles. "Special cat."

I smile too and add, "She takes pretty good care of herself."

Blue Boy frolics among us and gets all the attention. Then she darts away, just a vague streak in the twilight, and Neal is after her. They chase butterflies and grasshoppers and blowing leaves.

When we are back from the park, we sit on the floor of the living room, and I help Neal with reading. He mouths the words and touches his nose. "Still hurts," he says.

"You're imagining it."

"Can't smell."

I put my finger on the tip of his nose and he slaps at my hand.

"I might get an operation," he says.

"Nope. You're all better now."

"There's something wrong with me."

I squeeze his shoulder.

He stares, still rubbing the nose. He asks quietly, as though in an afterthought, "What they do with my mother?"

Later that night he creeps into my bed, and I let him. I won't allow the cat in though, get up and close the door. Blue Boy yowls three or four times during the night, then gives up. In the morning the cat just gives me a look, all at once greedy, sad and unforgiving.

*

On his eighth birthday we hold our first party. Four children show up. They are his new friends. He has joined the regular class now in the regular school. For the first week there he vomited up the school lunches. The doctors again. "The meat," they said. "That's all. Don't worry." So he went back and the teacher made certain he avoided the meat.

The teacher won't allow Blue Boy to come to school with him. "You're grown up now," she tells him. "Besides, we can't have everyone's pets running around, can we?"

"At the Center they did."

"Oh, but this is quite different."

So he goes to school alone, shutting Blue Boy up in his room so she won't get out and follow him. The cat grows thin and cranky. Some days we never actually see her. She hides and scratches and thumps the walls when she thinks we have forgotten her.

She is hiding the day of the party, too. Two boys and two girls arrive in casual clothes, without gifts. "Mommy says people don't give things anymore," one frowning girl explains. "Just a waste."

"But our mommy's not cheap," her brother adds.

They gorge on the blue superhero cake, and they watch rented videos for hours. In the middle of one, Neal drags out his violin to show the others. They demand he play. Neal obliges, but they cut him off when he hits the high notes.

"Too much sound," the frowning girl says.

I pat Neal on the back and tell him to bring out the games instead. He finds only a deck of cards. And soon the five of them are flinging cards and paper plates at one another. I decide there is nothing a decent father can do but let them play. When she hears the racket, Blue Boy races out, eager for a fight. The cat stands in the middle of the room as the cards fly everywhere. Then she begins to jump and claw. The frowning girl kicks her squarely in the rump and the cat bites her. The girl laughs and screams, saying her mother will kill me. Then the children tell her it is nothing, and she nods, shrieking that it's nothing. Soon they hurtle onto the deck of the house.

Later, when I go out to see them, Neal is crying soundlessly. He hunches in the corner and flicks pine needles off the edge, watching the others play jail. I break up the party and call the parents, who take the children home without a word. Neal just sits on the deck most of the night, freezing. I am in a chair nearby, huddled under a blanket. I offer him one. I offer some more cake. I tell him I'll make some hot chocolate. I tell him Blue Boy is lonely inside. But Neal won't come in. He sits rocking, pine needles stuck in his hair, and he hums gingerly. I think he hums the same tune he played for the children on the violin, only a little slower, perhaps a bit more in tune.

*

He says he is old enough to hear. He is at the TV, hoping I will explain some things. He concentrates and asks how it could possibly be true—all those things on the television shows. I begin to explain because it is my duty.

One day he makes a list of demands. "Other stuff I have to know," he says. It has nothing to do with TV this time. On the Saturday afternoon when he passes me the sheet of paper, we are sitting on the sun-drenched deck, Neal with his dark glasses and crossed legs clad in the neat blue pants bought with the money he earned helping the neighbor weed her garden. He is sixteen. He deserves to know.

It is like meeting with a lawyer. The cat slouches out. She comes straightaway to me. She hasn't gone to Neal in months. My lawyer son shakes his head. "Okay," he says. "Tell me about the beginning." I am too stung by the green eyes to hold anything back. I have rehearsed this very speech a hundred times, the truth-telling speech, a speech without malice. I do not know how much he understands because I know I am talking too fast. I am, in fact, talking all at once.

So I tell him that she was a teacher, a great one. I tell him that she was a brave woman. She was capable of so much generosity, truth be told. She was loved. At the grade school, at the children's park, in the neighborhood grocery, even in the town where she grew up and long ago left behind—she was loved in all these places. Her parents used to speak of her with a kind of strange reverence. I tell him that she was remarkably beautiful. She had the most unusual green eyes you would ever see. I do not him tell that she was loved and adored because she sourly demanded it of everyone. It was the price to pay to be in her presence. I tell him that she was hopeful. But she did not have great ambitions. We were never rich. She adored our rickety house, with all its faults. I complained about how mean and hard-hearted people could be, how ugly the town had gotten with its new buildings, how depressed my students were. I tell him that even her voice was hopeful. I do not tell him what she was not. I tell him about the last day.

*

I couldn't track her down. Tried and tried, called every single one of her relatives, hoping someone would know, but she had simply vanished without a trace. At times I thought she had died. Other times I thought she had hit her head in the accident and wandered off an amnesiac. The police helped, and then they gave up. I tell him that I gave up, too.

I tell him again about the last day. He was just a week old, newly hatched, still un-named. I do not tell him that he was not yet loved. I tell him none of it was his fault. There was nothing either of us could have done. It wasn't him. She didn't understand him. She couldn't hold him without shaking. But she smiled at him when he lay sleeping, and she never smiled like that before. I don't tell Neal that was the moment when I loved her most. I don't tell him she said she had nothing to give me. That's what she said on the last day, in the morning. She shoved me awake and said she could give me nothing more. Said our arrangement was over. She said she was going to India, of all places. I didn't believe her.

I tell him that she went off to work at eight. There was a car accident at eight-fifteen. That is what they told me. That was all I ever had to go on. They said she swerved for no reason, then slammed into that other guy, got out of her car and swore at him. They say she walked off, and the other guy tried to help her but she kept going.

Neal uncrosses his legs, and I ask him what else I should tell.

*

My body shivers. The whole house is freezing cold; the fog and chill having rolled inside. Neal has disappeared. The police come. The teachers say they saw him last standing in the school courtyard with the bigger boys who had cars. They say he was smoking with them, and blame me because these are all the horrors I was supposed to watch out for. I give the police an outdated photo. "He has kind of a mustache now," I say. "A little dark fuzz above his lip."

In a matter of hours, I see the picture everywhere—photocopied, posted, a plea underneath. I get calls from the other parents, offering sympathy. The police have a few early leads, some eyewitnesses. I ask them eyewitnesses to what, but they don't say.

Late in the evening of the second day I take a drive. I put Blue Boy in the passenger seat, and she sleeps balled up there. She doesn't miss Neal, doesn't sense the absence the way she used to when he was gone for even an hour. Now she is content to be driven up and down the streets and taken up into the highest hills where the deepest part of the night has pooled. I park the car in a familiar spot and rouse her. She scratches and complains, but I lift her out anyway, and together we sit on the hood of the car, looking out at the twinkling, surprised city and at the water laid out far below us. At first I try to say something to Blue Boy, something in a voice reserved for kittens and babies, something I used to tell Neal when he was small enough, but it sounds ridiculous now, to be muttering to this clever creature. So we are both quiet, the cat and I.

We get home after midnight, and there are messages on the machine from the police, who have nothing to say, and from the neighboring mother, who rattles on morosely for a few minutes. There is also one hang-up, just a raging dial tone, and I know it is Neal.

Not at all sleepy, I read for two hours, and I look at some old pictures. Then I pick up the phone and try the numbers again for the first time in many years. It is ludicrous. They are not angry now, merely puzzled. They pity me. They say I should remarry. When they ask about Neal, I tell them he has grown into quite a young man.

It is four o'clock in the morning here, and I call my mother because I know she will already be awake back in the Midwest. I have not called in ages. She asks over and over if it is really me.

"How is Neal?" she asks.

I tell her that he is missing, that I don't know what to do.

"He'll be back tomorrow," she whispers. "Children do this."

Then I tell her how I called the numbers in India again. There is a long pause. "You just remember that it's all my fault," she says. "I told you that from the beginning."

"It's not."

"I forced you to be with her. After all this time, why can't you let it go? My God! You are so foolish for still thinking...."

"But don't you think I should go back? I could look. If they saw me in person they might listen. I might find out some small thing at least."

"Go, go, do whatever you have to do! But don't whine like you used to. Not to me."

We talk like this for a long time, and then I tell her I must go looking for Neal again. She says I should call when I know something, and I promise. I fall asleep almost immediately. When the phone rings at ten, I let it go on and on, then the machine, the police saying I should come down, they have him safe. Neal won't explain where he's been. But he's safe. I hear all this, still lying in bed. The cat scratches at my door, whining, and I let her in. Blue Boy jumps on the bed, pawing my face, knowing nothing. And all of a sudden I start crying.

*

Once, in a village in the southernmost part of India, a still ancient place, there was a wedding to which a thousand guests came to bear witness. No family had spent so lavishly as far back as anyone could remember: an orchestra, a few elephants, a European limousine. It was beautiful and familiar and unseemly, all at once. It demanded an effort not to get carried away and be swept up in the old families' showy ambition. But for three days everyone ate and cried and believed. The guests, and even those who were not invited, would talk about it for months afterward.

It had been a difficult arrangement. Everyone wanted the match, even years earlier, but the young man and the young woman had other ideas. They had clothes and cars and beliefs, they lived on different coasts in America, and there was no stopping them. They mocked everything. The villagers had heard that, too. The young people thought they were so superior, thought they had licked the bad old ways. They stood grim-faced against the coaxing and cajoling, the threats and the tearing out of hair, the long and morbid letters. And yet somehow, finally, the children came to certain conclusions. They gave in.

Some said they'd heard that the couple had a terrible fight at the airport when they arrived. But there they were, not far from the beach, standing on the hot sand and grinning like they were happy, never mind the rumors. People would talk; it was just envy. Look at them: their families applauding and crowding around for a glimpse, the parents flanking them as a hundred pictures were taken.

The next day, the couple left—the young husband went to Spain, and the wife to England to see her friends. They wrote postcards to one another. They met again in America and promised themselves they would try married life. So they took long drives and cooked terrible dinners and walked the foggy streets of town thinking they could do worse. They called it our partnership, our mad duty, given the facts of our birth. When their parents phoned, they gushed and used fond names for one another. After those conversations, they would sit together in the kitchen, laughing hysterically about it, but they assured each other that they weren't deceiving anyone, they weren't running a sham, they weren't denying themselves happiness. They congratulated one another. Occasionally, they even slept together.

They lived like that almost two years: a part-time couple. Eventually, she became pregnant. In the last few months of the pregnancy everything grew different. The husband wanted to know what had happened. One night he called her into the kitchen while he was cooking. He had been at it for hours, and she teased him for it. Then he spoke, his voice trembling, and he stared intently at the cookbook. He reached over, patted the great stomach that enveloped a child that was not his own son. And he said—you owe me this, the truth. Then he talked about love, or something like it. But she merely shook her head.

"Shit," she whispered. "He's all we'll have between us."

Blue Boy

*

We take a flight that never ends. We are grounded in Tokyo. Mechanical problems, they say. In the airport Neal drinks three, four, five expensive Cokes, and he cannot stop talking. He talks to the uniformed men, to the tourists waiting listlessly, to the Japanese who try to understand him. Then we are back on the plane, and Neal starts asking about India. I tell him about the summers. He asks about the family, and I name names for him. He asks if we are going to find him a wife.

The boy is sixteen. His voice is cracking. He looks at the skinny female flight attendants and grins shyly. They give him a deck of cards, little packets of gum. He offers one of the women his baseball cap and asks her how far we have to go. She obliges, looking over at me, then draws him a map, as if he were a child. India is a triangle. She draws arrows and explains about the curvature of the earth. Neal shakes his head slowly, watching her breasts. The whole airplane shudders. The flight attendant slams down the paper and fastens Neal's seatbelt for him. He grasps her hand but she hurries off.

We land in the night at the dimly lit and sweating airport in Madras. We are many hours late. Our porter laughs. "We did not think plane will ever come," he says.

Another day passes before we reach the village, down in the center of a dry and rocky valley. There has been no monsoon yet, though the worst heat of summer has passed. As we ride down in the rented car our driver pokes his head out of the window and looking up at the sky, tells Neal to watch for bad omens. Neal still has the map, folds and unfolds it, and the creases begin to tear.

At the great arch in front of the estate, his great-grandmother is waiting, perched on a stool, and does not greet us. She speaks of God. Neal doesn't understand, and I translate her Tamil. She takes his hand and puts it to her cheek, tells him he is American and ugly and pale. I tell Neal that this is his mother's mother's mother.

She is eighty-three years old and blind. She sees with her hands. She tells me I am too thin, old for my age. She says I look nothing like the other men in my family. Eventually, she takes us through the compound and inside to the great room in the central house where pictures cover all the walls. From the sanctum she brings out the gods and the tins and the *vibuthi* and the camphor lamp and the incense.

So our days pass. The old woman remains as relations come and go. The relatives seem to have forgotten my calls, given up their irritation. They say they are happy to see the boy and me at last. But that's all they say. Only Neal's great-grandmother talks. She tells us about the old mistakes, the family's wasted fury. And every morning she brings us into the central room where she prays. I don't ask her anything until the third day. Spooked, Neal won't come in anymore. So I am alone with her, and I ask about her granddaughter.

"Sad," she says in English.

I ask again.

She shakes her head. The English words bring spittle to the corners of her mouth. "Leave it." And she tells me to kneel on the floor. We are kneeling together, and she is begging Ganapati to save us.

*

Neal is gone again. I have searched the village. A day and a moonless night pass. There are no other search parties this time; there are no police investigations. People in the village say he will return. They say people disappear like that in India, in the valley, but they return. On the second night I wait outside the arch, sitting on the old woman's stool with a kerosene lamp in hand. The cart drivers and the truant children and the old insomniacs all stare as they pass. They know why I have come, and they know why I sit outside. The eyes are unrelenting. Neal's great-grandmother comes outside to stand with me. I offer her the stool, but she shrugs. She sleeps standing up, but then asks suddenly, after I have drifted off myself, "He is not yours, is he?"

I don't answer. For the first time, I see her smile; a long front tooth edges out over a withered lip, and a dry laugh escapes.

At dawn she leaves me to go to the market to get milk and fruit, and she returns with Neal, who is carrying her canvas bag. He drops it and runs to embrace me at the arch. His hold is strong, nearly overpowering.

"I saw her," he says.

"What is he saying?" his great-grandmother asks.

"He saw her," I say.

Neal looks at the old woman. "My mother," he says.

"Tell the cook to fetch the doctor," she tells me.

The doctor says Neal has a fever and diarrhea besides. Pink pills and yellow pills. My son throws up for hours. I keep giving him water.

"Listen," he says. He tells me that he was running through the village alleys, snapping pictures with his pocket camera when he joined some boys at the roadside throwing pebbles at the chickens. A woman approached them and snatched Neal's hand. It was his mother, he says. She asked him to stop hurting the poor chickens. She took him to the sweets stall and bought him a bag of candy. They walked, he says. His mother started to explain things. She was not well. She wanted to go back to America. That evening she showed him the crumbling temple and the river she played in when her parents brought her to visit India. Then the two went up to Madurai on a motorscooter, he says, a real live motorscooter with a noisy engine. She keeps a school where she is teaching English. The following night they rode again, and she brought Neal back to the village.

"You don't believe me," Neal says at last.

"No."

"Fuck."

I slap him across the cheek.

He holds his head in his hands for a long time, and I finally touch his fingers, saying, "It's time to sleep."

"I have to go," he says.

So I lead him to the back where he squats and groans and shouts to me that his insides are burning up.

Finally he lies down. He says we ought to go home soon and I agree. I miss the cat.

*

The morning of our departure, the aunts and uncles and cousins are gathered in the courtyard. Neal's great-grandmother stands beside him, holding his head with both hands. I thank them all for having us. The children crowd around Neal and hug him. Neal's great-grandmother shooes the children away and thrusts Neal toward me, asking if I am up to being a father to this young man. I say I will do my best.

She comes very near me, her face in my own, and shouts, "You think no one can blame you for anything. That is what you do for a living." Then she steps away, looking at both Neal and me. "Two with sickness," she says. "You better leave before you give it to the rest of us."

The cook helps us carry the bags to the arch. Outside the compound the children gather again, reminding us to visit again soon. They say the weather will be better next time. They ask us to take their picture. So we have all of them line up along the graffiti-covered wall, crammed together and serious-faced as Neal takes the photograph.

*

We return to America. A quick and uneventful passage: no delays, no tremors, no maps drawn. Neal and I sleep through the whole thing. And then we are home. The friend who took care of Blue

Boy brings her over and frowns sadly. The cat has thinned. She wobbles when she walks. Neal picks her up, and she seems to sputter. The friend tells us she suddenly lost her sight. She bumps into the furniture and into the walls.

Neal says we must make the cat as comfortable as possible now. The cat sits morosely in the windowsill and her ears flicker as the traffic passes. Sometimes, Neal watches TV with her and turns the sound up.

If he is not with the cat, Neal flies. He rides about town with his friends who call him The Playboy. He has kissed a girl. On certain nights, I make him stay with me. I carry the cat in my arms, and the three of us head up to the park as we once did. Blue Boy lies very quietly, and we sit in the breeze. One evening we stay in the park until night has fallen and everyone has gone. There is only the dying cat between me and my son, and there is not much to say. Neal plucks blades of grass and dangles them in front of Blue Boy.

"I want to take her with me on the first day of school this year," he says.

"You know you can't. Remember? You asked a long time ago."

"Just once. She won't be around for much longer."

"You're too old for show-and-tell. The principal will send you home."

"You wait and see, even the principal will love her."

"She might get nervous. Who knows? She might bite someone."

Neal draws up his knees and looks at me. And who can tell in the dark what the color of his eyes really is. He laughs. "She's still a little monster, huh?"

"A terror," I say.

Chief Next Lightning's Phantom Hand

Michael Poore

An old Indian walks into Mesa Prosthetics on a Saturday morning. He doesn't have an appointment, so he sits down and waits all day.

The receptionist offers coffee, but the old Indian shakes his head. He doesn't speak until she asks his name, then doesn't say another word. "Phil Next Lightning," he tells her. "Former chief of the Sundog O-odham. I'm here because my arm left me."

He shows her the place where his arm used to be, and she writes his name in her book. Then he sits down and waits. He stares at the wall as if he finds it faintly amusing.

*

Only two people work at Mesa Prosthetics. One is the receptionist, and the other is Joe Ingram, who sees the patients and makes artificial limbs for them. The shop is located in southern Arizona, near the Pima reservation, so Ingram sees a lot of Indians.

Ingram finally gets Next Lightning in his office at four-thirty in the afternoon. He offers the chief an open-palm gesture he has learned, an Apache *hello*.

"Sometimes," Next Lightning tells Joe Ingram, "I can feel my arm moving and itching. I feel it returning greetings."

"'Phantom Limb'," says Ingram, nodding. "The nerves in your shoulder, your spine, and your brain don't know the arm is gone. The nerves get confused and send signals."

Next Lightning snaps his ghostly fingers.

Ingram makes a plaster cast of the Indian's stump, the arm having been chopped off above the elbow, and tells him to make an appointment. "Two weeks," he says.

"Two weeks," confirms Next Lightning, smoothing his long gray hair, adjusting his sunglasses, and Ingram knows he'll show up when he feels like it, not before.

*

Next Lightning has trouble remembering. He's had this trouble for awhile and it keeps getting worse. After he leaves Ingram's office, and no one is looking, he becomes a different person. His eyes grow sad and confused. He can't remember where he left his car.

He stumbles on it by accident. It's a rusty Cadillac convertible, an ancient roadship with a medicine bag hanging from the mirror. Next Lightning sits down in the passenger seat, trying to recall if he drove himself, or if his niece brought him. His niece doesn't like for him to drive anymore, because sometimes he forgets what he's doing right in the middle of doing it. After a while, he finds keys in his pocket and slides over behind the wheel.

He leaves the city at twenty miles an hour, thinking of ways to make himself invisible when he drives past his niece's trailer.

*

Dr. Ingram spends the next morning on his bicycle, flashing down the highway at competition speed. When his legs get tired, he thinks how lucky he is to have legs. He thinks about Next Lightning, and how the Indian doesn't seem to mind that his "arm has left him."

Ingram also thinks about his non-Indian clients, especially a young paralegal who lost a foot in a car accident. "Miss one red light and I'm fucked for life!" she had screamed. Then she whipped a pair of scissors out of her purse and stabbed herself in the offending leg. Nice and deep. There was hardly any blood at first. Ingram's hands had flown toward the scissors, then hovered around them, his eyes meeting hers. "They threw my foot in the trash. The fuckers didn't even bury it."

The young paralegal is now Ingram's fiancée, equipped with an expensive hydraulic prosthesis. When he remembers the scissors, Ingram rides his bike faster and faster and faster.

*

Next Lightning's niece, Becky Horse Practice, is a licensed therapist. Becky wants her uncle to join a support group for Indian amputees. "Lots of Apaches have prosthetics," she tells him urgently. "It's from diabetes. We drink too much, we don't eat right. Our circulation goes bad."

"Diabetes, my ass," mutters Next Lightning. "My arm is out wandering. That's all." *It's true*, he thinks. He can feel it, wandering between the thighs of young girls.

"Stop it," Becky barks, like she can tell what he's thinking.

Next Lightning jumps. It scares the hell out of him when she does that.

*

Ingram and his fiancée are afraid of each other.

Ingram's fear is buried deep. He doesn't know he's afraid.

Rachel, his fiancée, complains that he slams the refrigerator door. She complains about the pictures on the walls—which are mostly snapshots of Ingram on bicycles, crossing finish lines. When he's asleep, Ingram's fear whispers that this is because now that Rachel's living with him, she finds him diminished and ridiculous.

Rachel's fear is not secret. *He's with you because he feels sorry for you,* rasps her fear. *He'd rather have a woman with two real feet. Who wouldn't? He regrets everything; he's just too spineless to say so.* "Shut up," says Rachel to her fear, speaking aloud.

"Didn't say a goddamn word," says Ingram, leaving the room to get away from her. When he gets to the hallway, he can't think where else to go, so he just stands there.

*

Seven recent amputees sit in a circle, in folding chairs at the rec center. They look more bothered by the support group than by their missing limbs.

"Maybe you could start," says Becky Horse Practice to her uncle.

Next Lightning leans forward and warms his phantom hand over a phantom campfire. "Horror is nothing new to the Indian," he says. "There were monsters before there were men. In the beginning, the moon made women and set them on the world. The women burned with desire for men whom the moon hadn't made yet, so the moon showed the women how to pleasure themselves with smooth rocks and running stream water. The moon did not think what result this would have. When one woman pleasured herself with a smooth rock, she gave birth to a monster, who was like a round stone at first but he grew into a rolling mountain. The mighty monster rolled over the desert and over a lot of the women, crushing their arms and legs. Afterward, the limbless women gathered in a circle and talked. So it is to this day."

The Indians in the circle hide smiles with their real hands.

Becky presses her lips together until her mouth subtracts itself from her face.

One evening when Ingram and Rachel are eating supper on the back patio, two girls on horseback come riding down the wash beside the house. One of them eats a candy bar; the other waves up at the house.

Ingram waves back.

Rachel doesn't. Rachel watches the girls with narrow eyes, and when the girl with the candy bar tosses the empty wrapper on the ground, she leaps from her chair. "Hey!" she screams. "Shit! You pick that up!"

Both girls turn in their saddles. The litterbug dismounts, retrieves the wrapper, hops back into her saddle and gallops away.

Rachel hobbles through the back door and picks up her cell phone, jabbing at the numbers.

"What are you doing?" asks Ingram, following.

"Police."

"She picked it up, didn't she? We don't have to be assholes about it."

Rachel knows he's right. Secretly, moving her thumb behind her ear, she presses the *off* button. She hopes he'll go back outside before she has to pretend she's talking to the cops.

*

Becky Horse Practice drives her uncle to Ingram's office in the city, and reads magazines while Next Lightning's new arm is strapped on.

His elbow is a silver turnbuckle. His new fingers are hooks made of chrome. Suddenly whole again, Next Lightning's mind becomes sharp and clear. "You should talk to my niece," he tells Ingram. "She takes people with missing pieces and makes them talk in circles."

"Support groups," says Ingram, sounding interested. "Bring her with you next time. We'll talk."

Next Lightning nods, forgetting Becky in the waiting room.

*

That night, the old Indian sits behind the wheel of his car, parked in front of his trailer. He feels his death getting closer. It looks just like him, with long hair and deep black eyes. It hitchhikes and rides buses and trains, searching for him. Next Lightning considers his chrome fingers, feeling conspicuous.

Becky walks up from her trailer, sits down in the passenger seat, and bums a smoke. While she smokes, Next Lightning tells her his big idea.

"Work in the city?" she says. "You trying to get rid of me?"

"My death caught a ride in Flagstaff this morning," he answers. "With some girl in a Plymouth. You should think nice thoughts about me while I'm still here."

Becky pinches the bridge of her nose, feeling the birth of a headache. She shows Next Lightning her thumb and forefinger with less than an inch between them.

"This," she says, "is exactly how much I feel sorry for you."

*

Becky picks up the phone and leaves a message at Ingram's office. Ingram calls her back. They make arrangements.

Two days later, Becky and Next Lightning park his old Cadillac outside Mesa Prosthetics at twilight, after closing time. They sit down with Ingram in his private office in the back, drinking coffee and talking.

They talk about the weather and the news and how well Next Lightning is doing. Then they talk about people with missing limbs in general, and then how, in particular, amputees might benefit from a local support group. Next Lightning wanders away to find the toilet.

When he leaves the washroom, he sees his car keys sitting on a shelf above the coatrack.

He finds the Cadillac and drives away.

*

Rachel leans against her car at a filling station, pumping gas.

She is tired. Not just from a day's work, but the long, slow tired you get when fear whispers at you all the time. *Any day*, says the fear, *he's going to ask you to move out. He can't move out; you can't afford his place. The only reason he hasn't said anything yet is it would make him feel like an asshole.* Rachel turns away, balancing carefully on her stainless steel ankle, trying not to listen.

She is distracted by a spectacle amidst the traffic—an old man in a Cadillac convertible driving about four miles an hour, other cars whizzing around him or stuck behind him, honking and honking.

Rachel watches so intently that she fails to keep an eye on the gas pump, the automatic shutoff malfunctions and gasoline spurts over her hand, down her pants and into her artificial ankle, filling her shoe. Her screams distract the drivers behind the old man in the Cadillac, who figure there are worse things than being stuck in traffic.

*

"Shit," says Becky Horse Practice. "I knew this would happen someday."

Ingram stands in the parking lot with her. Their conversation has turned from lost arms and referrals to how Becky is going to get home. "I'll drive you," he says. "We can talk on the way."

And that's how Ingram comes to be getting into his car, long after office hours, with an attractive Indian woman, when Rachel's Honda comes roaring into the parking lot.

She gets out and stands there gaping at the two of them. *See,* says her fear. *It's finally happened.*

"I spilled gas all over myself," is all she can think of to say. "I came by to use your bathroom and get something to put on the car seat." She fights an urge to get down on her knees and see if the little bitch has real feet.

Instead, Rachel roars away again, radio blaring.

"What just happened?" Becky asks Ingram.

"Nothing," says Ingram. "But it's been happening for a while."

*

Chief Next Lightning meanders down the highway at forty miles an hour, the day and year swimming around him like a mirage. For awhile, he believes he is twenty again.

A Greyhound bus flashes by in the northbound lane. The Chief pays it no mind. In the very back seat of the Greyhound bus, Next Lightning's death brushes long gray hair from its eyes and stares back down the highway after the Cadillac.

*

Ingram and Becky sit at a table outside a Dairy Queen, halfway between the city and the reservation.

"Sorry," she says, trying to eat a chili dog without making a mess. "I get woozy if I don't eat for a while. Diabetic."

"It's alright," answers Ingram, digging into a banana split.

Becky points a chili-covered finger at Ingram's bicycle, upside-down in its rack atop the car. "You race?"

"Used to."

He doesn't plan on saying anything else about it, but before he knows it, he's telling her about the time he rode in a race up Mount Lemmon, and how his legs had burned and his lungs felt like he was breathing acid, and how his mind became a single coal, a tiny spark outside the pain. He tells about how he didn't win, but at least he finished. He had a photo of himself crossing the finish line, and Rachel had taken it off the wall. Ingram doesn't tell Becky that last part.

"I know about doing that thing with your mind," says Becky. "That thing with the hot coal. I did the same thing when I got tattoos around my nipples. Three concentric hoops."

A quiet space passes.

"Show me," says Ingram.

The quiet space widens.

She shows him.

Then she buttons up again, and they finish eating without a word.

*

Rachel gets woozy from gasoline fumes in her car. She screeches to a stop on the street in front of a mini-mall, and staggers out into the air, gagging, hauling in great, deep breaths. Her artificial ankle lurches sideways, wrenching its wet straps loose. As she collapses, she catches herself on the open door.

She doesn't curse. She doesn't scream. This time she's all action. With quick hands she tears at the remaining strap, struggling to free herself of the gas-soaked prosthesis. She can't. The strap winds around her lower leg. So off comes her belt, off come her slacks, over the real foot and the false one. Off comes the prosthesis.

Hobbling in her underwear, Rachel places her hydraulic foot behind the Honda's rear wheel. She gets in the car, hits the accelerator with her stump, and runs over the foot sixteen times.

Chief Next Lightning's Phantom Hand

*

Next Lightning is sitting at a picnic table outside his trailer when his death comes walking up the gravel road. Death bums a cigarette and sits down.

"A long time ago," Next Lightning tells his death, "before there were men in the world, there was a woman who made love to an old treetrunk in a stream and had monstrous children made of wood. When the monsters grew up, they walked around in the desert with no moccasins on, because their feet felt no pain. The stones in the ground wore away at their feet until their feet were gone, so the monsters crawled on their hands and knees. When their hands and knees wore away, they moved on the ground like snakes, unable to feel their wounds, until there was nothing left of them at all."

His death blows a smoke ring.

"My father told me that story," says Next Lightning. "I forget why."

The Indian and his death sit for a long time saying nothing, smoking and forgetting, smoking and forgetting, smoking and forgetting.

*

A police cruiser pulls up behind Rachel's Honda. When she sees the lights in her mirror, she hits the brakes and stops running over the remains of her foot, stops pretending to run over Ingram and his two-footed redskin slut. In a final gasp of frustration, she smacks her hand against the steering wheel, breaking a nail.

The nail points straight up in the air, blood welling beneath the cuticle.

A cop with a gigantic mustache walks up beside her, and when he sees her sitting there with no pants on and one foot missing, he says "Jesus" to himself.

Rachel thinks he's referring to the broken nail.

"Nothing," she says. "That's nothing."

*

Ingram's car pulls up in the dark outside Next Lightning's trailer. Becky gets out, and Ingram does too, to say *Hi*, since the old man is sitting at the picnic table. Walking up the hill, Becky and Ingram both imagine holding hands, but they don't, they just sit down.

Next Lightning doesn't say a word, which isn't unusual. Becky and Ingram don't say a word either; the chief's trailer and the hill it sits on both feel like it's okay to just sit and let the night turn around you.

Ingram thinks about going home, and gets a sour feeling in his belly. He rubs his mouth with his hand to keep from groaning out loud.

Somewhere on the reservation a pack of coyotes *yip yip yip*.

Somewhere else there's a gunshot and a radio turned up loud.

Becky thinks about patting her uncle's hand, but doesn't. Nothing seems to fit the way it should, which is normal, only suddenly it's worse, like being used to something your whole life and then one day not being able to stand it.

"I got a tattoo once," says Ingram in a whisper. "On my shoulder." He doesn't say what it is, but he draws a picture of it in the air, and without even knowing she's going to do it, Becky turns around on the bench and leans her head back against his shoulder. His arm drifts around her waist. Becky wonders what her uncle thinks of this, and decides she'll give him the finger if he says anything.

Next Lightning is as quiet as outer space.

Under Ganesh's Gaze

Helen Chandra

Ashok and I arrived in Benares on the Delhi Express in the middle of the night, and walked out onto a platform illuminated by over-bright lights, as if it were a stage. His father, Babuji, and his younger brother, Kumar, were waiting for us. Ashok gave me a slight nudge, and as we had rehearsed, I bent down and touched Babuji's feet, my face brought close to his yellow, horn-rimmed toes. Babuji, a large man with a regal presence, immediately raised me by my shoulders and said "No, no. No need for that." Out of the corner of my eye I could see Kumar snicker. Kumar was young, not yet out of college; I suppose the sight of an American woman dressed in a sari and observing all the formalities of a Hindu bride must have seemed to him comical, even unreal.

The sense of play-acting stayed with me as we continued on our way to Thatheri House. The family complex was located deep inside Thatheri Bazaar, the metalsmiths' market, and could be reached only on foot through narrow lanes now deserted. The station taxi took us as close as possible. At the road's end porters waited for us and rose clumsily out of their sleep to load our suitcases and bedrolls on their heads. I walked ahead in the procession that quickly formed, porters in front and behind me. Ashok strolled behind, chatting with his father and brother. Hearing their laughter, I struggled to remind myself that the acute loneliness I felt was the result of normal anxiety over coming to live with his family, not a premonition of what lay ahead. We had been married for several months, marked by a curious, do-it-yourself kind of ceremony shortly before leaving America. But after stops in London, Rome and Delhi, this was the first time we had visited his ancestral home. We had come to stay.

The shops on either side of the dark lane were shuttered, the street littered with bits of newspapers, leaf-packets, broken terracotta cups, cow dung, and splashes of red betel stain. The air was stale, as if all the life had been sucked out of it. We had not been on the way long when I saw something large and hairy scurry through the shadows at the side of the road. I stumbled, bringing the procession to a halt. At Ashok's command, Haridev, his old servant, rushed up to me, trained a flashlight onto the uneven path in front of my feet, and we started up again. The lane came to an end in front of Thatheri House, a tall, gray, imposing structure whose walls came down flush with the street.

Above the dim, arched doorway was a red and gold carving of the elephant-headed god Ganesh, just as Ashok had described it. Ganesh, the "remover of obstacles." I did not know the prayers appropriate to his worship, but liked the comfort his presence seemed to imply, and bowed my head as I passed under the deity's watchful gaze.

After passing through a dark hall, we walked into a well-lighted courtyard where the women of the house were waiting for us. I recognized most of them from photos Ashok had shown me: his married sister, his mother, grandmother, and a fourth woman that I could not identify. Ashok came up behind me and I heard him say "Ma, this is Sara," but before I could touch her feet as I thought she might have expected, she embraced me. Then she stepped back, put a hand on each of my cheeks and sobbed "*Bahu, bahu,*" which I knew meant *bride, bride*.

The next few minutes were a whirl of confusion, as I bent down to receive his grandmother's blessings, accepted a hug from his sister, and was introduced to his mother's friend, whom Ashok called 'Auntie'. It was by then very late, and we were soon allowed to retire to the rooms that had been prepared for us on the second floor.

My heart sank when I saw the room, almost completely bare except for two wooden cots isolated from one another by cage-like mosquito nets suspended from bamboo poles lashed to the bed posts.

"Never mind, we'll rearrange everything tomorrow," Ashok said, pushing the two cots together. When we were in bed, we each lifted the side of our mosquito net, creating an open space between us. We lay in the dark, our hands and sometimes our lips penetrating into the next bed.

"It has been a long day and night," Ashok said, stroking my shoulder. "How do you feel, meeting my family, the house, Benares, all for the first time?"

"A little scared," I admitted. "Do you really think I will fit in? That I can be the *bahu* your parents want, even though I'm hardly what they would have hoped for?"

"Of course," he murmured, kissing the inside of my elbow. "Believe me, I'm a little apprehensive too. I ask myself, how have I changed, going to school in America? What if I have become too Western for this place, too Indian for that? As I told you in Madison, give me a year, and if either of us isn't happy here, we'll move to another city, or even back to America. We will see it through together."

*

We slept late the next morning. When I woke I could see from the windows of our bedroom details of the house that were not visible to me in the night. I was enchanted by the peeling pink stucco walls, the brick-paved floor, and the small pavilion built onto a low platform in the middle of the courtyard. I knew from what Ashok had told me that the house itself stretched over a whole city-block, and in a maze-like manner, encompassed not only Ashok's family, but his father's cousins, and a few common rooms they shared.

Here on his father's side of the house all the rooms opened up onto this one courtyard. Ashok pointed out to me where his parents, Babuji and Ma, lived with his brother, Kumar, in a suite of rooms on one side of the courtyard. His grandmother slept in a room opposite them, next door to the *puja* room, where the family worshipped. The formal dining room and the kitchen were located on the second floor, just down the hall from us. But it was the courtyard, cool in summer and warmed by the sun in winter, that was the heart of the house.

Ashok appeared to have no trouble readjusting to life in India. Like all the men in the family, he dressed in immaculate white clothing, a wide pajama and a kurta, a loose shirt. He seemed more at ease in Indian dress than in his American clothes, and I had to look closely to find that edge, laced with curiosity and eagerness, that had drawn me to him back in Madison.

When we were first getting to know each other at the university, Ashok showed a talent for life in America. He spoke, read and wrote English perfectly; he charmed my family with his elegant manners; he relished new experiences—baseball games, Halloween parties, Easter egg hunts, and picnics at the lake—without giving up his essential Indianness. I was prepared to throw myself into Indian life with the same amount of confidence and abandonment.

"The one thing I cannot do," he said to me once, "is to eat beef. You look into the eyes of an American cow, she doesn't even look like an Indian cow. She has no soul. But I can't help it. It is ingrained in me, this devotion to the cow."

Ashok had something I lacked, I remembered thinking then, a religious belief that influenced all his actions. I had been raised a Protestant, and in our family religion was something we thought about on Sundays, at best. I loved animals, and I shared with most of my college classmates an admiration for the teachings of Mahatma Gandhi, but his concepts of non-violence and reverence for life touched me only obliquely.

*

After tea every morning, Ashok went off to join his father at the family factory, where they assembled fans and air conditioners using imported parts. Ashok hoped that with his American knowledge and contacts he could increase the range of imports and even perhaps export some of India's products back to the West.

I, meanwhile, tried to fit myself into the daily routine of the other women of the household, but I was excused, shrugged off, and otherwise discouraged from joining them in their work. I was not allowed to set foot inside the main kitchen. This room was the domain of the brahmin woman who was hired by the day. Since she belonged to the highest caste, any visitor to the house could eat food prepared by her. I was told that menstruating women were ritually unclean and would defile any food or utensil they touched. Since she didn't expect an American woman to be open about her menstrual cycle, it was simpler to keep me out of the kitchen at all times.

Sometimes I approached Grandmother, a frail woman who always dressed in white, the color of mourning, and who wore her sari pulled tight over her head. But Grandmother never had time for idle chatter, even if she could have understood my rudimentary Hindi. If she wasn't napping she cloistered herself inside the *puja* room, the family shrine. Scarcely larger than a closet, this room, entered from the courtyard, had shuttered windows and a door. Images of the gods favored with daily worship sat enthroned on a small, low, wooden table, while other sculptures, paintings, and ritual implements filled shelves all around the room. Here Grandmother sat for hours performing the elaborate set of rituals that made up her daily *puja*. Every morning she invited the main deity to inhabit its image, presented it with good sights, sounds, smells, and tastes, then concluded the *puja* by acknowledging that the deity had taken its leave. When she wasn't praying to the gods, Grandmother sewed clothes for the images, strung flowers into garlands to hang around their necks, and read sacred texts.

Often on Sunday afternoons the family gathered on the largest *chouki*, a room-sized padded sitting platform, to play board games or assemble jigsaw puzzles. The first Sunday or two they spoke some English, out of courtesy to me, but soon everyone, including Ashok, spoke Hindi exclusively. I could understand only a fragment of what was being said. Sometimes I could make out Ma complaining about the unusually large number of rats that roamed the courtyard. At other times someone would tell a story, provoking waves of laughter. I would smile politely as if I had understood the joke, even if I hadn't. Those Sunday afternoons were excruciatingly long for me, but I suffered through them as one would a broken leg, hoping time would heal the pain.

One Sunday Ma thought up a new game. "I wonder if we have time to make the Satyajit Ray movie?" she asked in Hindi. "Bahu, you make the call."

Obediently I crawled over to the inner circle, where she had placed a phone. Usually, I avoided making phone calls. Few of the operators spoke English, and without visual cues I had difficulty understanding their Hindi.

"Do you know the number?" I asked.

"No, just dial the operator."

Again and again I asked the operator to repeat the phone number of the theater while I tried to write down the long string of numbers. Then I began to repeat the number aloud and watched Ashok as he cued me by mouthing silently the English number. Next I called the theater and asked them when the movie would begin. By the time I got it all straight, it was too late for the movie.

Later, alone in our room, I told Ashok, "It's harassment. I think your family likes seeing me make a fool of myself."

"I can understand how you feel," he said. "Remember, we all had to learn English, and the Sisters who taught us were not always very kind. My mother may be trying to tell you to learn Hindi as quickly as you can."

He put his hand on my shoulder, but in my anger I shrugged

it away. He wasn't giving me enough credit for trying so hard to fit into his family. It had been easier for him when he lived in America. He already knew the language, and there were no mean-spirited family members to put him down.

"Well then, hire me a tutor," I said.

The next day Master-ji began coming to the house. He arrived every morning at 10:00, dressed formally in a white *dhoti, kurta*, and vest, and sat opposite me in the courtyard. He always looked so proud and pristine, I could never tell him about the fleas that I sometimes spotted on his collar. Each day I read to him from the text I had been studying or a Hindi newspaper, and we conversed for half-an-hour. After he left I carefully wiped off with disinfectant the chair in which he had been sitting.

With Master-ji's help my Hindi slowly improved. I began to enjoy some of the family excursions we took, a boat ride on the Ganges, or a visit to one of the near-by historical sites.

Despite my growing facility with the language, when Ma and the others were curious, they would forego Hindi and question me in cautious, but impeccable English. One day Auntie, who was married to one of the cousin-uncles who lived in another part of Thatheri House, joined Ma for the day and they motioned me to approach. Ma asked, "Do you observe the custom of dowry in America?"

I knew they were fishing to find out whether I had brought any money into the marriage and if so, how much. I chose to answer them in Hindi, saying no, we had different customs.

They persisted. "Your father and mother, they gave gifts when you were married?"

I thought my parents had been very generous; their gifts filled up many of the boxes and trunks that had followed us to the house and that were still stacked up in a pile in the courtyard. But I knew that those gifts, given to me as well as to Ashok, would not qualify as dowry. I began to enumerate things they had given and pointed to my watch, which I had received on the birthday preceding my marriage, but Auntie interrupted: "Gave to Ashok?"

I tried to wiggle out of the question by mixing up my Hindi with technical terms such as "calculator," which I hoped they wouldn't understand, but they bobbed their heads up and down in apparent satisfaction.

That night, after we had crawled under the mosquito net, I told Ashok about my conversation. He laughed. "I'm surprised they didn't ask you if we had a private bank account, and if so how much money was in it."

I persisted. "But do you regret sometimes what you've given up by bringing home a foreign wife? No dowry, no mother-in-law to fawn over you. . ."

He hit me over the head with a pillow. "Now I'm stuck with you—what can I do about it?" Then in a more serious tone he said, "The paying of dowry always seemed to me like paying a man to marry your sister or your daughter. And there is no way I could marry a woman I didn't love, let alone didn't even know. My parents knew how I felt, even before I went to America, and they finally gave up answering marriage inquiries. Still, I can't change how others think about it. I can only show by example what I think."

The only light came from an almost full moon that filtered in through the mosquito netting. Ashok, lying beside me, seemed both exotic and familiar. His warm brown skin glowed against the white bed sheets. Since we'd arrived in India he seemed older, and more confident, while I felt younger, paler, decidedly less in control. I joined my hand with his, as fascinated as ever with the interplay of skin tones, the interlocking light and dark fingers.

*

The conversations about dowry made the family newly aware of the unpacked trunks and boxes. Our small suite of rooms was adequate to sleep in, but what Ashok and I needed was a storeroom. Ma decided to open up a long neglected room on the third floor filled with old trunks, pots, and who knew what. For many years its door had been chained and bolted shut. The room was not suitable to live in since it was not connected to any other space in the house; it could be reached only by an open staircase on the far side of the courtyard.

Haridev took on the job of clearing it out. He tucked his loin cloth high between his legs and wrapped his head and face in a cotton shawl. Going up and down the staircase built into the stuccoed courtyard wall, he and the day laborers looked in profile like characters out of an Egyptian tomb painting.

Unbolted, the room gave out the unmistakable pungent smell of a rat hovel. The workmen filled countless buckets and baskets with dust, paper and cloth fragments, potsherds, and rat droppings. The tin trunks were pried open, moldy bedcovers and outgrown children's garments briefly examined and thrown out, then the trunks themselves discarded. Finally the walls, ceiling, and floor were scrubbed, and holes in the wooden shutters and door plugged up.

While the room was being cleaned and our trunks moved in, no one actually saw a rat, but at night we glimpsed their plump forms slinking along the edges of the courtyard. The brahmin cook took extra precautions in the kitchen storerooms and placed heavy weights on the lids of any containers that were not absolutely secure.

Many evenings Ashok, Kumar and I sat together on the *chouki* in a room off the courtyard. Our conversation would often turn to the rats and what to do about them.

"Rats are a sign of prosperity," Ashok said. "Think about it. Rats would naturally prefer to hang around a rich household that had storerooms overflowing with rice than live in a poor household. If you see a rat, you know it's there because it has found plenty to eat."

"But rats carry disease," I argued. "They're revolting. They spread bubonic plague to Europe." I shivered, while trying to disguise how strongly I felt about the rats.

"It's part of our respect for all forms of life," Ashok said, taking off his glasses and rubbing them with the hem of his kurta.

"From the time we're children, we're taught that all things, ants, birds, even rats, have souls and they, like us, are trying to live a good life so they will be born into better circumstances in the next life."

"I know, but is that what you believe?" I asked. I had heard all this before, but now, for the first time, I had something at stake in his answer.

Ashok shrugged.

"You know, Bhabi," Kumar broke in, calling me 'brother's wife.' "When we were small Grandmother would scare us with her stories. She would say, 'Don't step on that ant, you and he might have been cousins in a previous life.' She would tell us that the good karma we piled up in this life by not killing the ant would guarantee us a better karma in our next life."

The issue of the rats continued to haunt me, and I worried how I could possibly reconcile my point of view with the family's. The next day, I found Ma sitting with Grandmother looking through scraps of brocade to make into garments for the *puja* deities. I thought perhaps they could help me understand why the sanctity for life had to extend to all living things, even one as destructive as a rat.

"*Array Bapre* (Oh Lordy)" Grandmother answered, throwing up her hands at the very idea of killing rats. Ma was more patient with me, and explained that the rat is the *vahana* (the vehicle, or mount) of Ganesh.

I pictured a huge, pot-bellied Ganesh with the head of an elephant, sitting on the back of a tiny rat, one plump foot tucked under him, the other dangling over the rat's side. "But Ganesh is so big," I said in Hindi, opening my arms wide. Then bringing my hands closer together, continued "and the rat is so small."

"Yes, yes," they nodded vigorously, as if I had said something very profound.

Confused, I switched to English and asked Ma, "Why is such a small, lowly animal as a rat the vehicle of the mighty Ganesh?"

"Ganesh and the rat, the largest being and one of the smallest, they symbolize the macrocosm and the microcosm," she said. "Together they ensure harmony in the universe."

The rat problem persisted. One day, by mistake, a huge bag of Dehra Dun rice, newly purchased, was left out of the kitchen storeroom overnight. The next morning Ma discovered that a hole had been gnawed in the bag, a large amount of rice had been consumed, and a half-kilo strewn all over the floor.

A few nights later I woke up, feeling a prickly sensation as if something had just run over my leg. Terrified, I shook Ashok's shoulder, forcing him awake.

"You must have been dreaming," he told me. "Rats are not going to come onto our bed, here on the second floor."

I insisted that something had been on the bed, and forced him to turn on the light. We found the mosquito net torn and pulled to one side. Worse, there were small hard black pellets, unmistakable rat droppings, on the bed. I was too afraid to go back to sleep and spent the rest of the night huddled in bed with the lights on, though Ashok had no trouble returning to sleep.

That evening Ashok asked Kumar and me, "Do you suppose we could round up all the rats and let them loose some other place?"

Kumar shook his head. "Don't you remember? My friend Mohindas tried that at an archaeological site he was supervising. They had a problem with monkeys. So they caught the monkeys in cages, loaded them in a truck, and drove into the jungle. When they got there they opened the cages and the monkeys jumped out. Then when they were ready to leave and got back into the truck to go home, all the monkeys jumped back into the truck!"

Haridev listened, standing respectfully a few feet away. He cleared his throat to get our attention. "Sir, I was in the lane the other evening—the one that runs alongside the house down to the Ganges. A man came up to me carrying a large burlap bag and asked me, 'Is this the corner where you release rats?'"

I shuddered. "Oh Lord, you release the rats somewhere else and in the meantime new rats are deposited on your doorstep."

"I wouldn't ask anyone else to kill a rat, but I'm willing to risk being saddled with bad karma to get rid of them," Ashok said, after a pause. I nodded in agreement.

"Perhaps," Kumar mumbled, "though Grandmother and the others will feel very bad when they learn about it. How, Brother? How will you go about doing it?"

"Poison?" Ashok offered.

"I don't know. . . " I broke in. "Wouldn't poison harm other creatures also? Birds? Or cats that might catch a poisoned rat? What about a mongoose?" I suggested, remembering Kipling stories I'd read as a child. We contemplated an all-out war among rats and mongooses, with dead bodies strewn throughout the house, and agreed it was too appalling to consider.

Finally Ashok said, "If Haridev can trap the rats, I will kill them." I nodded quickly. Though I had always favored killing the rats, I understood that such a drastic solution would be difficult for Ashok, or for anyone with his childhood training.

We agreed the deed would be done the day after the next. That would give the servants time to buy equipment: traps, bags, and heavy clubs. Two days later Ashok returned from his office and changed from his everyday white starched kurta and pajama into blue jeans and a T-shirt.

Haridev had trapped three rats, two as large as full-grown cats, the other medium-sized. They had long curved claws, sharp pointed teeth, and bristles instead of hair, which stuck up straight from their bodies. They sat quietly in their wire cages, front quarters hunched over, watching us intently with red, beady eyes. Ashok told Haridev to put the rats in a burlap bag and take them upstairs to the passageway outside our bathroom.

"The family will feel bad enough that the rats are being killed," Ashok told me. "We don't have to do it in front of them. Afterwards I can get out of these clothes and take a bath. Where is Kumar?"

He had counted on his brother's help, but Kumar had not

returned home after his class and no one seemed to know where he was. I sensed that Kumar had stayed away on purpose. For a moment I wanted to run away too, and join the other women I knew would be sitting downstairs on the far side of the courtyard. But I couldn't do that to Ashok; I couldn't let him go through this alone. I didn't stop to question what I was getting myself into. "I'm here. I'll help," I said, pulling the loose end of my sari tight around my hips and tucking it in at the waist.

The burlap bag that Haridev dropped at Ashok's feet jerked and pulsed with life. It was impossible to count the animals inside the bag; its surface kept bulging out then falling flat, another bulge reappearing somewhere else.

Ashok picked up a heavy club and started to pound on the bag. Some of the blows landed with a crunch; most glanced off the squirming bulges and harmlessly hit the stone floor. Squealing loudly, the rats tried to bite and claw their way out of the bag. One poked its nose out of a hole.

"It's not working," Ashok exclaimed. "They're escaping."

"Quick, bring me a bucket," I cried out, "and a lid."

Haridev pulled an empty bucket out of the bathroom, and a wooden cover. Together we lifted the bag and forced the escaping rat through the hole it had made in the bag into the bucket, then clamped on the lid. I held the lid down while the rat thumped and struggled inside the bucket. "Now some water. Bring me a bucket of water, " I yelled, surprised at the urgency in my voice.

Ashok took the bucket of water from Haridev's hands, and while I pulled back the lid an inch or so, he poured water into the bucket, splashing me as he filled it to the top. The rat pushed its wet head and feet between the rim and cover, its claws scraping against the metal. Its efforts to escape made me acutely aware that this was something alive, struggling to get free. My hands shook.

"Have you got a brick?" I shouted. Haridev handed me a stone, which I put on the wooden cover to hold it down. The violent upheavals became less and less, and after several minutes there was no movement at all. I looked over my shoulder at Ashok, who was still beating on the burlap bag.

"Did you get those? Are they dead?" I asked.

Ashok nodded. Even from a distance I could feel his revulsion, oozing from him like sweat.

"Sir, I'll take them now," Haridev said quietly. He picked up the split and bloody bag and the bucket, its wood cover and stone still in place. He walked away slowly, his shoulders bent as if loaded down by the weight of bad karma.

Ashok and I slid down to the rough stone floor of the passageway and sat with our backs to the bathroom wall. I felt defeated—more at odds with the rest of the house than ever before.

"Never again," I murmured. "I don't know...but never again."

"Yes," Ashok agreed, slumped like a rag doll in the narrow passageway. "Let them take over Thatheri House, I don't care. But I can't go through this again."

*

The rats were clearly the winners, having lost only three of their own and forcing us to call a halt to the battle, but they never acknowledged their victory. With the old storeroom shut off from them they moved on to more hospitable quarters in some other compound. Rats continued to prowl the courtyard at night, but not in the same numbers as before.

No one ever said a word about the massacre, but Ashok and I were left feeling somewhat estranged from the rest of the family. No more impromptu calls for sugared cream from the bazaar, no last-minute boat trips on the Ganges with the family.

Sometimes I watched Grandmother and Ma from my second-floor balcony. I could tell from their glances toward our rooms that they were talking about Ashok and me. Were they blaming me for the killings? Didn't I blame myself? I thought Ashok and I were in agreement, but if I had been raised a Hindu perhaps I would have influenced his behavior differently. Still, I thought to myself, maybe he married me because he wanted help in breaking free of some of the ancient irrationalities and superstitions.

I tried talking to Ma, asking her for an explanation of an upcoming festival.

"Ask your husband," she replied curtly, and turned away.

Telling Ashok about this conversation, I said, "It's times like these that I know your family resents me, that they wish you had never married an American."

"But I did, didn't I? And I'm glad I did." Ashok smiled, but his lips and his eyelids drooped and in an instant the smile became a frown. "It's this business with the rats. I don't know what to do about it. After all, what's done is done. Now we have to live with the consequences."

The next Sunday Ashok and I went down to the courtyard after morning tea and found it strangely empty. Grandmother sat as usual in the *puja* room reciting prayers, but the others—Babuji, Ma, Kumar—were absent. For a while, we luxuriated in the privacy. I sat in the sun, pulled my sari up above my knees, and fantasized about how I would transform the courtyard if such decisions were left to me. First, I'd screen off the water tap so people sitting in the courtyard couldn't see the men bathing or the servants washing clothes. I'd put pots of bougainvillea on the second floor and let the vines trail over the balcony. I might even install a pool with water lilies and a resident toad.

Ashok broke into my daydreams by suggesting we visit his cousin Prithvi, who lived in the countryside on the outskirts of Benares. She had been asking us to visit ever since we'd arrived, and we had never gone. Today, with no other family obligations to claim our time, we could.

"Should we phone ahead?" I asked.

"No need," he said. "We're family. We're always welcome."

We walked to the end of the lane and hired a cycle rickshaw. The streets were quiet, as schools and many businesses were closed on Sunday mornings. As we drove away from the center of the city, the plots of land became larger with vegetable gardens of corn and squash and pole beans separating one house from another.

Ashok directed the rickshaw driver to swing in front of a moderate-sized bungalow on our left, and motioned for him to wait for us in case his cousin was not at home. As we approached the open door we heard conversation and laughter within: Cousin Prithvi must be entertaining other guests as well. Then as her guests turned to look at us and we at them, a stunned silence fell. There they all sat, Babuji, Ma, and Kumar. Babuji, who sat nearest the door, his broad white back partially shielding us from the others, turned and looked at us over his shoulder with surprise and disappointment.

Prithvi stood, welcoming us. "Ashok-ji, Bhabi-ji, finally you have come. What an auspicious day, to have all of you here with me together." She was a tall, commanding woman, the principal of a local high school. She wore her curly hair pulled back into a tight, no-nonsense knot, but the frizzled strands that escaped formed a soft cap over her head.

She clapped her hands to summon her servant and quickly produced cups of tea fragrant with cardamom and ginger. Ashok and I sat stiffly. How could we carry on a conversation here with the others when we barely spoke to them at home?

"Kumar, will you be the next one in the family to travel to America?" our hostess asked Ashok's brother, speaking in English as a courtesy to me. I could see his mother visibly flinch.

Kumar was not his usual buoyant self. He looked down at his tea cup and mumbled that he thought not.

"And you, Bhabi? How do you find life in Benares?" Prithvi asked me. I felt as clumsy as Kumar looked. My cheeks were warm, the beginnings of a slow flush. "Fascinating," I managed to answer.

"I think she sometimes finds us a little primitive," Babuji said in formal, high Hindi. The flush turned into a bright red blush. I thought, why is it that when people are speaking critically of you, no matter what language they use, their meaning is absolutely, unmistakably bone-clear.

Under Ganesh's Gaze

Soon Ashok stood up and announced we had to leave. Our visit today was a short one, he explained, as there was some office work he had to finish before the next day. We would come again soon, we promised Prithvi, and beat a hasty retreat.

*

After Ashok left the house each morning I felt unbearably alone. Chafing under Ma and Grandmother's disapproving gaze, I began to spend as much time as I could out of the house. Day after day I walked through the bazaar and down to the river, paying little attention to where I was going or how I would get back. I was not particularly worried about getting lost; I always carried some money with me, enough to pay for a cycle rickshaw that would take me back to the start of Thatheri bazaar.

One day on my way back from the Ganges, I walked through a part of the bazaar that sold *puja* objects. All around me I saw images of gods and goddesses, some made out of terracotta and painted in vibrant colors; others delicately sculpted in marble or cast in precious metals. Here also were solid brass lamps and bells used in worship. One stall offered only incense, advertising its wares by lighting fragrant sticks of the sweet-smelling *mogra* flower. Another merchant laid out rows and rows of auspicious colored powders: bright vermillion, golden turmeric, and bars of pale sandalwood paste.

I stopped, entranced by the assault on my senses. Then I saw on a counter in front of me a small silver figure of a rat, not more than three inches long from the tip of its nose to the curve of its thin tail. It was nibbling on a *laddoo*, Ganesh's favorite sweet, which it held in its two front paws. On its back it wore a saddle blanket. I recalled what Ma had told me of the rat's association with Lord Ganesh, and in a rush of understanding remembered that one of the god's epithets was "remover of obstacles."

I turned over in my mind the pairing of Ganesh and the rat. Ashok and I had to find a way to restore equilibrium to Thatheri

House. Could I entrust the problem to what seemed, on one level, nothing more than a couple of inanimate sculptures? It was a disquieting notion, one quite foreign to me. But I realized that deep down I wanted to be a part of India, not struggle against it.

I knew that Ashok would want that too, and I bought the silver image of the rat for Thatheri House, paying the merchant the first price he asked. That evening when I presented the image to Ashok he fondled the rat and turned it over and over in his hands.

"This is it." He raised his eyebrows and beamed at me. "This should do it. This should set things right again."

The next morning, after we bathed, we showed the silver rat to Haridev, our co-conspirator, and told him what we planned to do. He grinned with relief.

We waited until Grandmother had finished her morning prayers and had gone to her room for a nap, then we slipped into the family *puja* room. Arrayed before us were the images, pictures of gurus, and mementos that together formed a kind of map of the family's devotional history over several past and present generations. Ashok pointed out to me a small metal figure of the baby Krishna that his mother had received when he was a child, and that had been the recipient of her special devotion throughout his childhood illnesses. He showed me another image of Krishna that had entered the house mysteriously, snagged in the luggage of an ancestor who had returned from a pilgrimage to Brindaban.

We selected a large bronze figure of a merry, dancing Ganesh, his round belly swaying in one direction and his trunk in another, and placed in front of him the small silver image of the rat. Then, stepping back, we lifted our folded hands in homage to them both.

Alfalfa

Terry Thuemling

The fight started with a simple cryptogram in the Sunday Edition of *The New York Times*: FIND A WORD WITH THE LETTER COMBINATION X-Y-Z-X-Y-Z-X, but things escalated, as they inevitably did, and soon it was no longer a friendly contest to see who could solve the puzzle first but a battle fought tooth and nail across a glass coffee table, the outcome of which would be the surest sign yet of who was smarter, thus settling a furtive rivalry that loomed over their new marriage like a cartoon anvil and had recently intensified, thanks to comments such as, 'Oh come on, my twelve-year-old niece knows Bismarck is the capital of North Dakota,' 'Thirty-five across is *harebrained*, not *hairbrained*,' and 'Well sure, I used to think existentialism was interesting too, but that was back in high school,' and even though they were both educated and believed themselves above the things that most newlyweds bickered about, they found themselves arguing over equally trivial matters—the significance of SAT scores, who had actually read Baudelaire in French, or the proper pronunciation of Nabokov—at the same time they both knew these subjects had little to do with the questions they really wanted to ask, the answers they really wanted to hear, so then there they were in the middle of a row over a word game, saying nasty things about each other's parents and threatening to give up on the whole damn marriage, emphasizing each point by pounding the tabletop when suddenly the glass surface shattered into a thousand tiny pieces and they were left wondering what just happened, until one of them figured it out.

Christmas Cake

Mika Tanner

Toilets are my life. I wish this wasn't true but it is. For the past three years I have been working at the Omicho branch of the Ito Toilet Company here in Kanazawa, where I have lived since I was born. Maybe you have heard of Ito Toilets. They can be found all over the world. They are famous not only for their unrivalled comfort but for their clever features: there are models with a cushioned seat warmer, or a bidet spray, or a massage jet which pulses water to an appropriate area of one's choosing. There are models equipped with deodorizers, sensor-activated lids, and gentle blow dryers that eliminate the need for toilet paper. You can order one or a combination of any of these functions, although the bidet feature is the most requested. Each day I ride the bus into town, walk two blocks to the office and then change into the uniform that all the women employees are required to wear. The uniforms are different colors depending on what your status is in the company. I am at the very bottom of the ladder and so my uniform is purple. The skirt is a dark purple and the blouse is a lighter lavender shade with a dark purple bow around the neck. In the fall and winter I wear a purple blazer that is too small across the chest. The senior women get to wear a more appealing shade of blue although they have to wear the same unflattering style. The men don't wear uniforms at all. They wear suits and ties all year round.

Kanazawa is a small city in Ishikawa prefecture off the Sea of Japan. It is a quiet place for the most part, drowsy and serene. It is famous for its crab, *sake*, and for Kenrokuen Garden which is one of the three most exquisite gardens in the country. Because Kanazawa was not bombed in the war, you can still find passages of narrow streets lined with houses built before the turn of the century. The houses are made of wood, faded almost to gray, and are very small but beautiful. Downtown there are a couple of department stores and boutiques where you can find a select offering of the latest Tokyo fashions, and of course there is a McDonald's which is always filled with young people, the girls with bleached-blond hair touching up their mascara after they finish their burgers. I live on the west side of the city about a twenty-five minute bike ride, or a ten-minute bus ride, from downtown.

I began working at Ito Toilets right after graduating from college. I wanted to live at home to save money, and although I could have easily spent a few months lounging in my room reading comic books and magazines, my parents insisted I get a job, a job where I could learn some professional skills. I interviewed at several places, but with the recession, Ito Toilets was the only place that offered to hire me. And although I usually work about fifty hours a week there, my father still insists that I occasionally help him in the small restaurant he runs downstairs from where we live. My sister Kana, who is sixteen and in high school, is exempt from this duty, because my mother says she has to study. I do not think this is very fair, especially since Kana spends most of her time fooling around with her friends, but, seeing as how I get free room and board, there is not a lot I can do about it.

The restaurant is a traditional Japanese eatery, a place to drink as much as it is a place to eat. There are a good many regulars, mostly older men or blue-collar workers who come after work to sit at the counter and drink beer or *shochu* while they talk to my father. Decent, likeable men, many of them have been coming to the restaurant for the past ten years with the same stories, the same jokes. They almost never bring their wives.

Working here, running his own place, my father is happier

than almost anyone I know. He says that this congeniality comes from having only daughters; raising us has made him soft, has sloughed away the roughness of his masculinity the way a river's current can smooth the edges off of a stone. He claims that in order to survive in a household of women he has had to become agreeable and accommodating. Personally I think his cheerfulness is a reflection of his present happiness more than anything else, for when Kana and I were much younger he was not nearly so pleasant. At that time he was working for a large hotel near the train station, helping to cook extravagant Western-style dishes like Beef Wellington, rack of lamb, and fish smothered in rich sauces. He would come home late each night exhausted from preparing food he did not particularly care to eat, and the minute he got home he would drink a beer and smoke a cigarette. Then he would go to bed. He seemed especially fierce then, sullen and irritable, and Kana and I would avoid him as much as we could. My mother used to tell him she should have married a *salariman*. If she were never going to see her husband anyway, then at least he would be making more money. Now that things are better, she mentions her longing for a more stable sedate life only rarely, and only under her breath, and mostly when business is down or she has been especially busy helping in the restaurant. Most days things are fine and my father tolerates her occasional scoldings with imperturbable good humor.

My father grew up in Ishikawa prefecture, in a small fishing village on the edge of the sea, and he claims that Kanazawa is the best place in the world to live. "Everything you could ever want is nearby," he says, nodding his head with an expansive wisdom. "It has the countryside, it has the sea, it has the mountains. It has the best fish in Japan and the best *sake*. Why would you ever want to go anywhere else?" My father has not, in fact, been to many other places, even in Japan. The only time he has left Ishikawa prefecture was to drive me to my university in Kobe and then to attend my graduation four years later.

Christmas Cake

*

Things really pick up at the restaurant around this time, towards the end of December. It's when companies give out their bonuses, and generally business is very good for a few weeks until people realize they had better use the money more wisely than by spending it on alcohol. Most of the regulars are here then, and they chat with me while I clear their tables, bring them their drinks.

"Eh, Yoko," Mr. Sameshima says to me one night, loud enough that most of the customers looked up to listen. "How old are you now?"

I give him a look and continue to fill two large mugs with Asahi Dry.

"Come on, tell me," he says, taking a drag of his cigarette while I give the couple at the corner table their beers. "Twenty-two? Twenty-three?"

I turn and face him. "Don't you know it's rude to ask young women their age?" I say, which makes him and everyone else laugh.

Mr. Sameshima is about sixty-five years old, a retired gardener who shuffles into the restaurant about every other night. He is quiet until he gets drunk, and then he begins raucously carrying on with the people around him. Sometimes, if the mood strikes him, he will even sing.

"Hey, Toshio," he yells over to my father in a voice hoarse from decades of smoking. "How old is your daughter here?" My father only grins and turns something over on the grill.

"I'm twenty-five," I tell him.

"Twenty-five," he echoes, surprise widening his normally wrinkle-hidden eyes. "I knew you when you only came up to my knee. My, my. Twenty-five. I'm an old man."

"Ha," says Makoto, sitting at the counter. "Did you only just figure that out?"

"Oh, be quiet," Mr. Sameshima says, waving a dismissive hand in his direction. "Now, Yoko," he says to me. "Twenty-five is when you should be seriously thinking about the direction of your life.

You know, getting married, starting a family. Do you have a boyfriend who is going to take you away from here one of these days?"

I shrug, then bend over to clear away the empty dishes in front of him.

"I'll be your boyfriend," Makoto shouts. Everybody laughs. Makoto is a small man, shorter than I am, with thinning hair and a sweet, cherub-like face. When he is drunk, which is the only way I've ever seen him, he has a habit of making sweeping declarations about the Japanese national psyche. "Japan is an island culture," he will say. "We're isolated and that's a bad thing. We don't know or care what's going on in the rest of the world and that's why China will get the better of us someday." Most of the time, though, no one can understand what he is saying and eventually my father calls a taxi and helps him out the door.

"How about it?" he says. I smile at him and he raises his glass to me in a small toast.

"Don't pay any attention to him," Mr. Sameshima says. "You can do much better than that. Now, I'm serious. This concerns me. You've got to get your life on track here. So, what's the problem? It doesn't pay to be overly choosy, you know. Someone with your looks can't be too critical. You have to be realistic. It's just how life is."

I pinch up my mouth at him and say nothing, a prickly warmth spreading over my cheeks. Drunk, stupid old man. I move to go back behind the counter.

"Don't be mad now," he says. "Come here. Come talk to your uncle." For my father's sake I turn towards him once more, wearily putting my hand on my hip.

"All young people think of these days is romance," says Mr. Sameshima, tapping his cigarette into the ash-tray. "Marriage is not about being swept off your feet. It's a partnership, a way to get through life with the least amount of discomfort. You need to be with someone who is reliable and trustworthy, never mind what they look like." Mr. Sameshima purses his lips, regarding me for a moment under his grizzled eyebrows.

"Don't be too picky, Yoko-chan. You don't have much time left. Next year you'll be Christmas cake, and then your poor father will have to take care of you for the rest of his life." Everyone laughs at the hilarity of this, and I flick my wet towel at him and go back behind the counter. When my father isn't looking, I fill a glass with whisky and drink it back in one gulp.

Later, in the seclusion of my room, I take a pack of cigarettes out of a dresser drawer and open a window. Nobody knows I smoke, but I do, sometimes, at home. I almost never smoke in public, since I'm afraid someone from work will see me and word will get out that I'm *that* kind of a girl. So late at night I often stand at the window and exhale blue, swirling breaths into the air, watching them melt slowly into the darkness. I feel like someone of consequence then, as though my thoughts are original and profound, as large as the ink-colored sky.

But tonight my mind is taken up with a dense, closely-knit panic. Mr. Sameshima is right. Next year, when I am twenty-six, I will be considered Christmas cake. It is strange to compare a woman to the white frosted, whipped-cream filled cake that most Japanese buy and eat each year on Christmas, but it makes sense in a discouraging way. After the 25th, Christmas cakes grow stale, the frosting hardening in stiff lumps. No one will buy them, and ultimately they are thrown into the garbage. A woman, too, is past her prime after her twenty-fifth birthday. Women, like Christmas cakes, have a short shelf life.

It's only a saying, but I can't help but worry about it. I have had only one boyfriend, when I was sixteen, but he went to college in Nagano and I have not seen him since. And although I am not picky, like Mr. Sameshima seems to believe, it is hard for me to meet people. There is no one at work I could see myself dating, besides which the thought of being with someone else whose life revolves around toilets depresses me more than I can begin to say.

So on Thursday evening after work I'm going to a party, one where all the guests will be eligible single people hoping to meet their future spouses, and as always with these kinds of things I am trying to maintain a positive attitude. It's possible that I'll meet somebody nice, although I've been to one of these before and it was not a particularly enjoyable experience. All the men gravitated towards the two or three attractive girls who were there and the rest of us smiled tense, grim smiles and pretended to be enjoying the wine and finger foods. But still, you never know. This one might be different.

I know if I was beautiful I would not be so worried about all of this. I would have my pick of men; I would have so many to choose from that I could afford to take my time. Or, if settling down didn't interest me, I could have a glamorous career, perhaps be a stewardess and travel around the world. If I were beautiful I could set the terms of my own life.

But, as Mr. Sameshima so matter-of-factly pointed out, I am not beautiful at all. In photos I look like a moon, my face looming large and pale above the rest of my body. My nose and mouth are unremarkable, but my eyes are so narrow that they look frozen in a perpetual squint. Most likely my parents are worried that they will have to take care of me for the rest of my life, will have to speak of my disappointments in hushed tones with relatives and neighbors who ask what I am doing with myself. "I don't know what went wrong," my mother will say. "Thank goodness Kana, at least, has given us some grandchildren."

I'm beginning to think that if I don't get married I will stay at Ito Toilets for the rest of my life, my future swishing down a shiny, porcelain bowl. I will never leave Kanazawa and I will never leave this house.

*

At work on Thursday morning I deal with three irate customers before it is even ten o'clock. I am in charge of answering the customer complaint line. People from the Ishikawa area call in with their grievances about their Ito toilet, and if I cannot help them directly, I arrange for a repairman to go out to where they live and solve the problem for them. It's an awful job mostly because no one who calls is ever pleasant. They are always mad about their toilet and make a big fuss, and, if they feel their problem is not being handled in an appropriate way, they ask to speak to my manager. By the end of the day I feel like a toilet myself, a receptacle for all kinds of unpleasantness. So far, one woman has called in complaining about the pressure on her massage spray, another woman said that the automatic lid to her toilet did not open, that during the night she had narrowly missed peeing on it. My last call was a woman who declared that her toilet seat was too small. "I almost got stuck," she huffed. "They're not designed properly." I wanted to tell her that they were designed for normal-sized people and that from the sound of it she could probably stand to lose quite a few kilos.

The phone rings again, shrill and insistent. It is my friend Maria asking me what time we are to meet at the Riverview Hotel this evening. We are going to the singles party together.

I tell her to meet me there at six-thirty, which will give me enough time to change and to freshen my make-up. Maria is an American who is studying Japanese at Kanazawa University. She is not interested in finding a husband herself, only curious to see what a Japanese singles party is like. We met because she would come into my father's restaurant several times a week after she first moved here six months ago. At first, we didn't realize she was from America since she looks Japanese and speaks the language almost fluently. We just thought it was odd for a young woman to come in alone, and that sometimes she had a strange way of eating her food, like dipping things into the wrong sauces, that kind of thing. She blushed when I told her this, and defended herself by saying that many of the dishes were new to her. She had just ordered them and hoped for the best.

"I used to get really self-conscious in Japan," she confided to me once. "I look Japanese, so everyone expects me to act Japanese, all my relatives especially. That's why I stopped coming here with my mom. I just got sick of all the pressure. She was actually really surprised I decided to come to Japan to study. So am I, sometimes, when I think about it."

I can't imagine Maria being self-conscious. When I tell her this, she says that she decided before coming here not to worry anymore about fitting in or doing the right thing. "I'm an American, after all," she says. "And proud of it."

Maria is not pretty by Japanese standards but I think she is beautiful. Her hair is shiny-black and short and she wears no make-up of any kind. She has a commanding sort of face, with fierce eyebrows and a wide, mobile mouth, a face on which every emotion can be easily read. There is something about it that is exquisitely transparent and exposed, like a raw nerve that registers all tremors of pain and pleasure. Her face is marvelous to watch, so honest and alive.

Maria is my age but seems much older. I don't know what she used to be like, but now she's so sure of herself, filled with opinions and an energy that seems to crackle and glow from within her. The way her hands move when she talks, the way she leans forward in her chair when something interests her, the large silver hoops she wears in her ears, all these things seem so uninhibited and exotic and yet marks of a fully formed character.

Maria has been engaged twice, played the drums in a small rock band, traveled to Australia and Europe, and has lived on her own since she was eighteen years old. She cooks for me, making pastas and American breakfast dishes like pancakes and French toast. She gave me my first taste of Mexican food, using tortillas she brought from home and keeps in the freezer. She also teaches me about America, about the different people who live there, people from all over the world. She tells me how people are treated differently because of their color, that even she has been regarded with suspicion in her own country because of her Japanese face. She talks to me about human rights, about sexual equality, about movies, about drugs.

Being with Maria, my first American friend, I begin to feel that I could surprise myself. Nothing seems out of the question, the world seems larger and smaller at the same time, full of wonders that I could reach my hand out to touch. And when we are at her house listening to CDs of her American music, I feel as though I could be like her someday, confident and comfortable, in charge of who I am and what I want to be.

*

Before the end of the day, Mr. Yamashita, the director of our Ishikawa branch of Ito Toilets, gathers all of us together. He does this periodically, to inform us of developments coming from the head office in Tokyo, or to give inspirational talks when he feels morale is low. Mr. Yamashita is a tall, thin man with brush-like gray hair who has worked in this office, sitting at the same desk, for the last twenty years. He likes to send out quarterly staff reports that always have some bit of toilet trivia in them: Did you know that the Sun King, Louis the XIV of France, used to receive visitors while doing his business on the royal commode? he writes. Or, Most toilets in the world flush in E flat. One that I especially like is: When you open the lid of Beatles singer George Harrison's toilet, it plays Lucy in the Sky with Diamonds. I wonder what will happen to George Harrison's toilet now that he is dead.

This afternoon Mr. Yamashita tells us that the company is currently trying to expand its international public toilet sales, going after new markets in countries like India, China, and Vietnam.

"Even developing nations have recognized the importance of installing and maintaining clean, efficient toilet systems in public spaces," he says in an impassioned voice, his posture rigidly straight as though he was addressing a crowded assembly hall rather than fifty-five bored and distracted employees. "As these countries become more open to tourism and the global economy in general, they will realize that the public toilet is the window through which the rest of the world will judge them. Toilets are the critical difference between order and chaos, between civilized and uncivilized. Japan and Ito Toilets must be a part of this sanitary revolution, we must be leaders in making public hygiene a priority throughout the world."

We all listen, our hands clasped in front of us, our heads bowed as though in prayer. By working at Ito Toilets we are promoting the betterment of mankind! Mr. Yamashita, the Buddha of bathrooms, the saint of sewers. I want to laugh out loud, peal after peal, intensifying waves of mirth vibrating the air. Instead, I look down at my feet and take deep breaths.

*

After work I change into a pink wool skirt and jacket and meet Maria at the Riverview Hotel where the party is being held. Maria is waiting for me in the lobby, smoking a cigarette. She is wearing a black sweater and skirt, black stockings and black high-heeled boots. I look down at the dainty cream-colored pumps I bought on sale at Daiwa department store and feel frumpy in comparison.

"Yoko! Hi!" She gives me a hug, an American custom I'm still not used to. "So, are you excited? Do you think you might meet the man of your dreams tonight?"

I shake my head and laugh. "No, no. My friend Chiyo made me come. She's the one who put this thing together. She knows all these people."

Maria squeezes my arm as a hotel staff person leads us to the room where the party is. "You never know," she says. "This could be the first night of a very wonderful romance."

We are taken to an intimate Chinese-style banquet room, where two round tables of eight have been set up. About nine people have already arrived; they are clustered around the smaller drink tables lining the perimeter of the room, helping themselves to glasses of white and red wine, Kirin beer and soft-drinks. The men seem awkward and shy, clutching their drinks; the women, in suits very similar to mine, their faces pearly smooth with powder, avoid the men, talking to one another instead.

"Oh, boy," says Maria.

My friend Chiyo sees me and rushes over. "Yoko," she says. "I'm so glad you came!"

I proudly introduce Maria to her, and immediately Chiyo is both shy and impressed. "An American," she says. "How lucky you are. I would really love to go there someday."

"Maria just wants to see what Japanese men are like," I tell her.

"That's right," says Maria. "I don't ever get the chance to meet any. I hope you don't mind."

Chiyo looks at Maria apologetically. "Well, they're not so great. Compared to American men, I mean. American men are so handsome and tall! And so nice to their girlfriends, I hear. So romantic."

"Well. . ." Maria says.

Chiyo glances past us to the next group of guests to arrive. "Why don't both of you get some drinks. And Yoko," she adds, "I want you to mingle, okay?"

Maria and I go to one of the beverage tables and pour ourselves glasses of red wine. "What do you think I should talk about to a Japanese man?" she asks, looking surprisingly nervous. "Is there something I'm supposed to do or say at one of these things? And do I have to use *keigo*? I never learned how to speak it, my Japanese is totally conversational."

"No, of course not," I laugh. "No one will expect you to use formal Japanese. And anyway, just tell them you're from America. They'll be so impressed with you that you'll hardly need to talk at all."

Finally it is time to sit down and let dinner get underway. The seating arrangements are boy girl boy girl, so Maria and I are separated. I end up sitting between an engineer at Ishikawa Electric named Yukio Kanda, and a sales manager named Kazuo Matsui.

Mr. Kanda seems to be interested in the woman on his left, a pale, thin girl with frosted pink lips, so Mr. Matsui and I pour each other small glasses of beer and trade vital statistics: our age, what our fathers do for a living, where we went to school, what we like to do on weekends. Mr. Matsui says he likes to go fishing on the Noto Peninsula and I tell him I like to dance, although this is a lie. I just cannot think of anything more exciting. What else can I say—that on the weekends I like to sleep? Or eat? But Mr. Matsui listens attentively, taking discreet bites of his food as I talk. Everything about him radiates a calm preciseness: his clean white shirt, his slender hands, the careful side part of his thick black hair. He smiles encouragingly at me, thin lines crinkling pleasantly at the corners of his eyes.

I look across the table at Maria who is listening to a young man with long, shaggy hair who is not too bad-looking. She sees me watching her and rolls her eyes.

After dinner, which is a very mediocre five course Chinese banquet, everyone gets up to mill around again. Some of the guests, emboldened by alcohol, begin to form themselves into pairs. Maria comes over to me and hooks her arm through mine.

"Oh, my god, Yoko," she says. "I can't believe we each paid 7000 yen just to be tortured. Honestly, that was about the most painful thing I have ever had to sit through. I mean, can you believe these guys? The ones next to me didn't have one interesting thing to say. The only thing they knew how to do was refill my beer glass. Otherwise they just sat there looking embarrassed or talked about their jobs in excruciating detail. I haven't met people that socially awkward since I was a teenager!"

"Really? Was it that bad? I thought the person sitting next to me was kind of nice."

"What, that guy on your right? He seemed like such a boring little man. I swear, he just nodded the whole time. Did he even talk?"

"Of course," I say. "He works as a sales manager for a company that makes paper products. He talked to me about that for a little while."

"You poor thing," Maria says. "I wish I could have rescued you from him. He looks like the type of person who would wear his socks to bed." Maria pulls her pack of cigarettes from her purse, lights one with a lighter from my father's restaurant and inhales deeply. "Look at everybody," she says, waving the cigarette in front of her. "They're so desperate! They're all here to find the perfect spouse."

"But don't you have this kind of thing in America?" I ask. "Parties for single people?"

"Yeah, but in America they don't seem so, I don't know, obvious, they don't have such a specific goal. No one necessarily goes to them to catch a husband, or to meet the future mother of their children. It's more about having fun, meeting people. And anyway, only really desperate people go to that kind of party. Most Americans meet each other more naturally, through friends, or at bars or clubs. I just find all this a little strange. And are there always so many more women than men at these things? Are all women that eager to get married?"

"Well, I don't know. None of them wants to be Christmas cake, I guess, or maybe they already are, and they're starting to panic."

"Christmas cake? What is that?"

I explain. I feel a strange thrill when Maria's eyes widen in horror. She looks as though I'd told her I was to be sold into slavery. "Are you serious?" she says. "People actually say that?"

"Sure," I say, attempting a look of unflappable indifference. "It's a fact: nobody likes to eat Christmas cake after Christmas."

Maria looks around for an ashtray, and, unable to find one, taps her ashes into a nearby beer bottle. "I guess if there was something like that in America you'd be called fruitcake," she muses.

"No one likes to eat those after Christmas, either." She describes fruitcake to me and then frowns.

"No, forget what I just said. That's a bad analogy. Fruitcakes get passed from one person to another before they're finally thrown away and most people don't even like them to begin with." She laughs. Then she says, "But seriously, that is the most awful thing I have ever heard. No wonder all the women at this party seem so nervous! I didn't realize when you said it was a singles' party how much was at stake."

"Well, maybe it's not quite that bad," I say. "It's just a saying."

"I just can't believe how completely women are oppressed here," Maria says. "How can you stand it? I mean, in America, you're just getting started at twenty-six. And there's no great pressure to marry, either. None of my girlfriends are married, and a lot of them are in their thirties."

"Do they ever want to get married?" I ask.

"Sure, but when they're ready. They aren't going to let society tell them how to live their lives, you know? They're in control. In America, plenty of women get married and have babies in their forties. God, I'll be twenty-six next year, too, and marriage will be the last thing on my mind. I'm too young for all that."

I nod. "What will you do?"

"Go to law school, I think, if I'm lucky. I want to be an international lawyer. Besides, I love being a student. There's so much freedom in it, as long as I get scholarships and stipends, of course."

I nod again, remembering my college days in Kobe. They were fun, more drinking and playing around than studying, for sure. Nobody took it very seriously. I majored in English, but I'm embarrassed to admit that I can hardly string two sentences together. Whenever Maria comes into the restaurant, my mother keeps insisting that I speak in English to her, practice my conversation skills. I stammer out a word or two before they get hopelessly jumbled up in my head and I give up. My mother asks why I went to college at all. It is a question I am having more and more trouble answering, especially since, like most of my friends, I did not even manage to find a husband there.

"So, do you want to get married?" Maria asks me. "Is that why you go to these things?"

I shake my head. "No, not really. But it does seem like something I should do soon. I don't think I want to work at Ito Toilets much longer."

"Marriage isn't the solution, Yoko," Maria says sternly. "You just think it's what you want because that's what everyone's been telling you all your life. What is it that you want to do? Maybe you could go back to school."

I shake my head. "I don't know what I would study, and I'm not sure how happy my parents would be about that anyway. In Japan it is very difficult to get a scholarship. Graduate school would be a real luxury."

"Yoko, you have to do something. You're too smart to waste your life. I mean, all women seem to want to do here is go shopping, or look pretty. Or get married. Society judges them only by how they look, or who they're married to. Japanese women are just so passive! They let themselves be second-class citizens. I am so thankful sometimes that I was raised in America. I mean there are a lot of things that are wrong there, too, but at least I have a chance to make some kind of contribution to the world."

I had never really thought of myself as the product of oppression. My life has not been hard: I see movies, go shopping, have lunch at restaurants. I lie in bed on the weekends and rarely have to do housework. Does this mean I have been as shallow, as willing to be dominated as Maria seems to think?

"Listen, Yoko," Maria says. "Maybe you're unhappy at Ito Toilets because they have you doing such a stupid job. You've been doing it for three years! They can't expect you to do it forever. Maybe if you were given some responsibilities, you know, some challenges, it would be a lot more fulfilling for you. You'd learn things, you'd grow. It would give you the experience you need to move onto something else someday."

"Like what?" I ask doubtfully.

"I don't know. Anything! Maybe by working at a higher level you'd find out what you were really interested in. You're being stunted right now. It's not fair."

I nod, feeling a sudden tightness in my chest.

"You're the only person that can make changes in your life," says Maria, pointing her cigarette at me. "If you're not happy, you need to do something about it. You've got to be more assertive."

After leaving the hotel, we catch a bus home. I get off one stop before Maria does, so we say goodbye. It is cold outside, the stars are chips of ice in the sky. When I am about a block away from my house I can see the yellow glow of my father's restaurant, the sign in front still brightly lit. JINGO, it reads. It was my grandfather's name.

I go in through the kitchen door of the restaurant to tell my parents I am home. I am immediately enveloped in a swathe of cigarette smoke.

My father nods in greeting. "I'm glad you're here, Yoko," he says. He points his chin towards five or six small plates of sashimi, each one decorated by a small yellow chrysanthemum and shreds of white radish as thin and transparent as ice shavings. "Can you take these over to the corner table?" I look around the restaurant as I begin arranging the plates on a tray. Everybody is here tonight: Mr. Kuroda, whose head shines through the jet-black strands of his comb-over; Kenji, the permanent bachelor; and Mr. Shimada, whose face is already a beaming crimson from the *sake*. Mr. Sameshima and Makoto are at their usual places at the counter, watching the baseball game on the overhead television. It depresses me to think that these people have nothing better to do than to come here each week, year after year, that they find their happiness in heated cups of *sake* and a few pieces of grilled fish. They will come here and smoke their cigarettes and talk about the old days or

Christmas Cake

remark on how quickly the world is changing, although Kanazawa is the only part of the world they ever have, or ever will, see. They think they know something about life and how it works, without ever realizing they have experienced so little of it. Their thoughts are exactly the same as they were ten, twenty, forty years ago. And what about their wives, the ones they never bring here? Do those unseen women ever wish for more, or are they happy to cook and clean, take care of their husbands in the same way they take care of their children? And looking over at my father intently dropping battered shrimp into a vat of hot oil, I wonder if he, too, had ever imagined his life differently. But no, he is a man of small dreams and triumphs, comfortable only with what he knows. A beer and a cigarette, going to the hot springs bathhouse on weekends. The thought of going abroad, for example, would terrify him as it would all these men. My heart clutches as I think of him in a large city—New York or Los Angeles, perhaps, or even Tokyo—bewildered by the tall buildings, the speeding cars, the strange faces. He would be unable to eat the unfamiliar food, thinking wistfully of a bowl of rice and pickled vegetables, his place at the table in front of the television.

Just then, my mother, who is washing some beer mugs, nudges me in the ribs. "Hey, what are you standing there asleep for?" she says, irritated. "Get going."

I don't answer but take the sashimi over to the table of customers who are mostly sitting cross-legged on the tatami in their stockinged feet. They are joking and laughing and suddenly it makes me angry. Where are the women? The women like me, the ones in ugly uniforms, the ones who have probably never been invited to a night of alcoholic bonding with their male colleagues. The only professional social occasions women are ever asked to attend are the end-of-the-year company parties, but even those are not particularly inviting, as everyone goes to the boss's favorite hostess club after dinner. It seems that Japan, like my father's customers, will always be the same, that despite its modern sheen, all of its technology, things are as inflexible as they ever were. Japan makes toilets that can measure your weight, body fat, and the sugar content of your urine, a futuristic dream machine, but in the end a toilet is a toilet. It is used for the same purpose as it has always been used, the same as when it was nothing but a crude hole in the ground. Things never really change.

*

For several days I plod through my hours at work, my head in an existential whirlwind. What have I been put on this earth to do? And what if I never marry, never have children? What then? I do not want to die knowing that my sole achievement in life was to reassure disgruntled customers about the merits of their Ito toilets. At least if I were working in sales, for example, or in public relations, I could feel the satisfaction of being challenged, of learning something new. And, like Maria said, it would give me the experience I needed to move onto something else. Maria is right: Japanese women are too passive. We do exactly what we are expected to do, all we want is to fit in, not be the nail that gets hammered down. We don't question anything. We wear the uniforms, make the tea, have the children. We don't even bother to be ambitious.

It is a Wednesday when I decide to talk to Mr. Yamashita about my future. His office door is open but I knock before I enter. He looks up from something he is reading and stares at me over his glasses. "Yes," he says. "What is it?"

"Yes, sir," I say, bowing. "I'm Yoko Nakamura, I work on the customer complaint line on the second floor."

He is eyeing me as though he has never seen me before. "Nakamura," he echoes. "All right. What is it that you want?"

"Well, sir, I've been working at Ito Toilets for three years now, and I just wanted to tell you how much I enjoy it."

He removes his glasses and puts them on the table. "Okay, Nakamura. Good. Very good. I'm glad to hear it."

"Well, you see, sir, it's just that I've been working here for three years, like I said, and I would very much like to have a future

Christmas Cake

here at Ito Toilets, and I was wondering if there was any possibility for advancement, or for expanding my skills in a different area. I am very eager to learn what I can about this business."

Mr. Yamashita leans back in his chair, frowning. "What department did you say you were in again?"

"I service the customer complaint line."

He nods slowly. "Ah, yes. Well. That's a very important job, you see."

"Yes, sir."

"And you know, we need someone to keep on it. We need someone who knows what they're doing. When we hired you, we expected you to take charge of that position, that's what we saw as your niche here at Ito Toilets. And if we moved you into something else, we'd simply have to find and train another person to do what you've done so well for the last three years. It doesn't really make any sense. We need you to keep doing what you're doing."

"So, am I understanding you to say that the customer complaint line is to be my permanent position at Ito Toilets?"

He gives me an enthusiastic smile. "Exactly. That is how you can best contribute to the goals of this company. It's a very exciting future, let me assure you."

"Yes, sir. Thank you."

"I'm glad we had this talk, Nakamura. Keep up the good work."

I bow and scoot awkwardly out of the office.

I go directly to the ladies restroom where I look at myself in the mirror for several minutes. My skin is a pasty white and my nose is shiny. I press a paper towel to my face to blot the excess oil and then throw it into the trash bin. I go back to my desk where I sit down and do nothing for about a quarter of an hour. Finally I put on my telephone headset and prepare to get back to work.

My first caller is a man whose toilet makes a strange noise as it flushes.

"I'm sorry, sir," I tell him. "I will get a technician to come out right away. Now if I could have your—"

"Listen," the man says. "I paid a lot of money for this toilet and it's very upsetting that it's breaking down already. How can you people charge so much for such terrible workmanship?"

"I'm sorry, sir. Please accept my apologies on behalf of Ito Toilets. I will do my best to get—"

"It's always this way. Last week my television busted. A 100,000 yen set, top of the line, supposedly. And it's crap! You see what I mean? You people just try and rip off consumers, you have no conscience, no idea of how hard people work just to make a living these days. Who cares about your damn apologies? You people always think that's all it takes to make up for hours of inconvenience."

The man's yelling has become a sharp whine, like the buzz of a mosquito in my ear. It drones on and on. It's beginning to make me mad.

"Hey! Hey, you! Are you there?" he shouts.

"Yes, sir."

"I think I should get some of my money back, some kind of discount for buying this defective thing. Let me tell you, I did not pay for a toilet that sounds like someone in pain every time you flush it."

I have had it. I don't care what happens.

"Oh, dear," I say. "You know, now that I think about it, I bet that's the camera."

"The what?" the man says.

"The camera. There must be something wrong with it. I'm not supposed to tell anyone this, but sometimes, for research purposes, the company puts small cameras into their toilets. They like to get an idea of people's bathroom habits—you know, if they're regular, that kind of thing—so they can be sure to develop future models that suit the public's needs. Sometimes, as in your case, the mechanism goes haywire."

"You're kidding me," the man says, skeptical. "That's ridiculous."

"I know it sounds horrible," I say. "But it's for the greater good. It's to help people. But that's why Ito Toilets doesn't want the public to know because there might be some kind of protest and the research wouldn't be able to continue."

"For God's sake. That's—"

"—I'm telling you the truth, sir. Just be careful now." I hang up.

In the next two hours I tell a seventy-year old woman that the massage spray is to be used specifically for sexual pleasure (the pressure turned up to full volume, of course), and confide to a housewife that Ito Toilets were actually made using child labor in China. I tell another man that the service technicians double as male escorts, and then ask if he is interested in an evening of company. "I book those appointments, too," I inform him.

It is the best day at Ito Toilets I have ever had.

*

That night Maria comes into the restaurant. When she first started eating here, most of the regulars were nervous around her, never having spoken with an American before. Now they are much more relaxed, they like to chat with her after they've had a few drinks; they tell her for the hundredth time how wonderful it is for an American to be so interested in Japanese culture, how they are personally grateful and touched. Self-appointed diplomats, they teach her well-known proverbs and sayings, sing her the songs they learned as children, tell her about the Ishikawa of forty years ago. Unfortunately, alcohol gives them a tendency to slip into the local dialect, which makes it difficult for Maria to understand what they are saying. Nevertheless, there is a good-natured banter now when she enters, they call out her name and buy her drinks.

I decide not to tell Maria about sabotaging the customer complaint line. The truth is that I haven't decided how I feel about it yet. When I think about what I said to those people, at first I feel giddy, like I'm being tickled from the inside. Just as quickly, though, those pleasant flutters turn into waves of panic so strong I feel nauseous. So instead, I tell Maria about my conversation with Mr. Yamashita. My mother glares at me for sitting down on the job but I pay no attention.

"That is so unfair," Maria says. "In America I bet you would be able to sue him or something." She pokes at a piece of stewed pork with her chopsticks. "So, they just expect you to waste away at that job for eternity? You'd never even be able to graduate to a blue uniform?"

"It doesn't sound like it," I say.

"Well, you should quit. Or maybe you should come back to the States with me. You know, study English or something."

"My parents could never afford that," I tell her.

"Well, maybe you could get a job. Waitress at a Japanese restaurant."

"I don't know. That doesn't sound much better than staying here. And I'd have to get a green card or something, wouldn't I?"

"I have no idea. But, my point is that you can find something else to do."

"I don't know," I say once more. "Maybe getting married wouldn't be so bad. You know, raising a family."

"What? Yoko! Don't talk like that."

"Well, I would like to have a child someday."

"Yes, someday, but later, after you've lived your own life. Women were not put on this earth simply to procreate." Suddenly she calls over the counter to my father who is slicing up some vegetables for a salad. "Mr. Nakamura," she says.

The steady rhythm of his knife is interrupted for a moment as he looks at her.

"Do you think Yoko should get married soon?" she asks him.

He cocks his head a moment, considering. "Of course not," he finally says. "I'd miss her. She'd have to leave and then I'd be sad." He pretends to cry, his mouth turning down at the ends like

Christmas Cake

a clown's, and then breaks into a laugh. He goes back to his slicing but I notice the tips of his ears are pink.

"But seriously," Maria says to me. "If you try to live inside the box, it will become a coffin. You'll never get out." Then she leans forward and says, in an intense, almost chastising voice, "and anyway, you don't want to be just another Japanese housewife do you? Never seeing your husband because he works all the time, and raising your child to fit in, to be just another Japanese person who is unable to think for herself, has no personality."

I do not know how to respond to this. I look at Maria, her face so expectant and sure. What does she see when she looks back? A face devoid of expression, of any kind of human individuality? I know I should defend myself, list for her the ways in which I find my life to be enjoyable, the ways in which I am quietly unique. I think of the nights looking out the window of my room, when I am imbued with a sense of my own significance, an understanding of my place in this universe. I do not pretend to be a brightly burning star, shooting a path of brilliance across the atmosphere, but somehow I know that the fabric of the cosmos has opened up to make room for my existence. Yet although Maria's forehead is creased in well-meaning concern, I can see in her eyes that she will never understand.

So I don't say anything. There are too many thoughts in my head for me to speak.

*

Maria moves back to America in August. The next time I see her is four years later when she is in Japan for her grandmother's funeral in Hiroshima. On her way there, she makes a brief side trip to Kanazawa to see some of her old professors at the university. I am to meet her at the station for lunch before she catches the bus that will take her directly to the campus.

Miraculously, my moment of insanity at Ito Toilets went unpunished. There are twelve women who manage the customer complaint line, and although Ito Toilets advocates the most advanced technology in toilet fixtures, they do not have the same pioneering spirit when it comes to phone systems. Nobody could figure out who had behaved, as Mr. Yamashita put it, "in such a depraved and malicious manner."

But now I am married and no longer working at Ito Toilets. Nobuo, my husband, is a manager at the Toshiba factory in Toyama, a half-hour train ride away. There is the possibility that he will be transferred to the Saitama office, or perhaps to Singapore. Nothing will be decided for several months, so we try not to think about it. I have a six-month old son. I take him with me to the train station to meet Maria.

We decide on a tonkatsu restaurant for lunch. While we are waiting for our food, Maria ooohs and aahhhs over the baby. "Oh, Yoko," she says. "He's beautiful. What's his name?"

"Taro," I tell her. He is in his stroller, which I have parked at the table next to me. I reach down and proudly smooth the black strands across his forehead. For such a young baby, he has a lot of hair. He's also quite fat, like a little Buddha, and so far, about as good-natured. Maria eyes Taro wistfully, but when I offer to let her hold him she shakes her head.

"I'll drop him," she says, laughing. "I'll just admire him from here." She smiles at me and I can see faint lines at the corners of her eyes. Otherwise, she looks the same. Her expression is alert, intent. Unquenchable.

She asks me how it is to be married and I tell her I am happy, that being a wife and mother agrees with me. And generally, that is true. I feel rounded out, solid, an essential in the music of other people's lives. Nobuo and I met at an *omiai*, which a friend of his father's had arranged. When I first saw his photograph, I thought he was rather homely, and no doubt he was disappointed with me as well. But he turned out to be kind and intelligent, although somewhat shy, and after three dates the marriage was agreed upon.

Christmas Cake

Taro was born a year and a half after our wedding, and all the miracles of life now seem contained in each small toe, each perfectly formed little ear. We live in a large, recently built house on the outskirts of Kanazawa that has two Western-style bedrooms and two eight-mat tatami rooms. In our two bathrooms we have deluxe model toilets made by Japan Flush, Ito Toilet's most successful competitor. I am proud of our home, its spacious newness, the authority with which it stands in the middle of our street. My parents, too, are pleased with my life, the intelligent choices I have made. Now they mostly worry about Kana only, who, instead of going to college, is employed as a waitress at the local ramen shop.

Maria is now a lawyer working in San Francisco. She travels frequently, usually to Tokyo, sometimes to New York. She has a lover whom she met at a friend's party, and she tells me he is a mystery writer and likes to cook.

Watching her, listening to her talk, I am aware that there is something about Maria that fades me, makes me feel like a hazy outline of myself. Suddenly I feel as though I have been staring at the world through a microscope, one small detail at a time, forgetting to look up and see life as it really is. I imagine Maria in San Francisco, that sparkling city on the water I have only seen in photographs, picture her striding down its streets with swift, free strides. I imagine her with her lover, drinking wine together over dinner with the soft glow of twilight outside the window, talking about their dreams, their most-guarded secrets. Her future is wide and unimpeded, no decisions made that can't be undone.

"Are you in love?" I ask. She stares at me, her dark eyes unreadable.

"No," she says, pausing to light her third cigarette in twenty minutes. "I don't think so. He's a great guy, but I'm very focused on my career right now, so I'm not sure I want to get into anything too committed. Besides, I really like to have my own space and I'm not sure if I'm ready to hear his noises in the bathroom, see his dirty socks on the floor, that kind of thing. To be honest, I'm not sure he'd be into domestic life either—he's already been divorced twice. He's very cautious. We'll see how it goes, I guess. Who knows, maybe we'll fall in love and get married and live happily ever after." She laughs, as though she has just told a very funny joke.

I nod, trying to imagine a life like hers, neatly divided compartments of experience, like a *bento box*. Work here, romance there, friends and family in separate places all together. I wonder how she keeps herself from breaking into pieces, and in which of these compartments she feels most at home. I want to ask if there are any compartments that have not yet been filled, and if this worries her. I want to know if she is ever frightened at having such an unpredictable future, if she ever worries about getting lost while trying to claim it. My own existence seems so simple that it is hard for me to lose my way. I simply follow the path directly under my feet. And although I sometimes long to see a larger landscape, at least there are landmarks where I can stop and take stock of my life: cherry blossoms in the spring, Taro's first steps, Nobuo's first gray hairs. There will be persimmons in the fall and fireworks in the summer. One day Taro will go to school.

I look at Maria. She is as sparkling, as captivating, as she ever was. I listen to the soar and dip of her voice, riding its surface to places I never have been, things I never will see. She is telling me about her job when Taro gives a small yelp, as though he is testing out his vocal chords to make sure they work. He stares up at Maria, then at me, his eyes opening wide as he focuses on my familiar face. He pounds his stomach with his two softly dimpled hands and laughs.

Blue Roses

Carolyn Alessio

Antigone woke me the morning my brother died, pawing the comforter as though it were time for her kibble and a walk, instead of 4:48 a.m. "Shh," I said, trying to get her to go back to sleep, but she persisted, nosing my head and whining softly. "Okay," I said finally. I looked over at my husband, Derek, and saw that his eyes were still closed, his face dark against the yellow pillow. He'd been working late hours the past few weeks, and when he got home we'd been arguing. "Let's go," I whispered to the dog.

Gray light seeped around the kitchen blinds. When I moved in, my mother encouraged me to make curtains, but I never got around to purchasing the fabric and taking the measurements. I rarely even used my ironing board. Tiggy finished her rawhide bone, and the water for tea was beginning to boil when the phone rang. "I'll get it," I said, as though Tiggy were a person or Derek were awake and in the kitchen.

"Jill, Charlie's sick." It was Martin, my brother's lover, his voice far and thin.

"What?" I pressed the receiver closer to my ear, as though proximity could remedy the situation.

"He woke up and his head was killing him. He asked for water, but I could hardly understand him. So I took him to the ER and now he's unconscious." Antigone looked at me across the kitchen, her Shepherd ears raised into black teepees.

"A migraine?" I said. He had been complaining of headaches for the past few weeks.

"They don't know yet."

He told me which hospital and we hung up. I didn't replace the receiver. Instead I dialed the high school and left a message on the vice principal's voice mail.

"I won't be in today," I said, rushing the words. "Tell the sub to read from *A Raisin in the Sun*. I'll call if I have to cancel drama practice." I had never before canceled practice; a group of juniors and seniors were performing *The Glass Menagerie*, and the girl who played Laura needed as much practice as she could get. I hung up the phone. Antigone sniffed at my ankles.

I decided not to wake Derek. He was tired, I told myself, and we didn't really know how bad Charlie was yet. The truth was, though, that I worried if Derek got up we might start arguing about something petty. A few weeks ago, he had confessed that he kissed a paralegal months before at a conference. It was nothing, he said, but I pressed. I asked him what she looked like, if she were white like me, if she had longer hair than I did or wore muskier perfume.

But all he would say is, "I love you, it was nothing."

Now I opened the door to the bedroom. Derek slept on his side, one of his long arms thrown over the empty pillow next to him. Antigone pushed in beside me. "Keep Daddy company," I said, and shut the door.

*

I parked in a cement garage connected to the hospital by a long, above-ground passageway. As I walked its length, the early morning light angled through the window, and for a moment I pretended I was in an airport, going to meet my brother's flight.

A nurse in a peach jumpsuit directed me to a small room around the corner from the nurses' station. Inside sat Martin on an orange vinyl chair, talking to a woman in a plaid jacket.

"Where is he?" I said.

Martin looked up. His glasses were smudged and his cheeks shone red above the auburn beard. "Jill," he said. "It was a stroke."

Blue Roses

The woman stood up and put her hand on my shoulder. "We call it a cardiovascular accident."

"Who are you?" I said. "He's only forty-one. He didn't have a stroke."

"Please sit down," the woman said.

I looked above her head at a framed photo of a wheat field, at the bushy tops of the stalks and the way they brushed in one direction in the wind and sun. I looked at the wheat and I knew.

"Jill is Charlie's sister," Martin said.

"You're next of kin?" the woman said. "I know this is hard. Your brother was very ill. The doctors took heroic measures, but I'm afraid he's passed away."

I blinked. Heroic measures made me think of muscular cartoon characters.

"I'm Brenda Ralston, an organ recovery coordinator." She reached to touch my shoulder, but I shrugged her away.

"Jill," Martin said. "He signed his driver's license." His voice quavered, like a phone cord stretched too far.

"I'm sorry," the organ coordinator said, and this time I pressed my lips together, afraid my tongue would emerge like an angry jellyfish.

"Sit down," she said, but I didn't. I tried to grasp the idea: my brother's organs being flown across the country to children waiting desperately for just his heart or kidneys, but I was still thinking of Charlie as *Charlie*, alive.

"Let me see him," I said. They led me out into the hall. The lights flickered in one of the overhead fixtures, as though an indoor storm were brewing.

Fewer machines than I expected were hooked onto my brother, IVs and monitors that the organ coordinator had assured me were necessary to maintain organ support. The doctor, I was told, had pronounced him brain-dead not long after he arrived in the ER. I moved closer to the bed, Martin behind me. Charlie's neck looked more tender than I remembered. His blue eyes were closed. The last time I saw him he was mowing the lawn of his and Martin's house. I waved as I drove off and he tipped the brim of his baseball cap.

Somebody tapped me on the shoulder.

"Jill," said the organ coordinator, "when you're finished could I ask you a few questions? I know this is terrible timing, but I have to ask. I'll be in the lounge."

I shrugged and she left the room. "God, she's persistent," I said. "Vulture."

"He signed his license," Martin said. "I think we should honor that."

"I need more time."

When I left the room, Martin was running his thumb gently along Charlie's cheek.

Brenda, the organ coordinator, waited for me in the lounge, and when I arrived, she handed me a cup of coffee. "Cream?" she said and I shook my head.

"Time is really crucial," she said when I explained that I needed more time. "I know that's hard to hear right now. "

I sat down. The vinyl creaked beneath me and I wished Martin would join us. The organ coordinator set a form down in front of me. "Consent for Organ and Tissue Donation," it said in capital letters. Carbons were attached.

"This is called a family history," she said, and began her questions.

"Mom died last year of cancer," I said. "Dad, years ago, heart." I paused and watched while she wrote on a clipboard. The button pinned to her blazer said, "Give the Gift of Life."

"What about Charlie? High blood pressure?"

I shook my head. "He exercised," I said. "Went to the gym a lot."

The organ coordinator finished writing. "Okay, good," she said. "Now I have to ask a few personal questions. They're required for screening by UNOS, the United Network of Organ Sharing." Sharing, I thought, that was something only children tried to do.

"Did Charlie drink?"

"Well, wine," I said. "A glass or two a week. At most."

Not like Derek and me, I thought, who often ended our arguments with brandy snifters in our hands, sitting on opposite sides of the bed.

"Any intravenous drug use?"

For the first time in hours I felt like laughing: Charlie had always been so straight-laced that he refused even to smoke pot. "You never know," he'd said. "I might be one of those one-in-a-million people who freak out and are never quite the same."

The coordinator checked a box. "Here's the last one," she said. "To your knowledge has Charlie had sex with another man after 1970?"

I sat back, incredulous. "He was monogamous for God's sake," I said. "Martin was his only lover. Ever." I was embarrassed by the way my voice pitched, even more embarrassed by the vast difference between my brother's sex life and my own. I'd had frequent lovers in college and drama school; once I had ended up in the clinic for a social disease. I never told Charlie, but I think he might have figured it out.

"I'm sorry." The organ coordinator put down her pen.

"He didn't have AIDS," I said. "Look at his blood tests."

"I know," the organ coordinator said. "Sometimes I think these rules are way too strict, but I'm afraid this won't work out."

"Jesus," I said, suddenly convinced that I wanted to donate Charlie's organs more than anything, for his heart and liver and kidneys to be harvested from his body, packed in dry-ice and flown off to someone who waited, emaciated and desperate. Later, Martin and I might receive letters, thank-you notes that kept us updated on the recipients' progress. "Since I received your brother's kidney," I imagined a letter saying, "my life has turned around...."

"I think your brother would've been a wonderful donor," the coordinator said. "I'm truly sorry."

"Why'd you take us this far?" I said. "Who'd you think Martin was? His butler?"

The coordinator flushed. "We don't like to assume," she said, "until we talk to the next-of-kin."

I began to weep and she reached for a box of tissue but I waved her off. I couldn't look at her face; I was embarrassed by my own melodrama. If I'd been directing this scene in a play, I would have said, too sudden. What about foreshadowing, rising action, the curse on the city that nobody can seem to lift? Giving in, I grabbed the consent form and began to shred it. White and pink and gold flecks of paper fluttered around us like confetti.

He has gay organs, I wanted to shout as I emerged into the hall; make sure you say he didn't have AIDS in the obituary, because that's what everyone will assume. Instead I wiped my face with my hand and said to Martin, "Donation's not going to work. We need to think about a funeral."

Martin pulled out his wallet and began to go through a wad of business cards. I stood next to him, watching him flip, his hands moving clumsily, until he found it. "We had the same insurance agent," he said, holding it up. "I think I should call."

I looked around. Mid-morning light pushed at the windows. Somewhere people had gotten their sleep.

Martin said, "One of the nurses said I could use the phone at the station." I followed him over there, dragging my purse and coat, which felt as heavy as an X-ray apron.

I moved in closer to Martin. I wanted to lean against him, smell his cologne and maybe Charlie's too. What had they been doing that night? I wasn't looking for sexual details (if there were any), just some domestic information, like, they'd made spaghetti with avocado, one of their favorite dishes.

Martin reached for the phone but I put my hand over his. "What was the last thing he said?" I asked. "Try to remember."

Martin ran his hand through his hair. He turned to me, squinting his red eyes in the bright light over the nurses' station. "Jill," he said.

"Please," I persisted. Just before my mother died, she said, 'Take care of the cookie jars.' Charlie and I never knew if she was fully coherent or not, but it was something we talked about afterward, something private and funny and sad.

"Jill." Martin helped me up from the chair. "There's a vending room and lounge there. Please. I'll come down when I'm done."

Several nurses and an aide stared. One of them held a clean bedpan, an aqua plastic kidney. I put my head down. Everybody knew I had nobody in my life. I was pathetic and the lights in there were unkind. I pulled my coat around me and walked down the hall, following with blurred eyes the purple arrows painted on the walls.

*

Charlie and I grew up in a small town near Cleveland, not far from where we lived as adults. All the houses in our neighborhood were identical and aluminum-sided, like rows of oversized popsicle sticks. There were few businesses nearby, but several blocks away, near the turnoff to the expressway, hunched a bar called The Closet. Even from the outside it didn't make sense in our neighborhood; the tinted windows puzzled everyone and pretty soon they were smudged from the outside, too.

Nobody in town talked much about The Closet, but once, in the hardware store, I overheard two local men joking: "You take your lousy paws off me," one of them said, "or I'll haul your ass over to The Closet." They both burst into laughter and I turned back to running my hands through a bin of shiny wingnuts.

The Closet was constantly in the newspapers, and every few years around election time the candidates would start threatening to close it down. The headlines and the inevitable puns made me laugh: "McMurthy Says Close the Door on The Closet."

"Poor souls," my mother once said when we read about an altercation in an alley behind the bar. "Why can't we just leave them alone?"

Years later, when Charlie told us he was gay, I remember wondering if this would mean he would go to bars like The Closet, misplaced in a neighborhood of aluminum siding and swing sets. I imagined him getting beaten up in the alley out back, his ears buzzing from punches as he walked home.

The electric hummings of different cadences filled the hospital's vending room. The soda machine was loudest, but the snack machine cut in with a quicker tempo. I wiped my eyes again. Everywhere it was so bright. I couldn't believe I had answered any of the organ coordinator's questions. Intravenous drugs.

I scanned the snack machine: rows of gum and candy, pretzels, peanut butter crackers. My stomach rumbled and I realized how odd it was that I was hungry, that I had any of my normal sensations. I wondered if, at home, Derek had fed Antigone another breakfast by mistake.

The machine swallowed the coins I deposited and clicked. I heard the whirring increase, and I watched the box of Milk Duds push forward, as though the other boxes behind it had insisted. The box teetered for a moment but didn't descend, the wire loop hooked on its corner.

I stood back. My purse was filled with change but I could not scrounge again. I reached forward and with the heel of my palm slapped the machine. The box shook a little, but nothing happened. I watched it, yellow cardboard with brown lettering. I willed it to descend, but it remained caught.

I pushed again, this time slamming with both palms. My hands were beginning to sting, but I couldn't stop.

"Honey." I didn't turn around but looked in the dim reflection of the machine. Derek reached around my back, his breath on my neck. "I lost sixty-five cents," I said.

Derek reached for my stinging palms and pulled them up to his lips. He kissed them.

Martin was talking to a priest in the hallway when we emerged from the vending room. "Reverend Gates," Martin said, introducing us.

"Martin," I said. "I need to tell you something."

The priest looked up. He was wearing running shoes beneath his uniform. Derek looked at me.

"What about the liturgy?" Martin said, looking at the priest, who stared at me.

I felt the pressure of Derek's hand on my arm. "Charlie didn't have AIDS and I told them that, Martin, but they're paranoid and it's not fair."

"We can talk about it tomorrow," Reverend Gates said.

There was a pause, then Martin turned to the priest. "I've always found Psalms comforting," he said. "Is that too run-of-the-mill?"

I thought about Charlie a few rooms over, lying there in the sunlight as if he were only sleeping late.

Derek and I walked out to the parking lot, and I tried to think of a eulogy. I wondered if Martin would trust me to give one, considering the scene, but I tried to formulate one anyway. I could tell the story of how Martin and Charlie met: they were undergraduates, both out of the closet, but they didn't meet at a Gay Pride or support meeting; they met as members of the campus Young Republicans. It had been a joke for a long time in our family, who had always voted vehemently Democratic. "We nearly disowned Charlie," my mother would tell people, who'd nod solemnly, then she would add, "for voting Republican."

I had to get back to school. Stephanie, the girl playing Laura, couldn't dance, couldn't shuffle, even without the fake brace. I had asked the students in costumes to construct a light one that wouldn't impede her steps too much, but Stephanie balked. I had originally chosen her for the role because of a love poem about shy girls and cars that she wrote and performed for English class, but this character did not inspire her. "I don't get her," she said the night before, while I was locking up the auditorium after practice. "She dances with a man who's engaged and lets him call her that stupid name, Blue Roses."

Derek stood in front of the driver's door. "Let me drive you," he said.

I shook my head. "I'll be all right."

"We can leave your car here," he said, "Come on."

I pulled my purse closer. Derek pleaded with his eyes, but I could tell he was getting tired. I opened the car door and sat down on the seat.

"Don't go to school," he said, leaning into the car.

"She can't dance."

"We'll go home. Back to bed," he said. "I called the firm."

I blinked; this was the first time he had ever called in sick to the law firm. He had always worked long hours, but since he told me about the paralegal, I imagined every evening involved deceit.

Derek wiped his forehead. He was going to leave me eventually, I thought, perhaps for another woman and perhaps not. Though I wanted to pin it on race, to our overt differences that once had made me feel dangerous and smug, I knew that the problem was me. Forgiveness wasn't my forté. I slid in behind the wheel.

"Be careful," he said. I told him I would see him at home.

I started the engine. In the rearview mirror, I saw Derek standing in the parking lot, his magenta tie blowing across his white shirt like a long tongue. "Neither of my children are traditionalists," my mother once bragged about Charlie and me and our choices of partners.

Now I knew she was wrong. Everywhere in the world people were doing brave, unprecedented things and I was hurrying over to the high school. There were secrets I would never understand about the people I loved, but the only thing on my mind was my student who didn't understand how to dance. Imagining the steps as I pumped the gas pedal, I pulled out of the lot and drove.

Go

Stephen Dixon

She wants to go. Fine, let her. But he doesn't want her to. What does he want? Some time for himself, some easing of the work he does for her and all his other work, but he doesn't want her to go.

Why doesn't he want her to go? Ask yourself that, ask it, which he thinks he did but he'll do it again: why? It has nothing to do with love. He isn't asking what it doesn't have to do with but what it does. But he wanted to get that in, that he loves her, though what the hell's love anyway? He means, what's love? A feeling, of course, though much more, but what? Love is . . . ? Oh, what's he getting into, and he's losing this. Just snuff it and start from the top.

She wants to go, fine, let her, but does he want her to? No. Why not? Because he knows how he'll feel after. And that is? That he deserted her even though she was the one who left him. How's that? Because it was his actions that made her go. And he'd always be worried about her, would feel rotten he wasn't always there helping her when he could and as he has in the past, which was considerable. His help was. But he blows up too much because the work, all the work he does for her and also the kids and his job work and house and car chores and everything. It's work all the time, it seems, twelve to sixteen hours a day of it every day of the year or almost, so . . . what? Where was he? Talking of work and chores. His; endless, it seems. That he's conflicted about her going. He didn't say that but it has to have come out in what he said so far, and anyway, anyway, he is. If she left him, or let's just say was gone, he'd have some time for himself. Now he has very little of it, so some time means more time than just a little. But he'd feel so guilty she'd left because of him and certainly couldn't have the help, she couldn't have it, he gives her and best of all when he gives it without bitching, that he'd . . . but he's forgotten again what he was talking about. It was . . . he was talking about . . . no, it's lost, or would just take too much to get back, so start again at the top.

She wants to go, fine, let her, but not "fine" because he doesn't want her to. All right: he does and he doesn't. He knows his life would be simpler in some ways with her gone, or just less tiring he'll say, a lot less tiring, and being taken care of by professional people: she would be. People whose profession is taking care of someone in his wife's condition. But he also knows it'll be tough for her in a way where it wouldn't be if he were around and taking care of her. It wouldn't be the same, in other words. Not as natural as him doing it, he's saying: paying strangers to look after her all the time. Sometimes they might get rough with her or pretend not to hear her when she called out from another room that she needed them. He always came when she called, which is what he meant by the word "natural." That he was her husband, father of her kids, lived with her for many years, was in love with her all that time, so it was natural for him to respond whenever she needed him. Oh, maybe sometimes he took a few extra seconds to a minute or so to respond because he was in the middle of something—an interesting article or page of a novel he was reading, for instance, or involved in his own work—but no longer than that. Is that right? He thinks so. But he never got rough with her. Maybe one time he turned her over in bed a bit roughly and she hit her head on the night table. Actually, a few times, things like that. Lifted her off the toilet seat too roughly where she cut her foot on the wheelchair leg. Got her out of the

Go

front seat of the van too roughly where she banged her head on the door frame and got a big bump from it. But over the years, five to ten times he might have treated her roughly. Ten, he'll say, but no more than that, plus the ten or so times he was just careless in the way he handled her and she hurt herself but he's talking of many years of taking care of her: around fifteen. Ten times in fifteen years that he was intentionally rough—that flipping her over in bed too hard where she hit her head; cut it quite deeply, in fact, that it took some time for him to stanch it and almost reached the point where he was going to take her to hospital Emergency—isn't that bad, he thinks, though of course no times would have been ideal. But he isn't infallible or a saint. He tries his best, or tries most times to do his best for her. Certainly he thinks he started out every time to do his best—no, that's not true. Sometimes he started out angrily to do something for her—was angry the moment she called out she needed him and he knew he'd have to stop what he was doing to take care of her—so of course the chance of an accident or him hurting her intentionally was greater than when he didn't start out angrily. So let's just say he tries most times to do his best for her. He asks her what the problem is or she needs or he can do for her or knows or can see without asking and he does it, simple as that, or she just immediately tells him what she needs or wants done, though sometimes what he has to do for her is so hard or takes so much time that he gets angry while he's doing it and then becomes rough. He does have a little help in taking care of her, but only a little; he does most of it. "Only a little" because, for one thing, help can be pretty expensive. He also doesn't like these so-called professional home care people in his house—"so-called" because some of them come close to being inept, another reason he sees a problem and even a danger in her going and relying on them exclusively. But anyway, he doesn't much care for them in his house—though of course he has to put up with it, especially when he's out—reading a newspaper or magazine or cheap novel or religious tract or pile of catalogs or just clipping out coupons from this and that, waiting for something to do for her. Waiting for her to call out to them from another room that she needs assistance, is what he's saying. And, as he said, or didn't say but is saying now, when he's in a relatively good mood, which is maybe two-thirds to three-quarters of the time—not a good-enough ratio, or whatever it is, percentage—but certainly not the worst either. He could . . . he means, these so-called professional homecare people can't help her as generously and willingly and naturally as he can. That thought could be straightened out. But the point is—well, lots of those thoughts could—but the point is—the one he was making or trying to make . . . what? Forgets. Thinks about it but can't bring it back. So just go to the start again, the top.

She wants to leave him. Fine, for her, he supposes, though he's doubtful about that, but not for him. Why can't she just accept that sometimes he gets angry at all he has to do for her and everything else but that he always realizes how wrong he is and apologizes for the awful things he's said, the threats that he can't take anymore of this and has to get out of here, that he needs a few weeks at least away from her and the kids and cats and all the chores he has to do around the house day and night. That he's sick and tired of it, literally tired and probably getting literally sick. But that he always comes around and does what he has to do for her, meaning what she needs, and by "coming around" he means he eventually calms down and acquiesces and after that is always helpful and good to her and it's only rarely that he's in any way rough. But she's fed up with his periodic rages. She said—her actual words were—"I've had my fill of your crazy, dumb outbursts." That they're bad for her and the kids. That they might even make her physically sicker than she'd be without them. That he also embarrasses her when he flies into a rage in front of people outside the immediate family. And he knows he doesn't want to take care of her anymore, she said, so the best thing for her is to leave and get a small apartment in New York and someone there to take care of her permanently and he to stay in the house here with the kids and look after them, though for them to visit her often, she hopes, till they're grown and both in college. But he said she'd need three professional homecare people to look after her; more than three. Three a day for eight-hour shifts and another two for two twelve-hour shifts on weekends, or however these things worked out. At a minimum of twelve dollars an hour, for the year that'll come up to around . . . Well, figure it out yourself, he told her. How many hours in a week? Multiply that by twelve and then that figure by fifty-two. That's a fortune a year. Ninety to a hundred thousand. Maybe half of it paid for by the state or federal government, or both. But the other half they'd have to pay for, which means he alone, since she doesn't work. And that'll go on for years. Fine, let it, he wants her to be around for a normal life span and much longer. But that expense plus all the other expenses for her, not covered by medical insurance and federal and state benefits, will just about eat up every dime he earns. It'll eat up more than he earns when he also considers the cost of taking care of the kids for the next seven to ten years. College. How can he send them to college? How can he afford to continue making payments on the house? And New York. All right, she wants to be near her family and old close friends, but does she remember what apartments go for there? He'd have to get a second job to pay for it all. How can he do that and also see to the kids? So it doesn't make sense, her leaving. They have to stick together. He knows he's said too many times already that he'll change, but he will. He promises he won't go into anymore rages with her and that from now on he'll take care of her with greater . . . how did he put it? With greater patience, consideration and equanimity, he thinks, and without complaining, or with very little complaining. At least give him that, he said: the chance to complain a little, since he always goes back soon enough to acting affably or at least normally again. Because listen, he said to her in just about these very words, he hates the condition she's in, is distraught and depressed over it sometimes; that's not an excuse for his rages but just how he occasionally feels. But what gets to him also is all the work he has to do for her and all the other work he has to do at the same time. So what he's saying, he said, is that when it comes right down to it . . . what he's really getting to in all this . . . but he's stalling because he can't remember what followed it. Something to do with that they can't afford her living in New York by herself, meaning living there with professional homecare help sixteen to twenty-four hours a day. And "sixteen" because maybe she wouldn't need help between the time she's put in bed for the night and wakes up in the morning. No, of course she'll need someone there all the time. In case she has to use the bedpan or her leg falls through the bedrail or her feet get locked together where the pain's killing her and she needs them untwisted and straightened out. And to turn her, which he does at least twice a night, on her side or back so her muscles don't contract or go into spasms or whatever they do when they lie in the same position too long, but most importantly to prevent bedsores. So they have to stay together, if only because they can't afford to live apart. And for other reasons, of course. The kids; that overall he's the best one to help her; and he loves her, so naturally for that reason too he doesn't want them to split up. Though she has to know that sometimes—the work he does for her, and because he's far from being a young strong guy anymore, though he works out as much as he can to have the strength to do the more strenuous things—can be a bit too much for him, something he already mentioned but maybe needed repeating. What he hasn't said yet is that because of all this work, plus all the other things he has to do—kids, his job, etcetera—

Go

he has very little time to do the work that gives him a different kind of pleasure, if that's the right word for it—probably not—that helping her does. His creative work, he's saying. That's been his greatest frustration the last few years and what's led to or caused or is definitely partly to mainly responsible for all or most of his recent rages, he's almost sure of it, and maybe the rages the last few years too. He's no dope, though; he sees the conflict. Or "irony" or "paradox," he thinks would be closer to what he means. That even if they were able to afford her going because they suddenly came into a bundle or the federal and state social service agencies and his job's medical insurance plan kicked in a hundred percent of her living-away costs, he'd feel so guilty that he probably wouldn't be able to do . . . he'd probably be able to do even less than he . . . he wouldn't be able to do even the little creative work he does now. He'd constantly be thinking of all the things she has to put up with every day because of her illness. The obstacles and frustrations, he's talking about, and that he wouldn't be there to help her. That his rages forced her to go. That he knows he's the best homecare person for her overall because of his feelings for her and what she is to him and their kids and that he's not going to ignore her for more than a minute when she calls out to him or be anywhere near as rough on her physically as some of these homecare people have been. That she was probably getting used to living without him. It has its drawbacks, she'd think—separation from her kids, nobody much to talk to but the homecare people and medical personnel and physical therapists she goes to and a few friends and family when they come by or take her out somewhere—but she still finds that preferable to . . . well, there was a lot that was pretty good between them. The sex, which they continued to have, but not during the days of his rages; the meals he made and articles and pieces from books and newspapers he read to her, their talk about their kids and literature and movies they went to and other things and that he still always held her in bed at night, but even all that wasn't enough for her to endure his rages every week or more and anger about different things every other day or so. So . . . he's saying . . . but he's lost his flow of thought again. Lost the thought almost entirely again and whose voice he was trying—or "perspective"—to speak through then. He could get some of it back if he ransacked his brain hard enough, but best to start from the top again, he supposes, and maybe this time around he'll coast right through.

    She wants to leave but he won't let her. Meaning, he'll do what he can to stop her or, better, persuade her not to go. Convince her that it's in her best interest not to go: the kids, their mostly handicapped-accommodative house, not living with what are usually dull and often ignorant people all the time, that he wants her with him more than anything and will do anything to help her feel comfortable staying. For instance, changing his attitude somewhat and controlling his anger and other things, and what would those be? And changing his attitude now, and what's he mean, "somewhat"? Well, just changing it, being easier about things, not letting them upset him so quickly and so much, doing . . . just going . . . oh, damn, he's lost it again. Had something, for a while it was lively, clear and tight, but it got away from him. And as for "wanting her with him more than anything," he just wants her to stay, period; the rest should be obvious to her in everything else he says and his voice and expression and so on.

    She wants to leave him and live in New York but he doesn't want her to and will do anything he can to persuade her to stay. If he has to—if nothing else he does works—he'll get down on his knees and beg her to stay. He means it. She must stay, he'll say. "I'm on my knees: that's how much I want you to. What else can I do to convince you?" But she must from time to time, he'll say, accept his futile rages against all the work he has to do and that his life is no life but really her life or mostly hers that he leads and though he realizes he's in a way fortunate . . . very fortunate to be in a position to help someone in her condition . . . to help *her*, and this is no baloney he's throwing either. He does feel fortunate he's able to take care of her . . . was put on this earth, almost, or just happened to be the person who was there to help make her life as normal as it can be under the circumstances. But it's also true that from time to time, as he said . . . Oh God, he's really messing it up, really and right from the start, for nothing sharp and clear here. Everything was . . . let's just say he had a thought but let it run on and spill over to other thoughts till it was . . . what? Spilled, run over, making it impossible for him to get anything cohesive out of it. Just start from the top again but with a different tact.

She says she has to go. That there's no question of it anymore, she's going. When she said it, he said "Don't go; stay, please," and she said "There's no way that's possible," so he said "If not for me then just for the kids," and she said "Believe me, I've thought of that, but it's still impossible," so he said "Fine then, go; it'll probably be better for us both and might make life easier for me, if you want me to be honest about it, though of course it'll be awful for the kids." But it won't be better for them both, he knows that. For the kids, it's awful when he rages and it'll be awful if she goes. What would be better, he can tell her, is that he adjusts to all the work he has to do now and which will no doubt become even harder in the future, and tries to arrange things better, get professional help when he wants to do his creative work so he won't be frustrated he's not doing it, which would make things better for him and, in the long run, her, and, indirectly and also directly, their kids. But what the hell's he saying? And what's with this professional help, quote-unquote? Does he mean some kind of psychotherapy for him or just more homecare coverage for her, which they already have plenty of and is one of the reasons for his anger and rages? Not just the exorbitant cost of it they can barely afford, and let's say he didn't care about those costs anymore, or not as much as before, but that these people always seem to be in his way, cutting into his privacy, no time for him to walk around the house and think things out without bumping into them or seeing them out of the corner of his eye, and their generally being an interfering nuisance, for instance washing a single dish in the kitchen for a minute and blocking his way to the sink when all he wants is some water out of the tap to drink but what's he going on about now with this, since of course "professional help" meant them and not possible psychotherapy for him, but he was only saying that the way he said it could be misinterpreted. He means that he knew what "professional help" alluded to when he said it, but the way he happened to put it could have been—Oh, forget it—it's lost, the thought is, whatever he was getting at, the top too, the one just now and almost everything from the top too.

She wants to leave him. That's what she says she wants. He says all right. Said it, he means. Then he said, "No, what am I saying; you can't." She said "I'm sorry, but I've made up my mind. Believe me, it wasn't a hasty decision. I know I've said it before but this time I absolutely mean it." "You have said it before," he said, "and you've also said before 'and this time I really' or 'absolutely mean it' or 'plan to carry it out,' so why should either of us believe you're serious this time?" "Because this time is different. I've already—" and he cut her off with "Excuse me, I'm sorry for my sarcastic attitude just now. I apologize. It was totally wrong of me. Wrong attitude, words and tone. Wrong everything, even my expression." "Thank you," she said. "I accept your apology, but it won't change my mind. And I want to continue with why I think this time is different. I've already begun making arrangements to go. I'm in touch with someone who will look after me in New York. A very competent live-in homecare person who is also a nurse. I heard of the ideal apartment for me that will become available next month. It's affordable, though I suppose we'll have to incur some financial sacrifices, and it only needs minor renovation to make it completely accessible for me. I've talked this over with people whose judgment we both respect and they all agree it's a place I shouldn't pass up and a move I should definitely make. Even the kids reluctantly agreed that it's probably best I left, but because of their lives here and the size of my new apartment, they'd like to stay." He just stared at her, was heartsick over it, couldn't come up with anything to say. If he said "Have you seen this place?" what would be the difference? If he said...well, whatever he said, she was on her way. He had the same feeling in his stomach as when...but anyway, she said "I can't live with you anymore. It's obvious our marriage is finished. I don't want to make you feel even worse about it but my bad feelings to you and your overt and often demonstrated hatred of me and especially your violent rages are doing tremendous damage to the kids. Admit it. We'll all be much better off when you and I are split." "No we all won't," he said. She waited for him to say more, he shut his eyes and kept shaking his head, and she said "Believe me, we all will." "And I don't hate you," he said, with his eyes still closed. "Not one bit, and no one can take better care of you than me." "Perhaps you believe that—the last part, anyway—but I..." and so on. She also said then she does concede he can be considerate, helpful and quite warm and congenial to her sometimes, but he always reverts back, "and maybe this is too harsh a word for it but is the one that strikes my mind now," to the monster he's become the past year and, before that, the demi-monster the two years prior.

So there it is and this time he's almost sure he can't stop her. Words won't work, action neither, because what can he do, stand in her way so she can't get out the door? She'd call the cops—as a last resort. But first the kids would scream for him to let Mommy go if she wants to, "it's fair and you can't force people to do things they don't want to," and he'd have to step aside. Even if he got down on his knees—of course he wouldn't, but even if he cried, pleaded, said things like—well, said anything; that he'd even, "and this is no joke," see a shrink to try to work things out between them—all right, not a shrink but a psychotherapist, he'd say, a psychiatrist, whichever one she wanted him to go to, and work things out in himself, he means, because although she's the one who's sick, the problems in their marriage that came after it are all his, and by "sick" he means her physical illness—none of it would stop her from leaving him. He'll just have to get used to it. And be congenial and kind, not revert back to monster man, help her get her things together if she'll let him, even drive her to New York in their converted van and help her get set up. If she goes, it doesn't mean she won't come back. And certainly if the way he acts to her stays even, there'll be a better chance she'll come back. No, she goes, she's gone for good, he's almost sure of it. She'll see how much better life is without him. And in a year their older girl will be in college, and in four years, both girls. So one of the best reasons for them to resume living together would be gone. It's all his fault, he knows that, but there's nothing he can do about it. What's that supposed to mean? Just what it says, he thinks, or close to it. Maybe he can still stop her. Maybe it's only a matter of not having thought of every possibility to. By that he means . . . well, it's all there what he means, he's just too tired to put it in another way, just as he is with that last thing he said.

The Stones Also
Are the River

Sharon Balentine

My friend Jutta and I are walking in the Sierra of the Alpujarras south of Granada and the Sierra Nevada. Starting out from the village of Ogivar, we wind our way up through the steep streets of white houses and come out into clear country—high, falling ridges in the distance, and, before us, falling fields of olive and almond groves. In the clear morning air, we pass the last of the houses, where a few men repair a water channel, and we follow a dirt road around the base of a hill. I look down with pleasure at my six-month-old pair of strong boots, now broken-in, waterproof, high-topped; they cost a fortune, but they're worth it.

I am prone to spraining my ankles at the slightest opportunity, but what really decided me to buy the boots was my first trip with Jutta, when I wore what I thought were adequate boots, bought only the year before. That day we had walked with ten other people, six hours up a rocky arroyo and into another part of the coastal sierra, then back down the same granite-strewn river course again, having somehow strayed from the track we were looking for. I climbed painfully up and over beautiful pink granite boulders, across sharp rock beneath pricking vines of wild rose, breathing in the scent of pine, then eucalyptus and trying to look around me instead of at my feet. The last two hours were agony. I had a blister on my left sole the size of a large sand dollar. The boots were too short and too wide and my feet swam around in them while my toes turned purple—fine for one hour but not six. When we got to the road, the others had to leave me there and walk the last few miles into the village where we'd left our cars. I smoked a cigarette, drank the last of my water and nursed my feet until they came back. That's it, I thought. If I'm going to walk in the Sierra, I need good boots.

Jutta practices routes and trails for a job she's just gotten with a German travel agency that arranges hiking trips for tourists. The trails have been walked and written up by others before—she has pamphlets and books in German and English—but the directions aren't clear, and landmarks change over the years. Hence practice trips with volunteer companions.

After the first two walks, Jutta decided she wanted to travel with only one or two people. One German man—who ignored the exhaustion of his wife, stomping along ahead of her on his thick, sunburned legs—argued with Jutta over turns and forks in the trails during that walk up the arroyo. A Norwegian who had brought neither water nor food, though he'd been told to do so, went off on his own, taking two others with him. The whole enterprise stressed Jutta. "After all," she said, "I'm not getting paid for these walks. Why put up with this aggravation? When I'm doing it for money, that's another thing."

So this time we have come alone and are enjoying ourselves. No one has to prove anything. No man along needs to assert his "natural" authority. If Jutta isn't certain about the trail, poring over her maps and papers, we try a likely fork and if it seems wrong, come back and go the other way. Sometimes we talk, usually we don't. We walk, breathe in that pure air, and gaze around us. Soon the path descends to the river gorge, the river itself not visible from above, only the thicker concentration of dark-green eucalyptus and walnut trees, flowering shrubs and river reeds.

The river, fed by springs and snowmelt from the Sierra Nevada, is bigger than one would imagine from the dry land above. It rushes over rocks—an immediately refreshing sight. "Ah!" we say. "Time to eat!" We each choose a boulder to sit on, open our back packs and pull out fruit, wine, water. Jutta has dark bread she's made herself, a big carrot, cheese and grapes. I start with a hard-boiled egg, then eat my sandwich of ham, tomato and onion, and a pear. We chew and sip wine and watch the river, which seems to wash my troubled mood away with it, down to the distant sea, not visible from this spot tucked among the slopes.

Sitting there in the quiet company of my friend, I think, *the river is only itself. It follows its own way and doesn't bruise itself on stones.* I had been feeling bruised these past weeks. An emptiness that hurt, a void that seemed to open in my center and speak. The feeling would come suddenly, at odd times—washing the dishes or reading the paper. I would wake from a nap inside the void. I felt so alone. I had lost my love. I had lost him forever. The signs he had been looking for I never deciphered, or if I had—I never knew—I had not known how to display them. I felt adrift, floating through the days, my heart in exile, unable to return to a paradise I told myself I had only imagined. But telling myself didn't help. Some stubbornness would not allow me to listen. The hollow feeling would dissipate, but unexpectedly form again.

I sit in the blue air. A few white clouds make shadows on the earth and river as they pass over. It doesn't matter, I think. We flow, our lives are a flowing, from the source back to the source. Even the stones are flowing, back to what they were, only to be formed again, later, much later, some other way.

"The stones also are the river," I say aloud.

"What?"

"It's from a poem."

"Look," Jutta says. She points to a violet growing in the crevice of a boulder near her. I walk over and touch its delicate head and pointed fingers. So stubborn. So amazing. The beauty of being alive, of being here.

I feel suddenly how good it is, how miraculous, to be able to drive out of my home village to almost anywhere, up or down the coast, and walk into the Sierra. No matter what tangled knots I get myself into—what emotions from the past live in me like dormant viruses periodically giving me fevers and cramps, sickening me—all

I have to do is come to the Sierra and feel part of all this around me. My paradise. This is why I'm here. My heart is not in exile. I am home. I forget, immersed in the details of my life—fixated on something I think I need, suffering over my suffering and going in circles—who and where I am.

As we walk again, over another ridge, we pass ancient circular threshing floors paved with flagstones that explain the mysterious, narrow, leveled fields along the slopes where now only grass grows. I imagine the time when wheat grew here, green wheat high and waving in the breeze, people winnowing the ripe wheat on the threshing floors. The small *cortijos* dotted about the area would have been alive with whole families during the harvest threshing. We walk on, climbing, then dropping down again to the river.

Eventually we come to an abandoned hamlet and its enormous, empty church. We sit on the parapet that overlooks the river and valley, look at the river, think of the stones, and of the lives people made here. There is more work in the village itself now. Visitors come from afar to walk in the Sierra or stay in small hotels and relax. There are artisan shops. People make pottery, run restaurants and bars. The olive and almond groves and vegetable plots closer in are still worked, and there are signs of passing goat herds, but the wheat fields return to the Sierra.

I feel myself flowing with the day and all it holds, and I am happy, wanting for nothing. I have not lost my love—not now, not ever. When we pass each other in the street, or come upon one another in a bar, the force field of the one hits the other. I see him brace for the hit. He sees me. We are practicing, for over four years now, how not to bruise one another or be bruised. The force of the one attracts that of the other almost too powerfully. We practice delicacy, walking in the deep mysteries of who we are. I feel that sense of loss and need leaving me. There must be some meaning in all this. Or there is no meaning; it is how we are, how it is. We practice grace. When one cannot know or understand, there remains the possibility of, the necessity for, grace.

Margery's Will

Enid Baron

Next to Will Cunningham, whose droll commentaries on academia never failed to make Claire chuckle, her husband Henry seemed desiccated and dull, becoming animated only when someone made the mistake of asking him about his research at the pharmaceutical company where he worked. Whenever Claire and Henry got together with Will and his wife, Margery, Henry was odd man out.

She had married him after he completed his Ph.D. and life in their tiny apartment had been sweet, but somewhere along the line his job took over and soon Henry seemed distracted, even when they made love. Even after their son was born, Henry retreated to his lab at every opportunity, bringing home chocolates as a peace offering. "It's Henry's fault that my teeth went to hell," Claire had told her good friend Margery. "All those boxes of chocolates he's been bringing me all these years. He never wants to make love unless I'm wearing my dentures."

"What a shit!" Margery said fiercely. "What're a few teeth between friends?"

Easy for her to talk, Claire thought, with all those strong, solid-looking teeth. Tall and rangy, Margery had a lot of messy chestnut hair and large, somewhat protruding teeth. 'Horsey', was what Claire thought when she first saw Margery in the baby park, pushing her daughter on a swing next to Claire's son.

"Henry and I haven't been friends for a long time," Claire said.

When the couples got together, Claire found herself spying on Margery and Will, as if studying a marriage manual, observing their playfulness, the secret code they seemed to share. The more she studied them, the more she felt herself falling in love with the way they were together. In truth, she was falling in love with Will.

By the time her son entered high school, Claire, about to divorce Henry, had a full time position at the university library, where Will stopped in now and then to say hello. One afternoon, Margery dropped over with news that Will had been offered a full professorship at a small college in Vermont—an offer too cushy to turn down.

"You can't mean it!" Claire momentarily forgot where she was. "Oh God, I'm sorry, Margery," she said, regaining control. "No one deserves it more than Will!"

"Vermont's not the end of the earth, Claire," said Margery. "I know what you're thinking, but we'll be there for you during the divorce. If Henry decides to behave like a shit, we'll fly out and give him what for."

At the farewell party Claire gave, Will appeared in the kitchen to open a bottle of wine, although she could have sworn there were plenty of open bottles on the dining room sideboard. A little drunk, she threw her arms around him and told him she would miss him. Not them. Him.

"Come and see us in Vermont," he said, kissing her until her knees trembled.

Claire's husband bailed before Claire could file for divorce. Margery flew out and stayed for weeks while Claire stormed and wept and dissolved into hysterical laughter about Henry's having had her on while he carried on an affair with a colleague at work. "I'll bet anything it started after I got my denture," Claire bellowed. "No wonder he made such a fuss about my wearing it. He was sleeping with her."

Margery's Will

"You're lucky to be rid of him!" said Margery, hugging Claire. "Will says any man who'd walk out on you has to be an imbecile!"

"Will said that?" said Claire, staring at Margery.

"He says you're one of the most attractive women he's ever met!"

"Oh!" Claire felt immensely better, if only momentarily.

*

One evening not long after Margery and Will had moved to Vermont, there was a message from Margery on the answering machine when Claire got home from work. "I've got cancer," Margery said, in an eerily euphoric voice, when Claire returned the call. "It's in my liver."

"I'll get the next plane out," said Claire, feeling as if all the oxygen had been sucked out of her lungs.

"No, don't. It'd be too awful. You'd fall apart and then I'd fall apart, and what good would either of us be to Will, poor darling. He's the one who's going to be left. Watch over him, Claire. Promise?" Claire promised. They talked on the phone daily until Margery couldn't talk any more.

True to form, even at the last, Margery had made Will swear there wouldn't be a memorial service, just the family and a few friends. Knowing Margery's passion for Emily Dickinson, Claire had become so choked up at the service that she hadn't been able to read the poem she had brought which began. . . *Because I could not stop for Death/He kindly stopped for me.*

The first few weeks after she returned home from the funeral, Claire kept going to the phone to call Margery. At the sound of the dial tone, it would hit her all over again, the finality, the inconsolable loss.

*

The following year, Will invited her to visit him in Vermont. She had kept her promise to Margery, calling him regularly, writing notes, but this was different.

Silly, she scolded herself. It would be purely platonic, the two of them sitting around in front of the fireplace drinking sherry, talking about Margery. He had never given her cause to think he felt anything but brotherly toward her . . . except for that kiss at the farewell party, but both of them had had too much to drink. Days passed, a week, and still, she couldn't decide. Her divorce had been final for two years now, and it crossed her mind that Margery had re-enacted the classic deathbed scene with Will, in which the wife names her successor. But that was ridiculous; even if Margery had suspected Claire's attraction to Will, she would never have wrung a promise like that out of him. No, the invitation to Vermont was Will's idea.

What if he planned the opposite of platonic? Wouldn't she feel disloyal to Margery if she were to go to bed with Will? But how could she refuse him?

Come off it. Of course she wouldn't refuse him! But would it be over if he should find out about her teeth?

She went to the phone and called Vermont.

*

Will stood out in the small airport—straight and trim, his hair crisply graying at the temples. As she descended the stairs, Claire told herself to watch her step.

"Claire!" He swooped her up in his arms. "You don't know how glad I am to see you!" As her cheek pressed against the tweed of his jacket, she was sure she had done the right thing. "Let me have a look at you!" he said, releasing her and stepping back. "What have you done to yourself? You're not America's sweetheart any more. It suits you."

Her hair. She ought to have cut it years earlier, dumped the curling wand and the pageboy. Margery used to say that anyone with cheekbones like Claire's was crazy to hide them. Claire had been crazy, trying to please a husband who had stopped noticing long ago.

On the drive to his house, Will gave a running travelogue on local landmarks and before she knew it, he was pulling into the driveway of the rambling clapboard house with its dormers and chimneys. He led her inside. "The staircase is original," he said. "So are the fireplaces. 1789."

The house was Margery, all over—the antique hutch, paisley throws, faded oriental rugs. During the funeral, Claire had not paid attention to the house. Now she followed Will upstairs.

"You're staying in Betsy's room," Will told her. "The bureau's a real museum piece. Margery found it in Connecticut and made me schlep it back, strapped to the top of the car."

Relieved she wasn't going to be installed *ipso facto* in his bedroom, she relaxed. "Last time, I stayed down the hall with a cousin of Margery's who was full of tales of mad aunts and adulterous uncles."

"Eleanor. The family historian. We always thought she was a bit mad." A shadow passed over his face, pulling light from his eyes. "You can't know how lonely it's been. I wake up in the morning and expect to find her downstairs in the kitchen doing the crossword puzzle over coffee. When I come back from campus, I go looking for her in the garden. The only place I find her is in my dreams."

Claire started to say that she too knew about loneliness, but she stopped. There were losses and there were losses. "Dear Will," she said, going over and putting her arms around him the way one hugged a child. But he was not a child. She broke away.

"You'll want to unpack." He gestured toward her suitcase. "Shout if you need anything."

*

They ate at a quaint country inn, dim in candlelight, wood-panelled. "Have the duck," Will advised over a glass of Merlot. "You need fattening up."

"You should see Henry," she said, and then wondered why on earth she had said that.

"How is good old Henry?" Will smiled, as if the thought amused him.

"Positively sylphlike. The new wife's made a vegetarian of him. Jeffrey says there's never anything to eat at his father's house."

"Without Margery around to monitor my eating, I'm afraid I've given way to the sin of gluttony." He patted his flat stomach, looking anything but guilty.

"One of the lesser sins," she said, finding it hard to imagine Margery monitoring anyone.

"You're stealing my lines." He reached across the table for her hand.

She felt the blood rise to her face. They shouldn't be having a laugh at Margery's expense. She withdrew her hand and reached for her water goblet.

"It's OK, Claire," he said. "Margery had no interest in sainthood. I could never understand your being married to a dry stick like Henry. When it took you so long to answer my letter, I wondered whether it had been a mistake to ask you."

"I wasn't sure...."

"Sure of me? Or sure of you?"

"Sure of anything." How grim she sounded. She smiled. "Except for books."

"Claire the librarian." He threw his head back and laughed.

"No, really," she protested. "Books are faithful and reliable. You can take them anywhere. They're a lot less trouble than . . . dogs."

"You give a man no cause for hope," said Will, with a fake pout.

"I hope not!" she said, suddenly beginning to enjoy herself.

"You've got it wrong. It's *I* who hope not!"

"I stand corrected," she said, giving him a military salute.

*

After dinner, they strolled through the village, Will pointing out places of interest, the church with its needle-thin steeple, the town hall with its neoclassical pillars, the historical museum. "Margery was a docent here," he said, coming to a halt in front of the museum. "She was wild about the porcelain collection. Planned to take some courses at Harvard. Then she got sick."

"She told me she'd finally discovered what she wanted to do."

"Perhaps," said Will, his eyes narrowing. A glimpse of a Will Claire hadn't seen before. "She had a habit of getting excited about things and then losing interest. Early American textiles. Venetian glass. It got to be a little...well, a little old."

Don't do this, she thought. It wasn't fair to Margery. "I'm zonked," she said. "Would you mind if we called it a night?"

"Not a bit," said Will, putting his arm around her shoulders as they walked to the car. At the door to her room, he kissed her lightly on the lips. "May flights of angels sing you to your rest." He looked wistful as he turned and went down the hall to his room.

Sleep was slow in coming. If only Margery would come and perch at the end of her bed. There was so much Claire wanted to ask, so much she needed to know.

*

She awoke to the smell of freshly brewed coffee. Glancing at her watch, she saw that by Vermont time, it was almost ten. She dressed quickly and went downstairs to the kitchen.

Will turned from the stove where bacon was sputtering. "Morning," he said cheerfully. "Sleep well?"

"It was hard to get to sleep. I was thinking about Margery."

"So was I," he said.

The restaurant-sized stove barely made a dent in the enormous kitchen with its array of copper cooking utensils suspended from the ceiling. Margery's passions had never been culinary. On the contrary, it usually wasn't until late afternoon when she would mutter about picking up something for dinner. She was constantly amazed that Claire planned an entire week's menus. How could you know what you felt like eating on any given day? Margery relied on Sloppy Joes and macaroni and cheese from a box, except on those rare occasions when the spirit moved her to seriously cook.

Ah, what meals one could produce in this kitchen. Claire pictured cassoulêt simmering away in one of the heavy copper pots.

"Bacon and eggs?" Will's voice interrupted her thoughts.

"Why not?" she said, although she would have preferred *muesli.*

"Watching your cholesterol?"

"I just don't eat eggs very much these days."

"I'd rather give up sex. Well, not quite," he chuckled, winking at her. "The thing is, you can always count on an egg."

She felt herself blush. How could he be so flip when his bed-partner of a quarter of a century lay in the little country cemetery only minutes away? She had to remind herself that his irreverence was part of what had attracted her to him in the first place.

"Margery used to say I was pushing my luck," he continued. "But I'm as healthy as a hog." Was he flaunting his unclogged arteries, assuring her if she married him, she wouldn't wind up caring for a cardiac patient?

*

After breakfast, they hiked in the woods behind the house, calling out names of wildflowers to each other like children on a treasure hunt. When they got to the False Solomon's Seal, Claire said, "I've always wanted someone to tell me why it goes by that name. If it's not the real thing, why hasn't it got a name of its own? I should talk. I'm still using Henry's even though I'm not his wife any more."

"What's in a name?" Will bent to inspect the plant in question.

More than he knew, Claire thought, imagining herself as Claire Cunningham. They stomped around the woods for the better part of an hour and then returned to the house.

"I'd like to shower," she said, not having done so earlier.

"Use our . . . my bathroom," he said. "It's the only functioning shower in the house."

A flowered shower cap hung from the caddy inside the shower stall. Margery's, she assumed, unless Will had gone out and bought it for her visit. Or unless some other guest had preceded her. Determined not to let jealousy muddy uncharted waters, she pulled the shower cap over her hair and turned on the water.

*

Wrapped in a bath towel, she padded back down the hall to her room. As she stood puzzling over what to wear to lunch, Will came in.

"Excuse me," he said, looking flustered.

"Come on in," she said, not wanting to seem prissy.

"I wanted to read you Betsy's letter. Margery and Betsy . . . had a complicated relationship. I never really understood it." He sank down into a chaise lounge. "Margery must have told you about it. It was agony for her that she couldn't make things right with the girl. Before she got sick, Margery took Betsy away for a week, just the two of them. When they got back, Margery was radiant. She felt they had had a breakthrough. I don't know what's going to happen to Betsy . . ."

A wave of sympathy washed over Claire. She leaned down and put her cheek against Will's and stroked his hair. Sighing, he drew her down toward him. Her bath towel fell open. She clutched it to her breasts.

"Sorry. I didn't mean to embarrass you. I'll let you get dressed," said Will, letting her go.

"Don't worry, Will." She pulled the towel higher. "I'll be right down."

*

Downstairs, Will sat reading a book in the living room. He turned to the title page and held it up. "I still say no one's written anything worth talking about since Henry James."

It was an argument they had had over the years. "Come on, Will," she protested. "You can't still believe that."

"Name one." He seemed to be enjoying himself.

At first her face burned with annoyance. Then it became clear to her that he was trying to re-establish an old connection. She went over and sat on the arm of his chair.

"Go ahead, name one."

"Atwood. Ishiguro. Ondaatje," she rattled off, playing along.

"Very politically correct, my dear. Now name me one who will be read centuries from now."

She named Coetzee, Rushdie, Naipaul, Garcia-Marquez, knowing what he would say.

"Piffle and drivel. One or two may survive."

"You know what you are?" What she had always called him.

"An old stick in the mud," he answered, with a broad smile. He slammed shut his book. "It's like old times, having you here, Claire."

"Things were never the same after you left," she said.

"For me either," he said, looking into her face.

She flushed, at a loss for words. "I'd like to visit Margery's grave. No need for you to go if you don't want to. I could borrow your car."

"I thought you'd want to," he said, getting up. "I'll drive you."

*

"Why don't I take a little stroll and come back for you in about fifteen minutes or so," he said at Margery's grave. "Is that enough time?"

Claire had time enough to tell Margery about the new family Henry had started, how her son was doing at school, about her new condo, about everything except Will. She was relieved when Will returned.

He took her to see the college. "Just your prototypical New England institute of higher learning," he said, as they walked along.

"No big deal, right?"

"Not unless you like this kind of thing." He smiled, hooked her arm in his.

"How about letting me cook dinner for us tonight?" she said.

He stuck out his lower lip. "*I* was planning on cooking for *you*. Guess I'll have to let you in on the fun, won't I?"

At the market, he picked up a melon and held it up like a basketball player about to make a shot. "What do you think of this one?" he asked, passing it to her.

"Not quite ripe," she announced, sniffing.

He selected another and offered it up.

"Better."

Another stop at the fish store where he paced the display cases, trying to decide between halibut or swordfish, cross-examining the aproned man behind the counter as to which was fresher.

She could not imagine this Will having been satisfied with Margery's pick-me-up meals. Had he snuck out at night to sushi bars? Dreamed up academic duties that kept him from coming home for dinner? Or had he actually done the lion's share of the cooking at home? What had she really known about their marriage except what they'd let her see?

Back home, she found the potato peeler, tied an apron around Will and started him stripping asparagus. He said, "Margery used to say if the good Lord had wanted asparagus to be skinless, he would have made it that way."

"God, that sounds like her."

"She refused to eat peeled asparagus. She said it tasted slimy. Once, in a fit of pique, she said if I wanted gourmet food, I should have married you."

"I don't believe it," said Claire, dumbfounded.

"She thought you were one of the most capable women she'd ever met."

Claire never had felt she could measure up to Margery. "But . . ." she began, just as Will took hold of her shoulders and kissed her in such a way that, without thinking, she wrapped her arms around his neck and kissed him back. Next thing, he led her out of the kitchen.

"The swordfish," she gasped. "We can't leave it sitting out."

"Whoops. See what you do to me, woman?"

Dinner became a work of art: swordfish and asparagus with an excellent Vouvray; for dessert, tiny wild strawberries with sabayon sauce. They toasted themselves with champagne. Finally, Claire rose and began clearing the table.

"Not now." Will took her hand and she offered no resistance, felt no remorse as she followed him upstairs. Attacking his buttons with deft fingers, she took off his shirt, slipped out of her own sweater and slacks and climbed into Margery's canopied bed.

Moments later, Will, clad only in his boxer shorts, climbed in beside her. "No false modesty," he said, unhooking her bra and sliding it from her shoulders. As he gathered her in his arms, she tugged at the waist of his shorts. "You too," she said, pulling them down as far as she could reach without breaking out of his embrace. Like explorers charting unknown territory, they touched haltingly at first, taking their time, letting the heat between them intensify until they arrived at that moment when everything depended on Will. He fizzled like stale champagne.

"Too much wine, darling," he spoke against the hollow of her neck. "Make it up to you tomorrow." Moments later, he was asleep.

*

She awoke before dawn. Damn, she thought, cursing her aching gums. Gingerly, she lifted Will's hand from her thigh where it was resting, peeled back her side of the coverlet, and moved her legs crablike until she felt the floor under her feet. On tiptoe, she got halfway across the room when she heard his breath catch in his throat.

"Margery?" he mumbled.

"Got to pee." She said it as she imagined Margery would.

When she heard his slow, regular breathing again, she moved forward until she was past the threshold and into the hall. Shivering, she stood barefoot on the icy bathroom floor, her thumb against the inside of her denture. Using her middle fingers as anchor, she tugged at the teeth until they slipped from their mooring, a perfect half moon of lustrous white. She filled the bathroom tumbler with water, dropped in the teeth, and padded across the hall to Betsy's room where she climbed wearily into bed.

In the morning, she awoke to Will's voice. "Arise, my love, my fair one," it said. Her hand flew to her mouth as she yanked the

Margery's Will

quilt over her head. "Arise," the voice repeated. "We're expected in Putney for brunch."

She peeked out over the covers.

"Come now, Claire," he said, poking her in the ribs. "I've known about your appliance for years." He squatted and confronted her face to face. "Margery told me."

"She couldn't have," croaked Claire from her cocoon. Whatever had possessed Margery?

"Poor girl always hated her own teeth," he went on. "When she found out about yours, she said she ought to do the same. But she decided she was too much of a coward to go through with it. Now are you going to get out of bed or am I going to have to tickle you?"

"No," she cried. "I'm getting up."

Her hand clamped over her mouth, she flew into the bathroom and shut the door with a loud click. In the mirror, she saw her upper lip, caved in. Then, a voice that could only be Margery's: *What're a few teeth between friends?* as clearly, as if Margery were speaking from the other side of the mirror.

"Margery?" she whispered.

The drip, drip, drip of a leaky faucet, the only response.

"You better hurry and shower," Will called from the other side of the door. "Don't want to keep our hosts waiting."

She watched her lips form an absurd grin, a smile so ludicrous that it seemed to be mocking her own vanity. *Now or never.* She flung open the door and looked Will squarely in the eye. "If I go to Putney with you, I might *mith* my plane."

"For Christ's sake, Claire." He chuckled. "Put your teeth in. You look like the crone in a Booth cartoon."

Her cheeks burned and her eyes filled with tears. What a fool she'd been to expose herself. She slammed the door, snatched her denture from the tumbler and jammed it into her mouth. "You'd better phone your friends and say we're not coming," she called.

"Of course we are. Open the door."

"No."

"I'm coming in."

She threw herself against the door. Moments later Will had forced his way into the bathroom. "Do you think you can just drop out of my life because I said something that hurt your feelings?" His face flushed with anger.

She was the offended party. What right had *he* to be angry? "That was a terrible thing to say," she croaked.

"Come on, Claire. How did you expect me to react?"

"I expected more of you." She snatched a square of tissue from the box and blew her nose with a loud honk. "I thought you'd understand what a risk I was taking."

He came closer. "What about the risk I took asking you here? You can't imagine how much it meant to me whenever you called, finding a note from you in my mailbox. I didn't want to lose you."

She stared at him. "I never knew you out of context."

"*Out of context?* What am I, some character out of a novel?"

"What I mean is . . . I always thought of you as Margery's Will."

It took him awhile to answer. "I was Margery's husband, not Margery's Will," he said in a soft voice. "We can only belong to ourselves."

She sank down on the toilet seat and looked up at him. "I haven't had much faith in men since Henry."

"Henry was a schmuck. I'm not. Get dressed. We're going to Putney for brunch. After that, I'm going to drive you to the airport and put you on your plane. We'll talk in a couple of weeks and see where we are."

"Where we are?" she asked, not sure she understood.

"Whether we're willing to try again." He held out his hand and pulled her to her feet. In the cold, morning light, she saw the redness where he had nicked himself shaving. She imagined him alone in his house.

"I'll call," she said and touched the tip of her finger to his chin.

Storms

Andrew Porter

My sister has always had a certain power over me. Even when we were children and she was in and out of the hospital—even then, I made no move without her counsel. I did whatever she asked of me, said whatever she wanted me to say. And years later, it was always me who she told about getting pregnant, me who covered for her when she spent a semester living with her thirty-year-old film professor, me who inevitably defended and protected her from our mother. So it only seemed natural that I was the one who answered the phone last summer when she called from Paris to say that she would be flying back to the States without her fiancé Richard. The call came around midnight, just after I had fallen asleep, but as soon as I heard her voice on the other end of the line I knew that something was wrong. She spoke at length about her trip, but when the conversation got around to Richard and why he would not be returning with her, she refused to say a word. She simply explained that she would be flying into Philadelphia the following evening and that she would be travelling alone. "I'm coming home *sans* Richard," she said.

The next night a light rain slowed traffic on the interstate, and when I finally pulled into the airport, I saw Amy sitting on the curb outside the baggage claim, leaning against two framed backpacks. She looked pale and tired, like she hadn't slept in several days. Her hair was up in a bandana and her face bore that glazed expression of transatlantic passengers. I waved to her, and when she spotted me she stood up and hoisted the two heavy packs into the trunk.

"I want to die," she said, as she slid into the passenger seat.

"It's nice to see you too," I said. She looked out the window.

"Do you want to talk about this?" I said, starting up the car.

She shook her head.

"Are you sure?"

She nodded.

As we left the airport, I anticipated the long and silent trip back to our mother's house. Though I was certain that something had happened between her and Richard on their trip, I wasn't going to pry. With Amy, prying got you nowhere. It only made her retreat more. So I drove in silence, ignoring her, and then finally, as we were pulling onto the interstate, driving past the green farmland outside Philadelphia, heading north toward the wooded hills where our mother lives, she rolled down her window, lit a cigarette, and began to tell me the story.

She spoke calmly at first. She said that there had been a fight over in Spain. Not a bad fight, but a fight nonetheless. It was something about their hostel and who had paid, and a bunch of other bullshit. It had been building up for a few days, she said. What she did remember was that at one point during the fight Richard had stood up, dropped his backpack on the ground, and said that he was going for a walk. They had been sitting in a train station in downtown Barcelona, waiting for the afternoon express back to Paris, and Richard had just walked off and left her by herself. Twenty minutes later the express train departed. And so, for the rest of the day, as the crowd thinned out and the sky darkened, she just sat on the bench, waiting for him. She knew that he had disappeared on purpose. He had done the exact same thing to her in Paris, left her sitting alone in a café for almost two hours. He was trying to punish her, she thought, or maybe just make her feel guilty for whatever it was she had done to upset him. But the longer he stayed away, the less she found herself wanting him to return. By evening, it was only she and a few Spanish families, huddled under the outdoor platform lights. She stuck around the station for another hour, but when Richard never showed and the last train to Gare du Nord arrived, she just decided to get on. She had both of their backpacks, Eurrail passes, and all of Richard's money.

"Jesus," I said, when she'd finished the story. "Are you serious?"

Amy nodded.

"Does he even have a passport on him?"

She looked at me, then rolled down her window and lit another cigarette.

"Amy," I said. "Richard needs a passport to get out of the country."

"I'm aware of that," she said.

"How about money?" I said. "Does he have any money at all?"

She shrugged. "I don't think so."

I looked at my sister.

"I know," she said. "I know. I'm a terrible person." Her head was turned away. She was staring out the open window at the late evening sky, darkening beyond the hills.

"You know what he calls himself now?" she said.

I looked at her.

"*Rick*. Whenever we go to a party, he introduces himself as *Rick*. Can you believe that?"

I didn't say anything.

Outside the rain was picking up and as we exited the interstate, Amy rolled up her window and leaned back in her seat. "I don't want to marry someone named *Rick*."

*

Our mother's house is a large, white colonial hidden at the end of a private road in the wooded hills outside of Philadelphia. Our father bought the house in the late sixties, and in the years since he died it has become a tradition that every summer, regardless of how busy our lives may be, Amy and I return to it for a long weekend in August. Our family has never been close, but over time I think we've all come to take this weekend seriously and, in our own way, look forward to it each year. That summer the visit was planned as a celebration in honor of Amy and Richard's upcoming wedding. It was going to be me, my mother, her new husband Tom, and Amy and Richard. Only now Richard was stranded somewhere in Spain, Tom was apparently in the hospital with a foot injury, and to make matters worse, there was a serious storm which had been moving up the eastern sea coast that week. All the back roads in the county were being blocked off. There were detours along the river, and further up in the wooded suburbs where our mother lives police cars were blockading some of the side streets. As soon as Amy and I had made it back to our mother's house, we sat around the kitchen listening to the weather report. Our mother and Tom were still at the hospital, so we took our drinks and waited in the living room, playing cards.

    I had thought that being home might raise Amy's spirits. I had hoped that she might take some comfort in the familiarity of her surroundings. But she had said almost nothing since our arrival. We played gin in silence, and every time she lost a hand, she would put down her cards, sigh, then stand up and refill her drink. I was still having trouble processing what she had done to Richard back in Spain.

    To be honest, I had never really liked Richard. The first time I'd met him I knew the type of doctor he would be and the type of husband he would be to Amy. He was a tall, overbearing man who had a penchant for telling long, insipid stories about his experiences in medical school. And though I didn't like the idea of him joining our family, it bothered me that he had been abandoned in a foreign country and that no one had thought to do anything about it. I have always felt a certain sympathy for the men my sister has dated. It's as if there is a tacit understanding before we even meet, a consolatory nod to my sister's moods and temperament. She has never been an easy person to deal with, and I have never envied these men. But this was different. Richard was the man she was going to be marrying. In less than two months, they would be man and wife. And it seemed hard to imagine that either one of them would want to do anything to jeopardize that.

I tried several times to broach the subject with Amy, but every time I mentioned Richard's name, she would groan and bring up another thing he had done on the trip to annoy her. How he'd left her sunglasses at a restaurant in Bayonne. How he'd spent an entire day dragging her around Paris, looking for the grave of Victor Hugo. How he'd insisted on ordering every single meal in French. She spoke about him in the past tense and referred to their trip as if it were some type of pivotal juncture, an impasse, which they would never be able to move beyond. I said nothing. I watched my sister's face in silence, waiting for something in her expression to break. But her eyes remained stolid, focused on the cards.

When we finished our last game of gin, I helped her carry the backpacks up to her room, and the whole way up the stairs I listened as she complained about being jet-lagged and how she hadn't slept in two days, and then, as we stood outside her door, she put down her backpack and sighed.

I said, "I'm really sorry, Ame."

"Why?" she said. "It's not your fault if Richard's an asshole."

I touched her shoulder. "It's going to be fine," I said.

"No," she corrected me. "It's not."

*

My mother phoned around midnight. She and Tom had spent most of the day at the hospital, and now due to the storm they would be spending the night there as well. I could tell by the sound of her voice that she was distressed. She spoke for a while about Tom's injury, his surgery, and how he was now lying in post-op, sleeping. Then she asked how Amy and Richard were doing. I hadn't mentioned anything to her about Amy's phone call, and I saw no reason to mention it now. She had almost broken into tears earlier that year when Amy had threatened to call off the wedding, and I knew that she wouldn't quite be able to handle it when she learned that Amy had just abandoned Richard in Spain. I already had a vision in my mind of how the whole scene would play out: my mother crying, somebody slamming a door, the obligatory family heirloom shattering on the kitchen tile. I knew exactly how my mother was going to react, and I didn't want to be present when it happened. So I said that everyone was fine, more or less, and then asked how Tom was holding up. My mother explained that he was still in a lot of pain.

"He wishes you all were here," she said. "He keeps asking for you."

From what my mother had explained to me earlier, Tom had fractured a small bone in his foot playing mixed doubles at the country club that morning. Afterward, while he was still doped up on pain medication, he had blamed her, his partner, for not covering her side of the court and forcing him to make a reckless, last-second lunge at a stray ball. At sixty-four, Tom had over twenty senior tennis titles to his credit. He had a bookshelf full of trophies and a small plaque in the country club with a likeness of his pillowy face on it. I knew that his injury would be a major setback for him and that, in some way or another, we would all be held accountable.

I told my mother to give Tom my best, and then after we hung up I walked onto the back patio and flipped on the pool lights. It was raining hard now, the trees whipping around in the wind, the pool water spilling over onto the concrete deck. But it was a warm night, and despite the storm, there was something comforting about being back in a familiar setting. Across my mother's back lawn I could see my old school in the far distance, a cluster of large stone buildings at the edge of the woods, and beyond that the hills and the valley that led down to the river. In the years since our father had died, in the years since we'd been alone, this landscape had taken on an odd nostalgic quality for me. It seemed at times to belong to a different era, a different life. I could still remember, as a child, sitting on that lawn with Amy, waiting for our father to return from work. We would sit out there almost every night, as the sun went down at the edge of the woods and everything around us faded into darkness. We would just sit there patiently, laughing and talking, waiting for the headlights of his car at the bottom of the road, relieved when we saw them that he had made it back safely, assured in the knowledge that despite our worst fears, he was home.

After a while, I hit the pool lights and headed back inside. The house was dark now, and as I headed up the back stairs I could hear soft muffled sobs coming from Amy's room. I stood outside her door for a moment. But before I could knock, the sobbing stopped, and Amy said. "I know you're out there."

"Can I come in?" I said.

"No," she said. "You cannot."

*

The next morning, I stayed in bed for a long time, listening to the weather report. They were still issuing severe thunderstorm warnings, although it seemed that the eye of the storm was going to miss us now. Outside, there were large puddles forming on the lawn and a small tributary running down the edge of the driveway. I noticed that my mother's car was now parked outside the garage, but I had heard no sounds from inside the house. I lay in bed for another hour, reading, and then around ten I heard my mother and Amy talking in the kitchen. I couldn't make out what they were saying to each other, but from the elevated pitch of my mother's voice I guessed that Amy was spilling the story about Richard. In a moment I heard the back door slam and when I looked out my bedroom window, I saw Amy sliding into my mother's Saab and driving off in the rain. When I headed downstairs a few minutes later, the kitchen was empty and there was a large pile of dirty dishes in the sink. Through the patio doors I could see Tom in a wheelchair, tooling around the flagstone patio by the pool. He was decked out in his tennis whites, which were now soaked, and had a full cast up to his knee.

Like my sister, I found it hard to like Tom. For most of his life he had been headmaster at a prestigious prep school in Bryn Mawr. But some time after he met our mother, he'd decided to retire early and focus on the game of tennis, what he called "his true calling." Amy had been suspicious of Tom from the start. She was of the theory that he was after our mother's money. But I had tried to keep an open mind about him. And in truth, I had pretty much tolerated him up until the evening of my mother's wedding when he had panicked at the last minute and had his attorney draft up a prenuptial agreement. The whole incident had been upsetting and also absurd since it was our mother's house Tom was moving into, her car he would be driving around in, and her membership at the country club that would allow him to amass more of his coveted tennis trophies. In fact, it was her money that had paid for the cast he was wearing on his foot at that very moment. I watched him try to negotiate the flagstone patio in the rain. When he reached the edge of the pool, I turned around and headed into the living room, then out to the side porch where I found my mother sitting by herself at a glass table.

She lit a cigarette and regarded me absently.

"Are you okay?" I said.

She nodded, and then motioned for me to sit down at the table next to her. She slid her cigarettes across the glass surface and I took one.

"What's wrong with her?" she sighed. "Does she just hate everything?"

"No," I said. "She doesn't hate everything. I think she just hates Richard."

"My mother sighed.

I reached over then and took the lighter from her hand. I lit my cigarette and for a long time we just sat there at the table, not talking. My whole life there had been moments like this between my mother and me, moments filled with silence. She has always struck me as an intrinsically sad woman, a woman who in many ways never found a way to fill the absence our father had left in her life. For two years in high school it had been just the two of us in the house, and I could still remember how she would sit with me in the kitchen while I did my homework. She would smile whenever I looked up, but I could always see in her eyes just how thoroughly unhappy she was. That was how her eyes had looked most of my childhood and it was how they looked now—a look that told me there had been more disappointment in her life than pleasure. After a while, I leaned over and touched her hand.

"It's going to be fine," I said. "They're just fighting. It's probably just nerves. They're nervous about the wedding."

"There's not going to be a wedding," she said.

"We don't know that," I said.

"You really think he'll marry her after a stunt like this?"

"I don't know," I said.

"Would you marry someone after they abandoned you in Spain?"

I shrugged. I didn't have an answer for that one.

My mother shook her head. "I can tell you right now that he won't."

*

Later that afternoon, when I got back from running errands in town, there was a note on the counter that my boss Ellen had called. Ellen ran the non-profit art mag in New York that I had just started working for, and I knew that if she was calling me at home it must be something urgent. There wasn't a number written on the note, so I tried phoning the office in Manhattan several times, but there was no answer. After an hour or so with no luck, I grabbed a beer from the fridge and sat down at the kitchen table with a magazine. A few minutes later, as I was glancing through an article on Fritz Lang, the phone rang, and thinking it might be Ellen I ran to it—only it wasn't her. It was a male voice, faint and distant. There was a lot of static on the other end of the line and I could barely make out what the man was saying.

"Hello?" I said.

The phone hissed.

"Hello?"

"Hello," the voice echoed faintly.

"Richard?" I said. "Is that you?"

The connection clicked off.

I sat down at the table, wondering if it was Richard, if he'd call back. But the phone didn't ring again and I decided not to mention it, which would only upset my mother, and I didn't want anyone feeling any worse than they already did. Amy came home a few hours later with three shopping bags from Ann Taylor. She went straight up to her room and locked the door until dinner.

Around seven the worst part of the storm passed over our house. I was in the kitchen when I felt the force of it moving through the room. Outside the window above the sink I could see lightning splitting the horizon, crackling at the edge of the hills, and beyond that a thick set of dark clouds silhouetted against the night sky. There was some thunder and a loud crash, then a moment later we lost our power. My mother went around the house lighting candles, Tom began making phone calls to the power company, and I took a flashlight from the hall and headed up to my room. I lay in bed, and despite my efforts to distract myself, I couldn't stop thinking about Richard, wondering if it had been him on the phone earlier that day. The more I thought about it, the more it bothered me, and the more it bothered me, the more it seemed like a good idea to call his parents. I figured that he might have tried calling them himself. They might know something of his whereabouts. They might even know of a way to get him out of the country. But that evening at dinner, when I mentioned the idea to Amy, she said that under the circumstances there was absolutely no way she was calling his parents.

"They don't even like me," she said, sipping her wine.

"Just a suggestion," I said.

Amy groaned. "No fucking way."

We were all sitting around a candle-lit table in the dining room, drinking wine and eating braised chicken that Tom had somehow managed to prepare in the dark.

"No one deserves to have something like that happen to them," Tom announced from the end of the table. He had been quiet up until that point—most likely at my mother's admonition—but he was on his second glass of wine now, and I don't think he cared.

Amy pretended not to hear him and kept talking. "His parents told him he was making a mistake by marrying me," she said. "They told him he'd regret it. Can you believe that?"

"Well," Tom smiled. "Under the circumstances I think that you've provided sufficient evidence for such a claim."

Amy made a face, then went back to eating.

Tom shook his head. He leaned back and folded his arms. At times like this, it was easy to picture how Tom had once been a headmaster. "All I know . . ." Tom began.

"You know what, Tom," Amy said. "I don't really care what you know."

"Amy," my mother said.

Amy dropped her fork on the table, and stood up. "Look at him, Mother," she said, pointing at Tom. "A wheelchair? The man breaks his toe and he gets a fucking wheelchair."

"He's in a lot of pain," my mother said.

"It was the talus, not the toe," Tom said.

"Whatever," Amy said.

"Would you like me to produce the x-rays?" Tom said, raising his casted foot above the table, as if it was indisputable evidence.

"No," Amy said. "I'd like you to shut up."

My mother started crying. A moment later Amy left the table and disappeared up the stairs, and Tom and I were left alone, staring at each other. Tom winked at me, as if he thought I might find some secret humor in the situation; but before he could say a word, I excused myself and went up to my room to smoke. Through the wall between our bedrooms, I could hear Amy crying. She was saying, I hate you, I hate you, though I couldn't tell whether she was directing the statement toward Tom or Richard.

It bothered me, in a way, that I hadn't defended her at the dinner table. I couldn't pretend to understand my sister's logic all the time, but over the years I had learned to accept her moods, her mercurial temperament and her sudden, unexpected rages. It was something that had bloomed slowly inside of her in the years since our father had died. A difficult seed, was what our family therapist had called it.

I sat up in bed and knocked on the wall between our rooms. Amy stopped crying, sneezed, then told me to leave her alone.

"Do you want to talk?" I said through the wall.

"No," she said. "I do not want to talk."

*

The rest of the evening was a practice in avoidance. Amy stayed in her room, calling her friends to complain about Richard, Tom retired to the living room to listen to the weather report on a portable radio, and my mother sat by a small candle in the kitchen reading George Eliot. I stayed in my room and listened to the storm passing over our house. Around midnight I wandered downstairs and found Tom half-asleep in front of his radio. I turned off the sound and his head jerked up. He smiled and motioned for me to sit down.

I wasn't in the mood to talk to Tom. In fact, I tried to avoid it whenever possible. But at that moment it didn't seem like I had much of a choice. So I sat down on the couch across from him, and he began to grill me on the US Open, asking me who I favored to win the whole thing. He was drunk and it was hard for me to follow his train of thought. He said if "monkey face" Sampras didn't win it all he'd be surprised. On the women's side, he favored Hingis. From time to time he stopped and reached down to tap his cast, as if to reassure himself that his foot was still there. When he finished with the US Open, he started talking about his own career, his designs to play tennis on the pro circuit, his tragic knee injury in his early thirties, and later, his reemergence as a senior champion. The story of Tom's tennis career didn't seem to be nearing any type of conclusion, so after a while I sat up and explained that, to be honest, I didn't really follow tennis. He looked at me for a moment, then frowned.

"I imagine you must play," he said.

"Not since I was a kid."

"Well, you should take it up again," he said.

I shrugged. "Maybe."

Tom frowned again. Then he rolled over to the other side of the room and began refilling his drink. "You know, I'm not happy about the way I acted tonight," he said after a moment. "I mean that. Alcohol has never brought out my best qualities. I'll be the first to admit it. But I want you to know that I love your sister. I think of her as my own daughter." He cleared his throat and looked at me. "And you as my son."

I looked down at my feet.

"I've never had children before," he continued. "I've been a teacher and a headmaster. But that's a different type of thing altogether." He seemed to be waiting for me to say something.

"You know, it's late, Tom," I said. "I should probably go to bed now."

Tom rolled over to the couch and parked his wheelchair next to me. I worried that he might try to lean over and hug me, but instead he just put his hand on my shoulder and smiled. "Tennis," he said. "I want you to think about that, son."

*

The next day at lunch there was another phone call from Richard. We were all sitting around the dining room table, picking at the pesto-turkey sandwiches Amy had prepared as a peace offering for her behavior the night before. Earlier in the morning our power had been restored and Tom had gone into the kitchen to run the dishwasher as a kind of celebration. He was the one who had answered the phone call from Richard, and when he rolled back into the room, he handed the receiver to Amy with a face. It was drizzling outside, a light summer rain, but Amy took the phone out onto the patio anyway. Tom rolled up to his spot at the table, and we resumed eating, trying not to look out the window.

"Two months," Tom said, after a long silence. "Two months before I'm back in action."

"That's not bad," my mother said.

"Not bad?" Tom said. "That's only the entire summer season. That's at least three tournaments I'm missing." I could tell by his tone of voice that he still blamed her for his injury.

"Aren't there fall tournaments?" I inquired.

"Those tournaments are bullshit."

I looked out the window then and noticed Amy pacing back and forth by the edge of the pool, making large, dramatic gestures with her arm. I knew that whatever she was saying to Richard was not good. In a moment, she clicked off the receiver and walked back inside through the sliding-glass patio doors. She was dripping wet and I could tell by the puffiness around her eyes that she'd been crying. Nobody said a word, not until Amy sat down at the table. Then my mother, unable to restrain herself, said, "Is Richard okay, honey?"

Amy looked at her and nodded.

"Is he going to be able to leave the country?"

Amy nodded again.

"And you're sure he has enough money?"

"Jesus, Mother. Don't worry about Richard."

"Well, I'm just curious."

"Well, he's fine. In fact, he's totally fucking great. The person you should be worried about—if you're really curious, Mother—the person you should be worried about is me." Without excusing herself, Amy stood and trudged through the kitchen, up the back stairs.

Tom shook his head. "I'm not saying anything," he said. "I'd just like to point out that I'm not saying a word."

My mother gave Tom a look, then stood up and began clearing the table. "It's just as well," she said to no one in particular. "It's not as if we could've afforded a wedding."

Tom cleared his throat, and stared at her.

"What are you talking about?" I said.

"I'm talking about your father's money."

I looked at her.

"Tom made some bad investments," she said.

"Now, hold on," Tom began, but before he could respond, my mother walked out of the room and up the back stairs. I expected Tom to roll into the hallway after her, but he didn't move. He just sat there, looking bewildered and scared. He wouldn't look at me.

"How much money did you blow?" I said.

"This is between your mother and me," Tom mumbled, still looking down.

"Tom," I said. "How much?"

Tom looked out the window. Then, without saying a word, he turned around and rolled out of the room.

*

I spent the rest of the afternoon in my room, trying to process the slow and steady demise of our family. In the years since our father had died, it seemed that a cloud had descended upon us, a cloud the precise size and shape of our house, and that nothing in the intricate fabric of our future would ever be the same. In the books the psychiatrists had given to Amy and me as children, I remembered reading stories about people who claimed that after one of their parents died they were just never happy again. I understood this to be the case with my sister and sometimes with my mother. Life goes on, but it's different now. It's softer, duller. The highs are less high and the lows seem to have an endless depth to them, a depth you have to be wary of falling into. As I lay on my bed that afternoon, it occurred to me that Amy had probably spent most of her life on the edge of that depth, unwilling to let herself fall in, but frightened all the same by its presence. Now it seemed that she had finally given in. And that afternoon, as the phone rang off the hook, she stood in her doorway and instructed us not to answer. It was Richard, she said, and she was not talking to him.

Downstairs, I could hear Tom whining about the fact my mother had told the whole world about his investments. He kept saying, "The market's fickle, Helen. It's too early to tell."

"I'm not talking about this here," my mother said at one point, then a few minutes later I heard the door slam and saw them both head outside to the garage. My mother helped Tom into her car and then they drove off, leaving his wheelchair in the driveway.

That night was supposed to be the big celebration in honor of Amy and Richard's engagement. My mother had ordered an elaborate meal earlier in the week, and I guess she must have forgotten to cancel it, because at seven o'clock sharp two caterers showed up at the front door and dropped off several large food trays—salmon mousse, marinated veal chops, grilled eggplant, seckel pears poached in red wine. All this amazing food, and nobody here to eat it. I didn't have an appetite, so I left the trays in the dining room and went upstairs to knock on Amy's door.

"Dinner's here," I announced.

"Not hungry," she said through the door. I stood there for a moment, then turned the knob slightly and looked in. Amy was in her blue sweatpants and Amherst sweatshirt, smoking and paging through an old photo album. After a moment she looked up at me and smiled.

"Do you want to get drunk?" she said.

*

My mother has always kept a stocked bar. She and my father used to drink every night when they were younger. They drank straight scotch and then switched over to gin and tonics in the summer. A lot of people are social drinkers, but my parents were nightly drinkers. They'd start with a drink before dinner, then keep going till it was time for bed. My mother had cut down some since she'd married Tom, but Amy and I were still able to muster up a bottle of Tanqueray and a few bottles of mixer. The rain had stopped, so we took our drinks out on the patio where it was cool. Amy said that it had been a long time since she had gotten drunk, really drunk, and that she wanted to tonight. I could tell that she was upset, maybe even a little reckless, but I kept pouring her drinks, and she kept drinking them, and pretty soon we were both laughing about all the stupid stuff we'd done as kids. The time she had made me drink mud, the time we had almost burnt down the house, the time I had thrown an apple at a white-tailed wasps' nest and gotten stung seventeen times. Before long Amy was crouched over in hysterics, and I was leaning back in my chair, happy to see her in good spirits again.

"You know," she said, placing her drink down on the floor of the patio. "You're the only one who gets me, Alex. My whole life. You're the only one who understands me."

"I find that hard to believe."

"No, it's true," she said. "Not even Richard understands me. Not really. Not like you do." She looked out at the pool.

"I take it the wedding is off."

She smiled, poured more Tanqueray into her drink. "Can I tell you something?"

"Sure."

"Okay. But if you say anything, I'll cut off your fucking balls."

"Understood."

She lit a cigarette and leaned back in her chair. "I didn't leave him. He left me."

"What are you talking about?"

"Richard. When we were in Spain. He said he had some reservations about marrying me. That day at the train station, he took his passport and some money and said he wanted to travel some more, by himself. He left his backpack and everything. He said we needed some time apart."

"You made the story up?"

She nodded.

"Amy."

"I know," she said. "He just called this afternoon from Madrid to say that he misses me and that he can't believe what he did. He's begging me to forgive him now. One night by himself and he panicked." She laughed. "He's getting on the first flight home tomorrow."

I leaned back in my chair. "Jesus."

"Don't tell Mom," she said. "It'll be easier if she thinks it was my fault."

"Right."

"I mean it," she said. "You can't say a word."

"You got it," I said.

She nodded, then leaned over to reach her glass.

"So what now?" I said.

Amy shrugged and looked out at the hills. "I don't know," she said. "I'm almost thirty, Alex. Thirty years old." She paused to sip her drink. "Richard and I have been together for three years, right? Three long years. You get to know someone when you're together that long. You get accustomed to them, you know. And I'm not saying that he's perfect, because let's face it, Richard can be an asshole half the time. But last year he started putting away this money for us, you know, for when we got older, and it got to me somehow, the fact that he was already thinking that far ahead."

She sighed and leaned over and put her head on my shoulder. "I mean, really," she said after a moment. "What's the worst thing that can happen?"

I put my arm around her, and it felt good to have the full weight of her body against me. It had been a long time, years it seemed, since she had let me hold her. I touched her hair and ran my fingers through it, and after a while, as the wind picked up, she leaned into my chest and closed her eyes. And for a brief moment I felt myself drift back to those late summer afternoons when as children we sat on that patio, waiting for our father to return from work. I could still remember the way Amy smiled when she saw his headlights flash at the bottom of the hill. It seemed the simplest joy in the world—those lights, his car—the knowledge that the person you loved most was on his way home.

Touch

Laura JK Wilson

Linda K. came to me crooked. At first glance, it seemed to be her shoulders, left higher than right. But I had been doing this too long to be fooled. On my table, the miniature rock fountain bubbling behind me, my thumbs bumped beside her spine. Her naked back became the ladder to a secret hideout: the adhesions were rows of marbles from neck to pelvis and at the end, a massive bulge. Breathe, I reminded her softly. I focused on long strokes while her body moved beyond me in a peculiar way, the muscles like shadows mimicking my hands. Nothing mellowed her, not even compression, a sure thing with most newcomers. I shuddered with the excitement of unpredictability.

It was over too quickly. While Linda dressed, I glanced at her questionnaire in the office. Thirty-two years old. Ten years younger than I had thought. My fingers often told me that age was irrelevant, but this time, they tingled for days, as if they, too, were curious, or wished to capitulate.

*

The body, earth-bound in its impermanence, does not transform, but mutates. Mine did so with a rip, a severing distinct as book pages halved across an edge the day I tripped on a curb and wrenched my *Erector spinae*. When I finally stood, my posture imitated a boomerang. For months I cursed through physical therapy, muscles involuntarily contracting beneath electrode pasties, skin purpled from manipulation that was not of my choosing. And then, without warning, my body recalled the significance of equilibrium. It straightened. My legs were the same length, my hips re-aligned. After my final appointment bent over an enormous rubber ball, I smooched my P.T.'s rigid mouth, strode to Whole Earth Grocery, and quit my job. That afternoon I enrolled in three classes at the Center for Massage Therapy.

    The decision pushed dominos, a new life clicked into place. At the massage center, I made friends who consumed the sour wine and stinky cheese I served in my cubicle of a studio apartment. I met Gerry at the bus stop and soon fell in love with his quirky analytics. Once I moved into his apartment in Arlington that was not befouled with ceiling rot or half-empty cartons of Kung Pao chicken, my old self peeled away like artichoke leaves, revealing the somewhat fuzzy yet coveted heart. In the bedroom mirror I regarded someone reliable, a pal, a massage therapist, a live-in girlfriend. A person with a future that couldn't be blamed on the past.

    The past. Before the back incident, an evil personification: cruel, twisted, the Grim Reaper in drag singing the twisted lyrics of my life to the tune of There's No Business Like Show Business. After my malevolent foul-mouthed mother took off on the back of the exterminator's Harley, my dad silently vowed to never speak to anyone under the age of fourteen. He preferred the company of his drunk "photographer" friends who took candids from my closet while I changed into pajamas. I made a new family out of high school track team buddies and indolent boyfriends with whom I shared only a proximity to the wrong side of tracks. At college, I slept with anyone who could recite Keats, quote Martin Luther King, Jr., or run a mile in under seven minutes. I called myself "-ish" and blew off classes for an entire semester, studying instead the *Reader's Encyclopedia* I had stolen from the university book store.

Ultimately, I dropped out three credits short. Dad never asked, I never explained.

Even I thought I'd end up a drifter. But there it was, just months after my injury, a massage certificate hanging on the wall of my co-leased space in an alternative health center. The place was permeated with the pungent woodsy odor of the Middle Eastern grocery store on the first floor. It was perfect. Walls, rugs, and chairs the color of custard. Free spring water and herbal tea in the small lobby. During my first year, when Gerry lost his fourth job, the woman who shared the space left to have a baby and gave me her clients. I took another look at fate, an integral part of Gerry's theory that the scale of our luck rose and fell in diametric opposition. Again, I was unconvinced.

Gerry. Not a savior, but an ally. Gerry, who complimented the outrageous cartwheels of my red hair and grey eyes squinting behind small rectangular black glasses. Who lovingly traced the lines of cellulite cocooning like caterpillars under my burgeoning saddlebags. He was somewhat of a fuddy-duddy, I guess, a laid-off mechanical engineer working as a computer programmer who designed robotic food slicers as a hobby. Tall, thin, with mad professor light brown hair, he was kind of stooped before I started working on his deltoids. When we met, Gerry knew nothing of complementary medicine. He believed that acupuncture was meant for Chinese arthritis patients and all herbs were for spaghetti sauce. His diet consisted of overcooked meat and boiled starch, and his idea of exercise was biking four blocks to the ice cream shop. But he was affectionate and goofy, and he respected me despite my past, or perhaps because he was more concerned with the future.

He even sympathized when the disenchantment crept in. It snuck up on me, how I began to tire of clients whining about all-night corporate parties in high heels or neck cramps in the cherry picker. I made up games to distract myself: connect-the-moles, how many knots per square inch, guess the dermatologist. Soon I began to categorize people who came to see me for relief. Women who wore thong underwear and sighed in sing-song voices I called 'Monas.' The food-obsessed—vegans, ovo-lactos, macrobiotics with rice paper skin—were referred to as 'Vegiques.' Young women on the verge of an eating disorder whose fragility unnerved me I named 'China Dolls.' 'Mere Moms' were exhausted mothers who sought relief after hauling forty-pound diaper bags and holding toddlers above public toilets. There were inconsistent visits by 'Tight Asses,' attorneys with knots in their necks that were rooted, derisively and resolutely, to the part of the anatomy I dubbed the rectal cessation. 'Blue Boys' were plumbers and carpenters injured on the job, men who jabbered the entire session in an effort to make the experience asexual, adjusting their unzipped jeans and refusing to roll onto their backs after I touched them. Everyone else, usually my favorites for the quirkiness alone, I called 'Other.'

*

Linda K. transcended 'Other.' She showed up a month after her first appointment, on a Friday. That week, in addition to my regulars, I had accommodated three Mere Mom referrals and a few men from a Teamster's convention where some Blue Boy had distributed my number with the make-your-own-picket kits. My hands were beat. I called people by the wrong names. At night, I forgot to remove my lotion holster and arrived home with white globs on the crotch of my pants. "Blue Boy must have turned over," Gerry said.

Linda took a long time to undress. That first day she entered the waiting room, diminutive, with frizzy grey hair and downcast eyes, the part of my brain that stumbles toward logic (as Gerry calls it) clicked on mid-forties Vegique. Now as I entered the room and dimmed the lights, I was not so sure. She shivered beneath the sheet. I started with friction before carefully uncovering her. In the small of her back was a bruise the circumference of a peanut butter jar lid. Most people with that kind of injury would need a kidney replacement.

"Linda, I don't think I should work on you until this heals," I said.

"Oh, well that's why I came in," she whispered. "I can't sit comfortably at work."

"Work? You shouldn't even go!" My incredulity snapped. I started over.

"What happened?"

"I fell. Down the basement stairs."

I wondered what she landed on.

"There was a paint can at the bottom."

I couldn't imagine it. The edge of a paint can would have left a crescent-shaped bruise, unless it was quart-sized and she landed square, in which case the outer edge would be darker.

"I tried ice, then heat," she said. "Nothing helped."

"Did you see a doctor?"

"Oh, no."

She may have been a Combo, I thought: Vegique verging on China Doll. They both tended to bruise easily and repudiated meds. I gently rubbed mint salve on the purple skin, then started working on Linda's shoulders. Her upper back was riddled with adhesions larger than walnuts, and almost as hard. I spent a long time with straight strokes before I dared to work on trigger points. The woman was incredibly tough. She didn't evade me or wince.

Weeks later, Linda came in with her arm in a sling.

"Got in a little fender bender," she said, stretching out on her side. We talked during the session. She taught an organic cooking class at the community center and invited me to stop in sometime, promised not to mention my profession if I was overbooked. A slew of Vegiques, no doubt.

That night, I broke my rule about discussing clients with Gerry.

"She's a whacko," he said.

"How can you say that?" I asked. We were leaning against the lumpy brown sofa, picking fuzz balls from a navy rug he had found at a yard sale. The apartment reeked of the paint he'd slopped on after his fifth day testing capacitors in a hermetically sealed basement laboratory. Baby blue semi-gloss. I'd gagged.

"She's a nice person," I insisted. "You don't know a thing about her."

"What do you know about her?"

"She likes Asian food, has a sister in L.A., broke an ankle and a rib within the last year, has a chattering chipmunk laugh, and always wears white underwear."

"Is she married, divorced, gay?"

"I don't know."

"Have kids?"

"I don't know."

"What's her religion?"

"Don't know."

"Political leanings? Burning desire in life?"

"Geez, Gerry, I don't interrogate half-naked people who come to me for relief."

"I'm just emphasizing," Gerry smiled, "that based on your evidence, my assumption that she's a whacko is as reasonable as your assertion that she's a nice person."

I rolled my eyes.

"She seems unstable," he said.

"I never implied that."

"How can you be sure her kindness is sincere?" Gerry continued. "Unless you've made some definitive correlation between white underwear and nice people."

Gerry formed his fuzz pile into numbers on the rug. Hopeless. I got up to make stir-fried chicken and broccoli. Gerry put globs of butter on his basmati rice and flipped the green stuff onto my plate.

For dessert, we fooled around in the shower with peach yogurt (my choice) and caramel sauce (Gerry's).

When I awakened at 3:00 A.M., melancholy wrapped around me like a damp blanket. Why had Linda come to me? Me, who had forged a new life by accident. Still fending off the Grim Reaper's intrusions in flouncy pink prom gowns. I reached for Gerry, and his warm back allowed a memory to surface, vivid yet safe in the darkness.

It was my last year of college. I was on my way home to beg my dad for an overdue tuition check when a little boy on a skateboard was hit by a car right in front of me. The driver was shrieking, people scurried in the random patterns of wind-up toys. I dashed forward and grabbed the small, dirty hand, rubbed the cooling skin while the boy's brightness faded into the blue light of evening. There was the smell of fried food, and above me I heard a seagull cry. My mind spun with all the things that brown-haired kid would never have—first love, graduation parties, a beer with his dad—and it occurred to me that I hadn't experienced them either. The ambulance came and I was pushed aside. I watched the boy's stretcher fold into the back, saw the paramedic inside rub his arm, his head. Touch, a basic human reaction. Later it would occur to me: the sexcapades in high school, the rotating beds in college, the arms encircling me on rooftops I threatened to leap from—all for contact, for the comfort of touch.

*

Gerry and I had a fight. Initiated by a food issue, of course—this time his disgust with the quarter-cup of uncooked couscous he swept from beneath the table. Relax, I'd said, adding that I was the one who brushed his pubes from the sheets and shower every morning. Then we lobbed: my toenail clippings on the counter, his skid-marked underwear on the ottoman; my tofu wrap molded to the windowsill, his zit spray on the bathroom mirror.

Touch

At least I knew when to walk out, and to take public transportation so I could get blotto. Fortunately it was the first Thursday in August, night of the monthly massage-class reunion organized by my friend Marlene. On the *T* it came to me: Olé Grill. I would have preferred to eat a bag of cheese popcorn and a jar of Nutella while watching Love Story at Marlene's *feng shui* lair, but mediocre Mexican would have to do.

Marlene was at the bar in her usual dyed leather shirt, this one form-fitting dark purple. She resembled an eggplant, but I said nothing. Beside her, drinking dark beer, stood my partner from Session One of massage workshop. He was a short half-Dominican, half-Floridian, with spiky dyed blond hair, the threat of a paunch, puffy eyelids, and droopy jowls. Marlene once remarked that he looked like an overweight drug-addicted hound dog from southern California. We dubbed him Surfer Dog.

The first time Surfer Dog touched me in workshop, a shiver emanating from my internal organs nearly turned me inside-out. My teeth chattered. My orifices either leaked or clenched. He began effluage to get the circulation going, and the sensation approached—I couldn't believe it—orgasm. The instructor that semester had suggested mantras to keep focused, *Tender, tenderize*, and *Circulation, circular*, absolutely ridiculous but as difficult to get out of one's head as a 70s disco tune sung in falsetto. To shut down my ride, I hummed "Knock on Wood" (at least it had rhythm) and visualized spinning coins, orange slices, the lip of a cup.

His method was deliberate yet as random as a bird's wing in an air current. Variable pressure and arrhythmic circles united our skin by an unstable tether. His style, so unlike my own, made me wonder if the massage experience involved a combination of two sets of chemistry, maybe a delicate balance of pheromones and physiology. What could I possibly share with Surfer Dog—pulse rate, brain waves, tactile sensations? I whispered questions during session, which we weren't supposed to do. He liked red, I preferred green.

He liked spicy smells and food. I favored anything clean and fresh with a bite: eucalyptus, grapefruit, arugula. It was obviously a matter of biorhythms.

One snowy afternoon when I was recovering from a rotten flu, Surfer Dog changed his routine slightly, and he had me. My back was not skin covering muscle, but a silken fabric floating, the surface of a still pool skimmed by a flat palm. I became wax melting across the table. Surfer Dog pulled what was me right out of my body and took me to an unfamiliar but welcome place where I hovered like a thought, completely unaware of the smell of a pen on dry erase board, which normally annoyed me, or the squeak of sneakers shifting around the beds. I entered this place which completely defined every possible interpretation of the word serenity. *Timeless. Boundless.* No chance of encountering the Grim Reaper as Carmen Miranda. When it ended, I couldn't look at him. If Surfer Dog had stripped naked I would have yanked my pants off and screwed him on the table, oblivious to everyone in the room. I began to avoid talking to him in the cafeteria, only to seek him out in workshop. Once I even let the orgasm come, scrunching up my toes to conceal the rocking inside my body. Did he know, I wondered. But who would dare ask?

I hugged Marlene. Surfer Dog reintroduced himself as Joe and downed a shot of tequila. He looked a bit heavier, smelled of jalapenos and sandalwood cologne. When Marlene greeted a blonde I didn't recall, I ordered two dark beers and handed one to him. We talked about our jobs. He was doing corporate massage in the financial district. Manipulating the stiffs, he quipped. I liked him. He was witty and soft, but oh so unattractive to me, visually speaking. We did shots, bit lime.

At dinner, we didn't sit together. I drank close to a bottle of wine while Bonnie and Rayna talked about the use of Arnica for bruising. Rayna demonstrated by dripping red wine on the tablecloth and covering it with salt. The crystals soaked up most of the

Touch

color. Bonnie pinched my cheeks whenever my head lolled and told me to eat. My eyes welled up when I considered that the untouched cedar-planked salmon would be a good test subject for Gerry's Mousse-a-matic.

After a few spoonfuls of rubbery flan, Marlene suggested we all go dancing, but everyone opted to walk to a nearby bar to watch either the Red Sox or some insipid love-and-guts network drama. I lagged as the group clomped along the sidewalk. My ears buzzed and I knew I ought to go home and down the pint of cappuccino chunk in the freezer. Then a hand was on my shoulder. The fingers pulsed a bit. I honestly thought God had reached down to give me a wake-up call: STOP MOPING! My knees buckled and I crumpled onto the sidewalk. Surfer Dog appeared above me.

"Surf . . . Joe," I said. "You scared me!"

He looked like I had just slapped him. "I'm sorry, I was, well, I saw you back here and thought you looked a little lost." He reached down to help me stand. I'd forgotten I was a few inches taller, even as a floppy, drunken mess.

Up ahead, the group turned the corner. I grabbed Joe's hands, put them on my shoulders, and closed my eyes. Go, I thought. Immediately he started working, and the fluttering began. I was about to open the wrong door and stumble right in, about to tell him about the time that . . . which would lead to . . . then the awful declaration. . . But he saved me. He laughed and said, so completely unaffected, as if he were revealing his shoe size, that his hands had a way of giving people what they needed most. I had to admit, I was resentful that he didn't know he had it. The touch. A gift.

Then as now, I knew I'd never approach that realm. Most of the time, I saw the body as just that—a body—and at odd moments, not even a living thing. An inert conglomeration of bone, muscle, skin, a corpulent mass beached on the table like a manatee struck by a Chris Craft. Lately, my reactions were a source of consternation. Moments, for instance, while working on a particularly annoying Blue Boy who asked what a girl did to get such strong hands, when I envisioned my hands encircling his neck. I'd cup his sternocleidomastoid in webbed fingers and press my thumb against the vertebrae until he truly turned blue, his eyes finally opening, unbelieving. Such a small woman against such a massive man. Maybe I'd call him Goliath.

Surfer Dog walked me to the T, tripping as he waved while the train pulled away. What kept me going wasn't a desire to be like him. Nor was it the clients who hoped I'd identify things that they could not since, as one aptly remarked, they were inside the box. For me, it was the element of the unknown. The best massages were difficult to interpret, the movements so interdependent they comprised one indecipherable event. Same with sex, I told Gerry when I got home and we forgot why we were mad. Dark was mandatory. Now do what is least expected. The more intricately he worked with fingers, tongue, lips, the better. Complicate it so I can't figure it out. Confuse me. It's beyond trust, I said. After all, who can be trusted, really?

*

Linda came early to her next appointment and spilled her cup of water on the waiting room carpet. I thought she might cry as I blotted it with a white towel.

"Not a problem." I smiled too wide to stop myself from touching her forearm.

On the table, she twitched under the covers.

"Would you like a blanket?" I asked.

Her head slid from side to side.

When I put my hands on her back, they bounced back as if I had jammed two forks into a light socket. Sweat beaded on my upper lip, and I wiped my palms against my hips. A slight vibration like the idle of a car lingered when I replaced my hands. Closed eyes did not help me understand. She turned over and I noticed several red dots along her clavicle, as linear as fingerholes on a recorder.

My pinky brushed against them lightly. No reaction. Yet, the moment I began facial, a tear rolled down Linda's right temple. For most other women, it was commonplace.

"Are you alright?" I whispered, gliding my thumbs across her brow.

"Yes."

"I can stop now if you'd like."

"No, no," she almost smiled. "It's just that. . ."

I worked on her immobile face for a long time before she spoke.

"You're so gentle."

That night I called Surfer Dog. It was inevitable. Marlene would chide me for divulging patient information. Bonnie would offer a homeopathic remedy. Rayna would look for humor where there was none. And Gerry was . . . Gerry.

Surfer agreed to meet me for lunch at a vegetarian restaurant in the South End. We sat outside at a small metal table where whiffs of tangy charred meat reached us from the barbecue joint across the street. Red buds from the trees overhead dropped onto our hair. I ordered ratatouille, brown rice, and spring water. Surfer Dog had a grilled portobello sandwich with thick slabs of focaccia that reminded me of the styrofoam bricks used in amusement park buildings.

I told him about Linda, her mild nature, her injuries, her strange energy.

"For some reason, I don't think it's abuse," I said, picking at my ratatouille. "It feels almost. . . *internal*."

"Hmm." Surfer chewed. "Well, you could investigate. Get to know her better, invite her out but pick her up at home."

"I don't know." I pushed an enormous slice of onion to the side of my plate and put my fork down. "I did visit her cooking class. Everyone seemed to like her. She was calm, encouraging."

"Why not drop by her place?"

"Do you think I should I get involved in a client's life? Have you ever done it?" I tried to sound nonchalant, but I was curious about Surfer Dog's private life.

"Not really. I did have one guy come on to me, and it took a long time to convince him that I wasn't really gay."

I noticed he didn't say really wasn't gay.

"To get him off my back, so to speak, I agreed to go out with him one night," Surfer continued, "no strings attached. It was sort of ridiculous, me at a gay dance club beside a band of shirtless men with abs like upside-down ice cube trays. Someone said 'massage' and they set up a table right below the stage where a guy wearing a glow-in-the-dark g-string danced with a metal pipe."

The waiter cleared our plates and refilled our water glasses. Surfer Dog chugged his. I ordered a dessert to share, fresh berries with soy milk sabayon.

"Did you like it?" I asked.

Surfer leaned toward me.

"What was your first instinct with Linda?" He touched my hand and my fingers leapt toward his wrist.

"Leave it alone," I said, and he removed his hand. "I mean, do nothing."

"That's easy." He nodded. "And maybe smart. It reminds me of something a friend of mine who's studying philosophy told me the other day. I think he said it was William James who wrote it, whoever he is."

"Psychologist brother of the writer Henry." Facts from the *Reader's Encyclopedia* occasionally spewed forth.

"Yeah, whatever. Anyway, he wrote: The art of being wise is the art of knowing what to overlook."

"That implies that you've already looked, just chosen to ignore."

Surfer Dog said, "Hmm," and wagged his head.

A wine goblet of strawberries was placed between us. The fruit was tart, the cream a little gritty.

"I guess I'm looking for a sign when there isn't one," I admitted.

Surfer Dog licked his spoon and balanced it on his knife. "You know, when things like this happen to me, I try to remember what kind of person I consider myself to be—on that particular day, since it varies—and if my actions mesh with that identity."

So we did have something in common.

"Who are you today?" Surfer asked.

I stared at the smeared, empty goblet. "An observer, I guess."

There was no way to explain my apprehension. How I avoided peeling the scab back to see the depth of the wound beneath. Delving further might strike some survival mechanism. A warning signal would blare—RETREAT!—a flash of the brocade cape, the gaping skull topped with a synthetic platinum bouffant tumbling toward a mother taunting, *Shithead! Idiot!* before the door slammed against my head. A father working the night shift who told a neighbor there was no need for babysitters, the kid sleeps like the bump on a log. Weekends hiding from "guests" in the attic eaves where I read library books and fed Saltines to the pet mouse I'd found there.

Surfer Dog pulled at his jowls. "What's that quote, 'If you help just one person in your life. . .'"

I scoffed. "How do you know I'd be helping?"

"You would."

"Maybe I'd run. Forget about it."

"No, you wouldn't. You're too nice."

I laughed, thinking of Gerry, that I rarely wore white underwear.

"Well, maybe *strong* is a better word," Surfer Dog said. I looked at my hands. "Look," he continued. "Helping people in need isn't like coming down with the plague for them. You do it whenever you massage."

"No, that's what you do. You have the gift," I blurted.

Surfer Dog looked almost hurt. Then his expression shifted to gratitude. "So maybe your gift can be trying," he said.

"Sounds pretty lame."

"Not if you're the only one giving it."

*

Linda's duplex was a white vinyl-sided building behind a sub shop in Watertown. The metal doors were painted brown, the windows covered by dark shades. Someone had planted a few tulips along the foundation and mowed the brittle crab grass. I parked in front of the sub shop and went in to find something to bring, cookies or pastries. They sold only subs, drinks, and chips. I bought two bottles of lemon sparkling water.

Warm spring air was concealed beneath the dense aroma of newly poured asphalt. The atmosphere jittered with buzzing noises from a lawn mower, a chain saw, the telescoping bucket of a telephone truck. Suddenly my chest thumped with a jab of appreciation for my life, my job, for Gerry and our one-bedroom apartment with a view of the playground. For simple things—clean sheets, the ability, though rarely the time, to buy apricot soap and get a hair cut.

There was no bell. I knocked. The sound was shallow and I rapped a little louder. I couldn't hear anything inside. Next door, a dog on a chain approached the chicken wire fence. It had one soft brown eye but the other was a spooky whitish-blue. Around back, wooden stairs led to a small deck. Beach towels hung over the railing. A rusty charcoal grill slumped beside a box of empty cans and bottles, mostly beer. The back yard narrowed toward a wooded area with a thin dirt path, a place I would have investigated as a kid. I opened the aluminum screen door and knocked softly. A bee circling my head momentarily drowned out the other buzzing noises.

The door cracked, then opened. Linda wore a pair of cut-offs and a black t-shirt. She smiled, frowned, then smiled again. Her hands were covered with red rubber gloves.

"Hey, hi. I didn't expect to see you." She looked past me. "Sorry, I must not have heard you at the front door. I was washing dishes. Come in, come in."

The kitchen smelled delicious, of chili and baking bread.

"I was on my way to the mall," I lied, "and realized you lived along my short cut. I brought drinks."

I sat at the wooden table in the corner while Linda rinsed the last pot and put it on the rack to dry. She sat next to me and opened the paper bag, got up to get glasses and ice. The silence was insinuating.

"How are you?" I asked.

"Fine," she answered automatically.

She found mitts to take her bread from the oven. The screen door squeaked, and a man's arm protruded through the narrow opening.

"Lin! Oh, there you are. Get me a beer, would ya?"

Two loaf pans clattered onto a cooling rack. She found a can of Bud in the fridge, popped the top and handed it to the snapping fingers.

"Thanks." As he turned to go, the door creaked wide and I saw him standing there in jeans, no shirt, work boots. He was squat, well-muscled, with a thick neck and a receding hairline, his nose wide at the bridge, his lips pale and thin. In one hand was the beer tilting toward his mouth, in the other a greasy chain saw. He spotted me, clearly surprised.

"You didn't mention we had company," he drawled.

"Hi." I stood up. "I'm . . . from the cooking class."

Linda said, "This is my boyfriend, Danny."

I wondered if he'd put the beer down and shake my hand, but his gaze stuck to her. He lifted the chain saw to tap her chin lightly, and that split second after he walked toward the woods, her wide doe eyes scanned the floor. I knew. And she knew I knew. The Grim Reaper wore a velvet bustier with fakies, and for once I grimaced, and that grimace dissolved the oncoming image of my mother's twisted mouth, *Lazy Ass!*, her hands gripping the steamy mop above my body sprawled across linoleum. Instead, I saw Gerry's face, and smiled. I saw Surfer Dog, and thought, Okay, who am I right now? Hadn't it already been established that I was the one who touched? Not expertly, but with determination.

I looked at Linda's bent head. Had I helped her, changed her life even an iota? Maybe her body, but that was transient. What about her spirit? They were hardly the same, flesh and spirit. Flesh was so malleable. Could the spirit be, too?

My fingers rested on Linda's forearms. Her eyes were deep green with gold flecks shaped like wings. I wiped the black mark from her chin, then moved to her shoulders. My hands worked while she sobbed, until she stepped forward to shake one of the perfect loaves from the pan. She beckoned me to follow her through the darkened living room where she unbolted the front door with one hand. Squinting, we stepped together into the noisy air.

How Bluegrass Saved My Life

Kim Ponders

Bear, the navigator, had a five-string banjo with a reinforced neck. When I held it and plucked at the strings, it made a twangy, unhappy sound, but he could make it sing. His whole face listened as he played and his wet, pink lips moved silently over the words. On night sorties over the Al Jarha corridor, he would fold up his maps, and in the thirty minutes between checkpoints, he would slide his banjo out from under his console and twist around so that the neck would sometimes poke Rosey, the engineer, in the back. He played left-handed. Jago, the aircraft commander, and I, and the engineer would listen and sip coffee, watching the fires in Kuwait burning like the eyes of a hundred animals in the dark.

Sometimes the comm operator would tune up the BBC International on the high frequency radio, and the news of the war would come to us as we were flying in it, as though we were already a part of history. The radio with its static and whirls sounded like a 1950s sci-fi show. The war did not feel like a part of us. On the ground, I felt naked and slow, but in the air, I felt secret and anonymous, buttoned inside our metal skin.

Bear carried his banjo everywhere. He kept a snapshot of his pedigree Saint Bernard, Jo Dick, on his console during missions. Bear and Jo Dick had the same round, hungry eyes. Bear's girlfriend, Candy, had her arms around Jo Dick in the picture that was taken outside Bear's duplex in front of the wheel from his king-cab. Candy also had a round, soft face with wet lips and freckles that matched the auburn fur on Jo Dick's ears, but Bear always made it clear that the picture was of Jo Dick and not of the girl.

'See,' he would say. 'Here's my pup.'

And the crewdog he was talking to would say, 'Which one?'

Bear was a Congregationalist Baptist, and on Sunday mornings, if there wasn't a mission, he would attend the "meetings," as we had to call them, in the big sand-colored tent in the middle of the compound, and this gave Jago and me an hour and a half alone in their room. We would lie in bed, my unpinned hair stretching in tendrils across Jago's stomach, the sheets blown half across the floor like a parachute, and watch the light come through the shutters and form slats on the opposite wall. The shutters were always closed, so that even when the sun was high and full, the room was dark and cool as dusk.

'Let's get married,' I would say.

'If we do it in Saudi, does that mean I'll own you?'

We were already married to people back home, but we didn't talk about them or the letters they wrote us or the photographs we kept hidden in the backs of our aircrew aids. His wife's name was Pam, and Jago had introduced her at a Forth of July squadron picnic. We tried to shake hands, but she was balancing, on one arm, a tray of pig's blankets pierced with miniature American flags and, on the other, a little boy dressed in orange swim trunks. I could remember little about her except her short, practical hair and stocky legs (she had been a competition water-skier), and that we looked nothing alike.

Bear tried to stay out as long as he could. He went to his meeting, where, from under the canvas flaps, you could hear someone banging away at a piano, and then he went to chow and then to check the mail, but I was always still there when Bear came noisily into the villa. He would sit around in the living room picking at his banjo while I collected my clothes and crept out. An hour or so later, I'd arrive again, knocking on the door. Bear would have picked up my mail for me. Jago would have showered, and I would smell the dampness and want to rush up to him and put my hands on his wet hair and fresh clothes, but instead we would all sit around on the floor of the common room, feeling awkward and embarrassed.

One night, we were playing pigs on the floor of their villa with a British Jaguar Pilot and a Turkish NATO intelligence officer. The Brit's name was Heppotok. He was half Greek. He wore an olive green canvas jacket as old as World War II that hung halfway down his thighs. His hair was thick and black and his eyes were as dark as obsidian, and he tried to wrap me in their gaze as though it were a rich mink blanket. He'd traded his stash of Tempazepam for some distilled Kentucky bourbon that arrived in the kingdom through the wheel wells of a KC-135, and he kept splashing mouthfuls of it into our waxy paper cups.

The Turk, whose name was Sedami, was overweight and smelled awful, but he was kind, and he kept offering us the dates he'd brought to eat with the bourbon.

'The convoy looked like a snake,' the Brit said. 'A big-bellied anaconda with scales made of lights, winding out of Kuwait, its body stalled and trying to push the head faster.'

'Where were you guys heading out of?' Bear asked.

'Where were we heading *out of*?' the Brit asked. He was grinning and drunk. Bear was waiting for him to answer. He didn't seem to understand what the Brit had found amusing. 'We were heading out of Dhahran. Straight off, you saw the head advancing toward Basra.'

Jago spit some tangerine seeds into an empty Skoal can. Bear went back to plucking his banjo, absently, the arm of it resting on his shoulder like a cello.

'The only question,' Heppotok said, 'was where to drop the first round.'

'That's a beautiful story,' Jago said, and I laughed so hard that I had to look away.

Jago, lying back on his elbow, swallowed the whiskey in his cup and then reached forward and brushed his thumb lightly over my toes. Everyone noticed this but the Brit, who kept describing the run over the Basra highway and swaying forward, trying to capture me in his deep luminous eyes. He was very drunk.

'Beautiful.' The Brit wagged his head. 'More like fantastic.'

'Sedami was there,' Jago said. 'Was it fantastic, Sedami?'

Sedami raised his eyes. He'd been studying the two small plastic pigs in his hands that a marine had given him in Jubail after he'd surveyed the damage from the Basra highway bombing. Sedami had ordered one of the corporals to go around and shut off the music still playing in some of the jeeps that had been blown off the road. The corporal had climbed out of the charred and mangled openings in the jeeps where the doors had been, holding his cap over his eyes and retching. The marine had given him the pigs after hearing the story about the Basra highway because the marine had had nothing else on him to give.

'Please,' Sedami said. 'It's not important.'

The Brit eyed him hotly. 'What's not important, chap?'

Sedami grinned and shook his head. He was doing mandatory service in Brussels when the war started, and now he only wanted to finish his tour and go home to his fiancée, a civil engineer from Ankara.

Bear said, 'I wouldn't think pigs were the right kind of thing to give a Muslim.'

Sedami laughed. 'He didn't mean it that way.'

'This was a precious and rare opportunity,' the Brit said. 'The enemy turned their lights on in the middle of the desert at night.'

Jago rolled onto his back and began to gargle his whiskey. His fingers, holding a date, circled in the air over his mouth.

'Anyway,' Sedami said. 'I am Zoroastrian. Not that he would have known.'

Jago swallowed his whiskey. 'I didn't know there were any of those left.'

'Is anyone listening to me?' the Brit shouted. 'You all realize that it was an armed retreat.'

Jago dropped the date into his mouth and waggled it between his teeth.

'You have no idea,' the Brit said. 'You AWACS guys think you know what it's all about, lumbering around in the Hindenburg two hundred miles from the nearest missile. You think you can shake your head at the fighter pilots who do the nasty work. No offense.'

'We all do the nasty work,' Jago said.

We were supposed to be celebrating. The end of the war was near and we were all going to be going home. But it didn't feel like we were going home. It didn't feel like we were moving at all.

'How about you guys kiss and make up?' I asked. With that, the Brit began to leer and sway in my direction again. 'You're a small guy,' I said. 'That's why you get drunk so easily.'

'Small hands, warm heart.'

I think he said 'heart,' but I'll never know, because as he spoke, the room shook as though he had spit thunder out of his mouth. The floor trembled as if a clapper had struck the body of a tower bell housed in the walls. Sirens began to howl. A blast shot through my eardrums and nerves. We became a frantic flock of hips and elbows, sifting and sorting the chem gear in our trembling fingers.

'What's here?' Sedami yelled.

The blast itself answered, a second one, again like the clapping of a great bell surrounding us, piercing at first and then succumbing to a deadening hum. I tripped over a sleeve. Heppotok yelled. I saw his lips move. I saw the sound leave his mouth. It seemed to shimmer and dissipate in the air. I was still falling backward into Jago, bent at the hips. He had lifted his elbow to steady me. The air was thick and gray, and I seemed to be diving through it, and then my shoulder hit the ground. Something snapped. I thought it was the banjo. I pulled a nylon bag out of the way, and then I saw that it was not the banjo I'd broken, but my own gas mask. The canister felt loose, like a broken bone, under the hood.

Sitting on my shins, I lifted the straps off the faceplate and unfolded the hood, and the canister fell out in my hand. It had fractured in a clean line. I kept trying to fit the canister against the air nozzle, and it kept falling out in my hand.

'Is there any duct tape?'

The hum of a struck bell still filled the room. Sedami slid his canvas belt off and they tried to strap the canister on by wrapping the buckle around my neck.

'Take mine,' Jago said, ripping his mask off. His face was flushed and the imprint of the rubber had begun to form along his jaw.

'Don't be stupid,' I said.

The Brit was fumbling with his booties. He had put his rubber gloves on and the fingertips kept getting caught in the laces.

'I'm ordering you to take it.'

'You're ordering me?' He was trying to push the mask into my hands. Bear was grunting and waving his hands at us, his over-suit bunched like fishing gaiters at the waist. I tried not to think of the pictures they had showed us of blackened and bubbling skin. I hoped death would come quickly without too much thrashing.

'You're not brave,' Jago yelled, his face purple. 'You're stupid.'

'I'm not the one holding my mask in my hands.'

I wanted to take the mask more than anything, but I would not. If I took the mask, Jago would sit and think about Pam and the little boy with the orange swim trunks.

'Don't make me do this,' he said.

I turned from him and began to put on the over-suit and the booties and the cotton and rubber gloves. I didn't look at him again until I was sure the mask was over his face. He was breathing hard and I could see the sweat trickling along the bridge of his nose.

Sedami had put some M8 tape on the wall, but no one looked at it. He made a motion that I should put my mask on anyway. I shook my head. The mask was no good without the canister, though I understood it would make them feel better to see me wearing it.

My eyes stung. I sniffed for the smell of almonds and fresh cut grass. They were all trying not to stare at me, and I pretended to be alone in the room, looking at anything except their faces pale as prairie dogs in the shadows of the masks. I shut my eyes. It occurred to me that I didn't really know any of them. It would be horrible to die in front of these huffing strangers. It would be humiliating.

I saw that Jago would go on living, go back to Pam and the little boy, and then I saw that he would do this regardless of whether I lived, and it made me furious to die in front of him. Alex would have died for me. He would have pressed his mask into my hands, ignorant of the consequences. They were blinking behind the smooth plastic of the faceplates. I pinched the collar of my over-suit around my throat.

The sirens stopped blaring. Outside, the MPs would be testing the compound for chemicals. It occurred to me that I was going to live. I started to laugh. My aquatic friends kept huffing. I reached across Hepotok's lap and took the bourbon bottle. The Dixie cup felt soft and wet. Bits of wax had separated from the side and floated in the whiskey.

'*Sanguis Domini Nostri Jesu*,' I said. 'Drink and be whole.'

I pinched a date between my gloved fingers and brought it close to my face. I had never looked closely at a date before. I did not like the look of it, the wet brown body of an insect. I rolled over on my stomach and bit into the date while I looked at Jago. I looked at him with what I hoped was insolence and fortitude while the thick film of the date stuck to my teeth. I finished it and then I licked the tips of my gloves.

'Bear, I think I've been born again,' I said.

From the klaxons on the rooftops came the call for all-clear. There was the sudden sound of breath as the others pulled their masks off their faces. Nobody said anything for a minute, and then Heppotok said, 'To think I almost died without getting a kiss from Annie.'

I lifted up to my knees and kissed him hard on the mouth.

'There,' I said. 'Now you can say you've truly lived.'

My legs were shaky and I sat down hard. Sedami and Jago had begun stripping out of their over-suits. Bear picked up his banjo and leaned it against the bare wall away from us.

'Drink this,' Sedami said, twisting the cap on a bottle of water.

'I'm fine,' I said.

'You better go over to life support,' Jago said. He was gathering his things into his helmet bag. I felt annoyed I hadn't thought of that myself. 'I'll go with you,' he said.

'I don't need you,' I said. Jago frowned, but he kept folding his things and putting them into the bag in the right order.

'I'll take her,' the Brit said. I didn't like the way he seemed to be negotiating with Jago.

'I'm fine,' I repeated. I collected my gear quickly, but Jago had his bag zipped and he was waiting. There was no sense making a scene. I let him hold the door and I walked out and down the cement steps through the courtyard to the street. The moon hung crookedly over the Patriot battery on the north side of the compound. Everything was quiet. I took one step onto the road and then I threw up.

'I'm not so good,' I said.

'You're too good. That's your problem.'

'I didn't realize I was so drunk.'

'That's the thing about being drunk. You're always the last to know.'

We were crossing what was called the minefield in the middle of the compound. There were no mines in it. It was just a barren patch of dirt and rock where even the succulents wouldn't grow. There was a thin crack of blue light near the runway. Some things in the back of my pack kept clinking together and I swiped at it a couple of times but couldn't get a hold of the metal.

'I'm not drunk,' I said.

The heaviness of our packs made our boots sink into the sand, so that crossing the field took a long time. I walked as fast as I could. I kept stumbling on the uneven ground, but this only made me want to walk faster.

'You afraid Heppotok is going to catch up?' Jago was out of breath. He had braced his thumbs against the harness of his pack.

'Fuck Heppotok,' I said.

'I'd say that's what's on his mind.'

'Fuck Heppotok and fuck you.'

'You're so tough, Annie.'

In my room, there was nothing but a cot with a scratchy mohair blanket folded over it and my canvas bags that I'd propped against the wall. I never turned on the light when we were together but this time I did. I hadn't been in this room in days. We sat on the bed because there was no place else to sit. He put his hand on my shoulder and tried to pull me to him. It wasn't his fault, I kept thinking, it was just bad luck. But all I saw was the mask secured on his face, the four of them in their amphibious costumes, waiting for one of two things to happen.

'That's not my mouth,' I said when he tried to kiss me.

'Whose mouth is it?'

'It's Pam's mouth.'

'What do you want me to say, Annie? Do you want me to file for divorce from Saudi? Do you want me to make a decision right now in the middle of the war?'

'I thought you had.'

'What made you think that?' He unclasped the canister from his belt and took a swig of water and offered it to me. 'Have you?'

I shook my head. 'I know what I want,' I said.

'You might be disappointed, Annie. I'm lazy around the house. I have a bloodhound named Rosco who's so lazy I have to mow around him. But I like to take him out dove hunting in the fall. Ever go dove hunting, Annie? We take the pick-up and go out to Lovelace Ridge near Arkansas. I use a Remington double-barrel but my buddy's got a Winchester Supreme I'd like to get my hands on. Arkansas wouldn't be a bad place to settle down in, really.'

'You trying to scare me?'

'I'm just saying that we have to go home sometime.'

'Then why wait? If this is all so transient, why don't you go home right now?'

Then he stood up, took his pack and walked out, closing the door softly, and I wanted him to walk in again not because of what he'd told me but because he was strong enough to get up and walk out without looking back. I lay down and tried to imagine living on a ranch with a bloodhound in the backyard and the fillets of wild carcasses in the freezer, and the scene looked comic but not impossible. I had lived in a colonial house out of something in *Yankee* magazine, and in a dilapidated saltbox in central Texas surrounded by a chicken yard, following my father into the houses of women he took up and then abandoned, so why not on a ranch in the hot American heartland? I lay there in the dark, reinventing myself, without giving a casual thought to Alex.

But then I saw Jago sealed inside the safety of the mask. He'd done the right thing, and that irritated me. I told myself it was just bad luck that my canister had snapped, and that he had done what any pilot would do. You're a pilot first, I thought, and I tried to fill the shell of myself with the convictions of a pilot, the confidence of someone who could walk out the door without looking back.

How Bluegrass Saved My Life

'Fuck Heppotok and fuck you,' I said to the ceiling and fell asleep grasping the canvas ribs of the cot. But in the morning, I saw the mask over his face and then I saw our whole affair as a mask that Jago was wearing and would cast off when the war was over.

We flew that night. We went through the checklist under the red filter of the flight deck lights. The cockpit smelled dusty and also of old familiar metal that had been worn down from rubbing. My headset hung over one ear so that I could hear the ground and tower and also hear Jago, in a cool and neutral voice, run through the checklist. It was as quiet and professional as if one of us was getting an eval. There was none of the usual horsing around. Even Bear stayed turned toward the INS panel, punching numbers with the efficiency of a stenographer.

On the climb out, as soon as we turned north, you could begin to see the fires popping up in Kuwait. I started a letter to my husband. Dear Alex, it read, How are things?

Jago was staring straight ahead. I crossed out the first line and wrote, I hope everything is fine. I miss you. Then I crossed out that line and wrote, I've been thinking of you.

Jago's hand was curled over the throttles, resting. I looked at his articulate knuckles and missed them, and then I turned and wrote, You wouldn't believe what happened.

We refueled twice and spent the long hours rooted in complacent staring. Bear didn't even play his banjo, as if waiting in protest for the easy harmony of the cockpit to resume. Just before sunrise, we listened over the radio to a Prowler and a couple of F-16s hunting for mobile surface-to-air missile batteries near As-Salman. I scanned the sky for their shark tooth bellies glinting in the orchid smoke that hung over the desert, but the air was too thick with haze to see anything but the great boulders of soot rising from the oil fires in the east. When Jago hit the aft bunks, Bear and I had a long talk about why we had joined the Air Force. I had never really talked to Bear before, and I liked him more than I thought I would. I told him how my father had been an F-86 pilot and that I had joined because of him, not that he wanted me to, but that I thought he would admire me if I did. He told me he had come in on an ROTC scholarship and that his father had been a chief master sergeant. Really, I thought, this is how things should have been throughout the war. I should never have started that whole business with Jago, and I was feeling strong and virtuous when Jago came back up to the flight deck and said, 'How long have we been off course?'

The autopilot had skipped a turn point and neither of us had noticed. I had my hand resting on the throttle, and by the time I noticed that we were 80 miles north of our orbit, Jago had jumped into the left seat, brushed my hand off the throttles and said, 'My airplane.'

He pushed the throttles all the way forward and pulled the yoke up hard and to the right. The SAM hunters were no longer northeast, but low off our nose, looking for a missile that could at any moment open its eyes and launch at our broad belly which had no business lumbering over the skies of As-Salman.

Over the radio, the Prowler called off the coordinates of a SAM whose radar had begun to scan the skies.

'Did you get those?' Jago asked Bear. 'Where is it?'

I felt a sickening repugnance, so utter and wordless that I could not seem to reach back to a time when I had not been inept and foolhardy, and I swore that I would not speak for the rest of the war except in the line of duty and would welcome the humiliation that would come provided we only got the crew and the jet back to safety.

'Mud Six. Mud Six. Scoot 21, naked,' the Prowler called over the UHF. The F-16s called that they were naked too, which meant the SA-6 had launched onto a target they could not identify.

'Christ!' Jago yelled. We had no gear to tell us if the SAM had locked onto us or someone else. He pushed and twisted the yoke to force a quicker turn, and the jet responded as well as it could, rolling its left wing skyward and moaning into the wide, slow arc of a humpback whale.

I saw the missile come. Gray and thin as a barracuda, it flamed high into our two o'clock. Jago slammed the yoke forward. The broad, brown earth opened below us and for a moment I went blind with blood rushing into my head.

'SAM!' yelled Rosey leaning in hard and pointing over my right shoulder.

Jago banked even harder to pull the SAM across the nose and to the left side where he could see it. He called in a voice tight with the weight of gravity in his chest, 'Sentry 45 engaged Mud Six.'

'Sentry who?' called the Prowler.

We were diving hard now. The lead F-16 launched a missile at the SAM battery. But the battery already had at least one missile in the air, and so it became a race to see whether the F-16's missile could knock out the SAM's guidance radar before their missiles killed us.

The first SAM flew high and straight over.

'It's gone,' I said.

'There's always two,' Jago said, and as he said it, I saw the second one climbing at our one o'clock, smoke fanning out in its wake. Jago banked to the left, and the last I saw of the missile was its obliging arc, pursuing us like an urgent messenger. Then the earth skipped and floated across the windshield and we were thrown into a hurricane of sky.

I didn't know if we'd been hit dead on or just shaken by the blast of a proximity fuse. The jet seemed to twist and yaw, an unfriendly and bulbous bit of crag plummeting through the sky. The altimeter shuttered and spun. The horns and sirens began to scream. 'Pull up,' I yelled, though I had no idea where up was. The sun ricocheted from one part of the sky to another. The firelights leapt out on engine three. I pulled the extinguishers without waiting for Jago's call.

'Are we still flying?' I yelled.

Even in the cockpit, the air rushing through the back of the jet was deafening. There was a puncture in the cockpit, and this led me to hope we'd been hit by the shrapnel of a proximity fuse missile and not with a full impact.

'Mission crew status,' I said over net one, but I could hear nothing over the air hissing through the shattered window to my right. I pinched my nose and blew to force air into my eardrums, and then I looked at Jago. His windshield was intact. His checklist had tumbled out of his lap under the rudder pedals, and he was trying to kick it away. I keyed the mike, but still I heard nothing. Jago put an oxygen mask over his face. His lips were moving and he looked at me, but I couldn't hear anything. He pulled on his mask to indicate I should get mine, and I reached up with my right hand and saw my comm cord had been shot clean through, and whatever it was had taken a chunk out of the hose that connected my mask to the system oxygen and caught the tip of my shoulder too. A small, dark stain of blood dribbled over the fray in my flightsuit, but I felt nothing. I put my mask on, gang-loading the oxygen, and covered the rip in the hose with my right hand.

Rosey was up and leaning over my seat, flipping the forced air switches on the overhead panel. I tapped my headset and shook my head and Jago nodded. He had his fists wrapped around the yoke, his elbows trembling with strain. By then we were at eighteen thousand in a controlled descent. The throttles were up on three of the four engines, which meant we could probably land, and I began to think that things were okay when Rosey pointed toward the grille under Bear's feet. The radios in the lower lobe were golden with fire.

'They down there?' I yelled to Rosey, and he nodded, meaning the fire team had gone through the aft grille. There was no way to know if anyone in back was hurt. As we descended, the entrails of the ground smoke began to lap at the side of the fuselage. We were descending into Saudi Arabia toward what I assumed was King Kaleed airstrip. I looked back at Bear. He'd taken his gloves off and he was zipping his banjo into its soft vinyl case. I poked him on the arm and held my hand up to show that he should put his gloves on, but he shook his head and kept working the zipper around the rim.

I reset the alarms to silence them. In spite of the air whistling through the cracked windshield, the cockpit became hazy with smoke. In the narrow corridor behind the cockpit, the two firefighters crawled back through the open grille next to the first row of consoles. They made a sign that the fire was out but that the wires were smoldering. Jago pointed toward the flap indicators and cocked his hands in opposite directions to show that we had asymmetric flaps.

I nodded, and then I sat dumbly in the co-pilot's seat. If he'd told me we had only one wing, or that the back half of the jet was gone, or that we'd just set the whole war effort back six months, I would not have been surprised. I assumed this would be my last flight, that I'd either die or be stripped of my wings and court-martialed. I saw myself standing at the center of gray, austere rooms, dressed in Class-As before councils of senior officers, reading formal apologies while right and rank were stripped one-by-one like so many insignia from my uniform, and what shamed me the most was not enduring that ritual but the moment when I would stand in civilian clothes facing Jago, who would never have fallen upon his own mask, never let the course of an aircraft slip out of his hands. He would regard me as all pilots do when they see comrades fall from their station—with pity and loathing, as the strong regard the weak.

The airstrip was broadening. We were crabbing at forty-five degrees and running too fast. None of this scared me. Fear of death is a sharp, heart-pounding jolt, but what I felt was the cold, heavy bladder of dread. I longed vaguely to get everyone out of the jet. I prayed for the crew, though my prayers had nothing to do with faith.

They were just pleas of desperation, the kind you make as a child when either wonderful or horrible things loom out of your control.

At five thousand, the smoke was as thick as vapor inside the cockpit.

'We're overshooting,' I said. The lights from the crash trucks flashed along the runway.

'Gear!'

I pulled the gear handle, and we got two green lights on the main gear. I didn't have to call it. Jago was staring at the lights and I saw his lips move next to the mike and knew he was calling tower to ask if our nose gear had come down also. Then he shook his head at me and I knew we were going in anyway and that Jago would try to keep us rolling on the main gear as long as possible and edge us down gently on the nose.

Even with bad flaps, he kept us straight on the runway, and I thought about how good he was, how instinctual and calm and how he would save the crew from my recklessness. We rolled past the off-ramps, past the crash trucks and fire engines. The nose remained high as though resisting the day's final affront. Jago gave a final push on the yoke and the nose tumbled down, jolting us forward and slamming Rosey into the back of my seat. We kept sliding, so close to the ground that I could see the speckles in the paving and the variations in the skid marks.

We skidded like a derby car off the end of the runway into the dust. Jago hit the evacuation bell.

'Out,' he said. 'Out now. Bear, I want you to—'

Bear was tucked under the nav console working the banjo free. It had gotten wedged between the bulkhead and Jago's seat.

'Leave it!' Jago screamed.

'Fuck you,' Bear yelled.

'Forget the fucking banjo.'

The radios in the lobe under us had caught fire again. Smoke bubbled through the grille in the floor. Jago slapped at the breakers over our heads.

'Get out!' he yelled at me. Rosey was half-squatting on the floor with his arms thrown over the throttles.

'He's hurt,' I yelled.

'Get him out of here.'

'I can't move my arm,' I said. 'You have to help him.' He looked at me and the logic of the solution registered, and he seemed to resent me for it. 'I got it,' I said. 'I'll shut down. Go.'

Jago climbed over the throttles and pulled Rosey's arm over his shoulder. Rosey was breathing hard and clutching his ribs, and they shuffled out of the cockpit toward the forward port door where the radio operator had already pulled the slide handle.

I looped the oxygen hose over my seat where I could stand at Rosey's console and slap at the breakers with my good hand. I couldn't close my right hand over the gash in the hose now, and a pungent smoke began to slip in with the oxygen, but I had to make sure the engines and electricity were shut down so that there was no explosion in the few minutes it would take the crew to egress. Bear pulled himself up from the floor and knelt on Jago's seat, his feet flopped over the throttles, trying to work the banjo out of the niche between the bulkhead and the seat rails. I was still hitting the breakers, and I pulled my leg up and kicked him hard in the ass. That only made him jerk more frantically at the instrument. His broad backside jiggled between the yoke and the chair back and I kicked the soft flesh over and over until he straightened up, his red face huffing under the mask, and said, 'Let me be!'

'Don't be stupid!' I yelled. My voice echoed inside the auditorium of my mask. I had the urge to smash the banjo to pieces, stomp out the possibility of rescue but also the lunatic desire that kept Bear lingering over the kind of death that would seem pathetic and suicidal, full of bad judgment, and one that even Bear, in a saner moment, would see as indulgent and embarrassing.

'I can't tell where it's hung up.' His face was scarlet. He blinked, his eyes tearing in the smoke. I could see the brightness of the windshield and imagined, well beyond the nose, the crew assembling for the head-count and the medics working over the injured. My hair was damp with sweat and I felt a burning in my eyes and the edges of my ears and in my right shoulder where the blood had seeped into the green nomex along my arm. I began to cough with the acrid fumes in my throat. It felt as though the cockpit had closed up around us, as though we'd stumbled into a treacherous ocean cave, and now in the thickening smoke, Bear seemed to be moving away from me, deeper into the cockpit whose shapes and instruments no longer felt familiar but like sinister, startling hazards.

'Do you want to die here?' I shouted. 'Is a banjo worth dying over?' He didn't answer me, but in a sense he did, because if you have to hesitate after that kind of question, the answer is already clear.

'It's my fault,' I yelled. 'Hate me, but do it outside.' We both sucked twice on the oxygen and let the masks slide over our heads and onto the seats. I followed him through the cockpit to the port side door where the sun burnt a halo in the hazy smoke floating in the dark aft of the airplane. The radios in the forward lobe hissed under the grilles. Punctures like buckshot holes pierced the starboard side of the fuselage. Some of the insulation and panels had fallen down, but the heavy cabinets were intact and the jet looked like the dark, empty hull of a dying whale.

Outside, the firefighters had begun to spray the jet with foam. Bear leapt first, launching himself almost halfway down the slide where he bounced and tumbled to the bottom. I braced my right arm and jumped, sliding into the brightness that burned through the sweat in my eyes. Then I was up and running toward the voices calling our names.

Jago caught me. I bent down and spit black mucus on the ground.

'What took you so long?'

'Bear—,' I began, but I couldn't breathe with running and the images of the cockpit that now seemed surreal and indescribable.

'Medic!' Jago yelled.

'It's okay,' I said.

'Stay here,' he said. In the moment he was gone, I noticed the circus of flashing lights parked well away from the edge of the runway where our jet lilted beached with its nose in the dust. Three of our operators lay on stretchers attended by clusters of medics and officers from the squadron.

Jago returned with a thick pad of white gauze folded in his hand.

'How is everybody?' I said.

'Everyone's fine.'

'Rosey?'

'Cracked ribs, that's all.'

'Nobody dead?'

He shook his head. He tried to put the bandage up to my arm, but I shook him off. 'I want to know,' I said.

'Everyone's fine,' he said again. 'Lancey broke his wrist. Grady bent his knee up pretty bad. Just you and Bear were—what took you so long?'

'We were goddamn lucky,' I said. The other crewmembers, ones with lesser injuries, sat in the shade of the emergency trucks holding clothes or ice packs to their faces and legs, or stood staring at the jet.

'It wasn't your fault. Not entirely,' he said. 'The E-3 skips turn points all the time.'

'Save it,' I said. 'I'm ready for it, as long as the crew is okay.'

'We'll all testify,' he said. 'They should have seen it in the backend, that the jet was off course.'

'Forget it,' I said. He was still holding the cloth in his hand. I took it from him and pressed it to my shoulder, and then I said, 'I wouldn't have done it, either. Given up my mask. If things were reversed, I would have done what you did.'

Jago looked down at the ground for a moment. 'It shouldn't have happened like that. I don't want to remember that mask as the last thing between us.'

I shrugged. 'The result would have been the same when we got home, only it would have taken me longer to understand.'

There was nothing else to say. The blunt steel feeling of dread was gone. I would lose Jago, and I would lose my wings, but the crew was safe and I welcomed the punishment that would come. It would be the first time I would stand up as myself, not hidden behind the armor of my wings, and I was ready for that.

My wound began to sting under the hot morning sun. I walked over and sat in the shade of one of the fire trucks. Rosey and two of the other crew had already been lifted on stretchers into the ambulance. A young-looking medic with strawberry hair squatted over me and began to clean my shoulder, and it burned down to the bone.

'Nasty scratch,' he said. 'You'll be able to show your kids a battle scar.'

'I don't have kids.'

He smiled. 'Well, you've got time.'

The jet sat limply with its chin buried in the dust. Bear stood off its nose, so close that a fireman had to keep waving him off. I sat watching him and yearning for Jago, the freshness of a love affair whose only consequence was the daily uncertainty of battle and the innocence of never wanting more.

Contributors' Notes

CHRIS ABANI'S latest novel, *Graceland*, from which "Weeping Madonna" and "Blooding" were excerpted, will be published by Farrar, Straus & Giroux in Spring 2004. Other novels include, *Masters of the Board*, which won a 1983 Delta Fiction Award, and *Sirocco*. His short fiction has been widely anthologized and he has written and produced two plays, *Room at the Top* and *Song of a Broken Flute*. A 2001 book of poetry, *Kalakuta Republic*, received the 2001 PEN USA West Freedom-to-Write Award and the 2001 Prince Claus of the Netherlands Award. *Daphne's Lot*, 2002, is a meditation on war. Abani is a Middleton Fellow at USC and teaches in Antioch University's MFA program.

CAROLYN ALESSIO'S fiction has appeared in the *Pushcart Prize Anthology*, *StoryQuarterly*, *Boulevard* and *TriQuarterly*. She is prose editor of *Crab Orchard Review*, and of the bi-lingual anthology *The Voices of Hope*, a collection of writings from the children of a Guatemalan squatter settlement. She teaches high school in Chicago's Pilsen neighborhood and lives in Chicago with her husband and daughter Charlotte (whose picture graces the *SQ* webpage).

JEFFERY RENARD ALLEN'S books include a poetry collection, *Harbors and Spirits*, and a first novel, *Rails Under My Back*. The novel received the *Chicago Tribune's* Heartland Prize; was cited as a *New York Times* Notable Book, One of Best Twenty-Five of 2000 by *The Village Voice*, and One of Ten Best Books by *The Chicago Tribune*; chosen as a selection by the Book of the Month Club and the Quality Paperback Book

Club. He received a 2002 Whiting Award; fellowships from the Chicago Public Library, the Center for Scholars in the New York Public Library, a John Farrar Fellowship at Bread Loaf and a Walter E. Dakins Fellowship at Sewanee. Forthcoming is a second collection of poems and a collection of stories, and another novel is underway.

STEVE ALMOND'S debut story collection, *My Life in Heavy Metal*, went into paperback this Spring, with stories widely published and anthologized in *Pushcart Prizes 2002*, *New Stories from the South 2002*, and the *Best of Zoetrope II*. Algonquin Books will publish his next two books, a fiction/non-fiction book, *Candyfreak: A Journey Through the Chocolate Underbelly of America* in Spring 2004, and his next collection in Spring 2005. Steve lives outside Boston and eats too much candy.

SHARON BALENTINE'S fiction has appeared in *The Missouri Review*, *Tulane Review*, and *Rosebud*. She holds degrees in Microbiology and English Literature. "For as long as I can remember, I've been interested in how the natural world can regenerate the spirit."

J. T. BARBARESE, a Harry Potter scholar, recently appeared on CNN on that subject. He has authored three books: two of poetry and one translation of Euripedes, *Children of Herakles*. Fiction has appeared in *StoryQuarterly* and *North American Review*, and over 50 poems have appeared in *The Atlantic*, *Georgia Review*, *Southern Review* and other journals. He is marketing a novel and collection of stories and is Assistant Professor at Rutgers/Camden.

ENID BARON is author of *Baking Days*, a collection of poetry. Stories have appeared in *Doubletake*, *Calyx*, *A Room of One's Own*, *Whetstone*, *Descant*, and *Creative Nonfiction*. A story collection is seeking a publisher. Baron founded and continues to direct the popular *Hands on Stanzas* program, poets teaching poetry in the Chicago public schools.

KATE HILL CANTRILL, a native Philadelphian, lives in Austin, Texas, where she works as a theater set painter. The inspiration for this, her first published story, came from a very good friend.

JOHN CASEY is the author of *Spartina*, which won the National Book Award, and *The Half-Life of Happiness* as well as other books of fiction. His work has been widely published in commercial and literary magazines. Casey teaches literature at the University of Virginia.

HELEN CHANDRA lives in Chicago, where she studies writing with Fred Shafer. This is her first published story. She spent several years in India in the 1960s and continues to seek clarification of that experience by writing about it. Use of the elephant-headed god, Ganesh, suits a first story, for Ganesh is a special patron of writers.

JOAN CORWIN won Chicago NPR's *Stories on Stage* competition with "Hindsight," which will be read on WBEZ in October 2003 and is forthcoming in *River Oak Review*. She has co-authored four screenplays, written short stories and a two-act play, and is currently at work on a novel. She has published essays on nineteenth century travel writers, an academic specialty which she used to teach in Chicago schools.

STEPHEN DIXON has published 22 books of fiction, 13 story collections and 9 novels. Two more finished novels, *Leonard* and *End of I*, are seeking publishers. He is deep into a new novel, *Phone Rings*. He teaches in the Writing Seminars at John Hopkins U. "'Go' is my 13th story in *SQ*, or maybe I'm wrong and there are more."

RICHARD FORD was born in Jackson, Mississippi and grew up there and in Little Rock, Arkansas. He is the author of five novels—*Independence Day*, *Wildlife*, *The Sportswriter*, *The Ultimate Good Luck* and *Piece of My Heart*—and two collections of short stories, *Rock Springs* and *Women With Men*. Ford was awarded the Pulitzer Prize and the PEN/Faulkner Award for *Independence Day*, the first book to win both prizes. In 2001 he received the PEN/Malamud Award for excellence in short fiction. He is a member of the American Academy of Arts and Letters.

AMY SCHILDHOUSE GREENBERG, writer and translator, has published translations in *New Writing From Mexico*, *Tememe*, and *The Vintage Book of Latin American Stories* (edited by Carlos Fuentes). Her translation of Angeles Mastretta's book, *Women With Big Eyes*, is due out from Riverhead Press in November 2003. Greenberg's poetry, prose and fiction have appeared in more than 50 publications incl. *Poets & Writers*, *StoryQuarterly*, *Short Story Review*, *Into the Silence* (an anthology) and *Best Ohio Fiction*.

KAUI HART HEMMINGS grew up in Hawaii and now lives in San Francisco, where she is a Wallace Stegner Fellow at Stanford University. She is currently finishing a collection of stories set in Hawaii and beginning a novel about a resort town in the Rockies.

CHARLES JOHNSON, author of five novels, along with books of non-fiction, received the National Book Award for *Middle Passage* in 1990. Johnson currently holds the Pollock Professorship of English at the University of Washington in Seattle.

DREW JOHNSON returned to his hometown, Oxford, Mississippi, after nine years spent in Massachusetts and Texas. "Delta Interval" is his first published story. "Some things that were left out of this story: a great deal of chicken corn chowder, Ray's thoughts on cooking, half-a-dozen Chinese headstones, an 8-foot water moccasin, and a general discussion of the relative bodily cleanliness possible in the field."

CHRISTY KARPINSKI'S photographs have been exhibited nationally. Currently she is an MFA student at Columbia College in Chicago.

N. S. KÖENINGS was born in Belgium, raised in East and South Africa, attended college in the U.S. and published fiction in *Glimmer Train*. Her writing reflects concerns about relations between kin growing up far from each other, and the different countries that even people who share one place can inhabit. She lives in Bloomington, Indiana, where she is finishing a novel set in the 1970s in Tanzania. She has a Ph.D. in anthropology and publishes scholarly and human rights work under the name Nathalie Arnold.

ANGELES MASTRETTA created a sensation in Mexico when her feminist collection of fiction, *Mujeres de Ojos Grandes*, or *Women With Big Eyes*, became a national bestseller in 1990. A translation of the book, by Amy Schildhouse Greenberg, is due out from Riverhead Press in November 2003.

MORGAN MCDERMOTT'S stories have won competitions from the Dana Awards, *Phoebe*, *New Millennium Writings*, and Random House. He lives in Evanston, IL with his wife and muse, Wendy Parks. An Iowa graduate, he teaches writing at Adlai E. Stevenson High School in Chicago. "Evanston is a confluence of cultural, social, and financial rivers, pressures which carve a landscape of dichotomies. A high-population miniature city, where high-rises spring up overnight, it is also a bedroom suburb, a college town where many homes sell for over a million dollars. 'Traction' examines how a close-quarters environment—a city, a neighborhood, a house—shapes interactions of the people there. Ridge and Veronique appeared in a story published in *Mississippi Review* last year and I realized then that they needed some space, a room of their own."

KEITH LEE MORRIS'S stories have appeared in *New England Review*, *The Sun*, *Georgia Review*, *Puerto Del Sol*, and *New Orleans Review*. His first novel, *The Greyhound God*, will be published in September by University of Nevada Press. A short story collection, in which "San Diego Dreams" is included, will follow in 2004.

RAMU NAGAPPAN is a writer based in San Francisco. His previous fiction has appeared in *India Currents*. He is writing a novel and employed at the School of Medicine at the University of California, San Francisco, where he teaches writing and is developing a program in the medical humanities.

PENNY NEWBURY'S fiction has appeared in *Mississippi Review, Wisconsin Review, Conjunctions, Gargoyle* and other publications. She taught writing at the U of Connecticut and is currently Training Director for the U.S. Peace Corps in East Timor. She invites anybody reading this journal to please come visit.

RICHARD NEWMAN'S poems, stories, and essays have recently appeared in *American Literary Review, Boulevard, 5 A.M., Laurel Review, Poems & Plays*, and other periodicals and anthologies. He edits *River Styx* magazine, reviews books for the *St. Louis Post-Dispatch*, and teaches at St. Louis Community College. "Gristlehead" is from a monster sonnet series he started last summer. "I've tried to bury it several times, but it keeps resurrecting itself."

DAN O'BRIEN'S first published story was anthologized in *25 and Under: Fiction*. Still under 30, O'Brien has had plays produced nationally and published by Samuel French, Dramatic Publishing, and Playscripts. Subsequent fiction has appeared in *Greensboro Review, Bellevue Review, Ellipsis*, and elsewhere. He spent last year as a Tennessee Williams Fellow in Playwriting at the University of the South. He lives in New York City. "In 'Apocrypha,' I tried to communicate the sense of feeling lost, or of buried memories affecting a family, showing how these memories are unearthed through mythmaking and storytelling—telling elliptically and elusively, but hopefully richly, and rewardingly."

BRIGID PASULKA has previously published work in *ACM–Another Chicago Magazine* and *Shenandoah*. She won the AWP Intro Award for

2002 as well as the Charles Goodnow Award for Fiction (2002). "The Lemon Tree" is part of a collection of short stories with recurring characters. She is currently working on a novel titled *Wide Is The Vistula*.

KIM PONDERS is a former flyer with the U. S. Air Force and holds a Masters in International Affairs. Her work has appeared in *Chattahoochee Review*. This story is part of a linked series exploring the life of a young woman transfixed by the arcane and largely male-dominated world of flying. "The beginning of the story came very easily because Annie had been heading toward some kind of collision. Her avoidance of difficult issues had been so extreme I needed a grand rebirth to make epiphany possible. Images of fire and of the empty hull of a whale kept resonating—I think she had to walk through death to see life clearly."

MICHAEL POORE'S recent work has appeared in *Hayden's Ferry Review*, *Highway 14*, *Black Warrior*, *Southern Review*, and *Handy-Capable Lifestyles*. Poore currently teaches writing and wheelchair volleyball at the Cedar Lake Center for Spinal Rehabilitation in Jupiter, IN. The character of Joe Ingram is loosely based on his stepbrother, a competitive cyclist who fashions prosthetic limbs. "The rest is smoke, and ghosts."

ANDREW PORTER is a former James Michener Fellow. His stories have appeared in *Story*, *Antioch Review*, *Epoch*, *Other Voices*, *Press* and *Green Mountains Review*. He currently teaches creative writing at the University of Maryland, Baltimore County.

SYLVIA SELLERS-GARCIA, Third Robie Macauley Fiction Award Winner, is a fact-checker at *The New Yorker* and begins a Ph.D. in History at Berkeley in the fall. "A Correspondence" is her first published fiction.

KATHERINE SHONK'S short story collection, *The Red Passport*, from which "Kitchen Friends" was taken, will be published by Farrar,

Straus & Giroux in November. Shonk's fiction has appeared in *StoryQuarterly*, *Tin House*, *Best American Short Stories 2001*, and is forthcoming in *The Georgia Review*. She has received an award and a fellowship from the Illinois Arts Council, and lives in Evanston, IL.

MIKA TANNER'S fiction has appeared in *Glimmer Train* and she is at work on a novel. "I got the idea for this story living in Japan with my husband and we noticed how indignant Americans got over Japanese women passively 'accepting' their traditional roles. Being raised by a Japanese woman myself, I wanted to show a more complicated way of seeing this issue, and that it was in fact possible to be a unique individual while at the same time living within the boundaries of convention. My other inspiration for the story was, of course, Japanese toilets, which do everything but go to the bathroom for you." Tanner lives in Los Angeles.

TERRY THUEMLING lives in Milwaukee with his fiancée. This is his first published story. Of the cryptogram in his short-short, he notes that "it could also have been answered 'entente,' but the definition of the word precluded it as a title. The way in which the story's final words reveal a double meaning was a welcome suprise for me—as I hope it is for the reader."

LARA JK WILSON'S short stories have been published or are forthcoming in *Indiana Review*, *Confrontation*, *American Short Fiction*, *Chelsea*, and *BookMagazine.com*'s Newcomers Fiction section, among others. She lives outside Boston with her husband and their four young children.

Past Contributors' News

The *StoryQuarterly* family has been on the move in a big way. SQ38's "Nirvana" by Patricia Lear, plus a story by Brock Clarke, one of our staffers, are both in *New Stories From The South: Best of 2003*; Brock Clarke again, and Richard Lange, another *SQ* staffer, are both in the issue of *Georgia Review* that made finalist for the National Magazine Award. Deb Olin Unferth, another staffer, is featured for her fiction on the August cover of *Harper's Magazine*, which also reprinted our SQ38 story by Robert Olen Butler, "Mother in the Trenches," in February. Guess we know to keep our Olins and Olens straight.

MARGARET ATWOOD'S (SQ4) latest novel, in 2003, is *Oryx and Crake*.

T. C. BOYLE (SQ35) has a new novel out, *Drop City*, and a paperback of *After The Plague and Other Stories* came out in February 2003.

FREDERICK BUSCH (SQ9) brought out *Memory of War* in winter, 2002-3.

ROBERT OLEN BUTLER'S (SQ38) novel, *Fair Warning*, is due out in paperback, along with *A Good Scent From A Strange Mountain: Stories*.

BROCK CLARKE (SQ38) has been prolific lately, with fiction in many good places. He's finishing up a novel, *An Arsonist's Guide to Writer's Home in New England*, and a collection, *Carrying The Torch*. Hmm.

QUINN DALTON'S (SQ37) novel *High Strung* kept her on a book tour all summer. Only place to catch her these days is www.quinndalton.com

LAUREN B. DAVIS'S (SQ38) novel *The Stubborn Season* became a bestseller in Canada, paperback out here in Spring 2003. Her next novel, *Radiant*

City, is due out in 2005. She's still teaching at WICE and the American U in Paris, plus workshops in Ireland, Geneva and Washington.

ANTHONY DOERR (SQ35) is hitting on all cylinders. His collection, *The Shell Collector*, was named Notable Book of 2002 by *The New York Times*, *Publisher's Weekly* and the American Library Association. He won the New York Public Library's 2003 Young Lions Award, Barnes and Nobel's 2002 Discover Award, and has stories in *O. Henry Prize Stories 2003* and *Best American Stories 2003*. If you want his autograph, he'll be a Hodder Fellow at Princeton this fall.

STUART DYBEK'S (SQ36) novel, *I Sailed With Magellan*, is due out soon (Farrar, Straus & Giroux). Currently, find Dybek's fiction, with other *StoryQuarterly* past contributors, in *Our Working Lives: Short Stories of People and Work*.

REG GIBBONS (SQ36) had time, between chairing the English Department at Northwestern and teaching at the Warren Wilson MFA Program, to publish a new book of poetry, *It's Time*, which won the 2002 Best Book of Poetry Award from the Texas Institute of Letters. He's busy on "new or maybe I should say still unfinished books."

GAIL GODWIN (SQ2, 3, 19 & 36) had a new novel out, *Evenings at Five*.

BETH GOLDNER (SQ38) had a first book out August 5, *Wake*, from Counterpoint Press which will bring out her first novel in 2004. Beth writes, "I'm on Amazon and everything! Surreal!" An exciting and busy year.

ALVIN GREENBERG'S (SQ37) new novel, *Time Lapse*, is out (Tupelo Press). He'll be doing a book tour, winter-spring, 2003-4.

KEVIN GRAUKE (SQ37) published fiction this year, finished his Ph.D. and had a baby girl. He's teaching at the University of North Texas. A huge year, Kevin.

JANA HARRIS'S new *We Never Speak of It*, a collection of Idaho-Wyoming poems dating back to 1889, includes one done in prose for *SQ35*.

ALICE HOFFMAN (*SQ33 & 38*) has two novels out this year, *The Probable Future* and *Green Anger*. Now that's energy!

THOMAS KENNEDY (*SQ35*) has had lots of attention paid to his Copenhagen quartet, publishing one book a year from the group. He'll do a book tour in the U.S. next fall and talk about the newest, his frame being stories all set in Copenhagen bars. Tom loves research.

TABISH KHAIR'S (*SQ38*) novel, *The Bus Stopped*, is out by Picador (London) in early 2004. His *SQ38* story was based on a section from the novel.

THOMAS MCCARTHY (*SQ36*) has a collection published, *Final Days and Other Stories*, and a novel, *Riding the Tiger* is looking for a home.

JAMES MCMANUS (*SQ35*) rolled a bestseller this time with *Positively Fifth Street: Murderers, Cheetahs, and Binion's World Series of Poker*. Another man who loves his research.

ASKOLD MELNYCZUK (*SQ36*) spun off a novella, *Blind Angel*, which was written by a character in his new novel, *The Great Hospital*, recently out from Pressed Wafer.

STEPHEN MINOT (*SQ36 & 37*) has a 7th edition out, *Three Genres: The Writing of Poetry, Fiction and Drama*, which still draws readers in 50 states, plus the new *Literary Nonfiction: The Fourth Genre* is doing well.

LOREN OBERWEGER (*SQ37*) appears in an impressive roster of New Orleans writers—Tennessee Williams, Andre Codrescu, Ellen Gilchrist, Richard Ford—with his story "Blue Elephant," in *French Quarter Fiction*.

PAMELA PAINTER (*SQ* Founder) and Anne Bernays are bringing out an updated edition of their popular craft book on writing, *What If*. A tremendous teaching tool, full of exercises and good advice.

RACHAEL PERRY (SQ36) has a first collection, *How To Fly* (including her SQ36 story), due out by Carnegie Mellon U Press in December. She and her husband have moved back to the States from Duesseldorf.

TODD PIERCE (SQ37) had great press this spring when his first novel, *The Australia Stories*, came out from MacAdam/Cage with wonderful blurbs from Thomas Keneally and Jim Crace. Todd finished his Ph.D. at Florida State and heads for a teaching job at Clemson U this fall. Check out his webpage: www.literaryagents.org.

SUSAN JACKSON RODGERS (SQ36) has a collection out, *The Trouble With You Is*, and won the 2002 Lorian Hemingway Short Story Competition.

STEPHEN SCHOTTENFELD (SQ38) teaches at Rhodes College, Memphis this fall. He spent the summer in Nova Scotia, on his honeymoon!

DEB OLIN UNFERTH (SQ37), also on a roll, has two stories in *Harper's* this year, and starts teaching in a new writing program at the University of Kansas in Lawrence.

AMY WELDON (SQ38) became editor of *The South Carolina Review* and will begin teaching writing there while she finishes her dissertation.

AMANDA EYRE WARD (SQ38) published her first novel, *Sleep Toward Heaven*, (MacAdam/Cage) in March 2003.

ANTOINE WILSON (SQ37) has new fiction out in *Quarterly West*, and completed a novel set among oil towns of the Persian Gulf. All that and he got married, too. A lot of marrying going on around here.

MARK WINEGARDNER (SQ36) followed up the success of *Crooked River Burning*, and recently a collection, *That's True of Everybody*, by winning an invitational competition to continue Mario Puzo's *Godfather* series. What a combination, Winegardner and international crime cartels. We can't wait to see his always thoughtful take on macro-politics.

Sewanee Writers' Conference

July 13–25, 2004

The University of the South
Sewanee, Tennessee

Workshops in Poetry, Fiction, and Playwriting

Our faculty has included:

Horton Foote	Claire Messud
Ernest Gaines	Marsha Norman
Robert Hass	Tim O'Brien
Barry Hannah	Francine Prose
Anthony Hecht	Mark Strand
Alice McDermott	Derek Walcott

✤ ✤ ✤

In addition to our prize-winning faculty, our program features individual manuscript conferences; readings and craft lectures in fiction, playwriting, and poetry; and a host of editors, publishers, agents, and other literary standouts. A limited number of fellowships and scholarships are available on a competitive basis.

**For information please visit our website,
www.sewaneewriters.org, or contact:**

Cheri Peters, Creative Writing Programs Manager
Sewanee Writers' Conference
310Q St. Luke's Hall • 735 University Avenue
Sewanee, TN 37383-1000
(931) 598-1141

RICHARD FORD
PULITZER PRIZE WINNER

"One of the country's best writers.... No one looks harder at contemporary American life, sees more, or expresses it with such hushed, deliberate care."
—*San Francisco Chronicle*

INDEPENDENCE DAY

"Powerful...as gripping as it is affecting.... Ford has galvanized his reputation as one of his generation's most eloquent voices."
—*The New York Times*

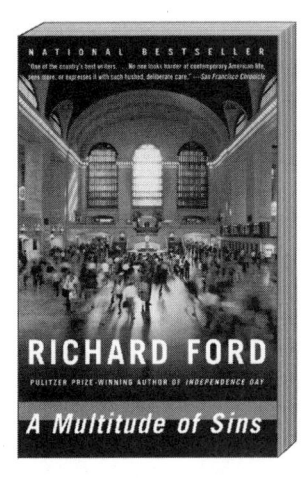

A MULTITUDE OF SINS

"Wrenching, intense, overflowing with compassion, *A Multitude of Sins* leads us into the restless ambiguities of the heart."
—*Newsday*

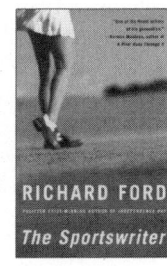

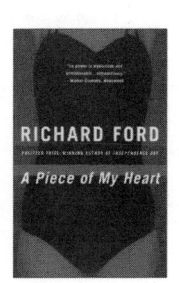

Available in paperback from Vintage Books
Find excerpts, interviews, and reading group guides on www.readinggroupcenter.com

the Carolina Quarterly

- Poetry
- Fiction
- Essays
- Interviews
- Reviews

Recent contributors include

Doris Betts • Ron Carlson • Fred Chappell
Michael Chitwood • Pam Durban • Clyde Edgerton
Marianne Gingher • Albert Goldbarth • R. S. Gwynn
William Harmon • Ha Jin • Michael Longley
Michael McFee • Robert Morgan • Lewis Nordan
Josh Russell • James Seay • Donald Secreast
George Singleton • R. T. Smith • Lee Smith
Cathy Song • Gary Soto • Elizabeth Spencer
Daniel Wallace • Richard Wilbur • Charles Wright

Interviews with

Russell Banks • Doris Betts • Larry Brown
Hal Crowther • Richard Ford • Lee Smith
John Edgar Wideman • Tom Wolfe • Tobias Wolff

For subscription information contact

CB#3520, Greenlaw Hall
UNC-Chapel Hill
Chapel Hill, NC 27599-3520
www.unc.edu/depts/cqonline
email: cquarter@unc.edu

$12/year (Three issues)

Bread Loaf
Writers' Conference

August 11-22, 2004

Michael Collier, Director
Devon Jersild, Associate Director

Faculty in 2003 included:
David Haward Bain, Andrea Barrett,
Charles Baxter, Linda Bierds, Maxine Clair,
Michael Collier, Cornelius Eady, Lynn Freed,
Linda Gregerson, Patricia Hampl, Edward Hirsch,
Randall Kenan, Margot Livesey, Thomas Mallon,
Cornelia Nixon, Sigrid Nunez, Peter Turchi,
Ellen Bryant Voigt, Dean Young

Special guests in 2003 included:
Paula Fox, Louise Glück, and James Longenbach

Financial Aid & Fellowship Deadline: March 1, 2004 (postmark)
General Application Deadline: March 19, 2004 (postmark)

Please note: The general application deadline is earlier than in past years.

To request the 2004 brochure & application:
Bread Loaf Writers' Conference
Middlebury College, Middlebury, VT 05753
E-mail: blwc@middlebury.edu Phone: 802-443-5286
For more information visit: www.middlebury.edu/blwc/

2004 Conference materials will be ready in December, 2003.

StoryQuarterly: All Story Anthology, 35-50 stories a year.

30 years of discovering talent early—

-Lee K. Abbott
Alice Adams
Margaret Atwood
Ann Beattie
T. C. Boyle
Rosellen Brown
Janet Burroway
Frederick Busch
Kelly Cherry
Stephen Dixon
Anthony Doerr
Eugene Garber
Gail Godwin
Angela Jackson
Pagan Kennedy
W. P. Kinsella
Jhumpa Lahiri
Paul Maliszewski
Lorrie Moore
Joyce Carol Oates
Melissa Brown Pritchard
Lore Segal
Nancy Zafris-

Take it to the beach, or take it to bed for the long cold winter.

http://www.storyquarterly.com

—and still at it!
*New Stories from the South, Best American Stories, O.Henr**Pushcart* and Ill. Arts Councrecognition in last 5 years

Send me a one-year subscription for $10; start with Issue_____.
Send me a two-year subscription for $18; start with Issue _____.
Send me a five-year subscription for $40; start with Issue _____.
Send me a life subscription for $250, start with Issue _____.
Send me ___ copies of SQ___ for the student/group rate of 5cc/$35.
   (Add $5/year for Canada; Add $6/year for International)
Name_____
Address_____
Address_____

Mail with check to: StoryQuarterly, Inc.
431 Sheridan Road, Kenilworth, IL 60043-1220